The Photograph

BY VIRGINIA ELLIS

The Wedding Dress

The Photograph

The Photograph

Virginia Ellis

BALLANTINE BOOKS • NEW YORK

This book is dedicated to my mother, Amelia—
a Winnie the Welder who lived parts of this story.
And to my father, George,
who survived three years in the Pacific—
once a Marine, always a Marine. "Semper Fi."

Acknowledgments

I would like to thank the usual suspects:
Pat, Sandra, Ann, Deb, and Martha;
the folks at the library—main branch—Miami, Fla.;
and the many members of the War Generation
who sat with me and answered my questions.

Chapter One

I've decided I'm not a good Catholic because I'll never forgive the Japanese for ruining my seventeenth birthday.

It was December 7, 1941—the day they bombed Pearl Harbor. *The* day that President Roosevelt proclaimed would forever live in "infamy" for every red-blooded American. That kind of sentiment didn't leave much anticipation or appetite for birthday cake, or for forgiveness. It was enough to make a girl good'n mad.

We were at war.

I suppose I should have counted my blessings that seventeen years earlier, Mother didn't have the imagination to christen me Pearl. She chose biblical names instead; David for my older brother, and Madelyn for me. I've always gone by Maddy.

As for my birthday cake, I did have one—on Monday instead of Sunday. But Mother cried the whole time she mixed the batter and poured it in the pans. The layers rose lopsided, and I swear I could taste a slight saltiness. Maybe it was just the metallic taste of fear. My brother Davey had joined the Marine reserves back in June, and now that we were officially at war, we all knew what that meant. He'd be one of the first to go.

The bad news didn't end there. At my halfhearted, one-day-late birthday dinner, my boyfriend, Lyle, announced that he had joined the Navy. To say this was a shock to me would be like saying the world had stopped spinning at 8:05 P.M. and would continue once more when this whole war thing was settled.

Lyle and I were "almost" engaged. He'd even kissed me in the back row of the movie theater during the newsreel before *It Happened One Night* with Clark Gable and Claudette Colbert. I'll never forget it because that very night we'd secretly promised to marry as soon as he had a good job and could earn my mother's permission. And now he'd gone and joined the war without even telling me first. Then, to announce it in front of the whole family—my mother, Davey, and his wife, Ruth—on a night that should have been my celebration, like he'd just grown a foot taller and we should be proud, added salt to the wound.

I'd had little experience with wounds in 1941. By the following year when my eighteenth birthday rolled around, however, I was a good bit more uncomfortably acquainted. What I didn't understand then and do now is, wounds are like ghosts—the initial pain might cut you to the ground, but if you can get up, sometimes with the help of others, you can survive and go on. Even as the phantoms follow in your wake.

My brother Davey got his orders a week before Christmas 1941. He was to pack enough clothes for three days, then report immediately to a place called Parris Island, South Carolina, for training. After that, he'd ship out to parts unknown. My mother was inconsolable. I hadn't seen her cry so much since we'd lost my father to a heart ailment (what he'd called his "bum ticker") when I was ten. Life in general, and my mother in particular, had never been the same after that. She'd seemed to decide that she had to take control of every detail in our world in order to make things safe. It was enough to make a girl, a headstrong girl like me, anyway, want to scream.

Unable to bear the thought of Davey traveling halfway around the planet to go to war, I suppose, Mother concentrated on South Carolina and how far her son would be from Pennsylvania and home. Ruth, Davey's wife, who had as much, or more, reason as Mother to weep, held herself together admirably. I'd never considered that being a wife and having babies could be a risky undertaking, but maybe Mother was right. Perhaps the world was a dangerous place. Ruth was barely out of the hospital after her second miscarriage, which had almost killed her. That and the large dose of sulfur they gave her for the infection.

If you ask me, I think it did kill her. I was there, I know— she'd nearly scared me into the next world, too. Since both of Ruth's parents were dead, our family and a few neighbors had taken turns sitting by her hospital bed when she'd been so ill. I'd been with her early one morning two weeks into her confinement when Davey had collapsed from worry and fatigue on the couch in the waiting room. The ward was quiet—the nurses and doctors off in another wing. I was minding my own business, thumbing through an old *Saturday Evening Post* I'd practically memorized when I heard what sounded like a sigh.

I looked up, but Ruth seemed asleep, as she'd been for two days or more. Niggling worry made me look closer. Moments before, her chest had been moving up and down. Now, it seemed still.

My heart took several labored beats. As I rose from the chair to move closer, I noticed a telltale brightness near the window. At first I thought dawn's sunlight had found the curtains. But then I saw her. It was Ruth, or the bright reflection of Ruth standing at the window.

Looking at me.

Seconds ticked by before she turned and floated through the glass.

I dropped the magazine and ran down the hallway wailing that Ruth was dead. Luckily, the nurses didn't believe me. They rushed back to the room with a doctor and did what I hadn't thought to try. They brought Ruth back, somehow. And Davey had been so happy he'd forgotten to strangle me for scaring everyone.

Ruth never mentioned being dead, but she did get better after that. She got to come home, walking with the help of a cane, right on time to help us send her husband off to war.

The morning Davey was due to catch the train south, my so-called boyfriend Lyle showed up, joining the men in war talk about how they'd make the Japs pay for their treachery. Mother made us take turns standing with Davey on the snowy grass in front of the holly tree so Mr. Jenkins next door, surrounded by an audience of other neighbors, could take snapshot after snapshot with his Kodak. Mother believed pictures were required on every occasion, happy or sad. I can't count how many times she'd said, "It's all I have left of your father."

I depended more on my memory, although, every year on the anniversary of my father's death when we got out the old photo album, there was a certain comfort in the fading images. When I was younger, I'd thought if I looked at them long enough, they'd move, or my father would speak to me. I swear once, I saw him smile. But after growing up, I realized they were only pictures.

As we posed for the camera, everyone acted happy, shaking Davey's hand or clapping him on the shoulder. Everyone except Mother and Ruth. Mother's smile seemed frozen on her face, and Ruth looked dreadfully pale as if she'd cried the whole night and had nothing more to say.

To me it seemed terribly romantic. Davey was going off to see the world, and Ruth would stay behind with us. Not for the first time I felt a twinge of envy. Boys got to do all the exciting things while the girls had to stay put. Lyle could quit school and announce he'd joined the Navy without so much as a "by your leave." I could just imagine my mother's reaction if I came home with the same news. She'd erupted like Mt.

Vesuvius when I'd talked old Mister Freed into letting me work at the drugstore after school. Not because we didn't need the money, but because it made me look too independent—a nice word for being headstrong. And it made it a little harder to keep track of her baby girl. In this gossipy town she'd usually known where I was going before I even got there. The possibility of me taking off to parts unknown to join the war effort seemed as remote and hilarious as running away to Hollywood to be a movie star. I had to turn my head and pretend to cough so Mother wouldn't recognize my improper laughter. She and I had been at odds so many times in the past year I thought I might die waiting for Lyle to fulfill our secret promise and rescue me with a mother-approved marriage proposal. The fact that my rescue had suddenly been postponed indefinitely, by Lyle's patriotic duty, soured my humor.

I couldn't wait for my life to begin!

"Can't you take me with you?" I said to Davey later, in a rare moment alone. I'd followed him a short distance down the train platform where he was checking the timetable while Mother and Ruth stayed warm inside the crowded station.

He turned to me, as serious as I'd ever seen him. "I've got the feeling I'm not going to like it very much where I'm goin'." Then he smiled and chucked me under the chin like the nine-year-old pest I used to be. "Besides, girls can't go to war."

I shrugged away from his hand. "It's not fair!"

"Yes it is, Squirt. This war is gonna be some bad business. And, anyway"—he went serious again—"I need you to help look after Ruth. You know Mother—"

"Yes, I know all about Mother." I rolled my eyes for effect. Mother could be a downright tyrant, especially when Davey wasn't around. "She drives me crazy."

"Promise you'll stick to Ruth and help her get through this."

I made my favorite gargoyle face at him.

"I'm serious, Squirt. Or, should I call you Madelyn since you're seventeen now?"

He was reminding me to act like a grown-up. I didn't

mind that so much as what his comment meant. Another fight I couldn't win. "Maddy will do just fine, thank you. All right, I promise. I'll stick to Ruth like the sister I wish I'd had instead of a brother."

"That's my girl," he said. "Cheer up, this whole thing'll probably be over by your next birthday." Then he did something surprising. He kissed me on the cheek. "I'm gonna miss you."

I was so shocked by his sentimental show of affection I didn't have time to return the favor or to remind him that he'd gone off and left me at home when he'd gotten married. "No you won't," I taunted. "You'll miss Ruth."

He glanced over my head toward the train station. When I turned, I could see Ruth sitting in a seat near the window watching us. "You bet I will," he said, almost under his breath. Then the station announcer called the arrival of the next train and we walked back to the depot.

That was the 18th of December. Come to think of it, the Japs had managed to ruin Christmas as well.

— RUTH —

Sitting at my mother-in-law's kitchen table, pen in hand, I tried my best to think of something cheerful to write to my husband. He'd been gone a month, one whole month, yet it seemed like a year to me. I couldn't tell him the truth. I couldn't write, *Oh Davey, I feel like such a failure. I know the doctors said it wasn't my fault. That the baby's blood and mine were fighting and he couldn't have been born alive. But I still feel responsible, and afraid. Because now you're on your way to this terrible war. You might not have been called up so soon if you'd had children to raise, a reason to stay behind besides a wife who could barely walk.*

No, I couldn't write that. It would only make Davey unhappy, and my one wish in life was to do the opposite. To make him the happiest man on Earth. Because that's how he made me feel. Blessed.

Except when I lost our baby. Once again I felt that deep, thrumming pain that always accompanied my memory of the loss. People think losing a baby before it's born is easier than losing a known child. Or maybe they think it *should* be easier. With words like, "Oh, you can try again soon." Or, "Next time will be the charm." All I can say is, the loss wasn't easy for me . . . in the least. And after two tries and two losses, I was beginning to wonder if I would ever be a mother.

At least I knew our babies were safe in heaven. I knew that because on the day I died, I saw them there. The memory has stayed fresh in my mind and comforting to my heart. I'd been so ill. I remember feeling lighter and lighter, then I floated out of my hospital bed. I could see myself, motionless and quiet on the sheets with Maddy sitting next to me, reading. I didn't have time to feel afraid, I was so happy the pain had left me. I'd wanted to float there forever.

Then, through the window, I saw beautiful green hills in the distance and sunshine so bright it stung my eyes. Something called me closer and I realized I could see people I knew. One man, Mr. Bledsoe, who'd worked with my father at the mine, kept waving and smiling. I remembered as a child meeting the men as they came home from their shift. Mr. Bledsoe always had chewing gum in his overall pocket to give to us. When he'd been alive he'd had one arm—lost his left one in a rock crusher. But when I saw him in heaven, he had both . . . and even though I was grown-up, he recognized me and seemed so happy to see me again.

The healing beauty of those verdant hills pulled me closer and closer, and the nearer I got the easier it was to breathe. I felt I could float into forever as more and more people walked toward me, waving, calling "hello." But I kept looking beyond them. I didn't realize who I was searching for until I saw him.

My father.

There he stood some distance up the highest hill, smiling. He had a baby in each of his arms. My babies. Mine and Davey's.

I started running. Me, who hadn't been able to take a few

steps or get out of bed for longer than I cared to remember. Barely halfway there, a voice stopped me.

"Not yet," the voice said in a very loving tone. "You must go back."

I shook my head, no. I didn't want to stop or think, and I certainly didn't want to feel the pain and grief I'd left behind. I wanted to stay there, in that brilliant light and breathtaking place with my father and my babies.

Then, Davey's face suddenly and clearly appeared in my mind. The next thing I knew, I'd opened my eyes and found myself back in the hospital with nurses and doctors crowded around my bedside, and my husband holding my hand. I knew I was alive because everything hurt again, and because Davey had tears in his eyes.

Losing our baby had killed me. But his love had summoned me back.

And now this war.

When Davey was called up for active duty I'd wanted to try to become pregnant again, but the doctor said no. The infection that had started in my womb and then settled into my right leg had done too much damage. He said he didn't think I could survive another miscarriage so soon after the other. He'd ordered me to wait until after the war and assured me I *would* be able to have children some day.

Davey took the doctor's orders to heart—no babies for now. He said it didn't matter to him if we ever had children as long as we had each other. But I have to say, it scares me silent to send my love to war without some part of him to stay behind. What if something happens . . .

My Darling Davey,

I miss you more than snow-covered grass misses summer. More than a clock misses tick tock. Ha. Ha.

I hope you are well. We are very fine. I'm getting stronger each day, able to do more to help around the house, which makes me happy, but worries your mother. She does allow me to fold some laundry and to do the mending, but beyond that she merely gives me that "look" and orders me to rest. I've secretly taken to walking a bit in the backyard, with the help of my cane, to toss crumbs to the birds when your mother is out of the house and the weather permits.

Poor Maddy is as restless as a cat. The war has severely curtailed her social life down to playing bridge with the neighbors or gang-of-girls movie nights. She seems to hold Lyle personally responsible for deserting her. I wonder if you should give another Marine her address? The mail seems to be our one bright spot in the day. The postman has never been in such delirious demand. Even your mother is not above stopping him at the sidewalk before he can visit the box properly.

I think of you constantly and wish I could kiss your dear face.
Your loving wife,
Ruth

My Dearest Ruth,

I swear, when I get back home, if I ever complain about the food, or the noise, or having an old pair of shoes, I hope you'll box my ears good. After what us men have faced at the hands of the U.S. Marines, going to war doesn't sound quite so bad. I understand they have to pound us down to size, especially some of these big-man hero types, but after marching five miles in new boots, and crawling what felt like another five, my feet and knees feel they have a right to complain.

And the needles. Ruth-E, I couldn't help but think of you and your terrible stay in the hospital when I was being prodded and poked by corpsmen with the tenderness of impatient prizefighters. I have bruises on my bruises.

I'm sorry about complaining when you've been through so much worse. I'm glad to hear you're getting on your feet again. And all kidding aside, nothing would bother me, not blisters or drill sergeants, or even hitting the deck before the chickens each morning, if I could only see your sweet smiling face.

I have to go now, five minutes to lights out.
All my love,
Your Davey

— MADDY —

Davey had been gone eight weeks before the telegram came. Oh, in the weeks prior, we'd each gotten letters and even a postcard or two with pictures of something called Battery Row in the city of Charleston. But this, this was a *telegram*. And, it was addressed to Ruth—Mrs. David Marshall.

Mother and I tried not to huddle around her too closely as she read it.

"DARLING," she began. Her cheeks blossomed with color but she went on, "TRAINING GOING WELL. BEING SENT FARTHER SOUTH. HAVE FOUND A PLACE FOR YOU. COME ON DOWN. LETTER FOLLOWING TELL YOU WHAT TO DO. BRING MADDY. LOVE= DAVEY"

I don't remember what my mother said because I was too busy hugging Ruth and whooping for joy. Davey wanted US to come visit him . . . somewhere south. Ruth had tears in her eyes when I finally let her go. She smiled for the first time in weeks.

"Can you do without us?" she asked my mother.

I held my breath as my mother's gaze settled on me. She couldn't stop Ruth from doing anything, but she could keep me at home. I had a fifty-fifty chance. Begging wouldn't help, or tears. My hope rested on Davey, Mother's favorite. Growing up, Mother rarely denied her son anything, especially after Father died, and now that he was going to war she'd surely give in. And he'd asked for me. I knew it had to do with helping Ruth, but I didn't care. *Thank you, brother.*

Eventually, after several eternal seconds of suspense, Mother nodded. "As soon as we know when and where, I'll ask Mr. Jenkins to arrange for the train tickets."

The letter with instructions postmarked Miami, Florida, arrived four days later, full of news to fuel our excitement.

Darling Ruth,

Miami is the greenest place I've ever seen—even now in what should be winter the palm trees flutter in the ocean breeze and the grass needs mowing. I think I've joined the Marines and gone to heaven. Sometimes we even do calisthenics right on the beach next to the water. The city itself is filling up fast with soldiers and dependents. The military has taken over some of the larger hotels for barracks. Everyone's here, Marines, Army, and Navy. There's hardly a hotel room to be had.

I've met a buddy who was born here and he's arranged with his parents to rent you and Maddy rooms for a month or so. I don't know how long I have and I don't like the idea of you living with strangers, but I want to see you too much to turn down the chance.

Leave your winter coats behind. You won't need them here. The salt air will do wonders for your good humor, and your beautiful face will do wonders for mine. Ha. Ha. I sound like I should get a job with the chamber of commerce. Maybe I will after this war is over.

Let me know your travel schedule. When you arrive, call Mrs. Charles Siler at LU-4287, she's expecting you and she'll supply directions from the station.

Please get here as soon as you can. I miss you more than I can say.

All my love,
Davey
PS—Tell Maddy she owes me one.

I did indeed. Since the day after my blighted birthday, life had taken a dramatic turn for the worse. Not in the same way as Davey and Ruth's had, of course, but enough to spoil the dregs of my good disposition. Not only had Lyle packed himself off to Navy training in Missouri, it seemed that most of the other boys had disappeared as well. From the Navy to the Army, even the Coast Guard, over half of the young men in town succumbed to the need to immediately join up. Walking down Main Street in Radley was like visiting a ghost town. People were worried. It seemed every conversation concerned what would happen now that we were in the war.

Gone were the Saturday night dances and Sunday afternoon get-togethers. Now, families and friends gathered around the radio to hear the latest on whether we would be bombed again, by the Japs or the Germans. I'd even had to give up my job at the drugstore due to the lack of customers.

I'd felt left out and left behind . . . until Davey's letter. Now it looked like this war thing might turn out okay after all. I was headed for Miami, Florida. First thing, I'd called Jeanne and Sharon, and they were practically technicolor with envy. I would have run through town shouting my good news, but the boys whose freedom I'd coveted were already gone. Besides, I needed to pack my suitcase.

Our trip was one long, tired blur. It took us three days to get to Florida by train. Because of the crush of people going south, Ruth and I were assigned coach seats, which meant a long and uncomfortable ride. The heat was turned up too high in our car so we took frequent excursions to stand in the connecting platform between cars to cool off. The car behind us had no heat at all. We had to console ourselves with the fact that we were lucky to have any seat in any car since the military men had first priority. If one or two extra soldiers needed to board, the corresponding number of civilians would have to get off and wait for the next train. At one stop, several soldiers gallantly offered to sit on the floor so as not to inconvenience other travelers. They didn't look much older than me and I wanted to talk to them, ask them where they were from, but I'd taken the seat near the window at the other end of the car—too far away to strike up casual conversation. Besides, my hair was a mess.

Sometime in the middle of the night after a stop near Greenville, South Carolina, an officer's wife boarded and demanded to be given a sleeper compartment. She gave the conductor a whole speech about supporting the war effort and refused to take no for an answer. When the railroad accommodated her, she gathered three other military wives, along with Ruth and me, and the six of us squeezed into the small space. At least we could close the door for some privacy. We gratefully took turns sleeping two in a bunk for the rest of the trip.

Ruth and I arrived in Miami dusty, wrinkled, and bone tired. Instead of being greeted by Davey, or even by swaying palm trees and a green oasis, we found an overcrowded station and had to stand in line after official line before clearing the red tape.

"You're required to have a place to stay or you can't leave the station," an official-looking matron explained when we reached the front of the line. Without acknowledging Ruth's cane or our tired faces, she went on, "If you don't have a place, you can sign up on the chamber of commerce waiting list." As Ruth dug in her purse for our landlady's address and telephone number, I glanced around. There were women everywhere, filling every vacant bench, some with several children in tow. A few looked as though they'd been there for days. I didn't want to imagine enduring a lengthy train ride then having to make myself at home in the station like a homeless refugee. Where were their husbands, the fathers of these children? But I knew the answer—going to war.

"Here's the address," Ruth said.

We watched the woman check the address against her map before nodding toward yet another line. "All right. You can use the telephone over there."

"It seems like every soldier in town has written home and invited his family to Miami without a thought as to where they might sleep," Mr. Charles Siler said as he drove us toward our new temporary home. Tall and thin, our new landlord reminded me of Ray Bolger in the easy, loose-limbed way he moved. At the station, he'd greeted us with a sort of resigned friendliness as though he didn't quite approve but would do his part.

"We're grateful to you and Mrs. Siler for your hospitality," Ruth said.

"Well, I should tell you my wife and I planned to rent to soldiers. The city is so full, it's our patriotic duty. And we can always use the extra money." He glanced back briefly in my direction with a frown before speaking to Ruth once more. "But since our Jack met your husband, he asked us to give you the place until they ship out."

Being reminded of the temporary status of our Florida adventure seemed to affect Ruth. Even in this sunny place, the dark cloud of separation wilted her smile. She looked down at the bag balanced in her lap. I spent my time gawking out the window. I wanted to see everything.

We'd left winter behind.

It was only the end of April, but it was already so warm the humid, salty air seemed to thicken every breath and weigh down each nonessential wool thread I wore on my back. My hair, dark like my father's, had taken on a life of its own and curled in all the wrong directions. It hadn't seen a pin curl since I left Pennsylvania. After spending three days on a train crowded into a sleeper berth with five other women, I was a bit rumpled and a lot tired. I couldn't have closed my eyes for a second, however. I tried to act grown-up and not ask too many questions, although Mr. Siler seemed happy enough to tell me the names of unfamiliar flowers or trees.

To me, every natural thing in south Florida seemed oversized and overgrown—from the feathery poinciana trees laced with fuchsia bougainvillea to the towering royal palms that lined the major boulevards like larger-than-life newsreel footage from Hollywood. Compared to the orderly, manicured, and stately streets of Radley, Pennsylvania, Miami was a temptress, gussied up and looking for a good time.

Our new temporary home turned out to be a big, rambling, two-story Mediterranean-style stucco house that fronted on the end of an overgrown road and backed on the Miami River. As Mr. Siler put it, "Close enough to the Atlantic to smell the salt tang in the air when the wind came out of the southeast, but far enough to require a bus ride across the causeway to take a swim."

Two huge, hairy-looking trees branched high over the house, shading out the grass in a yard of sand and ancient shells. A line of decrepit citrus trees weighed down with oranges and lemons formed a boundary, and a long wooden walkway connected what we learned was the Samuel place (where we would live) and the newer Siler house next door. Coconut palms crowded along the riverbank leaving fronds strewn on the ground like the decaying wings of some giant bird who'd flown too close to the sun.

My mother would have run screaming into the sunset at the general shabbiness of the paint and the scurry of bright green lizards along the porch. I could picture my mother uttering the famous Bette Davis line, "What a dump!" I was so tired, I didn't care. My future happiness depended on a bath, a change of clothes, and a nap.

I carried Ruth's smaller bag along with my own as we made our way to the front door of our temporary new home. Ruth seemed to depend on her cane a little more than usual, and I knew she had to be worn out.

Our new landlady pushed open the screened front door and held it for us to enter. "My sons Jack and Randy lived here before this war business came up," Mrs. Siler explained a few minutes later over cups of coffee and a plate of oatmeal cookies. "Now that Jack's in the Army, Randy lives next door with us again. You'll meet him at supper. He suffered a childhood bout of polio and lost the use of his legs, much like our President Roosevelt." She waved a hand around the sparsely furnished living room and changed the subject. "It's an old house—nothin' fancy. My father built it back in the twenties."

"I'm sure we'll do fine here," Ruth said, diplomatically.

I knew her well enough to hazard that Ruth would string a hammock between two coconut trees like a Seminole Indian and call it home sweet home if it meant being close to Davey for the short time he had left before shipping out.

As for me, I just hoped the bathroom was on the inside. I'd face worse than a herd of lizards before going home to my empty hometown and the iron thumb of my mother.

As though Mrs. Siler had a crystal ball, she gazed at me with a stern look not unlike my mother's when she demanded my complete attention. "I do have some rules," she said. "First, you'll eat evening meals at my house next door and share kitchen chores three times a week. That way you won't be wasting bottled gas or setting the house on fire."

It sounded like an equal possibility in her mind, and I couldn't dispute her. My cooking skills were less than Olympian. Mother had insisted on being the cook in our house. My job had been doing the ironing. I suppose I could have ironed the bacon to crispness but that was about it.

"There's some talk of more rationing. If that comes to pass then you'll have to turn over your coupons to me."

Ruth and I nodded companionably. I did my best not to fidget.

"Second, no men are allowed to linger after nine in the evening—eleven on the weekends." The tired slump of Ruth's shoulders suddenly stiffened. "Now I know you're a married woman, and this rule excludes your husband, of course," Mrs. Siler said quickly. "But your sister is young and single. In these times, with the city full of soldiers . . ." Her face flushed with color but she held her ground. "This house is my childhood home, and I have no intention of becoming the proprietor of any household of women who cause even a whisper of gossip in the neighborhood. We are members of the Presbyterian church and go to services every Sunday morning. Both of you are welcome to attend."

Ruth slid her hand over mine and squeezed. I didn't know if she meant it as comfort or to keep me from saying anything contrary—after all, we were cradle Catholics. "We won't do anything to disappoint you, Mrs. Siler," she said in an even voice. I knew Ruth would do whatever it took to be close to Davey. I myself would have scrubbed the woman's floors and washed the windows weekly rather than go back North. A few rules wouldn't hurt us. I took Ruth's cue and nodded my head in agreement.

"Good," she replied. "Now, lastly, I had planned to have a soldier or two live here to be some companionship for Randy.

He's confined to a wheelchair but he gets around fairly well. I'll expect you two to include him in any social activity that would be proper for him to attend, like movies or concerts. He loves to play cards," she added before pointedly looking at Ruth's cane. "You must understand how it is to be left out," she said.

I almost spoke up then. I was willing to do a lot, but poor Ruth could barely get around. I wanted to say something like, *Okay, first we're cooks and now we're baby-sitters. How about you paying us for staying here?* But Ruth beat me to the punch.

"Yes, I do understand. We'll do our best to entertain your Randy."

Later, after Ruth had used the Silers' telephone to leave a message for Davey at his barracks in the Regent Hotel, we took turns in the big claw-footed bathtub, which thankfully, was inside. I lingered in the long-anticipated bath until the water went cold, washed and pinned up my hair, then found I was still too excited for a nap. Ruth felt the same, so we took stock of our new home.

The old house had three bedrooms, two large ones downstairs and a smaller one upstairs, each with twin beds arranged against the eastern wall to catch the breeze off the ocean. Ruth and I each claimed one of the larger rooms leaving the upstairs vacant as Mrs. Siler suggested since the heat tended to gather in the attic. The dining room held an ancient but sturdy round table with six ladder-backed chairs, and the living room was decked out in chintz-covered wicker—a couch and two armchairs. But, in my opinion, the crowning addition to the living room was the big radio cabinet near the window. I fiddled with the dials until I found a station playing "It Ain't Gonna Rain No More" by Victor Young's orchestra. Then, with Ruth as my amused audience, I danced around the living room in my bathrobe and pin curls.

Even with her bum leg, Ruth could barely stay seated. I guess because she was too excited about seeing Davey again. I didn't blame her a bit. The love she felt for my brother was as plain as the long-lost smile on her face. As for me, I missed my boyfriend, Lyle, but being in Miami, seeing my own new place in the world went a long way to cheer me up. In fact, it could have been the weather or the many miles between me and my childhood home, but it seemed I could breathe easier. I felt grown-up and free for the first time in my life, and I determined right there and then to make the most of it.

We met Randy, the other member of the Siler household, at supper. The shock of seeing a young guy my brother's age confined to a wheelchair wore off by the end of the meal. It didn't take us long to figure out that Randy's bout with polio had left his legs disfigured but had done nothing to stunt his charm . . . or his sense of humor. Even in front of his parents he flirted shamelessly and seemed determined to outshine his disadvantages.

"There's talk of taking the sugar bowls off the restaurant tables since the Japs invaded the Philippines," Mr. Siler said as we sampled our chicken pie. "And candied yams are off the menus for the duration." He shook his head. "After kicking the dust of the Depression from our shoes, we're back in the soup lines."

"I imagine President Roosevelt knows what he's doing with this rationing. First gas and now sugar. Coffee will be next, I figure," Mrs. Siler said. "When the announcement is official, you girls need to go down and sign up for your new ration books."

"Yes, ma'am," Ruth answered.

She sounded agreeable, but to me she still looked tired. Both of us were bushed to beat the band. But the worst part for Ruth, I knew, was that we hadn't heard from Davey.

Conversation seemed destined to fail until Randy spoke up. "I don't know about the rest of you," he said with a challenging grin aimed directly at me, "but I think I'm sweet enough. They can toss those sugar bowls straight into the Atlantic."

"Why, I'm sure you're right," Mrs. Siler practically cooed. "You're my precious darling angel." Randy's mother gently patted his cheek like one might coddle a two-year-old, dimming the bright flare of mischief in his eyes.

I recognized the stamp of an overprotective mother—I'd survived with one my whole life. Before I could stop myself, I *accidentally* shot him the perfectly horrible gargoyle face I usually reserved for Davey. For one surprised moment, he simply stared back. Long enough for me to remember that I was picking on a defenseless cripple—even if it was for a good cause. Ruth's cough and discreet elbow to my ribs added to my shame. I could feel heat rising in my face as Randy's features shifted to a smile. He nodded, like a gunfighter calling my bluff. No doubt about it, I had tugged the lion's tail and would have to pay the price. Lucky for me, Mrs. Siler was gazing lovingly at her son rather than at her new mannerless boarder. I looked down at my plate rather than checking to see if Mr. Siler had observed the exchange.

A knock at the front door saved us from disaster.

Mrs. Siler frowned. "Now who could that be at dinnertime? Charles . . ." she prodded her husband.

Mr. Siler rose and went to find out.

Ruth, seated between me and the door, didn't turn to look. She seemed to freeze like she was holding her breath. As Mr. Siler swung open the front door I could see a man in uniform through the screen. "Davey!" I squealed and before you could say jack rabbit, I was on my feet. It took me a few seconds to understand I'd better help Ruth rather than stampeding over her. Instead of letting her depend on her cane, I gripped her arm and we both reached him at the same time.

Davey looked so handsome in his uniform. I mean he was still my brother and everything, but something about that pressed khaki and smart-looking hat made him seem different. Older or taller. I wondered if it would do the same for Lyle. He'd sent me a photo of himself wearing a cute sailor cap instead of the anchor and globe insignia of a Marine.

"There's my girls!" Davey said, barely inside the door before he threw an arm around each of us and then kissed Ruth on her cheek. I was close enough to see that for a moment, as he stared into her eyes a light seemed to go on inside her, as though my brother had done something magical to make Ruth forget being tired and stranded with strangers so far from home. I could also see that both of them had forgotten me. But that was okay. I'd gotten used to it.

Tears sparkled in Ruth's eyes before she composed herself and introduced Davey.

"Mr. and Mrs. Siler, Randy, this is my husband, David Marshall."

Davey gave me a breath-stealing squeeze before disentangling himself and shaking hands all around. Now that I could see him up close, he looked a little thinner, but there had been nothing weak about his grip on my ribs.

"It's nice to finally meet you, but where's Jack?" Mrs. Siler asked. "Didn't he come with you?"

"No, ma'am," Davey answered, shaking his head. "He's got duty this evening." He returned his gaze to Ruth. "I hitched a ride over, but I've only got a couple of hours before I have to be back."

Mrs. Siler, reminiscent of my mother—a woman in control—covered her disappointment quickly. "Have you had dinner? We were just sitting down."

"No ma'am. But I don't want to put you to any trouble."

"Nonsense. We always have enough to feed one of our fighting boys, don't we, Charles?"

In the blink of an eye we were reshuffling around the dining room table to make room, and Davey faced a heaping plate of chicken pie. Conversation shifted to the men and discussion of the expanding war in the Pacific and the new military support industry being built in Miami.

"Yes, sir. They've declared it an embarkation-debarkation port. Every county in Florida has some kind of military business going on. The weather makes it the perfect year-round place to train, especially Army pilots and Navy boys," Davey said. "Us Marines can go anywhere," he added with a saucy grin in Ruth's direction.

Ruth did her best to smile, but I had the feeling she wasn't excited about the prospect of Davey headed out to parts unknown so soon after walking in the door.

"I heard the Army is taking over all the hotels south of Forty-fourth Street," Mr. Siler commented.

"Yes, sir. They're turning out most of the tourists. I'm grateful to you and Mrs. Siler for taking in Ruth and Maddy. Why, I heard that one Army fella's wife is living in a chicken house with their two kids."

"That's disgraceful," Mrs. Siler said. "It's been reported over and over in the newspapers about Miami being filled to bursting yet those people keep coming."

A small space of silence followed her comment. Being one of "those people" I tried, unsuccessfully, not to take her statement as a personal condemnation. Ruth spoke up then and saved me from ruining our good fortune.

"We all want to believe there'll be room for one or two more," she said carefully. "Because it means one last chance to see our men before they go to war."

Mrs. Siler looked ready to put the kibosh on Ruth's sentiment, but our Ruth-E cut her off at the pass. "I'm sure you feel the same way about your son," she added.

"Well, I— Of course I understand," Mrs. Siler replied, her face pinkening in the effort of backtracking. "But a chicken house . . . Well, I never."

"Mother? Don't we have lemon pudding for dessert?" Randy asked.

Mrs. Siler, looking grateful for the change of subject, leaped on the suggestion. "Yes, darling, we do." She stood and began to collect the dinner plates.

Davey glanced at me and raised his eyebrows before pointedly staring at the other plates needing to be cleared. It didn't take a thump on the head to get the punch line. I pushed to my feet and collected the rest of the dishes before following Mrs. Siler to the kitchen.

As soon as decently possible after dessert, we left the Siler house, and I followed Davey and Ruth along the wooden walkway obviously built for Randy's wheelchair, which crossed the distance to the Samuel place. They walked arm in arm while I carried Ruth's cane. A breeze ruffled the palm trees and the sun, low in the west, glinted on the water. Marveling that we'd actually left winter behind and arrived in this exotic place, I drew in a deep breath of new air. The wind carried equal parts musty river water, grass, pine, and flowers. I couldn't wait to see the ocean.

"So, how was your trip?" Davey asked Ruth when we three were seated in the living room. We'd already given him a tour of our new home, and now that we knew the alternative— evicting the local chickens—we were much more lavish with our praise.

"Long," I said helpfully.

"Oh, it wasn't so bad," Ruth said, and only I knew she was lying. She still had that pleased look on her face, and she couldn't seem to stop staring at Davey, as though he might disappear at any moment. She left one hand balanced on his knee, to keep him anchored, I suppose. Then Ruth told him about Mrs. Albert Steele, the wife of the Army Air Corps' Colonel Steele, who'd given us a place to sleep on the train.

"You can bet *she's* not sleeping with the chickens," I said, remembering the woman's imperious tone with the conductor.

"I'm just glad you're here," Davey said, and I'm sure he meant both of us but he slid an arm around Ruth and pulled her closer to him on the couch. "How're you feeling?" he asked his wife.

I decided it was time to make myself scarce. No use sitting there and gawking at the two of them.

"I think I'll go outside and watch the sun set," I said, before Ruth gave him her answer.

"Good idea," Davey agreed, then winked.

Once outside the screen door, I kept an eye peeled for lizards as I slowly made my way along the walkway. The sun had dropped below the tree line along the river and looked like a bright, golden lantern shining through the leaves. But the clouds—the entire western sky was glorious in shades of pink and gold. And the trees were full of birds, chattering and fluttering, looking for their own private quarters I imagine. It was so breathtaking, I almost went back inside to get Davey and Ruth to come and see, but then I remembered the look on Ruth's face when Davey arrived. Ruth didn't need to see the sun—the light of her life was sitting next to her on the couch.

Besides, I wasn't alone on the walkway. Further along, a little closer to the river, Randy sat in his wheelchair, a pair of binoculars clutched in his hands.

"Want to take a gander?" he said as I approached. He held out the binoculars to me.

"What are you looking at?" I asked.

"Birds," he answered. He tapped the notebook balanced in his lap. "This time of year a lot of species are migrating. I have over a hundred on my sighting list already. You'd better hurry, it's getting dark fast."

I was more interested in the wondrous colors changing in the sky than the birds, but with my newly formed determination to see everything clanging in my head, I dutifully raised the binoculars and fiddled with the wheel until I could view the river. Suddenly a large, snowy white bird came into focus. He looked like he was walking on stilts.

"Oh, I see a big one! He's very tall, standing in the water."

"That's just an egret. There are lots of those around. Look up in the trees," Randy instructed. "That's where the rarer birds will be."

"*Just* an egret," I mimicked. "I think he's beautiful. I've never seen anything so strange." I continued to watch as the bird lowered his head and plunged his long sharp beak into the water. When he raised his head, a tiny fish wiggled at the end. "Oh look, he's caught a fish!"

Randy made a sound of disgust. "I forgot you're a Yankee," he said in a disparaging tone.

When I lowered the glasses to argue, I saw the same mischievous smile he'd worn at dinner. "And I was gonna apologize for making a face at you, but I forgot you're a scoundrel, so we must be even." I handed the binoculars back to him.

"I'm tougher than I look." He grinned then sat up a bit straighter in his chair before pulling the strap of the glasses over his head. "Too dark to see much with these now, anyway," he said, returning to the original subject. "Pull up a seat."

There wasn't a chair in sight.

To prove I was up to the challenge, I gathered my skirt and sat on the walkway next to him resting the heels of my shoes in the sand. The brilliant pink clouds in the sky had shifted to purple as the sun fell below the horizon. The trees were becoming lacy black silhouettes. In those moments I decided I could watch God's Florida artwork every evening for the rest of my days and be content.

"By next week I'll be looking for enemy planes rather than birds," Randy informed me.

Shaken from my reverie by the declaration of one more man in a hurry to go to war I answered, "What do you mean? Surely you haven't joined the Army."

I was glad the gathering darkness hid my warming face. I'd done it again. Of course a man in a wheelchair couldn't join the Army. Even men who could walk and wanted to go but had had rheumatic fever or asthma or flat feet were designated 4-F.

"No, they won't let me join, not even the Coast Guard. But they're setting up observation posts and air-raid filters. I've been studying the silhouette sheets of German planes. There's nothing wrong with my eyes," he declared.

I didn't know whether to apologize again or let it go. At this rate I'd be crowned the rudeness champion of the world if I kept allowing my mouth to outpace my manners. It seemed I was destined to lower his opinion of any "Yankee" he met in the future.

Keeping to a safer subject, I asked, "Do you really think Miami could be bombed?"

"There've been rumors that the Germans have planes flying within two hours of the Atlantic seaboard. And we know their submarines are right off the coast. They've already sunk five merchant ships in the Florida straits. Not long ago, thousands of new shoes washed up on the beach."

I gazed at the sky, which had darkened to indigo in the east and watched the first twinkling star appear. My adventure to see the world suddenly took on a different tone. I had told Davey it wasn't fair that girls couldn't go to war, yet thinking of the very real possibility that the war might come to me, gave me a shiver. I thought of all the women and children who'd followed their men south. Surely the Army, Navy, and Marine Corps officers and men, our husbands or brothers stationed in the area, would not have brought their families with them if there was imminent danger of attack.

"Davey wouldn't have brought us here if it wasn't safe," I said with utter confidence.

"Oh yeah? Tell that to the families who were stationed at Pearl Harbor and Honolulu." When I didn't reply he went on. "You know what? Most of those families are now evacuees who've been transferred by ship to Miami. I mean to make sure that after facing the scurrilous, yellow-bellied *Saps* and their sneak attack, they won't have to deal with the Germans."

It was now almost full dark, and I'd begun to feel rather small and far from home. Ruth or Davey had switched on the lights in the Samuel place but I remained seated and silent.

"I'm sorry, I didn't mean to scare you," Randy said. He seemed to shake off his serious mood. "I forgot you're just a girl."

"Oh yeah?" I countered, natural contrariness fueling my courage. "Well, how old do you have to be to volunteer? I'm almost eighteen," I found myself saying—only slightly a lie. "My eyes are as good as yours."

About then the screen door of the Samuel house swung open and Davey stepped through with Ruth. I clammed up quick so as not to have my real age debated, then stood, dusting my skirt as they came toward us.

"It's time for me to get back," Davey said, yet he kept his arm around Ruth as though he wasn't quite ready to let her go.

"Mr. Siler said he'd drive me over the causeway. I can't be late. I've got to be on my best behavior to earn a pass for the weekend." Davey gave me a brotherly hug. "I can hardly get used to the idea that you girls are here."

I nodded, feeling the same way.

Randy turned his chair toward the Siler house as Davey walked Ruth past him. "Hey, how about a push?" Randy asked before I could get by.

His smile said he was deviling me—payback for my smart-aleck mouth. He knew this game better than me. If I let loose with a wisecrack, I'd be up to my neck in trouble again, so I kept mum. But when I didn't answer, Davey stopped and turned. Even in the near darkness, I could see the message. I needed to earn points any way I could. Score one for Randy. He had the nerve to laugh. I felt like giving him a good pinch, but instead I dutifully gripped the handles of his chair and gave it a shove.

— RUTH —

*A*fter getting into bed and saying my prayers, I thought I'd fall immediately into dreamless sleep. All my wishes had been fulfilled. I'd seen Davey, not simply dreamed of seeing him as I had for these past months. Maddy and I had settled in and we seemed to be welcome, if paying, guests of the Silers. I don't believe I could have asked for more. Unless the war could be ended with a wish. I felt a totally inappropriate happiness mixed with guilt at being away from Davey's well-meaning but domineering mother. She'd made it her business to literally get me back on my feet after my last hospital stay. Then, Maddy and I had left her alone. The best I could do would be to write often and share a hope for the future I couldn't explain.

Being with Davey again was my heart's hope come true and pure torture at the same time. I swear, as soon as I'd looked into his eyes, the memory of the long, tiring trip and the fear of our uncertain future went right out of my mind. Davey has always had that effect on me. It wasn't fair really, or safe to love someone so much. But there you have it. He's been my weakness and my strength since I first set eyes on him back in the summer of '39.

We met on a blind date . . . sort of. One fateful weekend, three of the girls in the office at Talbot's where I worked, and I, promised to meet a bunch of guys Friday night under the clock at the Clarion Hotel in downtown Philly. We knew one or two of them but the rest were come-alongs. The evening nearly ended before it got going. It turned out our bus was late and the boys were early. We found them in deep discussion as to whether they should wait another thirty minutes or cut their losses and go to the movies alone.

You should have seen their expressions when we raced up the stairs laughing, like Superman to save the day—no, Superwomen to save the night.

That's when I spotted Davey. And from that moment, it was as though his face was the only one I could see clearly. The rest were a pleasant but unaffecting blur of smiles. Even after the bunch of us were introduced, he never took his gaze from mine.

In four months we were married, in six I was expecting and about the happiest woman walking the earth. We've had our trials since then. Some worse than others. But we love each other. And that's how I think of this war, as another trial that we need to get through to find our happiness on the other side.

But Davey is here now, I reminded myself, even though I was still sleeping alone. *We're both here in Miami.* "I love you, Davey," I whispered as though he were a hand's reach away. "I won't let fear or uncertainty darken however many bright days we have left together."

With that determination in my heart, I shifted onto my side and stared through the screen at the stars twinkling in this foreign southern sky. Even the unexpected gift of the balmy air ruffling the curtains conspired to lighten my heart. The thought that I could be happy here drifted through my sleepy thoughts. But then, I could be happy anywhere as long as I had Davey.

I felt so content, I almost had to remind myself that there was a war on.

Chapter Two

— MADDY —

By the weekend, Ruth and I had feathered our nest as best we could. After writing letters home to Mother (and to Lyle in Missouri), describing our good luck in the housing and climate gamble, we cheerfully folded our winter duds and stored them in the back of the closet. I'm not sure what Ruth said in hers, but in my letters I'd been careful to keep any whiff of my newly minted freedom to myself.

Dear Mother,

We've arrived safely. Our "quarters" as Davey calls them are in a house owned by a very nice family—the Silers. One son, Jack, is Davey's friend, and the other, Randy, lives at home. Randy is confined to a wheelchair due to polio. Seeing a young man so afflicted certainly makes one count her blessings. I'll never complain about having to walk to work again.

I'm sure you're wondering about our situation. Well, don't worry. We're being looked after very well, living in a house in a neighborhood not so different from ours in Radley although all the plants and birds are strange. Ruth and I even have our own rooms. The weather here is as glorious as Davey promised, although we haven't seen the ocean yet. I'm not sure I'll ever get used to the warmth so early in the year.

I miss you and Jeanne and Sharon dreadfully. I never thought I'd be so homesick. Tell everyone hello.

Your loving daughter,

Maddy

If I'd confessed to being happy, I was sure my mother would find some reason for me to return home. I'd also lost interest in torturing Lyle with my disapproval. How could I stay mad at him for deserting me when I was in the middle of my own adventure?

Darling Lyle,

You simply must see Miami. After this war thing is over, let's plan our honeymoon trip to include south Florida. I think it's ever more exciting than Atlantic City or Niagara Falls.

I hope you're not too unhappy about me being here without you. This trip has done wonders for my disposition. I've hardly been in the dumps once. It's hard to be sad with the sun shining and the birds chirping. I promise to send you a postcard a day as soon as I get to a drugstore to buy some.

Take care of yourself, sweets, and write to me at my new address for the time being.

Yours always,

Maddy

On Saturday morning the adventure took a new turn. Mr. Siler offered to take Ruth and me with him to run errands so we could see more of Miami besides Ninth Avenue, where we lived. Randy came along as our tour guide.

"Miami Beach is actually an island," Randy informed us. "We have to go over the causeway to get there."

There seemed to be water everywhere, from the river, to the bay, to the ocean. The causeway, it turned out, was the longest, flattest bridge I had ever seen. Randy explained that the span crossed the waters that separated the mainland from the largest of the three man-made islands, dividing Biscayne Bay from the Miami harbor. "It used to be nothing but swamp and mangroves," he said.

"What kind of boats are those?" I asked, pointing to the

sturdy-looking gray craft with large white numbers painted on their sides moored three deep along the bayside. They reminded me of a picture I'd seen once of logs caught in the eddy of a flooded river—pressed in side by side and stuck.

"Those are PT boats," Randy explained. "The Navy uses them to protect the coastline and the shipping lanes from the Germans."

"They have more boats than dock. Why do they need so many?"

"I suppose because there are a lot of ships and a lot of Germans."

Remembering our prior conversation about the possibility of being bombed took the wisecrack I might have made right out of my mind.

In the next minute, Mr. Siler slowed the car and pulled to the right to allow a bus to go by. As it passed I could see that it was filled with sailors.

"My boyfriend, Lyle, is in the Navy," I said, smiling at the passing boys who whistled and waved their white hats out every window like flags of surrender. "I wonder what kind of boats they have in Missouri."

"They won't train on boats in Missouri, silly. They have to go through basic training and probably gunnery school before they get to be on the ships. Hey, look at those planes!" Randy pointed toward the east at three tiny specks in the azure sky over the ocean. "I wish I'd brought my binoculars. Those are probably trainers out of Opa-Locka."

I hadn't informed Ruth of the possibility that we might be bombed. I figured she had enough worry in her mind over Davey going to war. And, I knew in my heart that German bombs and submarines were probably not enough for her to give up and go back to Pennsylvania. So, I simply ooohed and aaahed as the planes roared overhead, while my heart thumped in my chest.

On the far side of the causeway, we had to stop behind the busload of sailors at a gate guarded by two soldiers. By the time the soldiers raised the barrier and waved the bus through, there were at least four sailors hanging from the windows to get a closer look at Ruth and me. As brazen as could be, they called out their names and declared their undying love.

I had to laugh. Mr. Siler even cracked a smile. That kind of exuberance is just plain sweet. Once the bus turned the corner, we had an unobstructed view of the main avenue of Miami Beach. And compared to the main street of Radley, my almost deserted hometown, Federal Highway was a sight for sore eyes.

It wasn't the tall, royal palm trees, as Mr. Siler explained, or the stores and movie theater that impressed me. It wasn't even the ocean, although the greenish-blue water made me glad I owned a bathing suit.

It was the men.

Busload of sailors notwithstanding, there were men . . . everywhere. Most of them were wearing uniforms and marching this way or that between barriers set up down the middle of the street. The rest stood on corners, or waited in line at the diner, or drove by in jeeps and trucks. Even the two soldiers guarding the gate had seemed to take their time looking our car over before passing us through.

"To be on the safe side, if you were my daughters, I would advise either of you girls not to come over here alone. Day or night," Mr. Siler said as we pulled onto the main road. "This many men thrown together and facing God knows what later on are likely to forget good manners."

Heck, Ruth was twenty-three and too old to be called a girl. I was almost eighteen and the threat of bad manners didn't scare me one bit. Even on a good day, I myself remained likely to "put my foot in it," as Davey always said. Whether that meant my mouth or a hole I'd dug with thoughtless words, I would have to plead guilty. I decided not to dispute Mr. Siler's advice, however, due to his hospitality and the remaining tatters of my own good manners. My mother would have been proud.

First up on our trip, we delivered a sorely needed transmission part to a Sunoco station across the street from a tire store with a large sign reading OFFICIAL OPA TIRE INSPECTION. While we waited in the car, Randy explained that his father was an auto parts dealer which held certain advantages, one of the most important being he could get gasoline whenever he needed it—no rationing since it was vital to the government to keep military and civilian vehicles in good repair. Cars would have to be made to last since the factories were gearing up to make planes, ships, and tanks.

"Can either of you girls drive?" Randy asked, looking at me.

The good news was, yes, I knew how to drive. Davey had taught me the summer before he joined the Marines. The bad news was, I had no license—Florida or otherwise. I knew Ruth could drive as well, but her bad leg had put a halt to it until some future time. Randy being disadvantaged himself had probably already figured that out. "Of course," I answered.

"Great. So, whenever you girls want to take a ride or go to the beach, you let me know. I'll get my dad to let us use the car."

Randy didn't know it yet, but in that instant he'd made a permanent pal. A pal—me—who was very aware that this Miami "vacation" could end at any time and I'd have to go back home. I intended to have fun now. I just had to get my bearings first.

Once I grew accustomed to the sight of uniformed men sprouting from every foot or so of the sidewalk, the rest of our tour was relatively commonplace. Except for surprising glimpses of water between the buildings and the smell of the ocean in the air. We drove down Lincoln Road, which was lined by department stores, banks, and offices. Randy pointed out one of his favorite places, an ice-cream parlor next door to the movie theater. A marquee announced a movie called *Enemy Agents* starring Margaret Lange was playing through the weekend. That was one I hadn't seen.

You might call me somewhat of a movie fiend—a devoted

fan who'd worked every day after school in the drugstore back home to have my own matinee money. Movies had saved my life. I thought of myself as a prisoner and weekly matinees were my parole. Earning my own admission meant the warden, my mother, couldn't declare it a waste of *her* money. I think sometimes she admired my ambition although she had no idea how far I would go. Mother only "allowed" me to see musicals and comedies. But my friend Sharon and I had seen every film—sometimes three on a Saturday—that had made its way to Radley, from the silent, *Woman of Affairs* with Greta Garbo to the enchanting *Wizard of Oz*. I especially loved the romantic ones. We'd seen *Gone with the Wind* five times—Sharon had even renamed her tabby cat Scarlett. If mother had found out about the extent of what she considered an unsavory pastime, I'd still be doing some sort of penance. It was bad enough when I went to confession. My multiplying score of Hail Marys would've made her faint.

It was almost startling to realize that here, so far from mother and home, I could see as many movies as I wanted without having to worry about getting caught. I couldn't wait to write and tell Sharon. I managed to talk Mr. Siler into stopping at the drugstore to buy postcards to send home. Ruth and I sprang for ten each—most with photographs of the famed Miami Beach. I bought one for Lyle that had a cartoon of a big fish with a fisherman dangling from the wrong end of the pole. Since he'd joined the Navy I figured he must be interested in boats and fishing. Besides, the card was too comical to pass up.

Into the final leg of our tour, on the way back to the causeway, Mr. Siler drove us by the Vanderbilt Hotel, which had been converted to the Army's School of Aviation.

"That's where our boy Jack is training," Mr. Siler said, proudly. "He's gonna make a darned good pilot."

I glanced toward Randy, wondering, with his talk about volunteering, how he felt about not measuring up to his brother. I knew what it felt like to be second in line even though there was nothing wrong with my legs.

Randy stared back like the plane spotter he aspired to be, on guard for any sort of pity. "Jack said he's gonna get permission to take me up in his plane," he said. "Have to wait until after graduation though—as soon as he gets his wings."

"You girls will meet him tomorrow. He'll be home for church and Sunday dinner," Mr. Siler added.

Jack turned up sooner than that, although not in person. He called at dinnertime. Mrs. Siler was already frowning about having dinner interrupted again until she found out it was her son.

"But Jackie, can't you come home?" I heard her say into the phone. Then she listened, looking disappointed. Suddenly she turned to gaze at Ruth and me with an expression I couldn't describe. "Well, I suppose he could do that," she said, reluctance in her voice. "But are you sure? I'm not certain that's a proper place for someone Maddy's age." Her expression changed then, to one I would later dub "the calculator." As in who owes what to whom. She looked at me. "Yes, I know her brother is there. Well, I think he should bring Randy along as well."

Now both Ruth and I knew we were being discussed, though we had no idea what was coming. Hope and nervousness ran neck and neck through my thoughts while freedom whispered in the wings. Anyplace Mrs. Siler thought I shouldn't go sounded like the very place for me.

"All right, dear," she said, giving in. "I'll see you tomorrow at church then." After hanging up the phone, Mrs. Siler returned to the table, sat down, and straightened her napkin in her lap before giving us the news. By that time I felt like jumping out of my skin.

"Daddy," she said to her husband, "Jack wants you to drive Ruth and Madelyn down to meet them at the Servicemen's Pier after dinner." I was already grinning before she got to the good part. "He and Ruth's husband have a liberty pass until midnight—"

I'm afraid I let go of a very unladylike yahoo at that point and hugged Ruth. I knew her one pleasure in life was being with my brother, and escaping from Mrs. Siler to have some fun was fast becoming the new goal of my life. The Servicemen's Pier, whatever that was, sounded like a wonderful place to start.

"The pier is run by the Women's Auxiliary and the Red Cross," our landlady explained. "In the daytime they have classes and games, as well as a beach club for the soldiers. At night they have refreshments and music for dancing. I'm sure you girls will enjoy it."

In my mind I had already started going through the outfits I had brought for the perfect thing to wear when she added, "I told him you would be bringing Randy along as well."

That took some of the wind out of my sails. Not that I didn't like Randy or feel sorry for his affliction. I just didn't want to spend my first night of freedom baby-sitting and being polite. I'm not sure what kind of expression I had on my face but in the silence following her proclamation, I looked at Randy.

He blinked like a mind reader who'd finished tallying the contents of my head and found himself left out of the total.

In that silent moment of communication, I knew two things. One, I was definitely not going to heaven and two, Randy's heart was twenty-four carat.

"Mother, I don't feel up to it tonight," he said, without missing a beat.

Guilt and giddiness warred behind my smile. You had to admire a master. With one deft move, Randy had given us our freedom and diverted his mother. Mrs. Siler immediately moved to his side and began fussing over him. I gave him a wink and a silent promise—we'd take him anytime he wanted to go in the future.

How can I describe a place like the Servicemen's Pier? The building itself was built of simple, square concrete block and stucco, the only decoration being the cast insert of a pelican (another exotic bird to a Yankee) over the door and a temporary wooden sign stenciled with the name and the date of dedication. Nothing like it existed in my hometown, and I knew that in years to come, I would look back and know that this was where my life began. To me, it was Christmas in springtime. A mystery gift I couldn't wait to unwrap: music on the breeze, a tropical moon over the water, gay laughter, and freedom.

When we arrived, Davey and Jack Siler were standing out front with a group of ten or so men in uniform, smoking cigarettes. Judging by the reception we got as we stepped from the car, you'd have thought we were visiting members of the Rockettes.

"This is Maddy, my kid sister," Davey said to Jack. "And my wife, Ruth." That's as far as he got before soldiers and sailors crowded around with offers of help or guided tours. Davey and Jack had to assure the others more than once that they had our well-being under control.

"I'll be back at eleven-thirty," Mr. Siler said, as Ruth thanked him for the ride. By the time he'd pulled away, three soldiers had piled in his car for a lift to some important destination. And before we reached the entrance to sign in, I'd shaken Jack's hand and promised dances to four different men.

Heaven. I could hear music playing as we walked down the hallway toward the end of the pier. We passed smoke-filled rooms crowded with soldiers playing billiards or cards, reading books, or writing letters. Mrs. Siler had been right. In normal times my mother would've never approved of such a place, but thankfully, Davey had either forgotten that or figured the old rules didn't apply to wartime. Or maybe he just had his mind on Ruth.

A cool breeze cleared the air as we stepped onto the wooden dance floor built out over the water at the open end of the pier. As Ruth, Davey, and I looked for a table along the wall near the water, Jack went to the refreshment stand to wait in line for punch.

Before I'd even gotten my seat warmed, Davey pulled Ruth out onto the dance floor among the ten or so couples swaying to "Waltzing in the Clouds." Ruth wasn't much of a dancer with her bad leg, but it didn't seem like Davey minded taking slow steps and having her lean on him.

Some of the boys who'd greeted us outside showed up by the time Jack returned with our punch. He acted worse than my brother when it came to pulling rank and warning them off.

"Come on, fella. We just want a dance," one of them pleaded. "We haven't danced with a girl in months."

"Well, you don't have to trample her. Give her a minute to catch her breath."

I looked around the room and realized every available female had been claimed while men stood along the walls three deep in some places, watching the band and tapping their feet. After suffering the mostly empty dance floors back in Radley, it seemed like I'd hit pay dirt. If only my friends Jeanne and Sharon were here. I couldn't wait to write them the news.

Dear Lonely Hearts,

I have one important thing to say to you sad sacks. THE BOYS ARE ALL IN FLORIDA. Miami, to be exact. I've been dancing on a pier built over the ocean—with no less than fifty sailors, soldiers, and Marines. It's like being in a movie instead of watching one.

I swear I may never come home.

Have to run now . . . Ta Ta. I'll write again soon. Think of me under the palm trees in the arms of a handsome stranger.

Maddy

I wondered if Lyle was standing in a line of hopefuls in some Missouri dance hall. As a dance partner, he'd been reliable rather than flashy. Before this whole war thing, I'd been trying to teach him the jitterbug. I'd had better luck and fun with Sharon as my partner. "Dancing with these boys is my patriotic duty, I guess," I said, tempering my smile. I hadn't danced in months either.

"Okay," Jack said. He frowned mightily at my suitors. "Army goes first. You Navy guys stand back. And make sure you keep your hands to yourselves. Go ahead and pick one, Maddy."

His name was Larry and he hailed from Lincoln, Nebraska. When the first song ended too soon and another soldier tried to claim me, Larry argued successfully that he'd spent the first half of the music in negotiations with Jack. Then Larry proceeded to step on my new Spectator pumps twice during the next song as he told me how he missed his daddy's farm and his favorite bird dog.

An hour later I'd danced with a John, an Edwin, a Ralph, and a Richard. I lost track after that. I was finally getting around to the sailors who'd been waiting patiently when Jack cut in.

"Your brother sent me over here to check on you," he said as he slid his arm around me. "Are you doing okay? These guys haven't eaten you alive or anything?"

On close inspection, my first impression of Jack, other than his pro-Army sentiments, was that he smelled good. Old Spice, I believe. And I would have said he was taller than his brother Randy, but since Randy couldn't stand up straight there wasn't any way to know. "My feet are killing me," I answered.

"I'll do my best to stay off 'em, then," he said with a chuckle. "How do you like Miami so far?"

"Oh, I'm having a grand time," I assured him. "Other than my feet, I mean. And your parents have been really nice." A little family buttering-up never hurt.

He looked down at me with a knowing smile. "Is that so? I know my mother can be worse than a by-the-book drill sergeant when she puts her mind to it. So, you really like them?"

Hitler had nothing on Mrs. Siler, but I didn't think Jack

would be amused by the comparison so I kept it to myself. Randy, however, was fair game. "Well," I said, "your brother calls me a Yankee and gives me heartburn half the time, but yes, I like them fine."

Jack put his head back and laughed out loud. "That Randy. He's a pip, for sure. When I ship out, I think I'll miss him more than anybody." As the song ended, Jack gripped my arm and turned me toward Ruth and Davey. "Come on, let's make a run for it," he said and pulled me along as potential dance partners jostled for my attention.

"Maybe later," I offered to the new recruits, glad for the excuse to sit down for a while.

There were two other men who'd hauled chairs up to our table while I'd been dancing. They stood as Jack pulled out a seat for me.

"Maddy, this is Lt. Stephen Tull-Martin," Jack said. "One of the instructors at the aviation school, and—"

"Frankie Santorini, U.S. Marines." Grinning, the second man pumped my hand twice then held on. "I'm in Davey's unit."

"Nice to meet you," I said, waiting for him to let go.

When he didn't, Davey reached up and separated our hands. "She's off limits to you, Romeo."

"Aw, come on, Davey. I'm harmless. I'm a married fella." As we sat down, Frankie gave me a smile he must have thought looked innocent. Even I could tell he was pulling my leg.

"Lt. Tull-Martin is from England," Jack said. "He just got back from fighting the Germans."

The lieutenant's smile was closer to a grimace. I noticed a polished wooden cane leaning against the wall behind him. He tapped his right leg. "I'm afraid they made more of a dent in me than the other way 'round."

"Don't you believe it, ladies. He's got a Flying Cross to prove it. He's a genuine war hero."

"Everybody calls me Tully except for this mob," the lieutenant said as he shook my hand. "And the main distinguished thing about me is that I'm still alive." He briefly looked down at the drink he held in his hand, then smiled at Jack. "But now that you Yanks are involved, I'm happy to let you have a go at 'em."

"We'll have those Gerrys beat by Christmas," Jack announced, then added, "hey look! There's Bryan and Tuckerman."

Soon our table was surrounded by friends of Jack's from the aviation school, Marines from my brother's unit, and a few sailors left over from the sea of partnerless dancers.

I ended up dancing with another ten or twelve sailors and soldiers before pleading foot fatigue. Actually, I needed to visit the bathroom, and since the pier had been designed as a recreation center for soldiers most of the facilities were labeled for the men. I had to get one of the Red Cross volunteers to show me the way to the ladies' room.

"Hi. I'm Cleo—" She shook my hand. "—from California. My husband Johnny is in the Navy." Tall, thin, and almost boyish with her short, bobbed hair, Cleo nevertheless looked smart in her Red Cross uniform. Of course it didn't hurt that her legs could rival Betty Grable's even wearing sensible shoes.

"I'm Maddy. My sister-in-law Ruth and I came down to see my brother Davey before he ships out with the Marines." It seemed like we were all destined to be defined by our relationship to the men involved in the war. That wasn't much of a challenge to me since all through school and growing up in Radley, I'd always been Davey's little sister.

Ignoring the adoring looks and outright catcalls from a group of sailors near the door, Cleo led me down a dim hallway to a room back behind the kitchen.

"You need to get some nice sensible saddle oxfords," Cleo advised as she waited, smoking a cigarette, outside the stall in the ladies' room. "Otherwise these dances will cripple ya."

"I only brought my three best pairs of dress pumps," I answered. "They're pure torture." I straightened my skirt and moved to the sink to wash and dry my hands.

Cleo drowned out her cigarette in the sink before tossing it into the trash. "How long did you say you were planning to stay in Miami?"

"I don't know. Until Davey leaves."

She looked me over closely. "Are you eighteen?"

The lie wouldn't come out of my mouth so I nodded my head.

"Well, we're always looking for volunteers. If you think you might want to work with the Red Cross, leave your name and a phone number at the desk where you signed in at the front." She led me back to the dance floor. "Oh, and try Burdines on Federal for those shoes," she added.

The band had taken a break, so during the lull in the music, I migrated toward one of the open pier windows instead of going back to the table. The window itself was covered by a solid black panel that jutted out like an awning. I propped my arms on the window frame and leaned to the side so I could look between the frame and the panel. From that angle the ocean spread out before me like an invitation to the ends of the earth. I drew in a deep sample of the salty breeze and smiled into the wind. My parents had taken us on one or two lake vacations growing up. But they seemed uninterested in traveling to the ocean. I could hardly believe that I, Maddy Marshall, had journeyed halfway, top to bottom across the country, practically on my own, to visit the whole Atlantic. It seemed to me that if you boarded a boat here, you could end up anywhere in the world. I remembered that Lyle had been to the Jersey shore one summer, and I wondered if that's why he'd joined the Navy.

The drone of a distant plane, out over the water, caught my attention, causing my heart to give an extra beat or two. Surely it was one of ours. The dying edges of twilight held on against the first few evening stars as I squinted to find it in the gloom.

"That's an Army P-23 trainer, probably out of Homestead," a voice behind me said. "Those boys would train twenty-four hours a day if you let 'em," the voice continued.

I turned to face the source of the information but I'd already identified Lieutenant Tull-Martin by his accent.

"Do you mind?" he asked, before propping an elbow on the sill next to mine. I shook my head no. He smiled and then gazed out over the water.

"It's so beautiful," I said.

"That it is," he said, slowly, as though he wasn't sure he meant it.

"I feel like if we could look hard enough, we'd see England or Europe and Africa."

He chuckled and I immediately felt like a silly schoolgirl, dreaming dreams out loud.

"There's a good bit of water between here and there," he said. "But if you could see that far, you'd see the white cliffs of Dover."

"Like the song," I added, helpfully.

"Yes, exactly."

"You must miss your home?"

He turned away from the water then and gazed at me. "I'm not sure how to answer that. Yes, and no, I suppose. You see, on most beautiful, clear nights like this one, the Germans used to cross the channel in their bombers. And every time they did, a bit more of my home was destroyed. I've always felt rather helpless, stuck on the ground." He frowned. "But here I am with a beautiful young lady, talking about war. Let's just say it does no good to miss home. So, I try not to. I know I can't go back until the war's over because I'm no good to anyone at home except when I'm away. Does that make sense?"

"You mean away fighting the Germans?"

"Yes, or training Yanks like our Jack to fight them. He's pretty good, you know." His eyes shifted back to the plane as it flew into the darkness headed north. "They're all pretty good. I hope they're enough."

For a few seconds Lt. Tull-Martin seemed a million miles from Miami beach, the Servicemen's Pier, and me. I wanted to say something brilliant and witty. "Davey says we'll have 'em beat by Christmas," I offered, hoping to cheer him up. The following moment of silence was filled with the pounding of my heart.

"Ah, yes. Well, I hope your Davey is right." His smile looked more polite than hopeful, and I had the feeling he'd run out of small talk. "Shall we join the others?" he asked, then offered his arm like he'd been asked to escort the queen of England.

"Of course," I said, doing my best to sound older and sophisticated. I slipped my arm in his and, after a jaunty stab with his walking stick in the direction of the table that made me laugh, we were on our way.

Frankie Santorini and Jack were deep in a discussion about the merits of the Packard Club Coupe versus the Chrysler 41 Windsor as Lt. Tull-Martin pulled out a chair for me. Unfortunately, it was between the two of them. I felt like the net must feel in a tennis match. I'd barely settled when the discussion grew louder, and the best-looking-car claims more outrageous, as though I would have to settle the score and choose or there might be trouble. Heck, I wouldn't know a carburetor from a carbuncle. And watching them made me think of two little boys who, at any moment might say, "Oh, yeah? Well my old man can beat up your old man!" They'd reached the *oh, yeah,* stage, when a Red Cross volunteer showed up at the table carrying a camera. It was one of those big square ones like the photographers in the newsreels lug around.

"Cleo sent me over. I shoot pictures and sell copies. The money goes to the Red Cross fund. Are you kids game?"

After a few moments of everyone talking at once, she had those of us who were seated: Ruth, Davey, Jack, Frankie, and me, scoot our chairs to one side of the table while the rest of the men, including Lt. Tull-Martin, crowded in behind us. It was a rowdy group, a mix of Army airmen, Marines, and sailors, most of whose names I either didn't know or couldn't remember. The band had returned to the elevated stand at the other end of the room and the trumpet player played a bit of reveille to bring us to attention as though we were part of the show. There were wolf whistles and wisecracks from the peanut gallery of onlookers doing their best to make us laugh and spoil the shot. At the last second, Frankie Santorini slung an arm around my shoulders. The camera flash went off and I saw spots in front of my eyes for fifteen minutes.

I was sure this is what it felt like to be a movie star.

All in all, we had a swell time. I'd already determined that I'd just enjoyed one of the most memorable nights of my whole life. Jeanne and Sharon were going to absolutely scream when I sent them a copy of the photo. Of course I'd have to think about how to accomplish that without my mother finding out. Her unnatural nose for trouble would certainly pick up a whiff of any proof of my long-distance joy. And, she'd have conniptions if she knew I'd been within ten miles of a place like the Servicemen's Pier.

Well, like Scarlett O'Hara, I'd worry about that tomorrow.

— RUTH —

What a blissful evening! I can't remember the last time Davey and I went dancing. Of course I couldn't dance very well, but the music overcame my lingering weakness, and having Davey's arms around me lightened my heart. Slow dances have their benefits. The hours flew by until the band announced thirty minutes to curfew which meant the military men had to return to quarters. And Maddy and I had to go home.

After a long, slow, regretful good night to my husband, Mr. Siler drove us back over the causeway with the lights of his car shaded halfway to comply with blackout rules. He explained that headlights, along with streetlights and outdoor signs, had to be shut down to prevent outlining ships off shore by the lume or glow of the overpopulated

Miami area. The unusual darkness was a sobering end to a marvelous night and left me feeling even more of an outsider to our host city. Maddy didn't seem to mind, however. She opened the car window and laughed like she didn't have a care in the world as the wind wreaked havoc on her pageboy. In the past, she'd always been very particular about her hair. If I didn't know better, I'd think someone had spiked her punch.

We seemed to all be a little drunk. Having Davey back in my life after the longest separation of our marriage had wrapped my mind in a blissful cloud. So much so, I hadn't thought to worry about Maddy. She'd conducted herself as a grown-up and suffered the sacrifices of the train trip well. Her mother would have been proud. In the main I was glad to have her with me and knew Davey felt better knowing I wasn't alone in this new place.

Everything seemed fine. And I'm not sure what started me worrying, but I do know when it occurred to me that I needed to pay more attention. It was when we'd had our photograph taken. As the crowd of us gathered closer to pose, I'd glanced in Maddy's direction. There she sat with Davey's buddy Frankie on one side, Jack Siler on the other, and Lt. Tull-Martin standing behind her chair. Various other servicemen squeezed around them. An unexpected fear seized me then—as though cool fingers belonging to the patron saint of disaster had brushed the back of my neck in warning. At the shock and the realness of the touch, I turned to face our doom, but found Davey's smiling eyes.

His beloved features calmed me, and I did my best to shake off the uneasiness and smile for the camera. Yes, we were being relentlessly drawn into the war—and nothing spoke more of the changes to come than being surrounded by men in uniform. Yet there was something beyond that, something more personal in nature. Not only our lives had changed, mine and Davey's, everyone's including Maddy's, but our hopes for the future had altered as well.

We would never be the same.

I wished to be wrong. Life had become so uncertain and busy, there wasn't time to wonder about significance or whether this might be the last or perhaps the only time we'd be together in the same place—smiling. There would be plenty of time to wonder later.

Chapter Three

— RUTH —

The next morning, as we dressed for church, Maddy seemed like her old self. She spent thirty minutes in front of the bathroom mirror, pinning and repinning her hair while I pressed a skirt with an iron we'd borrowed from Mrs. Siler.

We'd be attending the Presbyterian church a few blocks away. According to the nuns in school, it was a sin to miss mass, but as with many things in our new situation, Maddy, Davey, and I would make do with what happened to be available. On my visit to heaven when I'd lost my baby, I don't remember seeing a sign that included or excluded Baptists or Presbyterians. Personally, I was looking forward to a relatively normal Sunday, if not with mass then with services and a family dinner. I'd been taught there was one true church, but I'd discovered I didn't care what church we attended, as long as my husband would be sitting next to me.

"Mother isn't going to be happy," Maddy said, as though I'd spoken out loud. "You know how she believes our church is God's favorite."

I knew Mrs. Marshall was a stickler for following her own rules. And in Maddy's world, breaking those rules held consequences. But I intended to go to church with my husband and the family who'd graciously taken us in. "Would she rather you stay home on Sundays?" I asked, although I knew the answer.

"I doubt it," Maddy said with a laugh as she searched through her bag for lipstick. "Ah, well, when in Rome, do as the Romans do. What she doesn't know won't hurt her. Like my friend Sharon always says, 'Half the truth is better than none.' I'll write Mother and say we went to church and leave it at that. When I get back home, I'll go to confession."

I wasn't sure what my responsibility in all this would be. Keeping track of half-truths could get us both in hot water. Technically, Maddy was grown-up, yet this was her first time away from home. I didn't relish trying to mother her. For one thing, I didn't always agree with Mrs. Marshall's rules. For another, the whole subject of motherhood tended to silence me. If God had intended motherhood for me then why had my babies died? I decided I might be better at sisterhood for the time being. Then I remembered the feeling of foreboding I'd experienced the night before.

I walked over to stand behind her at the mirror, rested my hands on her shoulders, and met her gaze in the reflection. "Promise that between you and me, we'll always tell the whole truth. Like sisters," I said.

Maddy rolled her eyes once and started to speak—probably a clever remark—but something in my manner must have stopped her. She turned to face me. "What do you mean?"

I reached for a tissue, then handed it to her to blot her lipstick. "Your mother isn't here to worry about you, so it's up to me. I have to know what you're thinking and doing. That way if you need advice, we can talk things over." She looked surprised and a little reluctant so I went on. "I may need your help as well. The two of us should depend on each other because we both know there are things your mother doesn't understand." I hoped that would do the trick. "If nothing else, I have to know what *not* to say in my letters."

"Why does anyone have to worry about me?"

"Because we're family. Being an orphan in the world, that means a lot to me. I want to see you happy and secure. And I would hope you feel the same toward me."

She squeezed my hand. "You know I do, Ruth. I'm just so tired of people telling me what to do. I've decided to have some fun before I have to go back home."

"I know. And I want you to have a fine time, but make sure you remember that no matter what, I'm on your side."

— MADDY —

I had no idea what had gotten into Ruth. For some reason, on this, our first sunny, warm Sunday in Miami, she'd gone altogether maudlin on me. And all because I'd admitted to planning a little white lie for the benefit of my mother. I mean, the lie did have to do with church but, gosh, it wasn't like I was spying for the Germans or something.

It was nice to know she cared. We'd never really had any heart to heart conversations since she'd come to live with us. My mother seemed to always stay in the middle of everything. Almost as though she didn't want us to be sisters or friends. Besides that, back home I'd had my own friends in Sharon and Jeanne, plus Ruth had been ill.

As Ruth and I walked across the walkway to the Silers' I realized that now, there was just the two of us, and I'd promised Davey I'd treat Ruth like the sister I wished I'd had. Here was my chance, the proof of the pudding. Was I a winner or a welcher? Right before we reached the ramp to the side door I leaned over and whispered, "I hope Lt. Tull-Martin comes with Jack and Davey today. I think he's a dream. He reminds me of Cary Grant."

"Or, maybe David Niven," she commented without blinking an eye.

Our sisterhood was born.

* * *

At precisely ten o'clock Mr. Siler drove the four of us to church. He told us he'd arranged return transportation with two of their neighbors for Jack and Davey along with as many other soldiers as they could fit. If nothing else, any extras could walk the few blocks.

"I'll make two trips if I have to," Mr. Siler said. "These boys have enough hard work ahead of them. I don't mind ferrying them back and forth."

Sitting in the backseat with Randy and Mrs. Siler I was determined to appear calm and grown-up and only mildly interested in who the extras at church and Sunday dinner might be. Under my cardigan jacket, however, my heart was pumping like a majorette in the drum parade.

I could feel Randy watching me with puzzled concentration. When I met his gaze he waggled his eyebrows, to let me know he was onto something. I controlled the impulse to react. I'd been told a thousand times that teasing and bickering was unladylike. Acting like a brat on the way to church was probably a mortal sin. My mother, had she been in the vicinity, would have ruled this the perfect occasion for me to pray like a sinner and behave like a saint. And I suppose some of her discipline had sunk in, because when we arrived at church and Mr. Siler helped Randy from the car to his chair, I found myself volunteering to push him up the walk.

As with most other things in Miami, the Presbyterian church was unlike any I had seen back in Pennsylvania. The large, boxy-looking building rose out of a foundation of solid rock toward a sky so clear and blue it hurt to look up. The rough stuccoed walls made me think of a giant, square wedding cake frosted a foot thick with white sugar icing and surrounded by ten-foot sprays of candy-pink bougainvillea.

Pretty enough to eat.

I had skipped most of breakfast at the Silers' and now my stomach rumbled in revenge, making Randy laugh.

"Sounds like you've got a motor in that boat," he teased.

I was too nervous to do anything but laugh along with him. Then a bell tolled from the rectangular steeple taking my mind off my appetite and reminding me why we were there.

The sun seemed to grow brighter and hotter with every step, and I could feel my blouse sticking to my back under my jacket. I parked Randy's chair on the part of the walk under a large shade tree to wait for the others. Several small groups of churchgoers were gathered along the walk and near the entrance. There wasn't a soldier in sight.

Ten minutes later a bus marked Miami High School pulled up in front of the church and opened its doors. Jack got off first, then Davey, then there were two other Army fellas. Lt. Tull-Martin was next.

In the bright morning sun, he looked even more handsome than I remembered. His RAF uniform set him apart from the soldiers around him, and the cane he carried seemed more like a debonair accessory than a necessary crutch. I did my best to look cool, calm, and collected when in fact I felt almost faint. If I'd been expecting an introduction to Clark Gable himself I couldn't have been more nervous. When Lt. Tull-Martin looked toward the church and our group waiting on the sidewalk, I quickly shifted my gaze to the back tire of the school bus, anywhere, so he wouldn't catch me gawking. But then Ruth waved to Davey and I knew they were headed in our direction. My usual nerves of steel had completely deserted me so I trained my eyes on the back of Randy's head.

Ruth casually leaned toward me and said, "They're here."

I knew she meant *he's* here. I slipped my hand in hers and squeezed.

After introductions to Mr. and Mrs. Siler and Randy, Lt. Tull-Martin said, "Hello, Maddy. It's nice to see you again."

"Hello." My voice sounded almost normal. I shook his hand and managed a brief smile.

"I wonder, did you dream of adventures on the high seas last night?" he asked.

My silly conversation about seeing Africa and England coming back to haunt me. I could feel my face getting warmer. I had to say something, so I told the truth. "No, but I did dream there were three fat seagulls on my windowsill singing me to sleep." Lt. Tull-Martin smiled and I felt dumber than I had the night before.

Then Randy leaned his head back to look at me. "Seagulls don't sing."

"Time to go inside," Mrs. Siler declared.

Rather than try to recover my dignity, I shrugged my shoulders like a good sport and pushed Randy's chair forward.

Ruth, Davey, and the others continued toward the front door to the sanctuary as Randy directed me along to a side door that had a wooden ramp built over the steps.

"Jack built this before he joined the Army," Randy said. "So us crippled people could get in the church to repent and pray."

"And you need it more than most," Jack commented. He and Randy obviously had a comfortable rivalry going. "But I built it so you could get out and see people. As much as I hate to do it"—Jack shook his head sadly—"I'm gonna have to take over from your pretty driver. This ramp is steeper than it looks."

I might be working on sainthood, but I decided to let Jack do the uphill pushing. Halfway to the top he said to his brother, "I think you're getting fat on Mother's cooking."

"That's because she misses you. She feeds me my own dinner and yours on top of it. By the time you get back from the war I'll look like Tubby Smith on wheels."

At the high end of the ramp, Jack paused and waited for me to open the door. "Hey, I sent you Maddy and Ruth, didn't I?" He grinned at me before entering the church. "They might not eat as much but they're a lot easier on the eyes."

I followed Jack as he parked Randy's chair next to a pew near the front of the sanctuary. Mrs. Siler had saved a seat for Jack, then came Ruth and Davey. Lt. Tull-Martin stood when I arrived then sat down next to me. My sainthood was in jeopardy from that point on. Used to hearing Latin, at first I was surprised to hear the Bible readings in English. But to be honest, I don't remember hearing much of the service. I was too conscious of sharing the hard wooden bench and hymnal with a real war hero. A man, not a boy like Lyle. And a handsome Englishman to boot. It didn't help that Jack and Davey obviously thought he could win the war single-handedly.

I couldn't believe the Presbyterians were going to force me to sing in front of him. By the time we stood to do so, I had to let Lt. Tull-Martin hold the hymnal on his own since I knew my gloves wouldn't cover the fact that my hands were shaking and I didn't want him to think he made me nervous. Even though he did. I was so rattled, I laughed after singing the wrong verse of "Before Thy Throne, O God, We Kneel" and was awarded a straighten-up-and-fly-right frown from Mrs. Siler. Like a bucket of cold water, the idea of being sent home to my mother cooled my humor.

For the rest of the service—a sermon on being good Christians and patriotic citizens, a call for sacrifice, a warning of eternal damnation for black marketeers, and prayers for our men in uniform—I kept a demure and devout face.

Outside, a group of neighbors gathered to meet the soldiers and the men took over the conversation. The talk was about war. In the past week, the Philippines had fallen to the Japanese and the Germans had the Russians on the run. Our merchant ships were being sunk all over the Caribbean by what the radio announcers called the German "rattlesnakes" of the Atlantic, and in London, due to fabric shortages, civilians were allowed to have only one pocket on their coats.

By the time we loaded up for the ride home, I was feeling a little maudlin myself. Not entirely because of the dreary war news, but because Lt. Tull-Martin, after one polite nod in my direction, seemed to be completely ignoring me.

At Sunday dinner, I finally pulled myself together. Mostly with the help of Mrs. Siler's decree about kitchen chores. I did my chores and Ruth's as well so she could sit with Davey those few extra moments. I found it a lot easier to set the table, pour water, and fold napkins than to entertain distinguished guests like Lt. Tull-Martin. It was one thing to talk to him in a gang of people like the night before at the Servicemen's Pier, quite another to eat in front of him and worry about fumbling a forkful of peas.

In the middle of dessert, as I shakily poured coffee, I suddenly understood my mother's admonition about idle hands. And why when tragedy struck, when she was nervous or unhappy, she found something to do to occupy her time.

Unfortunately, after dinner, Ruth and Davey excused themselves and walked arm and arm over to the Samuel place. Jack and his father moved to the porch to discuss the shortages facing the family auto-parts business, and Mrs. Siler set to work in the kitchen baking ginger cookies for the church social we would attend later. Randy had been determined to skip his afternoon nap so that left me to *occupy* him and Lt. Tull-Martin. Getting what you want sometimes is a scary thing.

"Tell us about your home, in Pennsylvania, isn't it?" Lt. Tull-Martin asked.

"Well, I uh—" For the life of me, I couldn't think of one exciting thing to say about Radley. The streets and the people were as familiar as the lines on the palm of my hand and just as humdrum. "It's a small town, pretty boring," I hedged.

"Oh, that can't be true. In England, the small towns are quiet, but if you get to know the people they are rarely boring. What do you do for fun in—"

"Radley," I said, helpfully. "I used to work in the drugstore." Having a job seemed more grown-up than finishing high school.

"Was that fun?" Lt. Tull-Martin persisted.

"She has a boyfriend," Randy said.

I know it isn't kind to want to kill a crippled person, especially when there were so many others like Hitler and Mussolini who deserved killing, but in that moment Randy was fair game. I *never* should've told him about Lyle. He was worse than Davey about teasing, and as far as Lt. Tull-Martin's opinion of me was concerned, humiliation was no laughing matter.

Lt. Tull-Martin smiled and I felt like Davey's "baby" sister all over again. *Oh, isn't she cute?* "What's his name?" he asked.

I'd seen an old Ray Milland movie once, a courtroom

drama. I now knew the true meaning of "reluctant witness." Other than my mother, the last person I wanted to talk about was . . .

"Lyle," I answered but my voice cracked. I cleared my throat. "Lyle," I said again. I shot Randy a look that should've set his hair on fire. He merely smiled like his mother's "precious darling angel" and remained quiet. In the seconds following, I thought I did a bang-up job of keeping my temper. "His name is Lyle Nesbitt and he's in the Navy," I answered like an adult. I didn't mention that I had had dreams of being Mrs. Lyle Nesbitt. The plans I'd made to leave home and be Lyle's wife seemed as far away as the war.

Lt. Tull-Martin didn't notice my reluctance. "A Navy man, eh? Is he stationed here in Florida, then?"

"No, he's in Missouri right now. I have a picture of him." In for a penny, in for a pound. I dug around in my handbag until I found my wallet and the photo Lyle had sent.

"Well, he looks like a stalwart young man. You must be very proud of him."

When Lt. Tull-Martin handed the picture back to me, I gazed at Lyle's boyish face and realized I was proud of him. His new white sailor's cap didn't have the effect of making him look older. In fact it made his ears stand out farther than I remembered. But his hometown-boy smile was the same. And from his letters I knew his loyalty belonged to me, even though he'd chosen his own destiny and volunteered to fight for his country rather than stay home and get married. I thought of Lt. Tull-Martin's words the night before about his home being bombed by the Germans, and the anger I'd felt at having my own plans spoiled seemed even more childish.

"I am proud of him. We're supposed to get married when he gets back." There, I'd confessed, and I immediately felt better. Unfortunately, my proclamation had an odd effect on Lt. Tull-Martin. He looked like he'd been delivered a message with bad news.

"I wish you both a happy future," he said, then quickly changed the subject. Before I could ask about life in England

and any girl in his hometown who might be keeping his photograph, Randy brought up the subject of flying.

"I have a lot of dreams where I can fly just like the birds. Jack says flying is kind of like dreaming when you're wide awake."

Lt. Tull-Martin smiled and said, "I agree. Flying is the closest any of us will get to heaven. At least I used to feel that way. Now, for most of us, flying has become a means to an end. An important tool in the business of war."

"Jack is a good pilot, isn't he?" Randy asked, although even I could tell by the look on his face that he already knew the answer.

"Jack is very good, perhaps one of the best I've trained." Lt. Tull-Martin chuckled. "He goes at it with your typical American devil-take-the-hindmost attitude. I worry sometimes that he doesn't treat the whole subject very seriously."

"What don't I take seriously?" Jack said from the doorway. "I'm in the Army, we're very serious fellas." He sauntered into the room with his father following.

"I was talking about the aerodynamic forces of air flight. You have no respect for gravity. You seem to think you can keep a plane in the air and going forward by sheer force of will."

"That's something coming from a man who brought in a Hurricane that had fifty reasons to crash."

Lt. Tull-Martin shook his head as though they'd had this conversation before. "Landing that plane rather than crashing into the sea wasn't force of will, it was abject terror."

"You were shot down?" Randy asked.

"Well, a couple of times, but—"

"I'm talking about landing a plane with the engine blown to hell—excuse me, Maddy—and leaking oil, while nearly bleeding to death yourself."

I must have made a sound because Lt. Tull-Martin's eyes were suddenly locked on to me with a concerned expression. "I doubt if Maddy wants to hear about that."

"Yes, I do," I said, calm as you please. "I want to hear everything about it."

He stared at me for a long moment. "Are you sure? It's not a pretty tale."

I nodded. Jack and his father sat down and we faced him expectantly.

"Well—" he said as he leaned forward, elbows on knees, and balanced his hat between his two hands. "That particular landing happened during the evacuation of Dunkirk."

Even in my small world of Radley, Dunkirk was famous. Two years before the newsreels had been filled with heroic stories about the hundreds of thousands of British and French troops trapped between the advancing Germans and the sea.

"We had orders to intercept as many German planes as we could before they reached the coast. You see they had a shooting gallery of sorts. Thousands of our boys facing death or capture, and hundreds of ships trying to get them out. The lot of them crowded thick as ants along a few miles of barren coastline. The German bast—" He gave me an apologetic glance. "I mean the German Messerschmidt pilots could strafe with their eyes shut and hardly miss a target. Those heavy caliber guns on the 109s cut through steel like paper. It was a bloody mess, I tell you.

"Our B section had been conducting operations on a small airfield near Rouen. We had eighteen planes, mostly Hurricanes with a few Spitfires. And we had four new pilots, barely out of training. To be truthful, none of us had proper training."

Barely out of training. I found myself staring at Jack. The look on his face gave me a shiver. Even sitting there in his pressed khakis he seemed as starstruck as a ten-year-old baseball fiend listening to Lou Gehrig talk about home runs. This story, however, was about war.

"Well, we did out best," Lt. Tull-Martin continued. "I tell you, when our group met up and got our first look at what we faced—there had to be at least twenty Heinkels. Those are German bombers," he added for my benefit. "And the 109s . . ." He shook his head. "I stopped counting at fifty.

"That's when the training takes over, there's no time to

think. You push the stick, get in the fight, try to get them before they get you." Again, he gazed at me. "I'm sorry to say it, Maddy, but to stay alive one must become a cold-blooded fighter. Not only is your own life at forfeit, but all those men waiting on the beach, looking for help.

"And those back home . . ." He went silent for a moment, then straightened his shoulders and sat back in his chair.

"We lost eleven planes in two days. Eleven out of eighteen. And six pilots, including the four trainees."

"Oh, no . . ." I said before I could help myself. The war that had seemed so far away had suddenly taken a giant step closer. I felt like I had known those men who'd died because Lt. Tull-Martin had known them. And now I knew more soldiers. I had talked to them, danced with them . . . men like Lt. Tull-Martin, and Jack . . . and Davey, my own brother. And Lyle.

"Who shot you down?" Randy asked.

"I imagine it was some German chap," Lt. Tull-Martin said, his humor returning. "But I couldn't say for certain. I never saw him. Heard two bangs and felt the plane shudder. Then something punched me in the shoulder like a hot poker—could've been a piece of my own engine because right about then it began to come apart rather noisily. But the worst was my knee." He straightened his right leg. "I could feel the blood running into my boot but nothing else. What I knew for certain was that I wouldn't be able to swim, or walk for that matter. Training demands you get out of the airplane. But a parachute among all those fighters would be worse than a floating duck with me as the bull's-eye. So I withdrew and decided to make some sort of landing before the fire reached the cockpit. Luckily, I wasn't far from the airstrip.

"In the final count on the 30th of May 1940, one of those eleven planes lost was mine. It burned on the field. It was my good fortune to be pulled from the cockpit by my two armorers and the squadron cook ahead of the plane's demise."

With that fiery vision in my imagination, I realized it was

so quiet I could hear a clock ticking somewhere. It seemed that none of us could think of a thing to say. Faced with silence, Lt. Tull-Martin went on.

"It was later reported that our confirmed kill ratio was 4 to 1. That's at least respectable even if it made little headway in stopping the Luftwaffe. I don't like to think about the thousands of men who perished either there on the beach or in prisoner-of-war camps because we couldn't do more."

"But you've made it back alive," I said, thinking the war was over for him and how glad I was of it.

"A little worse for wear, but yes, I have survived for the time being. And I'm determined to give you Yanks," he nodded toward Jack, "the benefit of everything I've learned about the German—"

"Bustards!" Randy added.

"Excuse me?"

Jack laughed. "My brother is a birdwatcher—has been since we were kids."

"I'm afraid I'll never understand you Americans," Lt. Tull-Martin said with a smile.

"Randy used to always be in trouble with our mother for his rough language." Jack winked at his brother. "For the life of me, I can't figure out where he picked it up."

"So I started changing the words to birds," Randy said. "I call the Japs yellow-bellied 'Saps,' and the Germans—"

"That'll be enough of that," Mrs. Siler interrupted. She had a plate of cookies in her hands. "I thought you boys might enjoy some of the first batch of my ginger cookies. They're still warm." She glanced at me. "Maddy, why don't you come in the kitchen and help make the lemonade?"

— RUTH —

"We're nearly broke with the doctor's bills and this trip. Once I ship out, I'll get a pay raise. For now, though, living on Army pay is going to be tight," Davey sighed.

"I know. But by the time we go back to Radley I should be well enough to work and help out."

"I hate for you to have to do that."

I turned in his arms to look into his eyes. I tried my best to prevent my voice from wavering but it didn't work. "Why? You'll be gone and I have no children to keep me at home—" My husband gone to war, no children. It was enough reason to cause any woman to weep. None of it was Davey's fault though. I cleared my tightening throat. "I'll be glad to keep busy."

Davey hugged me hard. "You've had some tough breaks, sweetie. I wanted to make your life a cakewalk. Now I'm leaving you on your own."

"Not alone," I said. "I have your mother, and Maddy."

Davey shook his head. "Mother might drive you to drink, and Maddy . . . well, I have hope for Maddy. She's nearly grown-up and if she plays her cards right, she'll do fine. We'll just have to wait and see."

Wait and see. That's the best any of us could do. I had no idea how I would get along without Davey. The thought of it made me so sad I couldn't bear to dwell on it. Better to talk about happier times.

I changed the subject. "Remember our honeymoon trip? After the first night in that terrible hotel I thought we'd never get there."

He leaned his head back and smiled. "I wanted to drive all night. I remember reading that the mist of Niagara Falls is supposed to be a first-rate aphrodisiac." He laughed out loud. "After taking the tour and getting soaking wet, I thought I'd never get you thawed out, much less in the mood."

The falls had been glorious, majestic in a deep, primitive sense. But the love between Davey and me, rather than being diminished by the grandeur, had blossomed. We'd laughed and kissed and nearly caught pneumonia together. "Weren't those your lips turning blue along with mine?" I teased. "And tell me, why was it so important that we get married in early October? I can't seem to remember . . ."

Instead of smiling, or making a comeback, he studied me

for one long serious moment. I knew that look. "Because I was so crazy about my Ruth-E, I couldn't stand the thought of losing her," he said, before kissing me so thoroughly that I lost my place in the conversation.

"Hmmmm," he mumbled into my lips. "I think it's getting misty in here. Do you suppose we can disappear for a half hour or so?"

The word "no" never entered my mind. "I wish you could stay the night, I miss sleeping with you."

He grinned. "Sleeping isn't what I had in mind."

Between Davey's constant worry about leaving me alone and pregnant, and my own fear of Mrs. Siler's opinion—after all, it was the middle of Sunday afternoon—a half an hour had to do. After a blissful, too few moments of pleasure, Davey and I forced ourselves to rejoin the others next door. We found Maddy, Randy, the British lieutenant, and Jack having cookies and lemonade, discussing birds and planes. You would think after spending their waking hours training like the devil, that they'd find something else to talk about.

"The Spitfire sort of looks like a fat little seagull," Jack was saying.

"Ah, but it flies like a sparrow hawk," Lt. Tull-Martin replied. "I can't describe the sensation. It's like nothing else, really. Except to say it's like putting on a suit of clothes. Instead of being in the plane, you *are* the plane."

"I can't wait to take one out." Jack turned to Davey and me. "Hey Buddy, I think I'm gonna volunteer to fly with the RAF. Whaddaya think of that?"

I didn't know what to think of it, but I could tell by the sudden tenseness in Davey's posture that he didn't consider Jack's announcement good news. He said, "I think if you do you'll probably end up in bombers rather than fighters. You shoulda joined the Navy."

Jack put a hand over his heart like he'd already been wounded. "A Swabby? Never. What do you think, Randy?"

Randy gazed at his brother, hero worship in his eyes. "I dunno. Those German bustards deserve a good bombing. You could do either one and help win this war."

"How about you, Maddy?" Jack persisted. "Tallyho and all that rot," he said in a terrible falsetto voice. "Don't you think I'd make a rather *dashing* RAF fighter pilot?"

Maddy paled slightly as everyone faced her expectantly. Only I knew how uncomfortable she must have been since she had a crush on a very dashing RAF pilot already. The one sitting in the chair opposite hers. She composed herself quickly though. "It sounds very exciting—"

"Don't encourage him, Maddy," Lt. Tull-Martin interrupted. "He thinks the whole idea very romantic. The reality though is a different kettle of fish. The reason we need volunteers is because we've lost so many of our own. Besides"—he chuckled and shook his head—"your accent is atrocious. If you used it on the radio the other lads would probably shoot you down simply to keep you quiet."

"Hey, can't let you Brits have all the fun. A little bit of *Tallyho* works wonders on the girls down at the canteen," Jack announced with a grin that challenged anyone to say differently. "They think I'm IT."

I bet they do, I thought. But not because of some phony accent. Between his wit and swagger I was sure he'd broken plenty of hearts. Davey and Lt. Tull-Martin obviously held a different opinion and made several disparaging comments that sounded more like groans and coughs. Maddy wisely kept her opinion to herself.

After a pleasant day of getting to know each other better, the church social turned out to be rather dull. Over coffee and cake, everyone seemed to be trying too hard to entertain or to pretend everything was normal when what they really wanted to talk about was the war.

Maddy especially was at loose ends since Lt. Tull-Martin had had to report back to the aviation school for some kind of officers briefing. Davey and I kept her close to us as we were introduced to the Women's Presbyterian Auxiliary Committee chairwoman, Mrs. Brown, and the local air-raid wardens, Mrs. Archer and Mr. Zachary. Being newcomers, they felt we ought to be filled in on the various activities of our temporary home. Miamians were busy installing air-raid sirens, buying war risk and bombardment insurance, and volunteering. Recruiting offices were staying open twenty-four hours a day, signing up men who wanted to "get a crack at those Japs." The local men had formed the McCarthy Platoon, an all-Miami unit of Marines, and set up guards on the harbor and gasoline storage tanks. The local women, some one hundred so far, were volunteering to work three- to four-hour shifts, twenty-four hours a day at the air-raid filter gathering information from the hundreds of observation posts throughout the state.

"I report tomorrow to the southeast Dade branch, on top of the David Allen furniture store," Randy said proudly. "They have an elevator so it's no trouble for me to get up on the roof."

"That's the spirit," Mr. Zachary said. He raised his coffee cup in salute. "God helps those who help themselves. We must do our part."

Mrs. Siler, who was serving seconds of cake, happened to be within earshot. "I agree, Mr. Zachary, about doing our part, but I worry about my son, he's—"

"You'll be a great spotter," Jack interrupted. He thumped Randy on the shoulder. "You've been spotting birds since we were kids."

"But Jack, you know he's susceptible to drafts—"

"Hey," Jack interrupted again. He leaned over Randy. "It's about time for our evening constitutional, isn't it, buddy?"

Mrs. Siler, expertly diverted, took up the next cause. "Oh, Jack, don't leave so early . . ."

Randy nodded his agreement, and Jack grasped the handles of his chair. "I'm not going back to barracks yet, Mother. I'm gonna give Randy a push home. We can use the exercise. We'll meet you there."

My opinion of Jack Siler was already on the upswing when he turned to Maddy. "You feel like taking a walk?" he asked her.

— MADDY —

As I waited for Jack to push Randy down the ramp and into the balmy twilight I turned my face into the breeze. *Thank you, Jack Siler.* I felt like I'd been holding my breath for hours and now I could breathe. It was a beautiful night. The palm trees lining the walkway made a peculiar kind of clacking sound, like wind through venetian blinds. The heat of the day had cooled to the perfect temperature. It was hard to believe that back home I would've still been wearing a sweater. Jack stopped at the bottom and waited for me.

"No wonder everyone's coming south," I said when I reached them. "The weather here is absolutely perfect."

Jack glanced around as if I'd pointed out something he'd forgotten. Then, he chuckled. "You wouldn't think so in July or August. It's hotter than blazes when the breeze dies."

"Yeah, even the birds go north," Randy said.

I fell into step beside Randy's chair. "Oh, I don't think it could be too hot for me," I said. "It would be more reason to go for a swim in the ocean—or the river behind your house. A quick dip to cool off."

"Not in the river, Maddy." Jack's tone of voice had gone serious.

"Why not? Is it very deep? I'm a good swimmer."

"Because of Old Joe," Randy said.

"A gator," Jack added. "Very large."

"You mean a *real* alligator?" I didn't mean to imply there were fake ones. I just thought they were probably telling stories to scare the "Yankee." "I don't believe you."

"Have you seen him lately?" Jack asked Randy.

"Not for a year or so. Doesn't mean he's not around, though." Randy took up the story. "When our Grandad lived next door he used to raise a few chickens for eggs. Old Joe kept stealing 'em—not the eggs, the chickens. One at a time. Grandad would find a two-foot-wide trail of loose feathers and flattened grass leading back down to the river. Said he'd shoot the old walking suitcase if he ever caught him. But he never did. He had to give it up and buy his eggs at the store."

"I saw him several times," Jack added. "Sleepin' up on the bank like a fat, bumpy cypress log. He had to be eight or nine feet long. That's when I stopped swimming in the river."

Living with small green lizards was one thing, but a giant alligator was a different story. "Okay, I get it. No swimming in the river," I pledged. "He can't get in the house, can he?"

Randy looked up at Jack and waited for his answer. "Only when the moon is full," Jack said with a straight face.

I quickly searched the night sky to check the moon. Then he and Randy both laughed.

Forgetting to act like a lady, I hit Jack in the arm with my purse. That made them laugh harder. I swear, if anyone would've come along they'd have thought the three of us were a little, no, *a lot* nutty. "I'm serious," I said. "I won't be able to sleep a wink—"

"Alligators don't come in the house, Maddy," Jack assured me. "They rarely leave the river unless there's something easy to catch for dinner."

Jack gave me the once-over. "You don't look very easy to catch," he announced.

I wasn't sure whether to stay mad or be flattered. He probably meant I was too ornery for even Old Joe to take an interest in but I didn't care. I decided to put the possibility of being eaten by alligators out of my mind by changing the subject.

"How long have you known Lt. Tull-Martin?" I asked Jack.

He thought about it for a moment, then answered, "About six weeks. He'd just arrived from England after a convalescence leave when I started training." He shot me a calculating look. "Why?"

"No reason," I said, maybe a little too quickly. "I've never met anyone from England and he seems very nice." What I actually wanted to know was whether he was married or engaged. But I knew I couldn't ask. Between Jack and Randy, I'd never live it down.

"Yeah, he's a good egg. The Brits are taking a real beating from old Hitler's bullyboys. Tull-Martin is determined to stop 'em."

"Did any family come over with him?"

We'd come to the end of the sidewalk—from here on out we'd walk in the street. Jack didn't answer until he'd pushed Randy's chair over the grass border and onto the pavement. Then, he cut to the chase. "You mean a wife? No. I think he has a sister back in London and parents somewhere else. Why?"

I didn't know how to find out more without giving myself away. "Just wondering."

"Did you ask him about taking me up in your plane?" Randy asked.

"We talked about it," Jack answered. "You know the Army frowns on any unauthorized flights since we have to conserve fuel. But he said he'd try to find a way. If nothing else, I'll sneak you out to the field. Oh, and don't let Mother talk you out of plane spotting. It's important and you'll be good at it."

Even in the dark I could see Randy's glowing pride. The moment didn't last long, however, because Jack pushed down on the handles of Randy's chair and hiked his feet off the ground before spinning him around in a circle. "Make sure you don't get dizzy up there on the roof and fall out like Humpty-Dumpty," Jack taunted.

Laughing, Randy clutched the armrests of his chair and held on until Jack lowered him to the normal position. For a moment I could see the young boys inside both these grown men. I felt the need to be included.

"I swear, don't boys *ever* grow up?" I asked, with as much of my mother's inflection as I could muster.

They both looked at me in surprise before realizing that I was fooling around. "Look who's talking, little Miss I'll-hit-you-with-my-purse. I bet your boyfriend is as henpecked as they come," Jack said.

"Yeah," Randy added. "And he's a swabby to boot. Only sissies join the Navy, right Jack?"

Jack watched me, dragging out the moment. "Nah," he said, apparently tired of torturing me. "Some of 'em are okay."

"But I thought you said—"

"Hey, c'mon Maddy, we'll race you to the end of the block," Jack said before shoving Randy forward.

I kept up with them the best I could in my uncomfortable shoes.

Chapter Four

— MADDY —

On Wednesday, I met the postman on the front walk as usual. Since Ruth and Davey were in the same city, she'd lost interest in the mail. I, on the other hand, still looked forward to letters from Lyle and home. It tickled me to read how jealous Jeanne and Sharon were of my sunny situation, and Lyle, well Lyle wasn't jealous as far as I could tell. A little worried, maybe. He imagined, quite correctly, that I was having a grand time without him. I tried not to rub it in too much though. The thought of making him unhappy took some of the starch out of my stubbornness. Besides, I missed him.

The postman, a thin, older man named Mr. Frady, smiled when he handed me the mail. "Afternoon, miss."

"Good afternoon," I answered, but my mind was already on the delivery. There were two envelopes, one with Mother's handwriting, and the other postmarked from Missouri—Lyle. There was also a flat cardboard envelope with a Miami return address. It was addressed to Ruth. I handed it over when I got back to the house and opened the letter from Mother first. I'd always been that way—saving the best for last. Whenever there were more than two letters, presents at Christmas, or homework and chores, I took care of the less interesting ones first and waited for the good stuff. You'd think I was a Protestant or something.

Dear Maddy and Ruth,

Received your letter from the first. I hope this finds you both safe and well.

Leave it to Mother to worry about our safety. To her Miami might as well be the wilds of a South American jungle. Forget being part of the good old U.S. of A. Well, as far as I was concerned, the people here might dress differently because of the weather and speak differently due to the invasion of tourists with a mix of accents, but they seemed to go about their business in the same way as people in Radley, Pennsylvania.

I miss you girls. It seems so quiet around here these days. The only excitement has been next door over Mrs. Jenkins's cat, Puss. It had six kittens under the bed in the Jenkinses' spare bedroom. That was a surprise since Mr. Jenkins had fixed up a nice cardboard box in the basement for the occasion. Of course Puss ignored her human friends and did as she pleased. Maddy, I'm sure you'll want to look over the new arrivals when you return home. There may be one that interests you.

Now I knew how much my mother missed me. Before coming on this trip with Ruth, Mother had halted any talk about pets. I'd had a cat named Inky when I was in elementary school but he'd run away not long after my father died. Everyone in our house was so sad. I couldn't blame Inky for wanting a happier home—I'd dreamed about running away myself. But Mother added the loss to the many others in our lives and decided pets were too unpredictable.

The weather is much cooler today, a lingering reminder of winter. Right now I'm wearing my heavier cardigan and having a cup of tea. I can't imagine how it can be as warm as you describe down in Florida. I hope you girls are protecting your skin from the tropical sun.

I had a letter from Arva Booth. Her son's boys have both joined the Army. It seems like every family has had to adjust to the

*war. Please give your hosts, the Silers, my best wishes and tell them
I thank them for watching over you and Ruth.*

Be a good girl, and write soon.

Love,

Mother

Be a good girl. Gee willikers. She made it sound like I was five years old. How was I ever supposed to come into my womanhood when my mother did her best to make me feel like a child?

I was shaking my head at my predicament as I glanced toward Ruth. She'd opened the cardboard envelope with a kitchen knife and was staring at its contents. One hand rested over her heart and the expression on her face worried me.

"What is it?" I asked and crossed over for a closer look.

"Oh!" I exclaimed before she could answer. "It's the photograph we had taken at the pier. Let me see." I sat down on the couch next to her, dropped the letters in my lap, and pulled the cardboard mounted picture out of her hands.

There we were. Ruth, Davey, and I along with Jack and Davey's friend Frankie. And Lt. Tully. I like to think he wouldn't mind me calling him that. I took extra time to examine his face. He was wearing that same sort of sad smile that made mush of my sensible, nonchalant act. My slow and steady heartbeat echoed in my ears as I studied the shape of his mouth and the direct gaze of his eyes. After a moment I moved on to the left and noticed that Ruth's smile seemed wistful as well. Davey had his arm around her, however, and was the spitting image of the "happily married man." Both Jack and Frankie were laughing outright. Finally, I stared at my own face. I looked happier than my mother would condone. Like I'd just been nominated for an Oscar and—for once—my hair had behaved.

"This is great! I can't wait to send a copy to Jeanne and Sharon." I held the picture at arm's length to admire the whole group. "We should get a frame," I said. Then I noticed that one of the soldiers had been cut off at the edge of the photo.

You could only see one shoulder and half his face. He was wearing the uniform of the Army Air Corps. I brought the photo closer and read his name badge. *Edwards.* "It looks like Airman Edwards almost got left out," I said.

When Ruth didn't answer right away, I turned to her. She met my gaze but I could tell something was wrong. "Don't you like it?"

"Of course I do." She held her hand out for the photo.

I turned it over but felt like I'd missed a step or two. She didn't look as if she liked it. As a matter of fact, without a second glance she slipped it back inside the cardboard envelope before I had a chance to stop her. "The next time we go out, we'll shop for a frame."

That didn't sound too promising, but since the photo had been addressed to her, and Davey had paid for it, as usual I didn't have much to say about the matter. I did, however, decide to copy down the return address and drop a note to the photographer to get a copy made.

"Did you get a letter from Lyle?" she asked.

I'd forgotten all about Lyle. I fished around in my lap and came up with his letter. "And one from Mother." I handed the open page to her for her to read as I opened Lyle's.

Dearest Maddy,

I don't have much time to write. We are being sent to California at the end of the week. I've been assigned to destroyers. They are the mid-sized ships that guard the bigger ships. I have a four-day leave before I have to report and will be heading back home to visit my folks. I sure wish you would be there. Is there any chance you'll be home soon? If not, I'll try to call you from my mom's.

Yours always,

Lyle

"Oh, no," I said. "Lyle's going to California." The farthest possible point from Florida. "But he's going back to Radley first." I felt a very uncomfortable wave of homesickness. The thought of Lyle being back home and me not being there to see him hadn't entered my mind. Now I had it in black and white.

"Oh, dear. Does he say when?" Ruth asked.

"At the end of the week. He mailed this on the second. That's five days ago. He's probably already on his way to Pennsylvania."

"I'm so sorry, Maddy. I feel terrible that you came on this trip and missed a chance to see Lyle."

I knew there was no way for me to get home in time. My joy at being long gone from Radley lost a little of its sparkle and I didn't know what to do. But I knew one thing: it wasn't Ruth's fault.

"Don't feel bad, Ruth. I wanted to come on this trip, more than anything. I didn't think everything would happen at once, I guess. Poor Lyle. There's hardly anybody at home to give him a special send-off. Besides his family, I mean."

"I'm sure they'll make him feel special," Ruth offered. "After all, they love him, too."

My mind had barely registered the "L" word when I had an inspiration. I'd call Jeanne and tell her to gather any of our friends left in town and take them to Lyle's house. That way, even though I wouldn't be there, he'd see everyone else before he left.

"This is an emergency. I have to call Jeanne and tell her," I said, and went to count my change to pay for the call.

— RUTH —

I was glad Maddy had something to keep her occupied and didn't even caution about the cost of the call. I truly felt awful that she'd missed her last opportunity to see Lyle before he went to war. I knew how it felt to be facing an unknown future with or without the man I loved, and I wouldn't wish the feeling on anyone. But I had other things to worry over.

The photograph.

I waited until Maddy ran through the room and out the side door on her way to the Silers' before I picked up the envelope again. The first time I'd opened it . . . well, it had appeared normal. Davy, me, Maddy, Jack, and the British RAF pilot surrounded by the others, everyone smiling, looking happy with basic mug-for-the-camera grins. But then, as I watched, the photograph changed, just slightly. At first I had thought it was my imagination or a trick of the shadows in the room. The faces had moved—a turned-down smile here, an out-of-focus expression there. Blinking to clear my sight didn't seem to have any effect. The image continued to sort of flutter. Then Maddy had pulled it out of my hand.

After taking a few moments to calm myself, I knew I had to look at those faces again, to calm my uneasiness. Surely I'd daydreamed the whole thing. I sat up a little straighter and prepared to laugh at my own silliness. Out of habit I made the sign of the cross, though, to be on the safe side. My hand shook as I pulled the photograph out into the light.

The group did appear to have shifted slightly. Jack's smile wasn't nearly as broad as I remembered, and Frankie, Davey's friend, had stopped smiling altogether. I ran the tip of my finger over my husband's beloved face, then along mine and Maddy's. As I sat there watching, wondering what to make of the changes, a breeze ruffled the curtains and swirled past. A shiver went through me. I recognized the same feeling of dread I'd felt the evening the photograph had been taken. A worry. A warning. Intently, I searched each face for telltale changes before I noticed the biggest difference. The airman, the one Maddy had mentioned being halfway in the photo, Edwards I believe she said, was gone. Not half there, simply not there at all.

I turned the photo facedown and placed it on the coffee table. I had to take several deep breaths before I could think straight. My first thought had to do with whether or not my illness and my "death" had somehow affected my mind.

I hadn't told anyone except Davey about what had happened to me in the hospital. About flying out the window and seeing heaven complete with people I had known—my babies, my father. I'd thought Davey had a right to know. Because he'd lost those children as well, and because he'd been the reason I'd come back.

But I didn't know how to tell him about this. It was bad enough that I had to walk with a cane and tired easily, that we had to be so careful when we made love so that I wouldn't become pregnant again. How could I tell him I was seeing things? Or not seeing things in this case. A surge of real panic went through me. I was not crazy. I couldn't be crazy. Not after everything I'd already been through. I would not send my husband to war with worry about me occupying his mind rather than thoughts of his own safety.

Without taking time to consider, I snatched up the photograph one more time and stared directly at the spot where the airman should have been. He wasn't there. I squinted and thought I could see the slight outline of his shoulder and the brass wings on his uniform. But the rest of him had faded into thin air.

Tears filled my eyes as I slid the photograph back into the cardboard envelope. I couldn't look at anyone else—the ones I loved. I was afraid they might disappear as well.

By the time Maddy returned full of news from home and plans for her long-distance welcome-home party, I had pulled myself together as best I could. I'd placed the photograph against the wall at the back of my closet. I knew that hiding it wouldn't keep Maddy from asking its whereabouts, but in a very real sense I hoped that out of sight would mean out of mind. At least until I found some explanation. Luckily she was distracted.

"You should see Randy. He just got back from his first shift as a plane spotter and he's sunburned to beat the band. He looks like a boiled shrimp. He said they haven't finished the top on the observation shack so he sat there on the roof in the sun. Mrs. Siler is fit to be tied."

"Didn't he wear a hat?"

"Well, yes—a felt Fedora." Maddy smiled. "But he said he was looking up most of the time. Mr. Siler said he's going to get him one of those big straw hats like the Indians make and that would help. Or Randy could swap shifts with someone who spots at night—at least until he returns to a normal color."

"Did you speak to Lyle?"

Maddy pursed her lips. "No, he hasn't arrived at his mother's yet. I did get Jeanne though. Her mom had to run down to Sharon's and bring them both back to her house to return my call. It seemed like it took five minutes before they stopped squealing over the long-distance call and agreed to plan a nice surprise party for Lyle. I told her to get Mother to help since I couldn't be there."

"That's sweet of them," I said. Maddy looked so forlorn I decided to concentrate on her unhappiness rather than my own fears. "Are you okay about that? I know how much you must want to be there."

"They both know Lyle so that helps. The gang of us used to go to the movies together sometimes." She smiled for the first time since she'd heard the news. "Of course Lyle and I used to sit in the balcony."

"Of course," I said.

"Lyle's mother said she'd give him my message and phone number as soon as he gets in."

By dinnertime he still hadn't called. After eating and helping with the dishes, Maddy and I settled in the Silers' living room in order to listen to the evening news. As we waited through the last song from the Fred Waring Orchestra, Randy reported the news of his day on the rooftop of the David Allen store downtown. His sunburned face looked almost shiny, like an apple that had been polished.

"I worked with two girls from the Pi Sigma Sigma sorority. We pinned up our silhouettes for German and Jap planes then watched the eastern horizon. Mostly we saw seagulls, but I got to watch a few of the trainers go through their maneuvers," he said. "I wonder if Jack was flying today."

Maddy grimaced. "Just looking at your face makes mine sting. Does it hurt very much?"

Randy touched the end of his nose and smiled. "Nah. Mother put aloe on me—that's good for any kind of burn. It took the heat out of it." He gave Mrs. Siler a sheepish look. "I promise to stay out of the sun tomorrow though."

The evening news interrupted the expected argument from Mrs. Siler. The events of the wider world quickly over-shadowed any of our small troubles. Toyko was reporting that Mandalay had fallen. The British and Chinese forces had been divided by a strong Japanese invasion force.

Closer to home, three United States merchant ships and a Norwegian cargo vessel had been torpedoed and sunk by enemy submarines operating in the Gulf of Mexico and the Atlantic. The armed forces announced three major moves to make the tropical waters "too hot" for Axis submarines menacing American shipments of vital men and materials in the Caribbean area. It was announced that an air-raid siren and loudspeaker system had been installed on Miami Beach City Hall—the voice of which would carry many blocks.

Before I could come to grips with the war striking so close around us the local news nearly stopped my heart.

"An Army aviation cadet was killed this afternoon in an airplane accident. The crash occurred two miles west of Opa-Locka during what was called a routine solo flight. The identity of the pilot is unknown at this time."

The color drained from Mrs. Siler's face. Even Randy's sunburn paled.

"Not Jack—" Mr. Siler said. Then he patted his wife's hand. "Don't worry, Mother. I'm sure he's fine."

Mrs. Siler opened her mouth to speak but closed it again.

I thought of smiling, swaggering Jack but thankfully couldn't picture him any other way. Surely he was all right. He had to be.

The news continued with business highlights—mostly about the city being on full war-footing. Ten hotels between Fifteenth and Twenty-third Streets had notified guests they must vacate rooms in two days to make room for the arrival of "special guests" in olive drab.

Mrs. Siler, though visibly shaken, collected herself and pushed to her feet. "Would you girls like some coffee? I have some left from dinner."

"Yes, please," I answered although I wasn't sure I could swallow anything. "Let me help." Mrs. Siler didn't argue. We left Maddy with Randy and Mr. Siler as the announcer switched to sports and a profile of Shut Out, the winner of the Kentucky Derby.

Our landlady's usual bossiness in the kitchen had been replaced by a strained silence. I set up cups and saucers on a tray while she heated the coffee. When I couldn't take the silence another minute, I slipped an arm around Mrs. Siler's shoulders and squeezed. "He's fine," I said, although I had no idea other than the lack of information. No news is good news.

She turned and looked into my eyes, searching for hope, I suppose. "Do you really think so?" she asked, as though my opinion mattered one way or the other.

Where there is despair, let me sow hope. I took a deep breath. "Yes, I'm sure of it. You'll see." St. Francis would have been proud.

Her shoulders relaxed and tears sparkled in her eyes. "I worry all the time. What will I do when he goes to war? I'll lose my mind not knowing where he is or how he is."

"I know," I said. And I did know. The thought of Davey hurt or dying in some battle on the other side of the world was unbearable. And yet, families over the entire country had to bear it. I had no idea how to comfort her.

My silence gave her a moment to get settled. She sniffed, straightened her shoulders, and stepped away. "This coffee should be hot enough, don't you think?" she asked as she picked up the hot pad.

By the time we returned to the living room, the news was over and the familiar music from *The Lone Ranger* was playing. Mrs. Siler served the coffee then settled next to her husband on the couch. I took the chair near Maddy.

I think we were merely dutifully drinking our coffee and halfheartedly listening as the episode began. By the first gunfight I felt ready to jump out of my skin. So, when the telephone rang, I nearly dropped my cup. I don't remember what the Lone Ranger and Tonto were doing, but Mrs. Siler leaped to her feet. After jumping up though, she couldn't seem to walk to the sideboard and simply stood there staring at it. Mr. Siler set down his cup, moved across the room, and answered the phone after the next ring.

I held my breath. *No news is good news.*

"Why yes, this is the Siler residence. Yes, she's right here." He looked at Maddy. "It's a Lyle Nesbitt, for you." The air seemed to go out of Mrs. Siler. She sank down on the couch and gathered her hands together in her lap.

Maddy's initial smile of joy faded as she faced Mr. Siler. She hesitated like it might be bad manners to be too happy.

"Come on, girl," Mr. Siler said trying to lighten the moment. "This call is costing a fortune." Randy made a face, then grimaced because of his sunburn.

With a grateful grin, Maddy took the receiver. Mr. Siler gathered up the phone and extra wire and placed it next to a chair closer to the window and farther from her unwilling audience.

Maddy did her best to keep her voice at a low level but I could hear her excitement. I tried not to listen. She'd missed her opportunity to see Lyle in person; the least I could do was allow her a private conversation. The Silers seemed to feel the same. Randy asked his father about the work he had lined up for the next day. But *The Lone Ranger* had gone to commercial break by the time Mrs. Siler recovered enough to talk.

"I've been meaning to ask you, Ruth. Do you have any experience with children?"

That tripped me up. Of all the ways to make conversation. "Well," I said, "I used to work in the church nursery and help out during catechism, back in Radley."

Mrs. Siler nodded and went on. "I received a call from our pastor yesterday. He said the Red Cross is looking for volunteers to baby-sit with children whose mothers are going to work for the war effort. I know you and Maddy will only be here for a short time, but I was wondering if you would be interested in helping out. The volunteers will be paid," she added.

I thought of the conversation Davey and I had had about money. Every little bit counted. And, as long as I could see Davey whenever he had a free moment, I didn't mind staying busy the rest of the time. "Why yes, I think I could manage the younger ones," I answered before patting my bum leg. "The ones who can't outrun me. We could use the extra money."

"I thought so. I'll pass along your name, then."

"Hi, Jeanne!" I heard Maddy say. She obviously had an audience on both ends of the phone line. She lowered her tone once more and I lost track of the rest of the conversation. *The Lone Ranger* ended with another wrong righted before Maddy said good-bye to Lyle. "I miss you, too. I wish I could be there."

Randy waited until Maddy replaced the receiver in the cradle before sing-songing, "Maddy's got a boyfriend. Maddy's got a boyfriend."

Maddy playfully pinched him on the arm but obviously hadn't taken offense. "Yes, I do. And practically my whole hometown will be at the party for him day after tomorrow." She took a seat next to me again and sighed. "I wish I could be there."

I squeezed her hand preparing to comfort her when the phone rang again. This time Mrs. Siler remained seated but the worry had returned to her eyes. Randy rolled his chair closer to the phone as he waited for his father to answer it.

Mr. Siler smiled. "Jack! I'm so glad you called." He motioned for Mrs. Siler to come to the phone. "We heard the news and—" She took the receiver out of his hand.

"Are you all right, Jacky?" Mrs. Siler asked breathlessly. "We were so worried. I'm sorry the line was busy—" She listened then, adding a few yesses and uh-huhs before saying, "That's terrible. Yes, I understand. War is dangerous business." She frowned. "All right, here's your brother."

Randy spoke to Jack a few more moments, then said good-bye. Mr. and Mrs. Siler both came back to the couch smiling. "He's fine," she said to me. "The pilot who was killed was someone he knew though. Brian Edwards. I think he said he was from Illinois."

Brian Edwards. *Edwards.* For a moment, the room seemed to go off-kilter.

"Ruth, are you all right?" Maddy asked.

I looked at her but my thoughts were on the photograph. The disappearing airman. Brian Edwards. I begged her with my eyes not to say anything.

"Yes, I'm—" Mr. and Mrs. Siler and Randy were all staring at me now. I knew I needed to get out of there before I did something very silly, like fainting. "I'm a little tired. I think I'll put my cup away and go lie down."

No one argued. "Don't worry about that, dear," Mrs. Siler said. "I'll clean up."

Maddy moved to my side and helped me to my feet. Then she took my arm and walked me next door.

— MADDY —

I hoped Ruth wasn't getting sick again. She was acting so strange. Maybe it was the scare about Jack. I'd been worried too, although Jack seemed pretty darned indestructible to me. I was so happy to hear from Lyle—whether or not we'd had to talk with everyone listening. I'd even heard some clicks on the line, which gave away the party-line eavesdroppers. It turns out that Jeanne and Sharon had set their own watch for Lyle's arrival and had filled his parents' house with friends as soon as he'd hit the door.

I was glad they were following my wishes and looking out for him. I wish they'd waited until I'd had him to myself . . . on the phone at least. He'd promised to call back around dinnertime before the party a few days later. I intended to guard the Silers' phone and commandeer it as soon as the call came through.

It appeared that until then, all I could do was wait. Wait, wait, wait.

The next two days were the longest days of my life until that point. Ruth and I did our best to keep busy. We did kitchen chores and helped with the shopping. Ruth stood in the rationed-only lines while Mrs. Siler and I compared prices between butchers and greengrocers. The three of us also went to meet a Mrs. Dowland—Leah as she asked us to call her—and her son Nickie who lived in a travel park a short bus ride from the Silers. Ruth was going to look after Mrs. Dowland's little boy starting Monday so that she could work at Trident Tackle, which had been converted into a munitions factory.

"My daddy's in the Navy," Nickie said. "I'm gonna be in the Navy, too, when I get big." He picked up a wooden boat and streaked through the room rumbling a child's version of a motor.

He looked big enough already to be a handful for Ruth. She must have been thinking the same thing. "Nickie?" She called him over to her and took the boat out of his hands. "Will you mind staying with me while your mother is at work?"

I'm not sure what I expected him to say, but what came out surprised me.

"My daddy told me to take care of my mom. But I guess if she's gots to go to make bullets, I can take care of you."

Ruth smiled and gave him a hug. "That would be very nice of you. We can look after each other."

Mrs. Dowland seemed ready to cry, and even Mrs. I'm-older-and-tougher-than-you Siler cleared her throat before getting down to brass tacks negotiation. When we left the Dowlands' small one-bedroom trailer, Ruth had the job, weekdays from seven to four, for as long as she wanted—at five dollars a week.

By the time the night of Lyle's party rolled around, I could barely contain myself. Although to be honest, it wasn't so much missing Lyle as it was feeling left out again. My friends were having a wonderful time without me. Even Ruth had had some good news. Davey had gotten a whole weekend pass, which meant he would be staying with us—with Ruth actually—but in our house starting on Friday night. I helped them plan a little Sunday afternoon tea but felt like a loner.

I waited through dinner, through dessert, before starting to fume during the evening news. Lyle had promised to call. The party should have started by now.

"Maybe he's waiting until everyone is there," Ruth said, trying to make me feel better.

"But I wanted to talk to *him*, not everyone else." She patted my shoulder, but instead of being comforted, I bristled. "I'll just call *him*," I proclaimed and went to ask the Silers' permission. If I kept this up, I'd owe the Silers more for phone calls than we paid for rent. But . . . I *had* to speak to him. This time I pulled the phone into the kitchen and leaned against the closed door. With each number I dialed I reminded myself to be calm. He probably got busy or, in the excitement, forgot with everyone around him talking at once.

After what felt like an eternity, the phone began to ring. In three rings, it was answered by a woman's voice.

"Hello?"

I didn't hear any music or laughter—sounds of a party. I was beginning to think that I'd hurried too much and dialed the wrong number. "Hello," I said. "Mrs. Nesbitt?"

"Yes."

My heartbeat calmed down. This was the right house—maybe the party *hadn't* started yet. "This is Maddy Marshall. Is Lyle there?"

"Oh, dear," she said in a tone that made my heart lurch. Had something happened to Lyle? Had they called him back early? I searched around inside for normal.

"He was supposed to call me tonight before the party," I said, sure that having a plan made any interruption impossible.

"I'm so sorry, dear. I know he was supposed to call you but something has happened." She sounded tearful.

I completely lost patience. "What? What's happened?"

"He and Jeanne Sharpe eloped last night."

Chapter Five

— RUTH —

"Ruth? Where is the photograph we had taken at the pier?" Maddy asked.

Instead of being worried about the subject matter, I was almost happy she'd spoken. After coming out of the Silers' kitchen looking like a death had occurred in the family, then telling me the bare facts of Lyle's desertion, she'd locked herself in her room for the rest of the evening and most of the next day. I was relieved to have to answer any question. Even if it was about the eerie photograph.

"I'll get it," I said and promptly went to dig it out of the closet.

She sighed when I placed it in her hands. "I looked so happy then."

Taking a seat next to her on the couch, I gingerly glanced at the familiar faces. That's when I knew for sure that something was definitely wrong. To me, Maddy's image in the photograph was completely different than she described. She wasn't smiling. I suppose the warning I'd felt that night had become the present heartbreak. I remembered my plan to look out for Maddy so I slipped an arm around her shoulders. "Do you want to talk about it?"

"Poor Airman Edwards," she added, ignoring my offer. She ran a finger along the edge of the photograph. The edge where she must see the airman, but to me looked like an empty space. A stab of fear caused my heart to flutter in my chest. How could I take care of Maddy when my own mind seemed to be slipping into confusion?

"Maybe you should go back home," I said.

Maddy looked at me then, seemingly calm. "I can never go home," she said as tears welled up in her eyes.

If I hadn't been so worried about the both of us, her child-like finality might have made me smile. "Why of course you can." I hugged her.

"You don't understand. Everyone knows Lyle and I were semi-engaged. They'll all know he ran off with Jeanne. It's too humiliating. I'm never going back."

I wanted to say, don't be silly you're only seventeen, but I didn't think going down that road would be helpful. I did try to turn in that direction, however. "In a week or so the excitement will have died down. People forget."

"I'll *never* forget," Maddy vowed. It sounded like a declaration of war.

"And you shouldn't," I agreed. "But think of it this way, at least you found out Lyle's character *before* you ended up married to him."

"I thought he loved me." Maddy sniffed.

"Lyle probably thought he loved you, too. He might still love you. But now he's a married man, and—"

"To my best friend! How could she do this to me?"

Betrayal on every side.

"I'd tell her off but I'm never speaking to her again," Maddy said. "And Lyle—I hope Lyle—"

"Maddy! Don't you dare say it!" My tone of voice was one I'm sure she'd never heard before. I don't think she could've been more surprised if I'd slapped her. I didn't care—some inner alarm made me stop her. "Lyle is going to war and—I won't let you say anything you might regret later."

Clutching the photograph like she could recover the happiness of the past, Maddy buried her face in my shoulder and cried for all she was worth. The result was uncanny since when I'd looked at the photograph I'd seen tears in her eyes.

For a thousand reasons, Friday night and Davey's weekend pass couldn't come soon enough for me. I wanted to be with my husband, to get back to the way things used to be. It worried me a little though that Maddy might feel left out, but Davey and I would think of something. Surely if anyone could sort out the mysteries of the photograph and of Maddy's broken heart, it would be Davey.

He planned to grab a bus or hitch a ride to the Silers' as soon as he could get away. Then we'd borrow Mr. Siler's car to go to dinner and maybe a movie. There'd be no need to hurry since we'd have the whole night, all weekend. To me the idea resembled heaven—and without the necessity of dying to get there.

Maddy's mother called late in the afternoon. As Maddy had feared, news of the elopement had spread around the town. In small-town Radley it had become the most important subject right after war news. As I waited to speak to my mother-in-law, I watched Maddy's face. She mostly listened with an occasional "yes, ma'am." I could tell that whatever Mrs. Marshall was saying was going in one ear and right out the other. I felt better—at least I'd gotten a reaction. Suddenly, Maddy's face changed.

"No, Mother. I'm not ready to come home." She gazed directly at me as she repeated my words. "I've decided it's a good thing I learned about Lyle before we were married." She listened for a moment. "Yes, and I think I should wait until the gossip dies down before I come home. Yes, ma'am, I know. Here's Ruth." She shoved the receiver in my direction like a baton in a relay. I had no choice but to take it.

After assuring Mrs. Marshall that we were both faring well in Miami, even under the circumstances, she gave me a stern lecture where Maddy was concerned. I needed to keep an eye on her. She knew her daughter and was certain that as soon as Maddy got herself together she was likely to do something wild in retaliation.

"Like what?" I asked.

"Well, once she and Jeanne wanted to get their hair cut like Greta Garbo. They wanted to dye it blonde, too. Mrs. Sharpe allowed Jeanne to cut hers but insisted on no dyeing. I forbade Maddy from either one."

"What happened?"

"Nothing at first. I mean she cried for a couple of days and accused me of being the meanest mother alive. Then, when I thought the storm had passed, she came out of her room one morning with several large chunks cut out of the front of her hair. She'd taken the scissors to it and looked like a lunatic."

I glanced at Maddy and had to smile. I could imagine her planning the perfect way to get around her mother and have what she wanted. Looking like a lunatic would have been polish on the apple.

"I had to take her to a stylist to get that mess straightened out. Then I took her to the priest for confession."

"I see," I replied without further comment. I didn't want Maddy to know her mother didn't trust her. "Well, don't worry. I'm sure she'll be fine." Then I changed the subject. "I'll have Davey call you when he gets in tonight."

— MADDY —

I swear, it was like I had a deadly disease or something. Everyone seemed to be walking on eggshells around me. Randy stared at me like a heartsick puppy and followed me from room to room telling me knock-knock jokes as I helped with dinner. Mr. Siler patted me on the back after I sat down at the table, and even Mrs. Siler called me "Maddy, dear" when she asked me to pass the salt.

It was enough to make a girl cry in her soup.

Oh, Lyle—you rat! Not only had he ruined my future, he was wrecking my vacation!

"I think we should do something fun this weekend," Ruth said as though I'd spoken my thoughts out loud. "After all, Davey will be here and on Monday I'll be starting my new job."

"We could go to the beach, couldn't we, Dad?" Randy offered. "Davey could drive us over." Randy stared directly at me. "Would you like that, Maddy?"

I had to admit, things were looking better already. Lyle and Jeanne might be on their honeymoon, but they weren't in Miami. "Yes. I would like to swim in the ocean. How about you, Ruth?"

Ruth smiled at me, then patted my hand. "Sounds wonderful."

"I'll pack a picnic lunch for you," Mrs. Siler added. "You can make a day of it."

By the time Davey arrived, we'd planned out most of the weekend in advance. Beach on Saturday, dinner and tea on Sunday with Jack and Lt. Tull-Martin. I decided my heart might be broken but my spirit was beginning to recover. Even spending a Friday evening playing pinochle with the Silers didn't bother me. It kept my mind off my loss and my hands busy. I stayed out of Davey and Ruth's way and went to bed early.

Mother would have been impressed.

I woke up to the sound of a man's voice coming through the wall from the kitchen. It took me a moment to remember that Davey was "home" with us before I jumped up, pulled on my robe, straightened my hair, and headed in that direction. Surely he'd have a few unflattering digs about Lyle I could add to my own collection. Instead of a happy scene, I came upon a rather somber discussion. Ruth and Davey were seated at the table—Ruth looked like she'd been crying and Davey seemed worried. The photograph we'd had taken at the pier was on the table in front of them.

"Good morning," I said, halfheartedly. From appearances it didn't look good at all.

Ruth sniffed and Davey put an arm around her. "Good morning, baby sister."

He seemed sad. Surely this grim discussion wasn't over me and Lyle. I decided I better buck up before I ruined everyone's weekend. I pulled out a chair and sat down across from them. "I'm feeling much better," I lied.

Ruth picked up the photograph and casually turned it face-down, like my mother used to do when she didn't want us to see her Christmas list. "I'm so glad."

I stared at her for a moment. She was acting odd about the photograph again. I pulled it closer and brought it upright. "Doesn't anyone like this picture, but me?" I asked, thinking that Davey would surely speak up. I looked at my happy face, surrounded by men, and had a delectably evil thought. "In fact, I think I'll have a copy made and send it to Jeanne and Lyle as a wedding present."

"No—" Ruth said, before quickly clamming up.

"Don't be a dunce," Davey said, sounding more like his old self. "The best thing you can do is leave them to their own problems. You were raised better than that."

I'd been hoping my brother would at least offer to punch Lyle in the nose. But I guess the Army had taken some of the starch out of him. He sounded more like I remembered my father sounding.

"It's not fair that I don't even get to have my say." I wanted them to feel at least a little uncomfortable about trampling my feelings. Both of them had been my friends.

"Sometimes saying nothing is more bothersome. It makes them believe you have better things to think about," Ruth said.

"But I don't . . ."

"Yes, you do," Davey smiled. "We're going to spend the day at the beach and if you're extra nice to me," he grinned at Ruth, "I'll take you girls to dinner and dancing at the pier tonight."

I have to admit my general attitude took a swing upward from that point on.

Heaven must have sand and sun and water. After loading Ruth, Randy, and me then squeezing in Randy's chair along with lunch and a couple of beach chairs into Mr. Siler's car, Davey drove us over the causeway. Ruth and I had sundresses over our bathing suits, and Randy had worn shorts and a big woven palm leaf hat his father had bought him. Davey asked him if he was going on safari and Randy, without blinking an eye, said the hat was his "bustard-watching" hat. It kept the sun out of his eyes so he could hunt for German submarines.

We looked like a bunch of gypsies in a caravan, minus the horses and the pots and pans swinging from hooks. I didn't care though. It was another perfect day in paradise, bright sun and huge fluffy clouds in an aquamarine sky, a cooling breeze ruffling the palm trees, and water as far as the eye could see. I was beginning to think it never rained in Florida and that suited me just fine. I'd had enough storms for one week.

Davey found a place to park not far from the pier, as close to the sand as he could, since he'd have to carry Randy from the car to the blanket. Ruth and I claimed a nice spot under two palm trees for our temporary camp and used our shoes to weigh down the corners of our blanket so the wind wouldn't flip up the edges and toss sand in our food. By the time Randy was settled and we were all accounted for I was ready for a swim.

That's when the wolf whistles started. There were mostly women with children scattered along the beach, but we were close enough to the pier for some of the soldiers at the swim club to notice us. As I waded into the water I stopped to wave in their general direction. Their attention warmed me like the sun. It felt good to be appreciated after being abandoned by Lyle. Unfortunately, remembering Lyle's betrayal put the brakes on my enjoyment. Now I would always wonder how many of those boys whistling and flirting with me had girl-friends or "almost" fiancées back home. The very idea made me want to stomp my feet in fury. Instead, I dove into the ocean and swam hard for Africa. If any of them wanted to talk to me they'd have to be good swimmers.

I let the warm water buoy me and my attitude, determined not to think of you-know-who. The drama of drowning myself over my broken heart only made me laugh and swim harder. Yes, I was hurt, but not THAT hurt. I would rather hold Lyle underwater for long enough to make him apologize. And Jeanne, well, I wasn't sure what I wanted to do to her. But drowning wasn't such a bad idea.

We ate our picnic lunch of cheese sandwiches, lemonade, and ginger cookies while Randy entertained us with stories of how he and Jack used to build sand castles—one facing the other. Then they would use rocks and shells like bombs, or sticks like battering rams to assault each other's castle until they were both destroyed.

"Girls are babies," he said looking at me. "They want to build things but they never want to knock them down."

I happened to be in the mood for some knocking down. "Okay," I said, snatching up my empty glass to use as a bucket. "Let's build."

For the next two hours, Randy and I labored on our castles. We even recruited a few of the children on the beach to help. We decorated the turrets with seaweed and broken pieces of coconuts, dug the moats, and gathered rocks and shells. When it came time for the battle, we readied our weapons—I'd put together a halfway decent slingshot using some derelict fishing line and two pieces of driftwood—then announced our intentions. I turned to signal Davey and Ruth who were up the beach on the blanket and saw they weren't alone. Jack and Lt. Tull-Martin were hunkered down next to them.

Jack waved. "Go get 'em, Maddy!"

Lt. Tull-Martin smiled.

Oh no. I felt heat rising to my face and it had nothing to do with sunburn. Of all the people to see me wallowing in the sand like a five-year-old. I was so out of sorts I let fly with my sling and hit Randy right in the nose with a fairly good-sized rock.

"Hey!" he shouted. "You're not supposed to aim at me!"

I felt bad since he was just getting over his sunburn. There wasn't time to apologize though. Rocks and sticks flew in retaliation and soon the castles were nothing but churned sand. The kids finished them off by stomping any remaining bumps. Since neither of us were willing to admit defeat, we were forced to call the battle a draw. When I stood up, I was covered in sand and my bathing suit seemed filled with it. I decided the best way to get clean was to get back in the water. It also kept me from having to face anyone.

I'd dunked under for the second time to rinse my hair when I noticed Jack and Lt. Tull-Martin, near the water's edge now, talking to Randy. The three of them were looking at me. After a moment Jack waved and yelled, "We'll be back in a few minutes." They set off down the beach toward the pier.

I was glad to see them go. It gave me the chance to put myself together before they came back. As my mother always said, if I wanted to be treated as a woman and not a girl, I needed to act like a woman. I waited until they were well away before leaving the water.

"Jack is coming back to take me swimming," Randy announced.

"I should hope so," I said. "You look like mister mudpie."

"No thanks to you," Randy replied then picked up a handful of sand as if he intended to throw it at me.

"Oh, no you don't," I said and scampered up the beach toward the blanket.

Jack was as good as his word. He and Lt. Tull-Martin came back dressed in swimming trunks. The two of them carried Randy into the water, then Jack held on to him so he wouldn't sink.

"Come on, girls," Davey said. "Let's join the crowd." He offered a hand to help Ruth up then looked at me. "You coming?"

I'd won the battle of getting the sand out of the most important places. And I'd combed my hair. The last thing I wanted to do was get mussed up again. But I didn't want to act like the queen of Sheba either—too good to join the masses in a little fun. It dawned on me then that swimming was a lot closer to civilized, adult behavior than sand-castle fights.

As the three of us approached the water, Randy whistled a perfect imitation of the wolf whistles we'd heard earlier. I stopped. Jack joined the refrain.

"Hey, that's my wife you bums are flirting with," Davey said, doing his best to sound outraged. Then he added, "And my baby sister."

"You can't blame a guy for tryin', can you?" Jack laughed. "You're not afraid of the water, are you, Maddy?"

I balanced hands on hips like my third-grade teacher, Mrs. Zinc, used to do when somebody was destined for the corner seat. I wasn't afraid. I was thinking up how I could give them a good dose of "what for," without wrecking my ladylike image. Unfortunately, the perfect words proved illusive, so I stood there with my mouth open like a beached fish. Davey and Ruth were already shoulder deep in the water when Lt. Tull-Martin waded through the breaking waves toward me. I did my best not to stare at the terrible scar running halfway down his right leg. It looked like he'd been struck by red lightning, and the thought of how much it must have hurt made my heart clench. He offered his hand.

"May I, milady?"

Well, what could I say to that? My castle had been trampled but a knight had come to call. Nothing came to mind but "Yes, certainly."

His hand was cool from the water, and my whole body was warm from the sun and from being the center of attention. This is what I'd wanted, to be treated like an adult, like a grown woman. It was almost too good to be true. Then I wondered if Randy had told them about Lyle and they were feeling sorry for me.

"Some blokes have no manners," Lt. Tull-Martin said with a smile toward Jack. He looked at me then and I knew he'd heard my bad news. But I didn't detect any pity.

"Tell me something I don't know," I concurred. Before I could stop myself, I stuck my tongue out at Randy. He smirked and looked like he might start a splashing contest but at the last second he pulled up. I swept past them into deeper water and did my best imitation of a future Olympic gold medalist.

My nose and cheeks were pink by the time we called it a day. We made plans to meet at the pier later in the evening, then Jack and Lt. Tull-Martin helped us carry everything, including Randy, to the car before they went to collect their clothes at the beach club.

"That was a perfect day," I said to no one in particular on the way home. It had been. I'd suddenly realized that if Lyle could change his mind so easily, then so could I. That meant I was free to flirt with anyone I chose, like Lt. Tull-Martin.

"Yes, it was," Ruth said. She picked up Davey's hand, kissed his knuckles, and sighed. "Wonderful," she added.

I poked Randy with my toe. "How about you, wisenheimer?"

"Couldn't have been better," he answered without the usual smart-aleck tone. "I'm really glad you girls came to Florida."

"Why, Randy, that's nice of you to say. Isn't it, Maddy?"

I was flabbergasted. I mean I knew Randy enjoyed picking on me but I didn't think he would admit to actually liking us being next door. Then I figured out that he was being nice because of Lyle. Well, that was okay. Nice equaled nice no matter the reason. "Yeah," I said, "that's sweet."

Chapter Six

— RUTH —

I insisted that Maddy take a nap before dinner. She looked so much better after our beach outing, but she still had faint circles under her eyes. I was sure she hadn't slept a wink the night before.

I had good reason to worry. I'd gotten out the photograph this morning to confess to Davey that I might be going off the deep end. As I told him about Airman Edwards and about seeing Maddy's tears, he'd asked me to look at the photo again to see if anything else seemed different. Sure enough, it had changed again—and not for the better. Maddy looked even sadder, and something else—her hair had been mussed and she seemed dazed, as if she'd seen a ghost. It had shocked me because I'd hoped Maddy was feeling better. Davey and I had discussed the possibilities of why this could be happening. But finally, as I knew he would, Davey calmed me with his determination that we should consider the warnings a kind of gift. Why else would God warn me of Maddy's unhappiness unless it was to help. That's why we'd gone to the beach and why we were taking Maddy to the pier tonight. To cheer her up and show her that there were plenty of other happy things in the world besides her ex-boyfriend.

She had so much to be thankful for, as did we all. Perhaps the photograph was there to remind us of that.

As we dressed to go out I spent a little more time helping Maddy than usual. I even loaned her one of my best rayon blouses. She seemed perfectly fine. She smiled when I showed her my sunburned ears and laughed when I dropped my last hairpin behind the dresser. But I kept remembering her face in the photograph and stuck to my plan of encouraging her. How could I know when I'd done enough?

We stopped for dinner at a little drive-in on Miami Beach called the Pig and Sax. It was crowded, even with the many shortages, and obviously a popular place for the soldiers and sailors. This was probably because of the fact that the carhops wore short skirts and rolled back and forth to the customers on roller skates. We ate hot dogs with sauerkraut and fried potatoes before driving down to the Servicemen's Pier.

I didn't breathe easier until I watched Maddy jitterbug with Davey's friend, Frankie Santorini, to a Glenn Miller tune. She laughed as he swung her around, and I hoped she'd found her footing again—her emotional footing, that is. There were plenty of soldiers ready and willing to help her forget Lyle.

It was nearly ten o'clock by the time Jack joined us. He said he'd had dinner with one of the girls from the canteen but he'd had to take her home early because she had first shift in the morning.

"Where's Lt. Tull-Martin?" Maddy asked.

Jack held a hand over his heart like he'd been shot. "Ow." He groaned like he was in pain. "Forget that Limey *bustard*," he said. "You need to stick to the red, white, and blue."

"Yeah," Frankie Santorini added. "Come on, let's dance." He clamped a hand on Maddy's arm and pulled.

She pulled back. "Hey," she said, frowning, and he let go. She looked past him. "Okay, Jack, you dance with me then," she challenged.

He smiled a beatific smile. "You got it, toots."

Frankie turned on his heels and disappeared in the other direction. I looked to see if Davey had been watching.

"Your friend Frankie seems a little edgy tonight," I said.

He frowned. "He's been making a few trips outside. I think he might have a bottle of whiskey stashed somewhere." Davey tightened his arm around me. "He's edgy because there's scuttlebutt going around that we might be shipping out soon—maybe this week."

I felt like my heart had fallen through the wooden pier and into the cold water below.

"Could be a rumor of nerves," Davey continued. "But I have a hunch it's not. We're taking a pounding from the Japs first in the Philippines, and now Corregidor."

"You don't mean tomorrow," I said, not even able to comprehend such a turnaround in our luck.

"Probably not on a Sunday, but we're on twenty-four-hour notice."

My eyes teared up. I couldn't help it. With Davey staying at the house I'd almost begun to feel normal again. And now . . .

"Don't cry, sweetie," he said into my ear. "I'm so thankful you're here." He squeezed me closer. "And we have some time left."

"Let's go home," I said, feeling desperate to be alone with him—to have him entirely to myself.

"Well, I don't know . . ." He looked for Maddy and Jack on the dance floor. The song had ended and they were on their way back to the table. "Let's see how Maddy is feeling."

Maddy was laughing. "You stepped on my foot, you big lug. I thought pilots were light on their feet."

"Only when we're in airplanes," Jack answered. As he pulled out a chair for her to sit down he leaned close to her. "Here comes your dreamboat."

Maddy's smile disappeared as she looked up.

"Hey, Lieutenant," Jack said with a smirk. "Some of us thought you got lost."

"Good evening," Lt. Tull-Martin said. "And I'm late, not lost. I went to the cinema with one of the other instructors and misjudged the time." He shook hands with Jack and Davey, nodded to me, then pulled out a chair. "May I?"

"Of course," Davey said.

"Hello, Maddy. I see your nose is pink from the sun," Lt. Tull-Martin said.

Maddy blushed even pinker. "What movie did you see?"

"Oh, a grand pirate epic, *Reap the Wild Wind*. It's about the shipwreckers who used to prey on ships from Key West to Charleston."

"Not unlike what the Germans are doing now," Jack added.

"Paulette Goddard and Ray Milland," Maddy said. Then looking embarrassed she added, "I saw the listings in the paper. I love movies—any movies, all movies."

The lieutenant chuckled. "Perhaps we'll have to go some evening."

Maddy looked so enraptured I thought she might float right out of her chair.

Frankie Santorini returned. He pulled out a chair on the other side of Jack and didn't look happy about losing his place next to Maddy. She didn't seem to notice. I decided that now was as good a time as any to broach the subject of going home. "Maddy, would you show me where the ladies' room is?"

She seemed a little pained at the interruption but nodded. "Sure." She stood and waited as I got to my feet.

I followed her toward the concession table. She waved at one of the women working there as we passed. "Hi, Cleo. Remember me?"

"Hi, kiddo. Back again, I see."

"Yup," Maddy laughed. "This is my sister-in-law, Ruth."

I said hello, then followed Maddy down a hallway behind the kitchen. I stopped her when we reached the door. "Maddy, Davey and I are almost ready to leave."

The happy expression on her face abruptly faded. "You mean now?"

"In a few minutes. I'm a little tired and—"

"Please Ruth, let's not leave yet." She took my hand and seemed truly upset. "Lt. Tull-Martin just got here."

"Well, I know, but Davey and I wanted some time alone . . ." I didn't know how to explain it without telling her that if Davey got orders to ship out this could be our last night together. It would also be the end of our trip, and Maddy's happiness would be over as well. We'd have to return to Radley. Perhaps that was the unhappiness I'd seen in the photograph. "I'm sorry," I said.

She got quiet then and I felt like an ogre. First a broken heart then her weekend disrupted. She remained outside the door while I used the facilities, thinking, I suppose, because on the way back to the table she perked up as we passed the concession table again. She waved me on and stopped to speak to the woman she'd introduced me to earlier.

— MADDY —

I didn't know what to do. It was Saturday night and I couldn't go home and have nothing to think about but Lyle. Cleo was my last hope. I mean I knew we were basically strangers, but surely I could prevail on her, woman to woman. I'd even tell her about Lyle if I had to. That should foster some sympathy.

Actually, I didn't want sympathy. I wanted a ride home, a way to stay another hour or so rather than going home with Davey and Ruth. I was nearly desperate. For some reason I felt like this might be my last chance for some fun.

It turns out it didn't take much to convince Cleo. She was living in a small motel on the other side of the causeway, and it wouldn't be too far out of her way to drop me off at Ninth Avenue. I was so happy I hugged her, then I dragged her over to help me convince Davey and Ruth.

Davey wasn't very keen on the idea, but Ruth stayed silent, allowing me to plead my case. When he'd asked Cleo what seemed like forty questions, he looked at me. "Mother would never forgive me for leaving you here alone."

"I'm not alone," I informed him. "And it's barely an hour."

He looked at Cleo. "You'll bring her *straight* home?" It sounded more like an order than a question.

Before Cleo could answer, I threw an arm around my brother's neck and kissed him on the cheek. "Thank you, brother dear." I grinned up at him. "You're my hero."

He gazed down at me for a long moment. He wasn't smiling. "Don't talk to strangers."

"Don't worry, I won't." I had no intention of talking to strangers. I wanted to talk to the lieutenant.

Davey turned to him and Jack. "Are you two gonna be here a while?"

Lt. Tull-Martin looked at his watch. "Until the bus back to barracks at eleven-thirty."

"All right, then." Davey nodded. Then he gathered Ruth close to his side. "We'll see you at home at twelve-fifteen."

I knew that meant he would be waiting up looking at his watch, but I didn't care. I'd gotten what I wanted. We'd all gotten what we wanted because Davey and Ruth went home and I sat back down at the table with Jack and Lt. Tull-Martin.

From that moment on, Lyle was almost the farthest thing from my mind. Jack seemed content to let Lt. Tull-Martin carry the conversation. And the first time I called him Lieutenant he insisted that I call him Tully. The evening could have ended there and I would have been content. But then the band began playing "White Cliffs of Dover" and he looked at me.

"I'm afraid with this leg I'm no Fred Astaire, but if you'd like to try a dance, this song seems appropriate."

I was too happy to speak, so I nodded. He pushed his chair back, stood, and offered his hand. A moment or two later, I was in his arms. I don't remember how he danced. I'm sure it was fine. I was more aware of the even pressure of his fingers on mine, the tangy smell of shaving lotion, and the warmth of his shoulder under my shaky hand.

"So, is there a girl waiting back home on the white cliffs of Dover?" I'm not sure why I suddenly felt brave enough to ask. I guess from being left alone, like a grown-up.

He gazed down at me looking very serious. "No. I'm afraid not."

"But why? You seem—" What the heck was I doing? One moment of feeling bold and I'd backed myself into a corner. What could I say? You seem normal? You seem wonderful? You seem like a man any girl would be happy to wait for? "Uh—"

He saved me by going on. "I've sort of kept it that way. This war—it wouldn't be fair to make promises I might not survive long enough to keep. And I wouldn't want to leave a wife and possibly a child behind to manage alone." His hand tightened on mine briefly. "You understand that, don't you, Maddy?"

I wasn't sure I did, but I nodded anyway. As the song came to an end he smiled. "Thank you for the dance." Before I could reply the band started playing "Into the Night," another slow one. "And since we're at it, how about another?"

We danced every slow dance after that. Jack spent his time flirting with one of the girls working with Cleo at the concession table. The band announced curfew call at 11:30—much too quickly.

I told Cleo I was walking Tully out front to the bus, then he took my hand. It was the closest thing to delirium I'd ever felt—even with Lyle. The night was breezy and quiet outside. Until the soldiers saw me and Tully holding hands that is. Then the catcalls started. One of the men yelled, "Kiss her good night!" The others around him took up the call. They made kissing sounds and talked baby talk. I could feel my face burning. Tully looked over my head toward the rabble-rousers, then he gazed down at me with a half-smile. He shrugged his shoulders then leaned over and kissed me on the cheek.

For one pulse-stopping moment, I thought I might have heart failure. The crowd around us seemed disappointed when he then picked up my hand and kissed my fingers before saying good night.

I waved as the bus pulled away and felt like I could have walked on water all the way across the Atlantic. The rowdy boys had loaded up and mostly disappeared. A couple of stay-behinds smoking cigarettes loitered outside the front of the pier. I headed back inside and had almost reached the door when I heard my name.

"Maddy!"

The sound had come from the corner of the building. I turned to look thinking it must be Jack. The outside lights had been turned off because of the blackout rules so I couldn't quite see.

"Hey, Maddy. Over here."

I walked in that direction. I remembered Davey's warning about talking to strangers, but this was someone who knew me, or my name anyway. When I got to the corner I found Frankie, Davey's friend. Or rather, he found me. He took my arm and pulled me around the building toward the ocean.

"Hey!" I said, pulling back.

He turned and I could see his white-toothed smile in the dark. "I want to show you something down near the water."

I smelled liquor on his breath. "I can't. I have to go find Cleo—" I didn't get to finish because he grabbed me and clapped a hand over my mouth.

I'm not sure how much later it was when the soldier patrolling the beach found me. Frankie was long gone and I felt like I'd had the air knocked out of me. Something had happened to my mind, I couldn't quite think straight. And rather than being helpful, the soldier dragged me up from the sand, waited a few seconds while I straightened my clothes and found my shoes, then pushed me in front of him toward the pier. I was getting a little tired of being man-handled. But no one seemed to care what I wanted or didn't want.

The officer in charge raked me over with a critical eye. "You know it's against wartime law to be on the beach at night. What were you doing out there?"

"I—I didn't know—" I couldn't tell them what had happened to me. Just thinking hurt my head. The rest of me didn't feel so great either. My throat was tight and I knew if I tried to speak I'd start crying and probably never stop. Then I heard my name being called again. For a scary moment I thought it might be Frankie and my heart nearly jumped out of my chest.

"Maddy! We've been looking everywhere for you. Where have you been?" It was Jack, and I'd never been so glad to see anyone in my life. I knew Jack would somehow make things right. He took one long look at me and the urgency in his voice disappeared. "What's the problem, Sarg?" he asked the man who'd been questioning me.

"We found her on the beach. I have to take her in, in case she's a German spy. It's the law."

Jack smiled but his eyes remained serious. "She's no spy. She's my little brother's girlfriend, visiting here from Pennsylvania. She doesn't know anything about war laws, do you, Maddy?"

I shook my head no.

"Here's my identification," Jack said and produced his wallet. "My family is local. Come on, Sarg, look at her, she's just a kid. Let me take her home."

My knees were beginning to tremble, and I wasn't sure how much longer I could remain standing. The sergeant surveyed me again then said, "You victory girls are nothin' but trash."

Tears were welling up inside me, but I couldn't speak.

"She's a good girl, honest," Jack said in a tight voice. He awkwardly patted me on the shoulder like a pet spaniel.

"Well, all right, missy. We'll let you go this time. But I'm gonna write a report on this. We better not catch you out there again."

I tried to say "thank you" but my voice wouldn't work. He turned to another soldier.

"Bring a jeep and drive them to—" He looked at Jack's ID, "—Ninth Avenue. And be quick about it. I'm putting your name on the report for being out past curfew," he said to Jack. "The two of you can wait over there where the buses load."

Without another word, Jack held out his hand and pulled me forward, supporting me as we walked. He waited until we were far enough from the soldiers before he clamped an arm around me. "Are you okay, honey?"

The flimsy wall holding back my tears burst. "N-no—" I managed, then I pushed my face into Jack's shirt and cried. Suddenly I couldn't seem to stop crying. I don't know if it was the shock or my gratitude to him for being nice to me, but between sobs and hiccoughs my voice started working.

"Somebody called my name and I— He grabbed me—I bit his hand and screamed but nobody heard m-me."

Jack raised my face in the dim light and seemed to be looking for bruises. I licked my dry lips and the bottom one felt swollen.

"Did the bastard hit you?"

"I-I don't think so. He held me down while h-he—" I couldn't say it.

Remembering what had happened and looking into Jack's worried eyes made my tears crank up again.

"I know what he did," he said, sounding murderous and miserable at the same time.

"Swear you won't tell anyone, especially Ruth and Davey." I knew Davey would never forgive himself for leaving me at the pier on my own, and Ruth would know that I was too stupid to be her sister or her friend.

"But they need to know. Something has to be done. And you might need help . . . later." He watched me, waiting, I suppose, for me to understand what he was talking about. All I knew is that it was over and I wanted to go home. I didn't care if I ever saw the pier again.

Cleo rushed out of the building then, another Red Cross volunteer in tow. "Are you okay, sweetie?" she asked looking worried. "We sent out a search party for you." She looked me over with knowing eyes then gazed at Jack. "Should we take her to the hospital?"

The word "NO" flew out of me like I'd been holding it in along with my breath. "No," I said, calmer. Hospitals meant calling my brother and my mother, then my humiliation would be complete. Lyle's desertion was nothing compared to this. I'd rather die than have everyone back in Radley find out what had happened to me.

Jack bracketed my shoulders with his hands and forced me to look him in the eyes. "Maddy? Are you sure? You might be hurt somehow we can't see."

Tears continued to leak out of me and again, for a moment, I couldn't make a sound. When I did speak the words came out shaky. "Please Jack. I—I just want to go home. I'll be fine. D-Don't tell Davey."

Jack looked at Cleo and shrugged. The soldier pulled up in the jeep then.

Cleo patted my hair into place on one side. "If you need help, come see me. I'm here every weekend. Or you can call the front desk and leave me a message."

I nodded. Reluctantly Cleo and the other volunteer walked back toward the entrance to the pier.

Jack frowned down at me. "I'll make you a deal. I won't tell Davey but you've gotta give me a name."

I kept my mouth shut.

"I promise, I won't say a word if you don't want me to."

Jack didn't move. He looked ready to wait the rest of the night if that's what it took. Too worn-down to fight about it, I gave him Frankie's name. For a few seconds he looked like he might have set his sights on Hitler himself. Then as quick as a blink he was handing me into the back of the jeep before getting in the front to give the driver directions. On the way over the causeway, I did my best to straighten my clothes. I had to take off my stockings because they were ripped. Jack kept his eyes on the road as he helped me put together a plausible story about why I was late and being delivered home by Army jeep.

I could see light shining at the edges of the blackout curtain at the Samuel place when we pulled up. "What time is it?" I asked, wondering how far I'd missed curfew.

Jack looked at his watch. "One-fifteen."

"Only an hour, then," I said but couldn't quite grasp the passage of time. It seemed like an eternity had gone by, not just a few hours.

"Cut the engine, will ya?" he said to the driver.

I could see Davey's silhouette inside the screen door as Jack escorted me up the walk. I did my best to walk on my own but Jack left his arm around me, as though out of habit. Halfway to the porch, the front door of the Siler house opened and Jack frowned in that direction. "I want you to laugh, Maddy," he said under his breath.

The last thing I felt like doing was laughing.

"My mother is watching, you don't want her asking questions. Now, laugh."

I felt like I had a giant bubble of air blocking my throat but I managed a grimace of a smile and forced a chuckle. Jack took over from there, his laugh sounding loud and clear. As Davey opened the door, Jack shook his hand and said, "Cleo had some car trouble. I talked this guy with a jeep into giving Maddy a lift home." He squeezed my hand to give me courage, I suppose. "Wait till you see what that wind did to your hair and your outfit." He grinned at me, then he waved. "Gotta get back. It's after curfew."

If Jack ever decided he didn't want to be a pilot, then I was sure he could go to Hollywood. He was a better actor than many I'd seen on the screen. And after all he'd done for me, I didn't even say good night. I watched as he trotted over to speak to his mother, then the jeep roared to life and took him back to Miami Beach.

Then I had to look in my brother's worried eyes.

— RUTH —

*I*nstead of the happy, carefree girl we'd left at the pier, Maddy looked like she'd seen a ghost. And her clothes were a mess.

"I'm sorry I was late," she said but kept moving. "I think I'll have a quick bath . . ."

I looked at Davey. Something was wrong.

"Maddy—" He stepped past me.

Maddy turned but continued forward toward the hallway.

"You can yell at me tomorrow," she said. "I promise." With a little wave she disappeared into her room.

"What the heck is going on?" Davey said, still staring after his sister. "You don't suppose she and Jack—"

"No," I said quickly. Even though Jack had brought Maddy home, I refused to believe the obvious. First, because I felt Jack wasn't the kind of man who'd take advantage of a kid like Maddy. But more importantly, I knew Maddy was harboring a soft heart for Lt. Tull-Martin. Then I remembered Mrs. Marshall's warning that Maddy might do something wild and my heart clenched. *Oh, please, no.*

I squeezed my husband's arm. "Leave it to me. I'll get to the bottom of it." As I'd hoped, some of the tension eased out of his face. He had enough to worry about with the war, and it was my place to look out for Maddy.

As we prepared to go to bed, I heard the bathroom door shut and water running. Davey went right to sleep, but I couldn't close my eyes. Lying in the dark my conscience warred with my sense of propriety. Should I go to her and demand to know what happened? Like her mother would do? Or should I wait for her to confide in me? Like a sister?

But then I heard her retching and the mother in me took over. I carefully slid out of bed so I wouldn't wake Davey. I closed our bedroom door and slipped down the hall to tap on the bathroom door.

"Maddy? Are you all right?"

She didn't answer. When I heard her choking again, I opened the door and found her sitting on the floor near the toilet with her knees drawn up.

I dropped to my knees beside her. "Are you ill?" I put a hand on her clammy forehead to check for fever. "Where does it hurt?"

She looked at me then and the naked emotion in her eyes nearly broke my heart. She blinked and tears rolled down her already damp cheeks. "I want to take a bath." The words came out in a cracked whisper.

I couldn't tell if Maddy was ill or not. She seemed beyond explanations or punishments. She looked like a lost child who needed an adult to put things right. I pushed the hair back off her forehead. "If you want a bath, then let's get you into the tub." I slipped an arm around her to help her stand and used the sink to pull us up. After putting the toilet lid down, I sat her on it. Then I filled a glass from the sink and held it out to her. "First, drink some water to settle your stomach."

She dutifully drank several sips before handing the glass back to me. I checked the water in the tub to make sure it was tepid before bringing Maddy to her feet to help her out of her clothes.

I recognized my own rayon chiffon blouse I'd loaned her. It had been new, but now as I unbuttoned the front I noticed that two of the buttons were loose and one buttonhole was ripped. I glanced up at Maddy to see if she'd make some sort of excuse but she seemed to be off in another place—waiting patiently while I undressed her. When I pulled the tail of the blouse from her skirt I caught my breath. She had scratches on her chest, near the edge of her bra and higher, on her neck. Determined to wait for explanations, I continued on by unzipping her skirt and helping her step out of it along with her slip. I found another scratch on her thigh and what looked like a bruise.

Oh, Maddy.

Tears filled my eyes as I turned her away from me to unhook her brassiere. I fumbled with the clasp and a fine sprinkling of beach sand fell to the floor. The picture was becoming all too clear. Whatever had happened, she'd fought against it. Doing my best to remain calm I sniffed back my tears and rested a hand on her shoulder. "Step out of your panties, sweetie."

Obediently, she did so and my worst fears were confirmed. Besides the bruises on her hips, which were obviously made by a man's hands, her panties were stained with blood.

An anger I hadn't realized I possessed rose up inside me.

For a few moments I understood the term "crime of passion." And I don't mean what had happened to Maddy. I mean the crime of wanting to kill a grown man who would hurt an innocent young girl. I intended to find out who he was and where I could find him.

I helped Maddy step into the tub, and as she stretched out in the water I wet a washcloth and put it over her eyes and forehead. "Is that better?" She nodded and rested for a few moments before she pushed upright. Without speaking, she picked up the bar of soap and started scrubbing. Face to toes, she washed until I suppose she felt clean. When she stepped out of the tub and I wrapped her in a towel, she warily looked me in the eye.

"Swear you won't tell Davey."

For once, she and I wanted the same exact thing but for different reasons. I would have done anything for her then *except* tell Davey. But I needed some leverage. "I'll swear if in turn you swear to let me help you. Whatever it takes."

Tears sparkled in her eyes again. "You've already helped me."

I gave her a quick squeeze. "We're sisters, remember?"

She nodded again. "Okay, I swear."

"I swear, too." I bundled her up in another towel and opened the bathroom door. "Let's get you into bed."

I believe everyone slept, for a few hours at least. When I made my way into the kitchen early the next morning, I found Maddy seated at the kitchen table, fully dressed. She looked more like herself, wearing a three-button suit with her hair pinned up under a felt bonnet.

I glanced over my shoulder and listened to make sure Davey was in the bathroom and not standing behind me. Hearing the water running, I pulled out a chair and sat next to Maddy. I rested a hand on her arm to remind her I remained on her side.

"How are you?"

She gazed at me with a sad, but calm expression. "I'm okay, I guess."

"Do you feel up to talking about what happened?"

Calm deserted her and her expression crumpled. She shook her head. After taking a deep breath she said, "I want to go to mass."

"If you feel up to it, I'm sure we can find a church close by."

I heard Davey in the hallway, then he stepped into the kitchen. "Feel up to what?" he asked. "Are you sick?"

Being unsure what Maddy might say, I stepped in ahead of her. "Good morning to you, too," I said, giving the words an inflection that would remind everyone in the room of Mrs. Marshall.

Davey nodded in understanding. "Good morning, Maddy. Good morning, wife. Now, who's sick?"

"No one," I answered quickly. "I *meant* we're a little wilted from being up so late last night."

"And whose fault was that?" Davey asked, advancing on Maddy. "You owe me an explanation. You promised to be home at twelve-fifteen."

I held my breath as Maddy straightened her shoulders and faced her brother. "That's why I want to go to mass this morning. Even though Cleo had car trouble, it ended up that I broke my promise. What else can I do?"

Well done. I hated the thought that Maddy couldn't tell us the truth, not yet anyway. But I also didn't want to see her fragile state of mind broken before she'd had time to come to grips with whatever happened to her.

Davey came around the table and patted Maddy on the shoulder. "Okay, Mads, I'll take you to mass. I was worried about you, that's all."

Maddy gazed up at her brother, eyes swimming with tears. She sniffed them back and cleared her throat before she said, "I'm sorry, Davey. I won't do it again."

Brother and sister remained eye-to-eye for a long moment,

and I began to worry once again. Davey seemed to be scouting for the truth, and he was hard to fool. I knew if he searched long enough he'd see something. "Are you sure you're okay?"

Sniffing once more, Maddy's mouth twisted into a slight smile. "It's a girl thing, okay?"

"Ah . . ." Davey backed off and I released the breath I'd been holding. I had no idea what Davey would do if he learned the truth, but I didn't believe it would help Maddy in the long run. Helping Davey's sister would be up to me. "Well, let me finish dressing," he said, "and I'll go over to the Silers' and get directions."

The Silers sent us off to the bus stop but insisted we return to their house for Sunday dinner before Davey had to report back to barracks. We took Maddy to mass, and I think each of us felt better afterward. Although Maddy looked even paler when she emerged from the confessional. The bus to and from the church was crowded, which precluded any sustained amount of conversation. I was watching Maddy when Davey mentioned Jack and Lt. Tull-Martin. Instead of her usual interest, she seemed nervous. Surely she wasn't afraid . . . Not for the first time I wished she'd confided in me. I could only hope the rest of the day would be uneventful so that when Maddy and I had the Samuel place to ourselves, she would tell me everything.

It occurred to me then that I should look at the photograph. I chose a moment when Maddy had gone to freshen up and Davey was occupied with the Sunday paper. Sitting on the bed in the room I shared with my husband, I slowly withdrew the picture from the envelope. After a deep breath and a silent prayer, I looked at Maddy first. Relief coursed through me. Maddy's expression, although not her original smile, had cleared. She looked calm and healthy—no more tears. But then Davey's friend Frankie claimed my attention. Originally he'd had an arm slung around Maddy's shoulders and he'd been grinning wolfishly. Now the arm was withdrawn and he appeared battered as though he'd been injured somehow. And his smile had vanished—hidden by a swollen lip. Lt. Tull-Martin seemed the same as I remembered, but Jack, Jack stared out at me with a deadly serious glower that gave me a shiver. A piece of tape had been applied to his cheekbone. I couldn't guess what it meant but I have to say I was relieved to see Maddy feeling better. Moving on, I couldn't stop myself from checking Davey. He seemed fit and solid, ready to do his duty even though he wasn't smiling. My heart lightened although I did notice something odd. We'd been sitting close together the night the photograph had been taken, touching. But now, after the image shifted and settled into place, there seemed to be some distance between us, as though his chair had been moved. And me, I wasn't smiling.

Suddenly I knew at least one part of the puzzle. The scuttlebutt was true. Davey's unit *was* shipping out—soon—and there was nothing I could do about it. My heart hammered out several labored beats, and I hugged the photograph to my chest as though I could keep him close. I'd known the day was coming but I wasn't ready to see my husband off to war.

"What's wrong, sweetie?" Davey had come to find me.

I sniffed back threatening tears, determined to act as if I was brave enough to let him go. "It's true," I said, as he sat next to me on the bed.

"What's true?"

"The scuttlebutt. You *are* shipping out."

He stared at me for a moment, then he pulled the photograph out of my grasp and looked down at it. "You can see that in here?" he asked as though he would believe anything I said.

I nodded.

My husband's expression became completely unreadable for a moment. I hoped beyond hope that he might see the same changes I had seen. But then he blinked and smiled at me. "Good. Then hold this close and you'll be able to keep an eye on me when I'm gone."

The fact that he believed me and had concluded that seeing visions was a blessing made me want to weep all over again. But I wouldn't. I'd be as fearless as I had to be—at least until he was out of my care.

* * *

As Davey called it, we *reported* to the Silers' for Sunday dinner promptly at 12:30. Maddy came along, subdued but cooperative. We were surprised to find that Lt. Tull-Martin and Jack had not attended church.

"They must've had duty," Mr. Siler said.

"Oh, what kind of duty could they have on a Sunday?" Mrs. Siler sniffed in disbelief, like the war would respect the Sabbath.

Davey spoke up then. "Well, it's up to the commanding officer—" he began but was interrupted by the phone.

"There's Jack now," Mrs. Siler pronounced.

Mr. Siler answered it. "Jack? Oh, hello, Lieutenant." He looked at his wife. "What happened?" He listened for several moments, then said, "Well, I appreciate you calling. Yes, I will. Thank you. Good-bye."

Mrs. Siler was speaking before he hung up the phone. "He wasn't flying today—he's all right, isn't he?"

"He's fine," Mr. Siler said then sighed. "He's in the stockade."

"What does that mean?" Mrs. Siler asked, her voice getting shriller by the moment.

"The stockade is the Army's version of jail," Davey said.

"Jail?" Randy repeated.

"What?" Mrs. Siler wailed.

"Now calm down, Mother." Mr. Siler crossed the room and sat next to his wife, probably to keep her from hitting the ceiling. "That was Lieutenant Tull-Martin. He said Jack asked him to call us and tell us where he was so we wouldn't worry."

"But why is he in jail?"

"Well—all the lieutenant knows is that he was late for curfew and in a brawl. Something to do with a woman."

I heard a small sound and turned to look at Maddy. The color she'd regained earlier had deserted her. If I'd been closer I would have been tempted to put an arm around her to steady her. But she was too far away.

Mrs. Siler was watching Maddy as well. "What woman?"

"The lieutenant didn't know any more than he told me.

Except that Jack would probably be confined to quarters for a while after he gets out."

"Is he hurt?"

"Not much," Mr. Siler answered. "But the lieutenant said, 'You should see the other guy.' "

The other guy.

A clear memory of the photograph appeared in my mind, of Davey's friend Frankie looking beat up, Jack's fierce expression, and Maddy. I gazed at her with new understanding, the pieces falling into place. Frankie had hurt Maddy, and Jack had hurt Frankie. *Bless you Jack Siler.*

"Maybe we should leave," I began, thinking to give the Silers time to sort out their family business. And time for me to become accustomed to the truth so I could decide what to do about it.

"Don't be silly," Mrs. Siler said, pulling herself together. "Dinner's almost ready and there's no reason to waste food." She faced Maddy. "Will you help set the table, dear?"

Maddy swallowed once but pushed to her feet.

"I'll help as well," I volunteered. I was reluctant to leave the two of them alone together. I had a feeling it would be easier to bluff J. Edgar Hoover than it would to fool Mrs. Siler.

By the time dinner was over and Davey was preparing to go back to his barracks I felt like a wilted dishrag. There were so many undercurrents hidden below the peaceful surface of the day, I could hardly keep up. But as Davey hefted his bag and picked up his hat, the fear I'd been holding down broke the forced calm.

"Wait!" I pleaded, clinging to his arm. I'm sure the others thought me a little crazy but I didn't care. I knew something they didn't know. I knew that my husband would be gone soon. He knew it, too.

Slowly he put down the bag and his hat and took me in his arms. "You know I love you more than anything," he whispered in my ear. "Forever and always, no matter what."

I wanted to speak but the sound that came out of me was a gasp I didn't recognize. Fear and tears were choking me. This could be the last time I ever saw him and I couldn't think of a thing that would be important enough to say. "Oh, Davey," was the best I could manage. I was shaking so hard I thought I would fly into pieces.

But my Davey held on, and he saved me by pushing back to look into my eyes. The words rushed out of me. "You have to come back, because I'll never love anyone else. You're the only one for me."

He smiled. "Well, now that *that's* settled. I'll be back. You can count on it."

He kissed me, and I swear it seemed like a combination of every kiss we'd ever shared—the newness of the first, the passion of our deeper love, and the sadness of good-bye. I didn't want to let him go, but before I could rally, the kiss was over and he was climbing into Mr. Siler's car for the ride back to the U.S. Marines.

Chapter Seven

— MADDY —

I felt like a walking mummy but somehow I made it through Sunday. It helped to know that Ruth understood what had happened to me. At least part of it. And I knew I'd always be grateful that she didn't insist I give her a name. Others, however, seemed determined to know.

Poor Jack. I should never have told him about Frankie. I just knew he'd been put in jail because of me and I felt awful. Frankie was the one who should've been in jail. The scary part was that Mrs. Siler seemed to sense it was my fault. As we'd set the table for Sunday dinner she'd gone into her landlady speech about having male visitors after nine o'clock. But as the visitor had been her own son, simply delivering me home, she'd let it pass. When she asked where we'd been so late, Ruth interrupted, saying she thought she smelled the potatoes scorching. When Mrs. Siler rushed to the kitchen to check, Ruth winked at me before handing me the silverware.

By that evening, when Ruth and I were alone in our place, I was too tired to talk. I'd used every ounce of my energy trying to act normal. Ruth seemed worn out as well. And since she had to begin her baby-sitting job early the next morning we decided to go to bed early. I'd been afraid to sleep the night before because I didn't want to dream. Tonight I was too tired to care.

As we each headed for our rooms, Ruth hugged me. "Everything's going to be fine," she said. "I know it."

I wanted to ask her how she knew but decided I'd sleep better if I just took her word for it.

Unfortunately, everything wasn't fine. Especially for Ruth. Oh, her first day baby-sitting had gone well enough. She and little Nickie had hit it off. Trouble came in the form of a phone call from my brother. His company was shipping out—immediately. There would be no time for good-byes.

Going to war.

After hanging up the phone, Ruth turned down dinner and shut herself in her room for the rest of the evening. It felt disloyal for me to relax and enjoy *The Lone Ranger* or *The Burns and Allen Show*. And I didn't feel up to hearing the war news, so I took myself to bed early and hoped for better days.

A light tapping on my door woke me before dawn.

"Maddy? Do you think you could drive me to the harbor?" Ruth's voice sounded husky as though she'd cried herself to sleep. "I'll go next door and ask to borrow the car."

I hadn't driven a car in months, and I wasn't sure if I could find the harbor, but if Ruth needed to go then I'd do my best. I pushed my hair out of my eyes and opened the door.

"Sure, I'll take you." It was the least I could do—not only for Ruth but for my brother. I noticed she was already dressed and ready to go, and I wondered if she'd slept at all. "Let me get some clothes on," I mumbled.

"I don't know how long we'll be there, and I'm supposed to watch Nickie today, so we'll have to take him with us." She rubbed a hand across her cheek trying to hide her tears. "Davey told me not to come. He didn't know what time or what ship. But I have to be there."

I grabbed a skirt and a blouse from the closet and headed

for the bathroom. By the time I came out, Ruth had the keys in her hand. She said she'd woken up the Silers, but Mrs. Siler had given her permission to use the car. The sky was already a pale apricot when we stepped out the front door. In the still air a mist hung along the river and the trees in the yard. There was a man standing next to the car—Mr. Siler. As we approached he held out his hand for the keys.

"I'm sure you girls know how to drive but I'm thinkin' you might take a wrong turn and end up in Georgia. I'll be your chauffeur."

Ruth glanced at me as though I would argue. "Thank you," I said. I wasn't ready to be an explorer with our last chance to see Davey at stake.

We were early to pick up Nickie, and when his mother heard our reason she did her best to get him ready. A serious child, Nickie seemed more excited about riding in the car instead of on the bus until he found out we were going to Miami Harbor. Then he was beside himself and would hardly hold still as his mother hurriedly dressed him in a miniature sailor suit. She barely managed to shove his sailor hat on his head before we swept him out the door.

The entire ride across the causeway Nickie asked questions and Ruth or Mr. Siler patiently answered them. At least one of us was excited about the day. When a jeep carrying four sailors passed us, Nickie informed us, "My daddy's a sailor. He's in the Navy. He's a radioman."

"Yes, I know," Ruth said. "He's very brave."

Nickie aimed his pointer and his attention on a large ship moored at the docks ahead. "Is that the kind of boat my daddy is on?"

Ruth looked at Mr. Siler. "I don't think so, son. That isn't a Navy ship, it's a freighter—carries supplies."

We were bombarded the rest of the way with stories about how Nickie's father was on a ship killing lots of Germans using his radio. His description would have been funny if it hadn't been so close to the truth.

On the far side of the causeway, we had to stop at the military checkpoint at the entrance to the harbor. A sign in the middle of the street said, "Restricted Military Only." I'd already had my own run-in with military authority. I silently wished Ruth good luck as she explained our mission.

The guard remained unmoved. "I'm sorry, ma'am. We can't allow any civilians beyond this point—orders straight from the admiral."

"But this is my last chance . . ." Ruth dissolved into tearful silence, leaving room for Nickie to add his unexpected two cents.

"Please, mister!" Nickie saluted the MP, nearly knocking off his own sailor cap in the process. "We've just GOT to see him!"

Balanced between laughter and tears, I reached over the seat and squeezed Nickie's shoulder.

The MP frowned, then saluted the little boy in return. "Wait here a second, ma'am." He walked toward another MP standing with a gun slung over his shoulder. They talked for a couple of moments, then the first MP returned.

"Okay, here's the deal, ma'am. I can't allow you to drive any farther and I can't tell you when or if any troops are leaving. But you folks are welcome to stand over there, across the street and wait. If any troops are shipping out, they'll march right down the center of this street to the ship."

When Ruth didn't answer right away, he added, "I think you'll want to wait, ma'am."

I saw Ruth pull in a deep breath. "Thank you so much," Ruth said.

"That's okay, ma'am. If he were my son, I'd want him to see me go to war."

Nickie remained blessedly silent as we drove past the checkpoint. Mr. Siler stopped at the curb the MP had indicated.

"Thank you for driving us," Ruth said as she helped Nickie down from the car. "We'll wait for a while then take the bus back."

I knew Ruth would stand there the whole day long if it

meant a chance to see Davey. Mr. Siler seemed to guess that as well.

"I'll find a place to park and wait with you a bit." He smiled. "It's too early to go to work."

Within half an hour, at least thirty other wives and family members were milling around on the sidewalk, waiting along with us. Nickie spent his time looking in the store windows with a little girl who'd come to see her father off. Ruth kept her eyes peeled on the distance, watching, hoping, to see Davey.

The sun was well up and already hot when Ruth raised a hand to shade her gaze. "Do you see something?" she asked.

My attention had wandered to the movement of several Coast Guard vessels gathering in the harbor. I shaded my own eyes and squinted down the street.

I didn't know if I was dreaming because I wanted to see something or not. "Definitely soldiers," I said.

Right then Nickie rushed up. "The soldiers are coming!"

"Those aren't soldiers, son," a man's voice said. "Those are U.S. Marines."

Ruth took Nickie's hand and pulled him to stand close in front of her. I stood between her and Mr. Siler. In short order we could see they *were* Marines, marching in formation, their seabags slung over their shoulders.

"It's got to be Davey," Ruth said under her breath. "Please let it be Davey."

In their excitement, a few spectators stepped into the street, but the MPs ordered them to stand back. Having arrived early, we had an unobstructed view.

As the first row of Marines passed by us, people here and there called out a name or waved. Ruth and I searched each face. Suddenly, she grabbed my hand. "There he is!" She pointed him out for Nickie and me. "Davey!" she shouted, standing on her tiptoes to wave, her bad leg forgotten. I waved with both arms and shouted as well, so he couldn't miss us.

"I love you, Davey!" Ruth called.

The men marching around Davey smiled slightly. You could tell that later he would be the butt of a few jokes. Davey himself did his best to look fearless and happy. Risking a reprimand from the sergeant, he turned his head and winked to let Ruth know he saw her.

I thought our day had been made until the last row of Marines came into view. My happiness deflated like a punctured balloon. There, marching at the end of the line between two MPs was Frankie.

I heard Ruth catch her breath in surprise and knew I must have done the same thing. Frankie looked terrible. Oh, his uniform was pressed and his hat fit well enough—but his face. One side was a brilliant red while the opposite side was more of a deep purple. He had a shiner that must have been administered by a boot and his nose was taped. One of his hands was bandaged up to the wrist and three of his fingers were wrapped together. And he was obviously under arrest.

My first impulse was to feel bad for him, but the notion passed. Because of him, I couldn't go back to Radley. Because of him, Jack was in jail. Because of him, I might never get married. I hadn't even figured out all the ways he'd hurt me. I refused to feel sorry for him, even if he was going to war under arrest.

We watched until they were a mere khaki blur in the distance before Ruth let down her guard. Covering her mouth with her handkerchief, she turned her head into my shoulder and cried. Mr. Siler signaled that he was going to get the car. Other people were sniffing and walking away, but I let Ruth take her time.

"I just don't know if I can stand it," Ruth said. She tried to pull herself together, but tears continued to fall. I did my best to think of something soothing to say, something Ruth might have said to me a few short nights ago, but a small part of me felt the same way she did—helpless and terrified. The whole world seemed to have gone crazy. As it turned out, Nickie had something important to say because he tugged on Ruth's skirt.

"Don't cry, Ruth," he said in his calm, baby-going-on-man voice. "He'll come back home."

Out of the mouths of babes . . .

Ruth succumbed to one more sob before bending to scoop up her young champion. The two of us hugged him until he squirmed to be let down. Then Ruth squared her shoulders and dried her eyes. With one last look toward Davey's ship, she took Nickie's hand and we headed for the car.

The days took on a kind of routine after that. We'd paid the Silers for the month so we had a place to stay . . . and Ruth had her job, but Davey had been the anchor of our ship, and now that he'd sailed off to war we had nothing to hold us in Florida.

I had no reason to go back to Radley. As a matter of fact, the thought of seeing my gloating friends and Jeanne—Mrs. Lyle Nesbitt—made my stomach queasy. Not to mention, facing my mother.

The truth of what had happened to me was finally beginning to sink in. What my mother had always feared had taken place—without my permission—but, I was ruined, nonetheless. No longer a nice girl any man would want to marry.

Ruined.

I'd barely started my life and now my future was over. I knew I was going to hell and did my best to feel ashamed. I even took the bus to mass three mornings in a row and went to confession afterward, but I ended up feeling mad instead. Mad at Frankie, and if truth be told, at God. How could this have happened to me?

By Saturday, Ruth had recovered somewhat from watching Davey go to war, or she was putting a brave face on her fears. She did one odd thing. On our customary Saturday morning shopping trip with Mrs. Siler, Ruth brought home a frame. Then she took the photograph she'd kept in the closet, put it in the frame, and propped it up on the radio cabinet.

"I thought you didn't like that picture," I said after she'd adjusted the position twice.

"Hmmmm?" she answered, obviously distracted.

"I thought you *hated* that picture."

She looked at me then. "No. I don't hate it. How could I? It has the people I love in it."

— RUTH —

I needed the photograph. It was my one connection to Davey. In the photo, the changes only I seemed to see, he'd already moved farther away from me, but he looked fine. The rest of the group, about the same. Maddy's tears had disappeared and she seemed less sad. Even Frankie looked a little better than he had as he'd marched between the MPs.

I needed to look at the photograph every day to see my husband, to see the future no matter what the outcome. But I couldn't tell Maddy or anyone. Why would they believe me? And how could I defend whatever magic the photograph held? I didn't know if it came from heaven or hell. And I didn't care. There was something else I couldn't confess either. I've always been a little superstitious. No walking under ladders or hats on the bed—normal things. But the evening before, when I'd decided to get a frame for the photograph, it had occurred to me that if I went home to Radley and took the photograph there, the magic might not work. Distance or different surroundings might break the connection like a phone line stretched too far. I couldn't let that happen.

"It's time for us to talk," I said to Maddy. She watched me warily as I sat down next to her on the couch. I chose my words carefully. "Now that Davey's gone, we need to think about going home."

Before I'd launched into my speech, Maddy blurted out, "I can't go home."

"Well, of course you can." I patted her hand. "Don't you miss your mother? Wouldn't you feel better if—"

"No." She clutched my fingers. "How can I go home and face everyone? Especially now." She gave me a meaningful look. "You know my mother, she'll have the truth out of me then drag me to confession. She's looked forward to my getting married and having grandbabies, especially since you and Davey . . . well, when she finds out what happened she'll cry for a year. The whole town will start talking again. Everyone's always thought I'd come to a bad end." She looked down. "I hadn't intended to prove them right. I thought Lyle and I . . ." She ran out of steam.

"I know, sweetie. I'm so sorry about what happened. I feel partially responsible, too. I was so busy thinking about Davey that I—"

"No, Ruth. You were *supposed* to be thinking about Davey. It wasn't your fault. Trouble is, I don't feel like it was my fault either, unless Mother is right and being too happy means you'll be punished. Is that the way life works?"

A shiver ran through me. I'd been so happy with Davey here . . . "I certainly hope not. There's no reason for you to think of going home as a punishment. This was our plan from the beginning. Only one thing has changed."

That got her attention. "What?"

I braced myself for her unhappiness and another argument. "I'm staying here in Miami. It's the last place I saw Davey and I intend to be here when he comes home." I also intended to watch the photograph like a hawk.

"Oh, please Ruth, let me stay with you. I'll get a job, I'll—"

I shook my head. "Your mother would never allow it. You know that. And, in case you've forgotten, we were only given this house until Davey left. Two more weeks and we'll have nowhere to stay and no money to speak of. I intend to ask Nickie's mother if I can stay with them—they don't have room for both of us."

"I'll ask Mrs. Siler, beg her if I have to . . ."

"Maddy." I stopped her. The thought of a tearful and probably unsuccessful plea from her to the Silers prodded my growing protectiveness. I hated to think of one more disappointment heaped on Maddy's plate. "Don't do anything yet. We have a little time. If you can think of a way to convince your mother, then *I'll* talk to Mrs. Siler." I doubted if either plea would be successful, but Maddy seemed so determined, I had to give it a shot. And I was afraid if I put her on a train alone she might run away and get into even more trouble.

Sunday brought us a surprise. During the week I'd been so caught up in Davey's departure I'd forgotten life would go on. At church the following Sunday when the bus pulled up, Jack and Lt. Tull-Martin got off. Mrs. Siler, of course, greeted them like long-lost family and immediately asked Jack about the two pieces of tape along his cheekbone. I noticed he had tape on his knuckles as well, but wasn't about to mention it.

"Ah, it's nothin'. I cut myself shaving," Jack answered as he kissed his mother's cheek. He didn't shake hands with his father, simply nodded.

"You must be joking," Randy said. "And the other guy you were shaving with? How does he look?"

Jack scowled at his brother but grimaced when the movement pulled the tape. Then he turned to me. "I heard Davey shipped out."

I did my best to look pleasant but seeing the serious expression on Jack's face made my throat tight. "Yes, he did," I managed.

"He'll be okay," he said, as the bell for services began to ring. Thankfully we went inside without any further conversation. I wasn't up to it and I noticed Maddy seemed determined to look anywhere but at Jack or the lieutenant.

No one mentioned the stockade until after dinner.

Mrs. Siler cornered her son in the living room as Maddy and I cleared the table. "Jack, please tell us what happened last week. We got the call you were in the stockade."

Dishes clanked and everyone glanced toward the source— Maddy. She quickly looked down. I reached in front of her and took the glasses out of her hands. "Bring the casserole," I said and waited as she picked up the heavy dish.

"Well, as you can see," Jack continued. "I had a little disagreement with a guy."

"A fight? But why would you get into a fight?"

"I didn't like the way he treated a lady," Jack said.

Maddy and I both stopped at the kitchen door. The Silers had their backs toward the dining room but Jack, Randy, and Lt. Tull-Martin faced us. I turned and met Jack's gaze while Maddy stared at the dish balanced in her hands.

"What lady?" Mrs. Siler asked.

Jack immediately relaxed back in his chair and smiled at his mother. "A damsel in distress. Does it matter which one?"

I prodded Maddy through the door and let it swing shut behind us. As soon as we'd delivered the dishes to the sink I raised her chin to gaze into her eyes. I remembered how battered Frankie looked in the photograph and marching to the ship. He'd looked as though he'd been fighting. "Did Jack have a reason to beat up Frankie?" I asked her, already guessing the answer.

Maddy's eyes filled with tears and she nodded. "He promised he wouldn't tell but I didn't know—"

A shot of very unrighteous joy filled me. I hugged her, hard. "Good for him. At least one of us got some satisfaction. I'd like to take a swing at the *rat* myself."

Maddy used the dish towel to wipe her eyes. She looked like she might say more but both of us jumped when we heard Mrs. Siler call Maddy's name. How would we explain Maddy's tears?

"Splash some cold water on your face. I'll see what she wants."

As I reentered the room I heard Jack say, "I'm confined to quarters. My commander let me come to church and dinner because Tull-Martin promised to keep an eye on me."

"I should thank you then, Lieutenant."

"You're welcome, ma'am. I always volunteer if it involves a home-cooked meal." He looked up as if he expected to see Maddy.

Mrs. Siler turned to me. "Mad— Oh, Ruth. Please check and make sure the coffee isn't burning."

"Sure thing," I answered before sneaking a look at Jack. He was smiling slightly, but his eyes were solemn. I couldn't say what I wanted to say so I stuck to the ordinary. "There's lemon pie for dessert. I'll bring some out as soon as the coffee's ready."

—　MADDY　—

I didn't get a chance to speak to Jack alone until after the dessert dishes had been washed and put up. I'd almost pleaded a headache and skipped dinner altogether because each time I thought of Jack knowing about what happened to me and Tully finding out, my heart seemed to have trouble beating. I couldn't look either of them in the eye.

After lemon pie, Tully got roped into entertaining Mrs. Siler and Randy with stories of the palace guard and the queen. I sneaked out and found Jack on the front porch smoking a cigarette.

"I wanted to thank you—" My voice faltered. I wished it was dark so he couldn't see me so clearly because I expected to burst into tears . . . again. It seemed like my body had more tears than blood.

He pointed out the bench next to him. "Sit down, Maddy." When I did, on the edge of the bench, he sat next to me. "How are you feeling?"

"I'm better," I said quickly then chanced a look at his face. Except for the tape and the somber expression, he remained the same old Jack and that was comforting. I felt completely different, while those around me were only a week older and a little bruised.

"So, everything's okay?" He waited as I thought about the answer.

"I don't know," I answered honestly. The words tumbled out of me. "Now that Davey has shipped out, Ruth and I are supposed to go back home. Except Ruth isn't going and I'm not either—"

He put a hand over mine to halt the flood. "I meant with you."

I still had some bruises and scratches but I wasn't about to talk about those. And any discussion about being *ruined* was out of the question. I just stared at him.

"Never mind." He pulled his hand away and raised his cigarette to take a drag. That's when I got a good look at his knuckles.

"Oh!" I couldn't help myself, I gingerly lifted his hand toward me. "Your poor hand! Does it hurt?"

He pulled the cigarette from his lips with his left hand and allowed me to examine his right. "Actually, it hurts more than my face. He landed one good punch." He wiggled his fingers slightly. "I got in a few more than that."

"I saw Frankie marching to the ship with the MPs. Did you have him arrested?"

"No, I didn't tell anyone what happened because I promised you and because I didn't want to deprive Frankie of the opportunity to serve his country. I didn't want him sitting out the war here at home in some safe jail cell."

"I'm so sorry you were put in jail."

"Yeah, well—" He looked toward the street. "The satisfaction was worth being locked up for a night or two. So don't you worry about it. There is one more thing, though."

My fingers tightened on his. "What?"

"They're promoting me out of flight school. I'll be leaving for England next week." He smiled and flicked his cigarette butt into the yard. "My commanding officer said if I'm so eager to fight, then I needed to go to war and fight Germans. I'll be attached to the RAF."

My usual gusher of tears began to flood my eyes. I had to blink to keep him in focus.

"Don't cry, kiddo. I'm ready to go—I've been ready. But I haven't told my parents and Randy yet. Thought I'd wait until I *had* to tell 'em. So we'll keep each other's secrets, how 'bout that?" He raised a hand to chuck me under the chin. In the same moment, the screen door swung open.

"What are you two doing out here?" Mrs. Siler asked.

I let go of Jack's injured fingers as though I'd grabbed the business end of Old Joe the alligator by mistake.

Jack sat up a little straighter. "Little Maddy was worried about me," he said.

If either Randy or Davey had called me "Little Maddy," I would have kicked them under the table. But Jack—Jack had earned the right to call me whatever he wanted especially if it put Mrs. Siler off the trail. I did my best to sniff back my tears and smile. Jack kept talking.

"Is Dad coming out? I thought we had some business to go over."

Mrs. Siler watched me; she was harder to distract than a cat cornering a mouse. "He'll be out in a minute," she said to Jack. Then to me, "Maddy? Why don't you come inside? We're setting up a game of pinocle."

With one watery smile in Jack's direction I pushed to my feet. He stood as well. "You take care, Maddy, girl." It sounded like good-bye.

"I will. You, too," I managed, then opened the screen door and fled into the house, leaving Jack and his mother behind.

That's when, ready or not, I came face-to-face with Lieutenant Tull-Martin.

"Is everything all right?" he asked after I'd practically run him down on the living room rug.

Surely this is how a bug on a pin must feel, I decided, surrounded by curious humans and unable to run away. I made a squirming stab at nonchalance. "Why, yes, everything's fine. Why?"

He studied my face. "Because you've been crying," he said in a low voice. "Did Jack upset you?"

"No," I said, probably too quickly. Did everyone know I was sitting on the porch with Jack? "I'm just—" I saw Ruth helping Randy set up the table for cards and nabbed her for an excuse. "Ruth and I have been upset because Davey had to leave and now we have to—" The look on his face stopped me.

I'd been so caught up in what had happened to me that night at the pier I'd forgotten the wonderful feelings I'd had dancing with Tully. As though Frankie had tainted everything before and after he'd ruined my future. The idea made me angry, and the urge to cry subsided.

"Would you be up to taking a walk with me, then?" Tully asked.

"Sure."

I felt Ruth's gaze as we crossed the room. I gave her a little wave to let her know I was okay. Tully and I went out the side door, down the ramp, and along Randy's walkway. The late afternoon sun had lost some of its bright heat. Even so, it was nicer under the trees. Tully had removed his coat but his shirt and tie had to be too warm.

"Let's go down by the river," I suggested.

When Tully stepped off the walkway and offered his hand to help me step down, I could feel the attention from the house behind us like a nudge between my shoulder blades. It seemed like today would go a long way toward closing the contract on my reputation as a notorious woman. In Mrs. Siler's mind anyway. First Jack and now the lieutenant. If she only knew . . . she'd never let us stay. And if she didn't, we'd have to find another place—scary but not the end of the world. But Tully . . . He'd already claimed a little piece of my heart. I never wanted Tully to know.

"I've missed you this past week," he said. "I've become accustomed to seeing your cheerful face on a regular basis."

He turned to smile at me, and I had to make myself hold his gaze and return the smile. In the movies, notorious women always seemed to be laughing at the world. I wanted to be cheerful, oh how I wanted to, but it seemed I'd forgotten how. And I wasn't a very good actress. When I pretended, I was afraid he'd look closely and figure out that I wasn't the same girl he'd danced with or kissed good night.

"I've missed you, too," I said before bringing my attention back to the river. "Look, there's an egret." I pointed toward the same bird Randy had named for me the first day we'd arrived. It turned out he was a faithful visitor to this part of the river. "Isn't he beautiful?"

Tully shifted his gaze, and I felt like a brat for changing the subject. But anything was better than talking about me. "Yes, he seems a fine gentleman in his white linen coat, but what if the *he* is a *she*?"

"I guess we could ask Randy," I said lamely and kept walking. "He knows a lot about birds." I was already sorry I'd brought up the silly topic of the bird.

We crossed the backyard in the shade of the palms and old lemon trees and reached a log that Jack had probably dragged near the river in younger days. As Tully dusted off the accumulated sand with his handkerchief, our white bird friend took wing and relocated himself farther down the river.

Tully took my hand to help me sit. When we were both settled, he propped his elbows on his knees and gazed at the slow, dark water eddying by.

"It looks like tea," he said with a chuckle. "What I wouldn't give for even half a cup of good English tea."

"I guess that's pretty hard to find around here."

"It's scarce in London as well. The ships are required to carry more important cargo. I make do with the American version." After a long moment punctuated by the plop of a fish in the river and the calls of other birds hidden in the trees, he spoke again. "You were telling me what you and Ruth will do now that your brother is off to war. Will you be returning to Pennsylvania?"

He didn't sound like it mattered to him one way or another and that helped me give him an honest answer. "We're supposed to. But Ruth's decided she wants to stay here in Florida, where she last saw Davey. The problem is, the Silers agreed to rent us this place until Davey left. After that they want to rent it to soldiers. So Ruth'll have to find another place to live."

"What about you?"

"I'm staying, too. I don't want to go home."

He looked at me then. "Surely your parents will object. This is no place for two women on their own without family or friends."

"I'll make friends," I said firmly. "And I have you—"

"I'm afraid you can't depend on any of us men for a good while. Davey is gone. Jack and I could be called at any time. I wouldn't be able to sleep at night thinking you were here in this crowded city alone."

Crowded with soldiers—men like Frankie. Little did he know the damage had already been done. If I had to be ruined, why couldn't I have been ruined by Tully? But I already knew the answer. Tully would never do what Frankie had done. So I tried out the speech I'd been composing for my mother's bene-fit. "There's really nothing to go home for. Remember? My boyfriend is married to my best friend. At least here I could do some good. I can get a job or volunteer—help the war effort." It sounded very noble to me. I waited to see his reaction.

"I see. So, you're determined then?"

I raised my chin and met his gaze. "Yes, I am."

He seemed to be battling a smile. "I'll see if Jack will speak to his parents on your behalf. Surely, now that they know you, they'll allow you to stay. Besides, we haven't had our outing to the cinema yet." I must've jumped or something because he added quickly, "Ruth is invited as well, of course."

Of course. Tully wouldn't even ask me to the movies with-out my family's permission. My water pump of tears cranked up again. I looked down at my hands.

"Maddy?" He reached across the distance between us and rescued one of my hands from the threat of falling tears. "Won't you tell me what's wrong? Perhaps I could help?"

I sniffed, staring at Tully's long-fingered hand holding my stubby-fingered one. I wished he could help. I wanted to tell him the whole ugly story, *If you knew what happened to me, you wouldn't ask me to the cinema or anywhere.* But instead of the truth and nothing but the truth, I gave him part. "I'm mad. And sad, and I can't stand the thought of you and Jack going away like my brother—"

"Shhh." He squeezed my hand. "I know. This war—" He swallowed and looked away. "Those of us who are able, have to fight. Otherwise, our world and everything we love will perish." He gazed at me once again. "Any man of honor would die to keep that from happening."

Man of honor. Not the kind of man who drags a woman into the dark.

"Oh—" I sighed in exasperation and dashed at the new tears forming in my eyes. I'd never understand war, or men. Maybe I'd never understand *anything*. I did my best to brighten up though, for Tully's sake. "What movie do you think we should go see?"

He chuckled and squeezed my fingers. "That's my girl. I think we should find a comedy. Perhaps for Friday night."

"Hey, you two!" A voice called behind us. We turned to find Randy sitting in his wheelchair on the walkway. "Mother sent me to get you."

"Ah, duty calls," Tully said as he pulled me to my feet. He grinned and bowed slightly. "Thank you, milady, for spending your time on me. I hope my company didn't cause you to feel worse."

His company had made me feel better, for a bunch of reasons. Mainly because I could tell that Jack hadn't told him my secret. When I looked into his eyes I could see the reflection of the old Maddy. And it took some of the sting out of my heart.

By the time we reached the house, Mr. and Mrs. Siler, Ruth, and Jack were in debate about whether or not Ruth and I could remain in Miami in the house next door.

"I've already cast my vote," Randy said. He rolled his chair over near his brother, facing his parents. He looked at me. "I voted yes."

I took a seat next to Ruth on the couch like the condemned facing a hung jury. Tully pulled up a chair to join the group.

"I don't see how the two of you girls will manage," Mrs. Siler was saying. Then Mr. Siler added, "And in these times, we'll have to sacrifice and suffer whatever the war brings. Anything left over needs to go to our boys in uniform." He looked at Jack.

"I'm sure Maddy and Ruth'll do their best to help. They have someone in uniform, too. Right, girls?" Jack said.

Ruth and I nodded. "I'd be grateful if you'd consider it," Ruth said. "We'll do our best to hold up our end."

Mrs. Siler's gaze was on me. "I'll have to think about this," she said. Her gaze narrowed. "Does your mother approve of you living so far away?"

"Yes, ma'am. She wants me to stay with Ruth," I lied.

Mrs. Siler tripped me up. "Well, have her call me."

I looked at Ruth. *Uh-oh.*

"She's visiting my Aunt Edna right now, but I'll have her call as soon as she gets back home." I didn't have an Aunt Edna, but Jeanne did. I figured if she could steal Lyle then I could borrow her aunt. I hoped Mother wouldn't accidentally call for some other reason before we'd convinced the Silers.

"All right," Mrs. Siler answered. Randy gave a whoop of happiness, which earned him a quelling frown. "I'm not agreeing. I meant we'll think about it."

Chapter Eight

— RUTH —

Dearest Davey,

Watching you march toward that ship nearly broke my heart. I already feel lost without you, but I'm very thankful for the hours we had together before you went away. In some ways our time in Miami seemed like a second honeymoon. But now that I'm alone, remembering makes me miss you even more. I can hardly think of anything else.

I know we didn't discuss this but I've decided to stay in Miami for a while. For some reason being here makes me feel one step closer to you—closer to the war you're fighting. And I believe staying busy and helping the war effort will keep my thoughts off my fears.

Maddy wants to stay with me and we hope to convince your mother to allow it. I know you worry about us both, but in the larger world I believe she and I are better off together. I hope you'll support us when you write home. Maddy has grown up so much, even in the short time you've been gone. I know you want her to be happy.

I pray you're safe and comfortable wherever you are. At least I know you aren't in the war quite yet although we hear daily about ships being torpedoed. Each morning I ask for heaven to watch over you.

I love you more than my life.

Ruth

As I signed my name I looked up at the photograph I'd propped in front of me at the table. I wanted to see my husband's beloved face. To smile into his eyes. No one else was missing, but my gaze was drawn away from Davey to something completely different. To Maddy.

Maddy had changed.

My breath caught as I realized what the photograph was showing. The future again, one I hadn't considered. One I *should've* considered. In the photograph Maddy looked healthy and serene and very, very pregnant. In awe I gently touched my finger to her stomach. For an instant, I thought I could feel the tiny flutter of that brand-new heart beating against my skin. Then a shiver of uncertainty shook me. I felt so alone. I missed my husband more than ever.

Oh, Davey. What should I do now? How will I break the news to her? What will we tell your mother?

"What's wrong?" Maddy said, appearing as though she'd heard me call her name. I shifted my gaze from the woman, the mother, in the photograph to the girl who'd shyly flirted with soldiers on the train to Florida. The lingering shadows in her eyes confirmed she'd grown up quite a bit since then, yet if the photograph showed the future, there would be a lot more growing up to do.

"I've been thinking." I removed my hand from the photograph and gestured for her to pull out a chair and sit.

"About a way we can stay?" She sounded hopeful.

I took a moment to pick through my thoughts and decided I couldn't tell her the truth, not yet. She probably wouldn't believe me and it would upset her. Better to face the future when there was no doubt.

"Yes. I'm going to tell your mother I'm expecting." I'm not sure where the inspiration had come from, although from past experience I knew pregnancy was the one argument Mrs. Marshall couldn't win.

Maddy sat forward and grabbed my hand. "Oh, Ruth!" Then she looked confused. "Should I be happy? Or is this terrible?"

I would have been thrilled if I'd been telling the truth. And not afraid. Better that I should be pregnant than Maddy. But Davey and I had been careful, too careful to hope. And Maddy. Well, Maddy hadn't had a choice. "What this is, is a way to stay in Florida for both of us. If your mother believes I'm pregnant, she'll want me to take every precaution. That means no long, uncomfortable train rides. And it means I'll need you here to help me."

She smiled. "That's brilliant, Ruth." As quickly as it arrived, the smile disappeared. "You're sure you're not really expecting, right?"

I'm not, but you are.

"I mean, I remember how sick you were, when you almost . . ."

"I'm fine," I said. "And I suppose there's the slight chance I'm telling the truth since Davey and I were together . . . before he left. But it's not very likely. The uncertainty does make it easier to—let's say—*speculate* about it to your mother." To soothe Maddy's concern I added, "You know most women have babies without any trouble whatsoever. I don't want you to worry about me." I didn't want her to be frightened by the process either since, God willing, she would sail through her own pregnancy.

That's when I realized that Maddy was carrying Mrs. Marshall's long-anticipated grandbaby and my heart lurched a bit. Davey and I might never have one, but Maddy would. She just didn't know it yet.

Maddy and I called Mrs. Marshall on Monday afternoon. We'd waited until the Silers were out before we commandeered their phone. As I dialed the numbers I swore to myself I wouldn't cry—that I'd be brave as I knew Davey would want me to be. And I managed fairly well as Davey's mother told me he'd called her to say good-bye. But when I described how brave Davey and his fellow Marines seemed as they marched to the ship that would take them halfway around the world to who knows what, my throat tightened and we both boo-hooed. Regaining her composure after a good cry, Mrs. Marshall asked when Maddy and I would be arriving home. I had to quickly pull myself together.

I took Maddy's hand and looked into her eyes before I answered. I needed her strength and more than that, I needed her resolve. I knew she wasn't going home no matter what her mother said. "We might have to wait a little longer before we make the trip," I answered.

"What do you mean, dear?"

"Well, I—I think I—" I stumbled to a stop finding it harder to lie than I'd imagined. But then Maddy squeezed my hand bringing me back to the reason for lying in the first place. "I think I may be pregnant," I said in a rush.

Mrs. Marshall drew in a huff of a breath like someone who'd been hit in the face with a shock of cold water. "What? Oh, that's wonderful!" Then she remembered my previous failures. "Oh dear. The doctors said not to—"

"I know. I don't want to worry you. It may be a false alarm but I don't want to take any chances." It wasn't truly fair to dangle the possibility of a grandchild in front of her like this but I soothed my conscience with the knowledge that she *would* have a grandchild—but not from Davey and me.

"Of course not," she agreed. "Davey would want you to be careful."

Feeling like I'd chosen the right argument for the occasion, I pushed on. "And I'll need Maddy to stay with me." As I watched, Maddy closed her eyes tightly and crossed the fingers of her free hand. I didn't know if she was praying or casting some kind of long-distance, wayward-daughter spell on her mother.

"Perhaps I should come down there," Mrs. Marshall said. "Maddy can be more of a bother than help sometimes."

"Uh, no. That's all right. I think we can manage. I wouldn't think of inconveniencing you with such a long trip." Maddy's eyes popped open and she looked ready to run. She shook her head no, vigorously. "I promise to call you if we need you," I added quickly. Then I crossed my own fingers.

"Well . . . I suppose. But you have to keep in touch—I don't like the idea of you living in a house with no telephone."

I tried to sound easy-breezy. "Oh, the Silers keep an eye on us and let us use their phone when we need it. By the way, that reminds me, could you write Mrs. Siler sometime this week and give your permission for Maddy to stay? She wants to be sure you're happy with our arrangements." A long silence followed. Time enough for Maddy to start fidgeting and for me to continue worrying. I had no idea what we'd do if she refused.

"I would *rather* speak to Mrs. Siler," she said, and my anxiety eased. "At a time like this, you'll need some extra care and I want to make sure you have it—"

"No! I—" I took a deep breath and struggled with a normal-sounding tone. "Please, Mrs.—Mother Marshall—*Please* don't mention the pregnancy. I don't want *anyone* to know in case—"

"I understand, dear. But I don't like the idea of you being alone. With Davey gone and this war business. I don't like it one bit. You should be here at home."

Pregnant or not I could agree with her on those points. "I'm not alone. I have Maddy. We've made a good temporary home here." I squeezed Maddy's hand again for good measure. Feeling the case was closed, I went on, "There's one more thing I have to ask though, and this one is difficult."

"What is it?"

"Please don't tell Davey about the baby." Before she could answer, I hurried on, "He'll only worry himself sick, you know that. And both of us know there is nothing he can do about the outcome. I don't want him thinking about anything but his own safety."

An even longer silence followed. "I'll agree on a temporary basis but reserve the right to tell him if I think he should know."

Not a victory but not total defeat either. I guessed that was the best I would get from her. "Thank you, Mother Marshall."

"Now let me speak to Maddy before we break the bank with this call. Oh, and Ruth, congratulations. I know how badly you want a child. Perhaps even more than I want a grandchild, if that's possible. Take extra care of yourself and keep in touch."

"I will." I felt like a fraud—head to toe. I knew I could never repay my mother-in-law for the care I'd received during my long illness. But I was certain of one thing. I intended to do my best to help Maddy have the healthiest, happiest grandchild Mrs. Marshall could imagine. I handed the phone to the unknowing mother-to-be. She was smiling when she spoke. "Hello, Mother."

From that moment on we worked on Mrs. Siler each afternoon at dinner. Maddy did extra chores and talked to Mr. Siler about available jobs, and Randy did his part by taking every opportunity to pretend he couldn't imagine life on Ninth Avenue without us around. But, Jack—Jack was the one who saved us. He showed up unexpectedly on Thursday afternoon carrying a cardboard box and wearing what looked like a forced smile.

It turns out he'd come to say good-bye.

"By this time tomorrow I'll be somewhere in the Atlantic," he said, making it sound like a grand adventure.

Mrs. Siler had a handkerchief pressed to her mouth as she shook her head. The expression of panic on her face made tears come to my eyes. I remembered the feeling—wanting desperately to keep the most important person in your life safe at home but having to be brave and let him go. Knowing it might be the last time you see him.

Jack did his best to put her mind at ease. He slipped an arm around her shoulders. "It'll be okay, Mother," he said, then gazed at his father. "You know we have to stop those

German bullyboys." Mr. Siler nodded, but he seemed speechless as well.

"Where are you going?" Randy asked, able to speak but unable to find his normal playful smile.

"I'll be attached to the RAF, based in England."

I remembered Lt. Tull-Martin's comment about the RAF, about how they needed volunteers because they'd lost so many pilots. Mrs. Siler must have remembered as well or maybe the reality of her son going to war had become uncomfortably real. She made a muffled sound like a sob and turned her face into the shoulder of Jack's uniform. I felt Maddy grip my arm. I nodded and stood, pulling her up with me.

"We should probably say good night—"

"Don't go," Jack said. "I can't stay long, and you girls are part of my family now, too." He gave his mother a brief hug, trying to shrug her out of her tears before adding, "Mother, I hope you'll let them live next door and help out around here after I'm gone." He grinned at Maddy. "They dress up the place a lot better than a bunch of bums in khaki. Besides, soon most of the soldiers are gonna be bunking somewhere on the other side of the ocean."

That seemed to be the breaking point for Mrs. Siler, and she burst into a full-scale storm of tears. "Oh, Jackie!" As Jack gingerly helped her to sit on the couch, I did the only thing I knew to do.

"I'll make some coffee."

When I reentered the room with a tray I heard Jack say, "I'm sorry I never got to take you flying, buddy." He was speaking to Randy. Mrs. Siler sat next to her husband on the couch, sniffing. "I kinda got myself in the doghouse with the CO," Jack went on.

"That's okay." Randy shrugged, doing his best to look devil-may-care. "You can take me up when you come back."

When you come back. The words hung in the air.

"That's right. When I come back I'm gonna get a job flying one of those new clippers to South America. You better bone up on your Spanish while I'm gone."

"Sí, señor," Randy said, and everyone tried to laugh.

But we all cried when Jack left. Standing on the front porch I ended up with my arm around Mrs. Siler, and Maddy stood with a hand on Randy's shoulder as we watched Mr. Siler back the car out of the drive. We waved until the car was out of sight then shuffled back inside like a group of hospital patients who'd gotten out of bed too soon. Weak and worn out by too many good-byes. This time when Maddy and I said good night, no one tried to change our minds about leaving. Mrs. Siler went into her bedroom and closed the door. Randy tuned the radio to a station playing classical music. No war news, no sad good-bye songs, just soothing sounds. Although I doubted anyone would be soothed tonight. Maddy and I let ourselves out the back door.

I wasn't feeling so chipper myself. Every fear I'd felt when Davey left had come back to haunt me through Jack. As Maddy and I walked across the walkway in silence I fought back my own panic. What would I do if something happened to Davey?

"I hope we get a letter from Davey soon," Maddy said, again reading my mind it seemed. She gave me a quick look. "I mean, I'm sure he's fine."

"He's already written us," I said. The first separation of our marriage had turned my husband into a good correspondent. Letters had been frequent and full of news—even if the news had to do with what he'd had for breakfast and lunch. Now that he was off to war I had no idea how often he'd be able to write. But I knew if nothing else, he'd write to say he loved us. "We'll have to wait and see how long it'll take for the letters to get here."

We seemed to be constantly reminded, minute by minute, that there was a war on. Everything from the mail service to the very food we ate—the war had to be taken into consideration. From the paper we learned that more and more men were streaming through the Port of Miami on their way to the Panama Canal and beyond to the Pacific or across the Atlantic to England or Africa.

After this sad night I desperately wanted to see my husband. Since I couldn't see him in person, I settled on the next best thing. As soon as we turned on a lamp in the Samuel place, I walked over to the photograph. Davey looked fine—the same—sitting next to me with a smile on his beloved face. I breathed a little easier. Some shifting and rearranging had taken place within the group. Jack had moved slightly . . . a little farther from Maddy. I knew that meant he was leaving. I picked up the frame and stared at Jack's cocky smile. The cut on his cheekbone had already begun to disappear. "Be safe, Jack. Come back home," I said aloud.

Maddy walked up behind me, leaned in and touched Jack's uniform with the tip of her finger. She had her own incantation. "Don't let the Germans get you."

Amen.

For the next week I watched Maddy. We'd had so many shocks in a row that I wasn't sure when she'd realize something else had changed. I'd had morning sickness early in my two pregnancies and by the second one knew almost immediately that I'd conceived. But Maddy was young and resilient. She'd recovered physically from the trauma of what had happened to her. I'd asked her to let me check her scratches for infection—always a danger. They'd healed. There was nothing more I could do, except wait for her to come to me.

So I dealt with our other immediate problems. After Jack's last request to his mother about letting us remain in the Samuel house, Mrs. Siler could hardly throw us out into the street. Her decision to allow us to stay came with several strings attached, however. First, we would need at the least one more roommate and possibly two. With people searching for accommodations all over town she considered it a sin to have empty beds. Of course more roommates would also bring in more money.

Maddy and I had to make a plan.

— MADDY —

I've decided that I never want to have children. After watching the Silers say good-bye to Jack I had a whole lot more sympathy for my own mother and every mother having to send a son to war. It was bad enough letting my brother go, even though he'd joined up. I never wanted to have someone else I loved at risk.

Tully popped into my head. I was so glad he'd already done his duty—been wounded and everything. And even though I hadn't had the heart to dream about him lately, I held on to the hope we could be friends.

Before I could be anyone's friend, though, Ruth and I had to settle our living arrangements. She called a powwow to decide what to do.

"I'll get a job," I said. "With all the new people in town and the war, there must be plenty of jobs available. Since you're gone most of the day watching Nickie I may as well make myself useful."

Ruth nodded but seemed unconvinced. "We still need a roommate. I wonder if the woman you met at the pier might know someone."

The pier. I'd done my best to put the whole night of my ruination out of my mind including the spot where it had taken place. "Maybe," I said, remembering Cleo had seen me after— Did she know what had happened? *No, don't think about it.* "She said I could call her," I said. *If I needed her.*

"Well, I'll ask Mrs. Dowland, but it's either your friend or an ad in the newspaper. Since we don't have a telephone, that would put Mrs. Siler in charge of finding us a roommate."

"She'd probably pick a nun or something," I said, only half joking. "A married nun."

Ruth smiled at my silliness. Then she said, "It'd be nice to have a nurse around."

That surprised me. "Why?" I asked, then remembered the whole pregnancy story. "I mean, you said you're *not* expecting, right?"

"I don't think so, but I guess I won't know for sure until I have my monthly. After the health problems I've had, I wouldn't mind having some good advice available."

"Oh," I said, not knowing what else to add. Ruth had been using her cane less and less and walking better and better. She continued to wear the heavy elastic stocking on her leg, but I guess I'd assumed she was nearly back to normal. "Cleo works for the Red Cross, she might know someone."

"Good. Let's start there."

Tully called to officially invite us out. As good as his word, he asked both me and Ruth to go to the movies—the cinema as he called it—on Friday night. He apologized about having to meet us downtown but promised to buy ice cream after the show.

Mr. Siler drove us to the theater on Miami Beach to meet Tully, and we brought Randy with us. He'd been kinda down in the dumps since Jack left. We decided all of us needed a bit of cheering up. On the way over we discussed the comedies that were playing. But I voted against *To Be or Not to Be* with Jack Benny and Carole Lombard for selfish reasons. I'd loved Carole Lombard—she'd had spunk. In the movies nobody got the better of her. Now she was dead—indirectly because of the war—and I was sure I couldn't ignore that fact long enough to enjoy the movie. We chose something light on its feet— *Yankee Doodle Dandy* with James Cagney. I wondered if the dancing might make Randy unhappy, but he seemed to enjoy it as much as the rest of us.

"I go to dances at the church social club," Randy said after the movie as Tully pushed his wheelchair down the sidewalk toward the ice-cream shop.

"But—" I caught myself before I said something really dumb like, "How in the world do you dance?"

Randy gave me a knowing look. "I like to dance with the normal girls. The ones who aren't in wheelchairs."

I didn't know what to say. How many "normal" girls would

be willing to dance with a crippled man? I couldn't think of many but then again maybe girls were different in Miami—not silly and stuck up like they were in Radley. So, instead of stating the obvious, I smiled a "good girl" smile—even though I'd lost the right to do so—and said, "That's nice."

I should've known Randy wouldn't let me weasel out of a comeback. "I like women who are taller than me," he said with an exaggerated leer.

I burst out laughing. It felt good. Even Tully and Ruth laughed, and for the first time in a long time the world seemed almost ordinary.

"Well, don't get any grand ideas about Maddy," Tully said. "I've already claimed the first few dances with her tonight. That is if you ladies feel up to walking a few blocks to the pier after we have our ice cream."

The pier. "I don't know . . ." I said, taking Ruth's arm as though I'd just realized she wasn't using her cane anymore. "What do you think, Ruth?" I was willing to let her give me an excuse not to go back to the "scene of the crime."

She patted my hand. "It *would* be a good time to speak to your friend about a roommate," she said, almost apologetically.

There was a line at the ice-cream shop. At least twenty or thirty soldiers had left the movie and had gotten there ahead of us. We were discussing whether the ice cream would be worth the wait when the last soldier in line said, "You can go ahead of me, ma'am," to Ruth. The one in front of him did the same. In a matter of moments Ruth and I with Tully and Randy in tow were hustled to the front of the line.

As I paused to study the chalkboard menu and make the important decision about what flavor, soldiers behind me called out their favorites.

"Get the strawberry, it's better than homemade."

"No—vanilla—it tastes like angel food."

"Then the chocolate must be the devil's own," another voice added.

Ruth and Tully ordered vanilla. Randy asked for strawberry. I still couldn't make up my mind.

"We've got one scoop of chocolate left," the server said, hoping to tempt me.

The offer had the opposite effect. I glanced over my shoulder at the soldiers waiting in line and shook my head. The crowd of men had increased in the past few moments. I thought of my brother and Jack and realized it could be a long time before these boys had ice cream again. "I think I'll pass," I said. "Let someone else have it."

A great groan went up from the crowd of men straining to see which I'd choose.

"Get the chocolate!" someone from the back yelled.

"Yeah, come on. We *want* you to have it!"

They wanted me to have it. I nodded to the server and a few seconds later he placed the sugar cone in my hand topped with the last precious scoop of chocolate. I turned to hold it up as the crowd cheered and whistled. Then I made a great show of sampling it. "It's the best I've ever tasted," I announced, causing another cheer.

It took us a good twenty minutes to get out of the store. The men who were so eager to allow us to get in front of them didn't seem as willing to let us leave. Most of them seemed to have a question to ask or a comment to make. I'd nearly finished my cone before we made it to the sidewalk again.

"Well, that was exciting," Ruth said, smiling at me.

"Gosh yes, I feel terrible for taking the last scoop of chocolate."

Tully chuckled. "Don't you understand that giving them the privilege of watching you enjoy it was better than having it themselves? There were moments there when I thought Randy and I might have to rescue you from their interest."

"Yeah, and they weren't after your ice cream," Randy said. "But I enjoyed watching you, too."

I socked Randy in the arm. "You watch me eat every day of the week."

He looked up at Tully. "Uh-huh, forget the ice cream. Eat your *heart* out."

The pier looked crowded. There were a number of soldiers

standing around outside the entrance, and a Red Cross bus was parked at the curb. I hoped that meant we could find Cleo. She'd certainly be here on a busy Friday night. I was determined to think of anything but what had happened to me here. In order to hold on to my game face I kept my gaze locked straight ahead. I wouldn't look at the darkness near the corner of the building, or think of the scratch of sand and the smell of liquor.

"Good evening," the volunteer at the door said. "Sign in, please."

"Is Cleo here tonight?" I asked as Ruth wrote our names.

"Why, yes. She's in the ballroom, working at the punch table."

"Thank you."

Ruth and I followed Tully and Randy down the hallway. Again, we passed rooms filled with soldiers laughing and talking, or playing pool. Had it only been two weeks ago when I'd been so excited to be in such an exotic place? I thought I'd have the time of my life. Now it simply made me feel sad.

A group of three soldiers cleared out to make a place at a table near the dance floor for Ruth, Randy, Tully, and me. But before we could settle in properly the band started playing and Tully pulled me up.

I allowed him to lead me out onto the dance floor where instead of letting go of my hand, he pulled me close to him.

"Ahhh, I thought I'd never have a moment alone with you," he said. "I might've had to start another war if someone asked you to dance before me."

I knew Tully was teasing, but after Jack and Frankie the idea of Tully fighting over me sent an uncomfortable shiver down my spine. In the movies a war or even a fistfight seemed romantic and righteous. The bad guys getting what they deserved. Now, after having lived through some of the cause and effect, I'd rather live without any reason to fight. Beating up the bad guys didn't seem to make a whole lot of difference, anyway.

"Promise you'll never start a war over me," I said.

He chuckled and gazed down at me like I'd asked for the moon. "I'm afraid the war is already begun and sometimes a good fight is necessary." After an extended moment his expression went serious. "I wouldn't fight over a dance, but I would never allow anyone or anything to hurt you. You know that, don't you?"

He meant it. I could see it in his eyes, feel it in the grip of his hand on mine. I knew I was going to cry . . . *again*. "Well, sheesh," I said. Trying to hide my tears I pushed my face into the spot between his chin and his neck. His arms tightened around me as my stupid, why-couldn't-you-have-been-there tears soaked into the collar of his uniform shirt.

We danced to three songs before the band picked up the tempo for a jitterbug. I didn't have the heart for it and Tully's leg made any fast moves awkward. We walked over to the punch table instead.

"Hi, Cleo. Remember me?"

"Sure, kiddo," she answered. She gave Tully a measuring look, a sort of character check, much like my mother might have done. "How're you doin'?"

"I'm fine." The Germans had nothing on us when it came to speaking in code. I knew she was asking about more than the present. "This is Lieutenant Tull-Martin," I said.

"Tully," he corrected as he extended his hand.

"Nice to meet ya." He must have passed the test because Cleo smiled.

The men standing in line behind us were getting restless. I knew we wouldn't be able to talk there. "When you get a break will you come over to our table? Ruth and I want to ask if you know anyone who needs a place to live."

Cleo perked up suddenly. "Sure thing." She looked at her watch. "In about twenty minutes."

When we returned to our table with punch for Ruth and Randy we found them surrounded by soldiers and sailors; Randy had talked two of the Red Cross doughnut girls into sitting down and watching as a soldier taught everyone—especially the girls—card tricks. It was quite a show. The men spent more time watching the girls than the tricks.

True to her word, Cleo showed up after the band had finished a break. I deserted the fledgling cardsharps and pulled my chair closer to Ruth and Cleo. Ruth explained we were looking for a roommate or two and how much the rent would be.

"Well, I know plenty of people who are looking . . ." Cleo began. "But to be honest I'd love to move out of where I've been staying. We have a regular hotel room with an extra mattress—that's three women in one room. The only place to store anything is under the bed. When we're all home at once we can hardly walk to the bathroom—we have to climb over.

"And I can afford the rent. I've been working at the aircraft factory for a month now. The pay is pretty good."

Ruth looked at me. "What do you think?"

I nodded and leaned toward Cleo. "You'd have to pass inspection by our landlady. She can be pretty tough. But you're married, right?"

"Yes. My Johnny is in the Pacific."

"That should make Mrs. Siler happy," I offered.

"How about Sunday? You could go to church with us. That would pave the way. When you come to talk to her, mention your husband and how much you miss him." Ruth gave me a guilty look and lowered her voice although Randy seemed to be in the middle of his own party and ignoring us. "They have a son, a pilot in the Army Air Corps, who recently shipped out. It wouldn't hurt to be extra patriotic. As a matter of fact, let's introduce you to their other son."

Ruth brought Cleo around the table and interrupted the trick in progress. "Randy? This is Cleo. If your mother approves, she might be our new roommate."

Randy gazed up at Cleo with a perfectly bland look. "Another tall woman," he said. "Suits me just fine."

"She's married, Don Juan," I countered and socked him in the arm.

* * *

I'd been taught that Sunday was supposed to be a day of rest—at least according to our priest back home. Rest *after* confessing your sins and attending mass, that is. But obviously our priest had never had to cook Sunday dinner, or serve and clean up after seven people.

On the one-month anniversary of our arrival in Miami, Mrs. Siler gave her grudging permission to oversee a houseful of women by announcing she would allow Cleo to move in. Cleo had shown up right on time for church—punctuality being a virtue—in her dusty and dented Ford Coupe. I admired her boldness. She'd listed off her assets to the Silers like an applicant for a job: Her husband was in the Navy, Cleo herself was a Red Cross volunteer, and she worked at the Intercontinental Aircraft Factory making bombers. She topped it off by confiding to Mrs. Siler that even though they weren't supposed to, she and her coworkers always wrote short "good luck" messages and signed their names on every plane they built.

"Have to take care of those fly-boys," she said.

Either Cleo was brilliant, or she'd had enough of the place she'd been living for the past six months.

By the time the food was served, the deal was done.

During dinner, conversation seemed to lag. For the first time we had more women than men. It was easy to see that everyone missed Jack. We had Tully though, and after dinner he made a surprise announcement. He wanted to take Randy flying.

"Before he left, I promised Jack I'd arrange a flight. That is, if you're ready, Randy, and," he gave Mr. Siler an apologetic look, "if your father will drive us out to Opa-Locka, we could go this afternoon. There's a bus but I'm afraid—" He looked at Randy's chair.

"I'll take you," Mr. Siler said.

"Oh, I don't know—" Mrs. Siler began. "I'm not sure that's a good idea. He might catch a chill or—" She reminded me of my own mother with forty days and forty nights of objections, but at least now I understood a little more. Mrs. Siler had one son at risk; she didn't want to worry about them both.

Mr. Siler patted his wife's shoulder then gazed at Randy. "Do you want to go, son?" he asked.

The expression on Randy's face left little doubt. "You bet! I'm sick of lookin' at planes. I want to fly in one." He grinned at Tully. The first one hundred percent genuine smile I'd seen since Jack left. "I can't wait." Then he turned to us. "Will you girls come along and watch?"

"Sure we will," I answered before I realized we had too many to fit in the Silers' car.

Cleo dug through her handbag and pulled out a ration book. "I can drive, but I have to stop and get some gas."

Mr. Siler smiled. "Don't use your stamps. I think we can squeeze in if we tie Randy's chair on the back. The lieutenant can help."

The Opa-Locka airport was so flat it looked like a card table with a little grass and rock around the edges, and a tall fence. Not a tree or bush to block the blazing sun—only runway and planes and above, blue sky. Mrs. Siler had loaned us three umbrellas so we wouldn't get sunburned but had refused to come along herself. She said it was bad enough that Jack wanted to fly in planes. Seeing Randy up in one might be too much for her heart. There was also the issue of space. Laughing, we loaded into the car like a bunch of clowns at the circus. Cleo, Ruth, and I squeezed in the back with Randy, who never stopped smiling the whole way. Tully sat in front with Mr. Siler and kept us entertained by quizzing us on great English actors and American comedies.

Gosh, I wouldn't have missed it for the world.

With a show of ID, Tully talked our way through two guard posts before we drove across the cracked pavement that led to the hangars. At least thirty planes were lined up along the road.

"We'll be going up in one of the old trainers," Tully said to

Randy before waving to a man in coveralls near one of the hangars.

"Afternoon, Lieutenant," the man said as he approached. By this time we'd opened our umbrellas and clumped around Randy by the Silers' car.

"Afternoon, Mac. We've got a VIP here, Jack Siler's brother, Randy, and I've promised him a demonstration flight." He walked over to Randy and put a hand on his shoulder. "He's also a volunteer plane spotter."

Mac extended his hand, then noticing it was covered with grease pulled it back. "Nice to meet you," he said with a nod as he wiped his palms on a rag he pulled from his back pocket. "Old Jack was one heck of a flyer," he added.

I guess it was the unfortunate choice of words that made Ruth give a start. I swear she was getting as jumpy as Mrs. Siler. I turned to look at her but she was staring at the planes.

"I imagine he still is one heck of a flyer," Tully said smoothly, then went on. "These ladies," he recited our names, "are friends of ours." He introduced Mr. Siler last.

"Well," Mac said after the formalities, "you know you're supposed to have the colonel's okay for any flight . . . But I seem to remember we need to test out one of the trainers we put back on the line yesterday." He winked. "Let's get this show on the road."

"How about cranking up old twenty-one," Tully said.

"You got it."

I felt a thrum of excitement for Randy. "This is going to be so much fun," I said in his ear.

"Yeah. I wish Jack was here, though."

The roar of an engine drowned out further conversation. As Mac pulled the blocks, a shiny red plane with the black number twenty-one painted on each wing rolled forward out of the line of its drab gray neighbors.

"That's a biplane," Randy shouted over the noise. "Jack told me it's the first plane most pilots learn to fly."

"Are you ready?" Tully yelled as he climbed down with an extra leather jacket in his hand. He approached Randy. "You're not worried about going up with me instead of Jack, are you?" he asked as he handed Randy the jacket to put on.

"Worried? About flying with a war hero? I don't think so. I just wish I could go with you to chase some Germans."

"If you spot any let me know." Tully smiled, then he looked at me. In that moment I decided there must be something dangerous about airplanes that changed a man inside and out. Standing there in the hot Florida sunshine wearing a heavy jacket with goggles slung around his neck, Tully smiled like Jack, like a pilot who knows he's a man with wings, immortal, and intends to prove it. A tiny fear fluttered inside me.

In very short order, Mr. Siler, Mac, and Tully got Randy situated in the front training seat of the plane and they were rolling down the runway. Randy smiled and waved until the wheels of the plane left the ground. Then I believe he completely forgot about the ones he'd left behind on the ground.

They buzzed the field—they even did a loop-de-loop. For nearly an hour we watched that tiny red dot fly through the bright blue sky. Then they were back. Number twenty-one floated down and touched the runway with the grace of a seasoned campaigner. Randy was talking a mile a minute as the men lifted him out of the plane.

"You should've seen it!" he was saying. "We flew over our house and over the ocean." Randy was only getting warmed up when Tully turned to me.

"Would you like to take a ride?" he asked. "I think we have enough fuel for an abbreviated tour."

"Oh, yes, I'd love to go," I answered. I wanted to see what all the fuss was about and frankly I would have gone with Tully almost anywhere.

Ruth touched my arm. "Are you sure?" She turned to Tully. "Is it very rough?"

A strange question. I turned to look at her and she seemed nervous. I guess she had a right to worry over me after what had happened. But I was fine now and I'd be safe with Tully. "Don't worry. If Randy can do it, I can, too."

"Some of the trainees say it's sort of like a roller coaster,"

Tully said. "But I can make it more like floating." He held out his hand and I took it. "I'll look after her," he said and we were off.

Flying is like dreaming, except it's noisier. First you're hot like sitting too close to the radiator in the wintertime. Then, when you leave the ground, the wind cools everything down, roaring through the propeller like a giant fan. It's impossible to talk, the wind blows the sound out of your mouth. I didn't know what to say anyhow. It was too beautiful for plain words. Florida looked green for as far as the eye could see—and from the air that was pretty far. And the green is surrounded by blue. The ocean was bigger and bluer from the sky than when you were in it. A bird who'd never flown north might think Florida was an island, floating in an endless ocean.

A dream I'd be happy to live, if I didn't know that the deep blue water connected us to the world and to the war.

"Hang on!" Tully yelled, then banked into a long slow turn. I could look down and see cars on the streets and occasionally a person staring up at us. Being red, we were hard to miss. We passed over an impressive building with a Spanish-style tile roof that looked like a small hotel.

"Jack told me that's the gangster Al Capone's house. The Army took it over to house WACs."

Leave it to Jack to know where the women were housed. I nodded and smiled. When we came out of the turn we were headed east. I knew that because I could see Miami Beach in front of us. The mist of a low cloud touched my face and my stomach gave a little lurch, not only from the floating sensation but from the view. I suddenly knew that this is where I would spend the rest of my days. Not in an airplane, but in Miami.

We made one run right along the water's edge before we turned back. I saw the Servicemen's Pier flash beneath us with soldiers relaxing on the beach or swimming in the waves. A few of them waved.

I didn't feel a thing, not nostalgia nor anger, and that was puzzling. I'd felt so many things in the days following Frankie's attack. Now I merely wanted to get on with my life—whatever kind of life that might be. If the perfect marriage and family were out of reach I would do the best I could.

Soon we were back over the airport. I could see our little audience had moved into the shade of the building. The air temperature seemed to climb the closer we got to the runway. We touched the ground with a bump and a bounce and my stomach did another little somersault. Returning to the ground didn't seem to agree with me. All in all, I think I would rather have stayed in the air.

"Thank you." I hugged Tully as he helped me down from the plane. He set me on my feet and seemed momentarily at a loss for words. I turned to Ruth, grinning ear to ear, but a funny thing happened. My head seemed to empty of any thought and I felt a cool clamminess, like the mist from the clouds, on my face and my arms. I saw Ruth step toward me but I lost her in the bright blue sky. Then, the sun went out.

Chapter Nine

— RUTH —

I thought my heart would fail when Maddy collapsed. One of those times when you're an unwilling witness to impending disaster but unable to stop it. It was a good thing Lt. Tull-Martin was standing close enough to catch her. As any hero in the movies, he swung her up into his arms and disregarding his own limp, carried her into the hangar. The building smelled of gasoline and grease but at least it was quiet and cooler than outside. Tully placed her on the sagging couch in the office, and Cleo provided a damp cloth I could press to her temples.

"Maddy?" I questioned when she began to come around. "Maddy, can you hear me?"

She opened her eyes but stared at me silently for a number of seconds. "Ruth," she said with a sigh of recognition before glancing around the room. "Where are we?"

"We're at the airport. Do you remember riding in the airplane?"

It took her another few seconds to reconstruct her memory. "Yes . . ." Then she jumped with the suddenness of a sleep-walker waking. "What happened? Where is everyone?"

"You fainted, sweetie," Cleo said. "Everyone's waiting outside."

A blush of color rose into her pale cheeks. "I've never fainted before," she confessed. "I don't understand, I felt fine. Well, maybe a little queasy but the ride was glorious—better than I imagined. I wanted to stay up there forever." With my help she pushed to a sitting position on the couch. "Now everyone will think I'm a baby."

Better that than for them to know you're going to have one. "No they won't," I assured her. "Don't let it upset you. You need to rest calmly for a few more moments. I'll get you a glass of water." I left Cleo in charge of making her stay put.

Outside, as I waited for Mac to find a clean glass for Maddy, I calmed everyone's fears. "She's fine. A little too much excitement, I think."

"Do you think we should take her to a doctor?" Lt. Tull-Martin asked. He looked in worse shape than Maddy. He was ready to take the blame for making her ill. I couldn't let him though because I knew the true reason.

"She's fine, really," I assured him as Mac returned. "A little embarrassed." I smiled at Randy. "No teasing when she comes out." He nodded and I went to deliver the water.

After taking a few sips, Maddy managed a halfhearted smile. "I bet you didn't expect to be waiting on me, huh?"

I patted her knee. "There's a lot of things in life we don't expect, but they seem to work out."

When we arrived back home Lt. Tull-Martin insisted on helping Maddy into our house. He would have carried her if Maddy hadn't been equally determined to walk. He'd not been in the Samuel place before, and I gave him a little tour after we got Maddy situated on the couch. When the tour ended we were standing in front of the photograph. He picked up the frame and studied it.

"Most of these boys have shipped out," he said as he pointed out two or three of the pilots who'd graduated.

In my sight, one of those pilots had already disappeared. I blinked, trying not to give away my shock. The smiling young pilot was gone—an empty space. I closed my eyes briefly and asked God's angels to be with his family. Then I wondered if his parents, his . . . wife . . . if they even knew the terrible news yet. I knew. Because of that, I decided I needed to hear his name.

"This one right here"—I pointed to the spot where he should have been—"His name was—is—?"

Lt. Tull-Martin studied the picture. "We call him Skeeter but his real name is Lt. Linton Streeter. Skeeter Streeter"—he smiled—"makes the names easier to remember especially in bug-infested Florida.

"And there's old Jack," Lt. Tull-Martin went on.

"We certainly miss him," I said, taking the frame out of his hands and replacing it on the radio cabinet. I didn't want him to point out any more men who might disappear before my eyes. "Don't we, Maddy?"

"Sure do," she answered. When Lt. Tull-Martin turned to look at her she went on quickly. "But now we have Cleo."

"Yes," Lt. Tull-Martin said before nodding to our new roommate. "I'm glad you're finding some friends."

"Cleo works at the aircraft factory making bombers."

"Is that so?" The lieutenant crossed the room and sat down. "B-17s?"

"Yes. I've been there about two months," Cleo answered. "I work on the machine that bends the metal for the wings. I'm getting pretty good at it. Some of the girls are old pros."

"I kind of like the idea of women making airplanes," he said with a smile. "They have a great eye for detail. Airplanes are dependent on trivial things—one small part can bring you down."

Off into a discussion of airplanes and parts, Tully and Cleo might as well have been speaking another language. Maddy looked a little pale to me, still. So, after a respectable interval I broke up the party.

Cleo moved in with us the following day. I'd barely arrived home from the Dowlands' when our new roommate pulled up, wearing her scarf and coveralls from work, her car stuffed with boxes and bed linens.

"The other girls were happy to see me go," Cleo said with a smile. Then she seemed to realize that didn't sound very good. "I mean, you know, to give them more space."

"Well," Maddy said, "if we don't get along there's a big old alligator named Joe who lives in the river behind the house. I imagine he has plenty of space for troublemakers. When I first moved here, Jack told me that Old Joe goes hunting every full moon."

"Shoot," Cleo said. "I bet Joe has relatives who work at Intercontinental. Some of the 4-F guys down there are toothy and always on the hunt." She laughed. "Don't worry. I'm sure us girls will get along fine; you can count on me."

The Silers welcomed Cleo as well—especially Randy. It took very little time for the "new girl" to be educated by our resident prankster. Barely a week after Cleo moved in, Randy wheeled himself over one evening with a jar of pennies in his lap. He announced his intention to teach us to play poker.

I didn't know if Cleo knew how to play or not, but she decided to honor part of our agreement with the Silers and go along with the evening's entertainment. But that was before we caught him cheating.

Like lambs to the slaughter, Maddy and I lost fifteen cents apiece and Cleo a dime. Even as Randy swore, after he was caught, that he'd intended to tell us the truth at the end of the night and give the money back, led by Cleo, we pelted him with cards and pennies until he raised his hands in surrender. After that, he learned to duck when he won—whether he'd cheated or not.

Maddy seemed fine after her fainting spell. I worried about her anyway, waiting for the inevitable time when she'd have to face the truth. Babies would not be put off. Against my better judgment I let her ride to work with Cleo one day so she could apply for a job. She came home full of excitement.

"Can you believe it? They're going to teach me how to weld!"

She sounded like she'd been invited to attend Harvard. "That's wonderful, I think . . ." I glanced at Cleo.

"It's one of the higher paying jobs, up to sixty dollars a week once you're on the line, and it doesn't require a lot of upper-body strength," Cleo clarified.

"I have to start out on the cleanup crew, but after that I get to train on the welding machine. I'll be doing my patriotic duty—building airplanes. I can't wait to tell Tully."

I hated to rain on her parade. "Didn't they ask your age?"

"I only lied a little," Maddy confessed. "I told them I was eighteen and a half."

"And a half . . . ? What did they say? Did they ask for your driver's license or your ration book?"

Cleo laughed before Maddy could answer. "Half the women in this city carry ration books that say they're twenty-one. The young ones want to be older and the older ones want to be younger."

"They didn't ask for anything. They just made me sign a paper that my information was correct."

"And take the oath to be a patriotic American," Cleo inserted. "They need as many workers as they can get. There's a rumor the plant may go on round-the-clock shifts."

Maddy raised her right hand then laughed, her excitement obvious. "Just think, Ruth. We'll have enough money to pay our rent and then some. Welding doesn't look hard. I know I can do it."

"I know you can, too, sweetie," I said. But I would've been much happier if she'd gotten the kind of job she'd be able to keep when we couldn't hide her pregnancy. And what in the world were we going to tell her mother? *Yes, Mother Marshall. The daughter you've always thought to be an independent tomboy is now working in the aircraft factory as a welder.* I could only shake my head. Approaching disaster was like approaching anything else—it required one step at a time.

"I'll keep an eye on her," Cleo promised, and I felt a little better. A *little*. I didn't find out that she'd joined the Red Cross until later.

* * *

Work dominated our lives after that. Each morning Cleo and Maddy would stop at the Silers' to pick up their bagged lunches, then wait on the corner for the "share the ride" car to drive them to the factory. Luckily, they put most of the women on the early shift so they wouldn't have to wait at night. I caught the first morning bus over to the Dowlands' house trailer. Nickie and I had become fast friends and we had many serious discussions about why the sky was blue or whether Hitler's mother knew the bad things he was doing. I did the best I could to answer his questions although sometimes, like when he asked if "my" Davey was on his way home yet, I had to hide my tears.

"I don't think so," I answered. "He only left a little while ago."

"He's gonna go get those Japs, huh? We should write him a letter. My mommy writes my daddy over and over."

My voice wouldn't cooperate, so I nodded. I didn't want to think about anybody *getting* anybody. But I knew every soldier had to do what must be done. Or die trying. "Okay, let's write." It was easy enough to find a pad and pen.

Dear Davey,

A friend of mine wanted to say hello to one of the brave fighting men in the Pacific. His name is Nickie. He's four years old and his father is a radioman in the Navy. Nickie was with me at the harbor the morning you left and he says to tell those bad Japs they're gonna get a good whippin'.

My little friend is definitely all sizzle and spark. He keeps me entertained. I hope to have several like him when you get home.

We're thinking of you. I hope you're safe and comfortable.

Love from the home front,

Ruth

Maddy had been working exactly two weeks when she threw up for the first time. I found out secondhand when she happened to mention that something must have upset her stomach. By the time she told me, she felt fine. I marked it on the secret calendar in my mind, though. How long did we have before I would have to tell her? Or at least bring up the possibility?

"Maybe you're just tired," I suggested. She'd been working full-time on the cleaning crew and was learning welding, and Cleo had talked her into volunteering at the pier on weekends. I didn't have the heart to say no and spoil any time she had left to enjoy life—before life limited her options.

— MADDY —

I was having a ball. I have to admit that at first I was hesitant to come back to the pier—because of bad memories. Because of Frankie. But I was determined to overcome that fear by smiling—at sailors, Marines, and hundreds of Army PFCs. I'm sure I'd smiled at some rotten apples like Frankie in among the others, but most of them were just lonesome boys away from home. I stuck close to Cleo and did my job.

As I helped three sailors sign up for a spot on the pool-table roster, I thought of Lyle for the first time in a while. I'd put his photo away and had some difficulty recalling his features, but something about one of the sailors reminded me of him.

"Where are you boys from?" I asked. A standard question.

"Illinois."

"Michigan."

"Pennsylvania."

"Where in PA?" I asked.

"Bucks County, ma'am."

I gave him an extra smile. "A farm boy, huh? I'm from Radley—outside of Philly." I handed over his ticket for a turn at the pool table. I'd learned the art of short conversations. "Knock 'em dead."

He stood there, staring, twisting his sailor hat in his hands. I kept smiling and figured I'd give him a moment before signaling to the next man in the line. One of his buddies wasn't so patient, grabbing the collar of his uniform and pulling. "Come on, farm boy. The lady is busy."

"Farm boy" stammered, blushed, then followed his friends. The next man in line was Tully.

"Did you want to sign up to play pool?" I asked with a smile.

He smiled back. "Why no, actually. I would like to claim you for a few dances later if you can leave your post. Is there a ticket for dancing with pretty Red Cross volunteers?"

Pretty. I would have given him the entire roll of tickets and the table they were sitting on if he'd asked. "You don't need one. I'll come and find you when I have my break."

It had become a ritual for us to ask the band to play "White Cliffs of Dover." As a matter of fact, the last couple of times we hadn't had to ask. The guys in the band would wave and begin the intro like we were an old married couple.

"I won't be at church on Sunday," he said. "I wanted to tell you now so you won't think I deserted you. Or that I'm in the stockade like Jack."

Nothing against Jack but I couldn't imagine a well-mannered man like Tully in jail for any reason. Then again, I couldn't imagine him shooting down German planes either. "Too busy to entertain the peasants?" I asked, doing my best impression of witty and sophisticated, like Barbara Stanwyck or Katharine Hepburn.

Tully smiled as though I had pulled it off. "Never that— too busy, or too entertaining for that matter." Before I could laugh, he went serious. "No, I have some meetings I have to be present for, that's all."

I looked into his eyes and waited. His gaze shifted to somewhere over my head for a moment and then returned. His fingers tightened on mine. "I'll be sure and tell them that from now on my Sundays must be kept free. That I have more important subjects beyond this silly war to occupy my time."

Silly war meant he was still joking, but he didn't smile. He pulled me closer and we finished the dance in silence.

* * *

I woke up Saturday morning sick again and had to beg off early doughnut duty with Cleo. I'd purposely eaten very little dinner so my stomach would settle down. It hadn't worked. As I washed my face after throwing up, Ruth knocked on the bathroom door. When I opened it, she looked worse than I did.

"What's wrong?" I asked, not realizing that she was looking at me with the same question in her eyes. Or at least worry. That gave me a scare. Did I look so sick that Ruth thought I might have some dreaded disease? I thought of my father and his "bum ticker." He'd been pale and tired most of the time, but I didn't remember him being sick to his stomach.

"Come sit down," Ruth said.

When we were both seated on the couch she pressed her hand briefly to my forehead. "Feeling better now?"

"I drank a glass of water, that seems to help." Ruth nodded but continued to watch me with concern. I really started to worry then. Heck, I'd never been sick for long and usually my mother knew what to do. "Do you think there's something terribly wrong with me? Should I go to the doctor?"

"Well, I'm not sure. I'll tell you what I know then help you decide what to do."

What I know . . .

"Remember when I decided to tell your mother I was expecting?"

I nodded, unable to speak.

"And I said it was possible because Davey and I had been together, meaning we made l-love?" She stumbled on the description and I could see a rush of color moving into her cheeks.

"Well, you and Frankie—"

Me and Frankie? My stomach heaved and I had to clamp a hand over my mouth and run for the bathroom. I kicked the door shut behind me.

Ruth was waiting in the hallway when I came out. She seemed tired but she took my arm and helped me back to the couch.

"I'm sorry to put you through this now, when you're ill, but you have to know. I believe you're going to have a baby."

My mind was spinning like a top. I knew Ruth had been pregnant . . . "But how do you know? Can you tell by looking at me?"

She drew in a fortifying breath and pointed toward the frame on the radio cabinet across the room. "Because of the photograph."

"What?" I could barely get the word out. The photograph she'd kept in the closet? "Ruth—"

"I know. It sounds crazy. But I can see things that are happening to the people in the picture. You and Davey, Jack and Lt. Tull-Martin." She swallowed. "Frankie . . . and the others."

I started to cry again, and for the first time I had a good reason. Ruth retrieved the photograph and held it on her lap. She waited as I wiped my eyes and blew my nose. I'd started carrying a hanky everywhere I went these days for that purpose.

"Do you remember when we heard on the radio that an airman had been killed in an accident? Airman Edwards?"

I nodded.

She ran a hand over the photograph like a blind person who could feel the faces. "Well I already knew because he'd disappeared from the picture."

"Disappeared?" Then I had a dawning thought—part of the puzzle solved. "That's why you hid it in the closet."

She looked a little sheepish. "Yes. I thought if I didn't look, I wouldn't see bad news."

"What changed your mind?"

"Davey," she said, then smiled sadly. "And you."

Fear rang through me like a fire alarm then. "Davey knows?"

"Not about the baby," she said quickly. "I told him about the airman, and that I thought I might be crazy."

"What did he say?"

"He laughed."

I felt like laughing, too. Calling Ruth crazy would be like calling my mother a cream puff.

My mother. After Frankie, I'd sort of come to grips with being ruined. I didn't feel especially different though, other than being mad, and I had decided that if I could keep my stupidity a secret, then life would go on pretty much the same. But having a baby . . . that would be impossible to hide. What was I supposed to do with a baby?

Then I remembered how sick Ruth had been, and that she'd almost died trying to have a baby. My sickness took on a whole new face. As my heart pounded out several frantic beats I discovered that even in this present darkness, I wanted to live. "Am I going to die, Ruth? Like you did?"

"No, of course not," she said quickly. "What happened to me was a rare thing."

I searched her face for the evidence of kind lies. "But you lost both your babies. What if that happens to me?"

Ruth looked down for a moment, then met my gaze. "We can never know what we might have to face in life." She smiled. "But you're young, and you're healthy as a horse. I believe you'll do fine."

Dear Ruth,

I pray this letter finds you well. I have to say that since hearing your news I have been on pins and needles with worry. I even spoke to Dr. Wellman about it—but only in hypothetical fashion. His main advice for any patient who is expecting is to rest and eat well. I confess I suspect you already know this but I had hoped for some newfangled baby science. It seems the woman still must do things on her own. He then asked me how Maddy was doing in Florida and I had to change the subject.

Between Davey's service and your pregnancy I'm sure to worry myself into a head of gray hair. I'm glad that Maddy isn't the cause for once. I wouldn't want her to feel singled out—after that business with her boyfriend Lyle.

Please write for anything you need and that includes money. I have a little put away and I won't hear of you going without and making yourself ill.

Drink plenty of milk.
With love,
Mother Marshall

Dear Maddy,
I hope you're being a good girl and taking care of Ruth. I know in those tropical climates laziness must be a great temptation. Just remember what Father Gus says about sloth and prove what a fine girl you've grown to be. Any effort on your part now will be paid back later when Ruth gives you a new niece or nephew to spoil. (I have no doubt you will try. I remember you feeding your cat roast chicken because he liked it better than ordinary table scraps.)
Speaking of cats, I've taken in one of the Jenkinses' kittens to keep me company in this empty house. I hope you'll approve of him when you come home since you weren't here to pick him out. He has four white paws and a white stripe on his face. A clown by all accounts. He'll be the perfect little man to entertain my new grandchild.
I miss you, Maddy and I hope the great responsibility you carry will not be too difficult to bear. Think of Ruth as your sister. I'm sure she feels the same about you. And call me right away if anything seems to be going wrong.
Love,
Mother

Everything had already gone wrong. "I'll have to tell my mother," I said, still in shock. I put a hand on my stomach but other than a tiny rumble of hunger, it felt the same.

"Why ruin a perfectly good lie?" Cleo asked. She'd come home after delivering the morning's ration of doughnuts to the boys down at the Red Cross center and found us in serious discussion. She'd been the one who'd brought in the morning's mail.

"A WAV told me that three girls in her barracks had buns in the oven and nobody knew a thing until one of them went into labor."

"How in the world did they hide it for so long?" Ruth asked.

"Bigger, looser clothes I guess. You know those WAV uniforms are nothing to write home about." She shrugged. "The girls had already gone through training so there wasn't much physical exertion in their jobs."

"Oh, no, my job!" I was beginning to get the picture of how Frankie had changed my life. I looked at Ruth. "What'll we do if I lose my job?"

"Calm down. The three of us can work things out." Cleo took the letters from my mother out of my hand and tossed them on the table like they were antennae for trouble. "Let's leave your mother out of this for now. What she doesn't know won't hurt her." She sat up straight and looked me in the eye before smiling a smile that would have made Mata Hari look innocent. "The men have their war. This'll be our campaign. Now, how do we hide a baby?"

Cleo and Ruth spent the next few hours making lists, discussing timetables, and basically plotting out the next nine months of my life. I wanted to help and did for the first hour or so, but like the low sound of buzzing bees, their voices made me sleepy. I ended up falling asleep on the couch. When Ruth woke me for dinner, I felt so much better I forgot to worry. Maybe it was the feeling that my two roommates were on my side—or maybe it was the growling of my stomach. I felt like I hadn't eaten for a week and wasted little time changing and making myself presentable for dinner with the Silers.

"That's your third helping of potatoes," Randy commented as I dug into the bowl. Caught with spoon in midair I could feel everyone staring.

"They're good." I put the spoon down and set the bowl closer to him.

"You're gonna get fat," he teased.

"They *are* good," Ruth commented. "I'll have to write down exactly how you make them, Mrs. Siler. Randy, could you pass them this way, please?" I watched in shock as both she and Cleo ate another helping of potatoes.

"I can see we'll need to make a larger grocery list," Mrs. Siler said, looking more pleased than annoyed.

I kept eating although my appetite had hit the road chased by nerves. I realized that from now on, I was going to have to pay more attention to everything I did or I'd be on a train to Radley faster than the charge of the light brigade, disgraced and defeated.

"I've had a letter from Jack," Mrs. Siler reported. "He's arrived safely and says to tell you girls hello."

I perked up at her news. "Did he say what England is like? Did he see the white cliffs of Dover?"

"No, dear. He wrote mostly about airplanes and his new assignment. He did mention there was a lot of bomb damage in London. A real shame." Mrs. Siler shook her head.

"He said the RAF can use all the help they can get. So you girls better get to work making those planes," Randy added. "No slacking off."

If I hadn't known Randy would have given anything to be making planes or doing something himself to help the war effort, I would have let him have it. He'd even been released from plane-spotter duty as the rumors of German bombers raking the East Coast turned out to be just that, rumors. Instead of trading wisecracks with Randy, however, I worried about being sick every morning and losing my job.

After an expectant interval, Randy realized I wasn't up to the game. "When you finish the next one, write my name on it, will ya? Write that Randy says hello."

"You got it," Cleo promised.

Later, when Cleo, Ruth, and I were alone in the kitchen washing up the dinner dishes, I saw Ruth slip into the pantry and come out with something folded in wax paper. She slipped it into her pocket before I could get a good look. I found out the next morning as we were getting ready for church.

"Here, eat this," Ruth said. She'd unfolded the wax paper and produced a soda cracker.

I shook my head. My stomach felt like it had been invaded

by Mexican jumping beans and the thought of food merely made them jump higher and faster.

"You have morning sickness—from the baby. Open your mouth," she ordered.

Ruth might not have had children of her own but she could already wield that mother-tone along with the best of them. I opened my mouth. She stuffed a cracker in.

"Chew."

The cracker tasted like salty dust in my mouth, and I wondered if I'd even be able to swallow. But then Ruth held up a glass of water and told me to drink. The cracker went down and within a few minutes my stomach settled. I ate two more.

"There, your color looks better. I want you to carry these with you everywhere you go. Whenever you get queasy, eat one and drink some water."

I nodded and took the package. "Thank you." My voice sounded like a croaking frog but my jumping beans had taken a vacation.

Ruth gave me a hug. "Let's go then."

Church made me nervous. I was glad Tully wasn't there. The being ruined part was bad enough before but now . . . How could I ever face him again? I had stared in the mirror, trying to see if I looked different somehow. I worried that everyone from the pastor to the organist would be able to look at me and tell that I was PG. But with Ruth on one side of me and Cleo on the other I made it up the sidewalk and into the pew.

I said prayers for Davey and for Jack and for Tully, for my mother and even for Lyle. But for me, I didn't know what to pray about except forgiveness. The damage was done. I expected to be punished—by something or someone. I wasn't clear on the charges though since I hadn't intended for any of this to happen. Every time I tried to prostrate my will I got weepy. Father Gus back home would have been disappointed.

"Remember, no heavy lifting. Stay off ladders," Ruth said as I stuffed the package of crackers into the pocket of my coveralls.

I'd slept well yet I couldn't seem to get my eyes open completely. I usually got my motor running after lunchtime but the mornings . . .

"Come on, kiddo. Let's go make some planes."

I yawned as Cleo pulled me through the door, then I waved to Ruth. "Don't worry, they have me on the cleanup crew for a while yet," I said. I'd been doing my best to do as Ruth advised and take life a day at a time. But I wasn't expecting more bad news.

On Wednesday, Tully called the Silers' and left a message with Randy that sounded more like a telegram. He wanted Ruth, Cleo, and me to meet him at six o'clock in front of the School of Aviation where he was stationed. STOP He had to attend a wedding at a friend's home and we were invited. STOP Sorry for the short notice. STOP He'd wait for us until seven. STOP.

Cleo got us there at 5:30.

Ruth and I had worn our best dresses but neither of us had brought anything suitable for a wedding. Cleo had donned her newly pressed Red Cross uniform. It was her conviction, she said, that the Red Cross would be welcomed anywhere.

"I'm sure the bride will be happy to have a few other women in attendance—no matter what they're wearing. Her family is from New York and they couldn't make it. Everything on such short notice and all," Tully said.

Tully looked downright breathtaking. He'd obviously taken even more care than usual with his appearance—pressed and polished, he smelled divine. Sitting next to him in the backseat of Cleo's car made me feel like a vagabond.

"So, it'll be mostly pilots and strangers."

"The bride must be unhappy to have such a rushed ceremony," Ruth said.

Tully shook his head with a rueful smile. "It was her idea. You see, our—I mean the groom's unit has received orders. It's either today or wait until after the war."

"Oh," Ruth said. I could see by the expression on her face that she was thinking of Davey. Tully glanced at me then quietly took my hand. We rode the rest of the way in silence.

Following a hand-drawn map, we found the house promptly at 6:15.

"Wow," Cleo said as she steered the car down the circular, crushed-shell driveway. "This is some joint."

I'd almost gotten used to the overgrown disorder of south Florida, but this neighborhood seemed to have tamed Mother Nature. My own mother would have been impressed. Huge trees hung over the house but they'd obviously been trimmed to give the perfect amount of shade without looking shaggy like our trees on Ninth Avenue. The yard and house were landscaped within an inch of their lives—combed and culti-vated. They'd even trained the bougainvillea on an arch along the garage. The house itself was one story and pale-pink stucco but large enough to encompass both the Siler and Samuel houses at once.

Then, as we walked toward the entrance, I saw the water.

"Is that the Miami River?" I asked, completely turned around in my directions. It looked wider and deeper than the river behind our house.

"I believe people call it the New River. It forms the water-way between Miami Beach and the mainland," Tully answered. He took my arm as we approached the front door. Once in-side, someone—a maid I suppose—pinned gardenia corsages on Ruth, Cleo, and me.

"Oh, this is lovely," Ruth exclaimed. "Thank you for bring-ing us, Lt. Tull-Martin."

"Yes, thank you," I echoed.

He merely smiled and squeezed my arm. "I'll be right back. I need to speak to the groom."

I don't know if the bride was happy to see us or not but I can tell you there were a bunch of happy airmen. When we first walked in it looked like they were standing at attention holding up the walls, worried about breaking something. But Cleo had been right—as soon as they saw her uniform we were surrounded. I didn't have time to be nervous. At least eight of them started talking at once and it took every bit of my con-centration to keep up with the shebang.

By the time the groom's father asked everyone to be seated I was winded. Tully presented himself to guide us to a seat as the groom and minister took their places. The ceremony itself was short and sweet, then rings were exchanged. The announcement would surely read: The bride wore cream-colored silk and held a bouquet of pink sweetheart roses. The groom proudly wore his Army Air Corps uniform—shiny new brass wings pinned to his chest.

"I pronounce you, man and wife."

A war whoop went up from the airmen as the groom kissed his bride. The hurrah seemed to startle the mother of the groom, but with a fluttering hand stationed over her heart, she smiled as her son kissed her cheek. I glanced over at Ruth and saw tears in her eyes. I felt teary as well but I'm sure for a different reason.

"You seem different somehow," Tully said.

At his suggestion, we'd walked outside, away from the music and conversations, down to the dock built over the waterway.

I nearly choked on the sip of punch I'd just swallowed. Could he tell? Could everyone tell? I cleared my throat and concentrated on breathing. In this case, lying would be easier than telling the truth. I set my glass of punch on a piling then squinted into the setting sun rather than look him in the eye.

"I think I've grown up a lot," I answered carefully. I hoped that part was true. "Is that what you mean?"

"I'm sure that's part of it." He took my arm and turned me to face him. "But you seem . . . I don't know . . . sad I suppose. You've been sad for weeks and you won't tell me why. When I first met you, you were as flighty and happy as a lark."

Damn. Damn. Damn. A thousand hours had passed since then and I'd changed forever. "I think I—" My traitorous eyes began to sting. I wanted to say I should go inside, but I blinked and hot tears rushed down my cheeks.

He rested a hand along my jaw, then with cool fingers

wiped away my tears. "You may as well tell me because I've already stumbled and caught my heart on you. I don't expect anything can come along to change that."

I couldn't move or speak. Of thousands of dreams I'd dared to dream, this was the best—and the worst. I thought I'd understood what Frankie had stolen from me. But until this moment I hadn't truly known what I'd had to lose.

"I can't." It came out in a whisper, but he sobered like I'd shouted in his face.

"I see." He brushed my cheek one more time then withdrew his hand. "Well, I have some news to tell you then. I wanted the right time, but there is no right time it seems."

I did the best I could to pull myself together even though my heart had hit the ground like Humpty-Dumpty. *All the king's horses and all the king's men . . .*

"I've received new orders. I'll be leaving for England in two days—with this new group of pilots." He nodded toward the house full of airmen, one of them a new husband.

The king's men.

I have to confess, I don't know what happened to me then. Suddenly, I couldn't breathe properly. One second I was standing on my own, and the next Tully's arm was supporting me. The sunset seemed to spin several times before returning to normal. I found myself staring into Tully's worried eyes. I guess I should have been afraid, alone in the dark with a man—after Frankie. But I wasn't. Not with Tully.

"Maddy? Are you all right?"

I couldn't think of a suitable answer, so I kissed him—right on the lips. I'm sure it was a childish and selfish thing to do, but I couldn't help myself. I guess I've always wanted what I couldn't have—as a girl, and now as a woman. Tully didn't seem to mind, and in a very short time I had learned a thing or two about kisses, and my arms were twined around his neck.

He pulled away first—just his lips, not his arms. "I'm about to confess something I swore I'd never say until this war was over." He struggled for a moment. "I want you to know what's in my heart, no matter what happens. But I won't tie you down with promises. You're so young and so beautiful, I'm sure there will be many other men who'll—"

"No." There would be no other men for me—for a hundred reasons. Tully was the one I wanted, and if I couldn't have him then I knew I'd spend the rest of my days remembering him. Wishing everything could have been different. I had the urgent thought that if I could keep him from saying the words out loud, I could stop the pain those words would bring.

"I haven't said anything yet." He smiled.

Equal amounts of fear and fascination fluttered in my chest. Here was my chance to interrupt—to never know how he really felt. My mouth moved, but no sound came out.

"I'm in love with you, Miss Madelyn Marshall. Whether you like it or not."

"Oh." I liked it all right but it didn't matter what I liked . . . or loved anymore. My choices had been narrowed to telling lies and keeping secrets.

"Now will you please tell me why you're so sad? It isn't because of me, is it?"

Rather than explaining or lying, I decided to ask for what I wanted most of all. "Will you kiss me again?"

I didn't have to ask him twice. This time when he drew away we were both a little breathless. I had regained my balance, but his smile had faded into serious business. He took a step away and captured both my hands in his. I could feel a tremor in his fingers.

"I said I wouldn't hold you to promises, and I meant it. But I have a promise for you." He swallowed. "When this war is over. When the lot of us come home for good. Look for me. I'll find you—and if you're not otherwise inclined—*then* I'll ask you for promises. Or vows."

The sun had dropped below the horizon and the sky grew darker by the second, like the joy in my heart. Soon we'd be standing in the dark and even sooner, I'd be alone. I squeezed his hands and pulled him a little closer. "Don't go. I'm afraid I'll never see you again."

His smile returned but seemed a little tarnished. "I have to go. I've known that from the start. I cannot rest until this business is settled. I've lost too many friends to stand back and stay out of it. We're all in it until the bitter end."

I walked into his arms again and soaked his shirt with my tears.

"Ah, sweetheart," he whispered into my hair. "I didn't mean to upset you. You've made me so happy and I've only made you cry."

"Not you— Never you—"

"Maddy?"

"There's Ruth calling you." I felt him wave. He set me back away from him. "Let's see how you look." He took out his handkerchief and dabbed at my face. "I don't want everyone to think I've broken your heart."

— RUTH —

After a silent ride home, Maddy went to her room and cried for three hours. I had to make her get up and drink a glass of milk. I knew it had something to do with Lt. Tull-Martin, but so far she wasn't willing to tell.

After tucking Maddy back into bed and saying good night to Cleo, I paced over to the photograph and picked up the frame. As always, I looked at Davey first. He appeared wind-blown, his pressed uniform mussed, but his smile remained. Neither Jack nor Lt. Tull-Martin were smiling. Jack wore the same deadly serious expression I'd seen when he'd gone after Frankie. I would imagine his battle face was aimed at the Germans now. And the lieutenant, the lieutenant had moved slightly—away from Maddy and closer to Jack.

Lt. Tull-Martin was leaving.

I put the photo down. How could that be so? We'd thought he would be a trainer for the duration since he'd already served bravely and been wounded to boot. Part of me hoped I was wrong, that the photograph had simply shifted. Another more selfish part of me, however, believed in what it showed. I had to believe in my one link to Davey.

As usual, before going to bed, I sat down to write my husband.

Dearest Davey,

I miss you so much, sweetheart. Cleo, Maddy, and I attended a wedding this evening—one of Lt. Tull-Martin's airmen. It was a simple affair at the home of the family, and if not for the attendance of so many men in uniform I would say it reminded me of how life used to be before this war. Young couples vowing to love and cherish. But even the perfume of gardenia corsages couldn't fool us for long. The groom has to leave in two days. The war goes on. And so does life.

I was thinking of Maddy. I wished I could tell Davey everything—we'd never had secrets between us. If Davey knew, I'd have at least one more member of the family to help Maddy and me make decisions. But I couldn't do that. Davey had enough to worry him without adding our problems. Maddy and I would have to do the best we could alone.

I believe Lieutenant Tully has been ordered back to active duty as well, probably to England. Maddy is broken-hearted. You know she had her sights on him from the beginning—even before Lyle disappointed her. I think the lieutenant has feelings for Maddy as well. I wish I could think of some comforting words to help her but I find I'm tongue-tied. I've yet to find the right words to comfort myself from your leaving. I promise to do my best.

In your last letter you asked about my health. I am very well. I think the warmer climate has helped me recover. I'm walking without my cane although my leg remains clumsy at times. On the whole I feel very lucky to have made such quick progress. I only wish you could be here to see me—and to hold me in your arms for a real dance rather than the two of us swaying like a Maypole in a bucket of sand.

I think of you each moment—waking or asleep. Take good care.
All my love,
Ruth

As I folded the letter I heard the click of a door latch. I turned to find Maddy standing in the door of her room looking rumpled and red-eyed. I stood and opened my arms and she walked toward me. After a hug, I pushed her hair back and asked, "Are you ready to talk about it?"

She nodded. I took her hand and led her to the couch.

"They're sending him back to the war," she said. She faced me dry-eyed, as though she'd run out of tears hours ago.

I squeezed her hand and chose my words. "He told us he might have to leave. Remember? They have to go, every one of them." I was trying to remind her that we were stuck in the same boat, but she flattened that argument with her next words.

"He said he loves me."

I couldn't help smiling as words spilled out of my heart. "That's wonderful."

She looked at me like I'd laughed in her face. "No. It's terrible."

"But why—"

"You know why. He loves me now because he doesn't know what happened. He doesn't know I'm— He says he won't ask for promises or expect me to wait for him." She pulled her hand away and twisted her fingers together. "I'd wait for him forever but he'll think— What do I do?"

I'd always been a great fan of the truth. But in this tangle of pain and love and war I wasn't absolutely sure the truth would be the best choice. Any man who truly loved a woman should be able to overcome something like what had happened to Maddy. On the other hand, raising another man's child was a lifelong commitment. The evidence of a crime revisited on a daily basis.

Maddy suddenly found her supply of tears. "Why couldn't it have been Tully?" she asked, sounding more miserable than I could remember. "Then I'd be having his baby and we could have a life together . . ."

I wiped at her tears. "The lieutenant would never take advantage of you. He's an honorable man."

She sniffed. "He wouldn't even kiss me. I had to kiss him. He probably thinks I'm cheap rather than honorable." Those words sounded like they'd originated with Maddy's mother at some point in the past.

"Did he tell you he loved you before or after the kiss?"

"After the first but before the second."

"I wouldn't worry about it then."

Maddy stared at me with eyes older than her years. "What should I do, Ruth? I can't let him believe everything's fine— even though I want to. I know how it feels to be thrown over. What if he does come back like he says he will then sees the baby. He'll think I— He'll think he never meant anything to me."

I tended to agree with her but then again, I wasn't in love with a man enough to give him up. I intended to keep mine. Maddy's choice had been taken away, however. As a woman, I wanted to say *Don't tell him. Take love when it's offered. Put the baby up for adoption.* But as a sister, and a woman who would never let anyone take her baby away, I needed to help Maddy find her own peace for the future. Being honest rarely caused regrets.

"If you want to tell him, it's probably best to write him a letter. That way you have time to put the words down logically without emotion spoiling the moment. When is he leaving?"

"Day after tomorrow."

I gave her a hand up and led her to the table where I'd left my supply of paper and pens. "Don't skimp on paper. Tell him what happened and what's in your heart." I hugged her briefly. "Especially what's in your heart."

Maddy looked tired the next morning. Tired but calmer. She went to work, but not before Cleo talked one of her girlfriends from the Red Cross into delivering Maddy's letter to the School of Aviation as an emergency message for Lieutenant Stephen Tull-Martin. That done, Maddy seemed resigned.

I spent part of the day with Nickie waiting in line at the

butcher. By the time Leah Dowland ended her shift, most of the meat would be gone. This way I could help her out and watch Nickie at the same time.

On the bus home people were talking about a new naval offensive in the Pacific—the Battle of the Coral Sea. One woman had a newspaper and we took turns reading the headlines: "Allied Task Force Stops Jap Invasion Fleet. Port Moresby Saved." I felt a guilty stab of relief. I didn't need to clip the articles—there were no Marines involved.

I was already over at the Silers' helping prepare dinner when Maddy and Cleo got home. They pitched in—still wearing their coveralls from work.

Cleo had actually coaxed a smile out of Maddy by pretending to light up a carrot like a cigar when there was a loud banging at the door. We looked at each other. Whoever was banging really meant it. The whole house seemed to shake. We couldn't all fit through the kitchen door at once so by the time we bumped together and shuffled the order, Mr. Siler had opened the front door.

Lt. Tull-Martin stepped inside. I felt Maddy's hand on my arm as she moved behind me. Cleo took the cue and stood next to me. We set our feet like an amazon battering ram and waited.

"I'm sorry to interrupt—" Lt. Tully looked as harried as I'd ever seen him. Instead of his usual polite greetings he looked past us, straight at Maddy and said, "I need to speak to you."

"Now wait a minute," Mr. Siler said. "What's going on?"

Surprisingly, Mrs. Siler moved over to stand with our little immovable group.

I had to wonder exactly what Maddy had said in her letter. But whatever the case, she'd been manhandled once. It would not happen again as long as I had breath in my body. It seemed that the rest of the women in the room felt the same.

The lieutenant rubbed a hand down his face and looked to be doing his best to find control. "Please," he said. Then he looked at Mr. Siler. "I know this is out of bounds, sir. But I've got barely an hour or so and I ship out tomorrow morning. I must speak to Maddy."

Mr. Siler turned to me. "Ruth?"

Before I could answer, Maddy whispered in my ear. "Will you come with us next door?"

I knew she didn't want anyone else to hear, and I'm sure Lt. Tully didn't either. I could go along to referee if necessary. Well, not referee. I had no reason to believe there'd be an argument even though I'd never seen the lieutenant quite so out of sorts.

"Maddy and I will meet you next door. Go to the front, I'll let you in." In those instructions I hoped the lieutenant recognized the order to calm down a little. I didn't want the Silers getting involved.

Lt. Tully nodded stiffly, turned, and walked out the door.

Randy gave a low whistle. "Who rattled his cage?"

Mr. Siler watched the lieutenant leave. "Probably the war, son," he said absently, as though he could understand.

Cleo gave Maddy a supportive hug before the two of us headed out the back. It suddenly occurred to me that we were shirking our cooking duties. I turned to Mrs. Siler. "I'm sorry, we'll be back to help as soon as we can."

"Don't worry. Cleo and I can finish up. Right, Cleo?"

Cleo winked at Maddy and me. "Yes, ma'am. I'm an officer in the Red Cross. I can make a meal out of cardboard and chocolate syrup if I have to."

"Well, tonight you're peeling carrots."

"Is this true?" Lt. Tully held out Maddy's letter.

Maddy and I were seated on the couch, and I had asked the lieutenant to sit in the armchair so he wouldn't be towering over us during this discussion.

"Which part?" I asked. I wasn't completely sure how much of the story she'd told him.

He handed the letter to me. "All of it, but especially the part about—about—" He gave Maddy a miserable look as though he couldn't say it out loud.

"About the—the baby," she said with no emotion in her voice. She stared at her hands. "It's true."

Lt. Tully left his chair and paced across the room, stopping in front of the photograph. After an indrawn breath he snatched it off the radio cabinet and turned to face us. "It seems I've chosen the wrong occupation." He stared down at the faces in the image. "Instead of killing Germans I ought to be staying here to protect the ones I love. Ruth? How could we have let this happen?"

I met him halfway across the room and took the frame out of his hands. "It isn't anyone's fault but Frankie."

Lt. Tully's face changed when I said Frankie's name. I was suddenly very glad I would never have to face the lieutenant in battle. "Now I know why Jack went after him. If I'd known then what I know now there wouldn't have been enough left of him to ship off to war." He seemed to realize he was scaring us. He looked away for a moment, visibly collecting himself. "I couldn't help you then, but I can help you now." He turned and offered Maddy a hand up from the couch. "Go change your clothes, Maddy." His words were gentle, like his old self.

"What?" Maddy said, confused.

"I don't know how, but we're going to find someone to marry us, tonight." His face softened. "I meant what I said yesterday, and I only wish the circumstances could be different—but I won't leave you behind on your own."

Even though she couldn't have been expecting this, Maddy stuck with whatever decision she'd made. In this case, going it alone. With a sad smile, she lifted his hand and kissed his knuckles. "No," she said, simply. "You know we can't get married tonight."

I think I was as surprised as the lieutenant.

"Maddy, don't be foolish. You'll be at the mercy of gossips and the baby—the baby will come into the world as a—" Too polite to speak the naked truth, he faltered. "Unprotected by a father," he said, struggling with the concept. "There's no need for that. I'm more than willing to—"

I watched Maddy's eyes fill with tears and felt my own begin to sting.

"Remember when you said you loved me but you wouldn't hold me to promises?" She sniffed, and in an automatic motion he produced a handkerchief and offered it to her. "Well, I feel the same way about you. You shouldn't be held to promises you weren't ready to make. How could I ever believe you married me out of love? And I want love. I don't want you to feel sorry for me because of what happened then meet someone new and wish you were free."

"I truly love you," he said.

"Then do what you said you would do. Come back to me when the war is over."

"But what if I don't make it back? What will you do then?"

"If you don't come back then it doesn't matter what happens to me. I'll never be happy again."

He threw his arms around her and buried his face in her hair. "Ruth, make her understand. Tell her she should go with me now." When he met my gaze there were tears in his eyes. "Tell her."

I rested a hand on his arm to ease my words. "These past weeks she's had to grow up and be strong. Strong enough to choose what's right for her life. I can't tell her what to do. But don't worry, she won't be alone. I'll be with her every step of the way. We'll get through whatever comes together."

I left them there with their arms around each other and went back to the Silers'. As I helped put dinner on the table I peeked out the window and saw the two of them sitting on the wooden walkway between the houses. It seemed the lieutenant was already guarding Maddy's reputation.

We didn't have the opportunity to watch Lt. Tully march bravely to a ship. We heard his group was transferred by plane to Jacksonville for their departure to England. It had been a little over two months since we'd arrived in Miami, and in what seemed like a moment, the men we cared about were gone. Luckily there was no time to stay miserable—we were too busy. Between scrap metal drives, war bond sales, and plotting around shortages, we developed a network of ways to keep our strength and do our patriotic duty.

As for Maddy, she was in the first stage of our plan to hide her condition. Since the Silers were used to seeing her in the baggy coveralls she wore to work, she took to wearing those most of the time around the house. She wasn't showing yet, but by the time she needed the extra room, there would be little comment or question.

Cleo and I insisted she cut back her Red Cross volunteering but for different reasons. Although Maddy was young and strong, I wanted her to save her strength for the baby. I remembered how much of my strength pregnancy had required—nearly all of it. Cleo's reasons were more practical.

"Some of those old bats have radar when it comes to the young girls volunteering. They watch 'em like hawks just waiting for any sort of impropriety. The diamond dolls don't want the Red Cross name trampled in the mud by a few victory girls, and they'll publicly trounce anyone they suspect."

When Maddy started to say something Cleo stopped her. "I know, you didn't do anything to be ashamed of, but they don't care. You stick to me—we'll be the doughnut Dollys on the weekends. It's easy work and you can hide behind the counter."

Mrs. Siler, with a mother's instinct I suppose, seemed to sense something was up. Maddy had explained away Lt. Tully's visit by saying that he'd felt responsible for her and Ruth since Davey and Jack were gone. I doubt if our landlady bought that bill of goods but at least she stopped asking questions.

We received our first letter from Jack a few days later.

Dear Boarders (Ruth and Maddy),

I'm writing to you to report the severe lack of female companionship in this part of England. The few women I get to see look to be about my mother's age. They are grand at running the command center and we love 'em for that, but they leave something to be desired—something ELSE. And let me tell you, Maddy, the white cliffs of Dover only look good on the return trip. On the way out we have to fly over hundreds of wrecked planes that didn't quite make it home.

I hope you girls are doing gangbusters. I miss our Sundays at the old homestead. Tell that loafer Tully I've learned a thing or two about the German 109s. And I'm still around to talk about it.

I think of home each sunrise and sunset and several times in between. That includes you girls. Please write if you can.

Your friend,
Jack

— MADDY —

Dear Jack,

We were so happy to get your letter. Your mother had read parts of the ones you wrote her but that's not the same as having our very own. Things are downright dismal with our friends gone. We think of you a lot and miss your smiling mug. We also miss Tully. I guess you haven't heard but he's on his way to England to rejoin the war. I swear it nearly did me in.

Did Randy write and tell you about Tully taking us flying? It was fabulous.

As for me, I have a job at the Intercontinental learning to weld airplanes. So rest assured we're doing our patriotic duty down here in the Florida sun to help all the boys come home ASAP. We are healthy and getting tan. Ruth has tossed away her cane and walks with only a slight limp now. By the time Davey gets back she'll be in true form.

I'll add one other bit of news mainly because you're so good at keeping my secrets—to the point of going to jail. Ha. Ha. I understand now why you kept asking me if I was all right after the pier "incident." You knew more than I did. Let's just say that now I have another secret to keep—for as long as I can, anyway.

Jack, I'll never forget your taking care of me. Ruth and I both send our love and prayers. Please be careful and come home soon.

Lv,
Maddy

PS—Jack,

If there's anything you need—please write and let us know. We've gotten quite good at scrounging. As Maddy said, we think of you often. You are in our prayers as well. This world would be sad indeed without your smiling face.

We'll write every chance we get.

Ruth

Chapter
Ten

The world felt like it was picking up speed, spinning faster. There never seemed to be enough time. And time for me had new meaning. It was marked by a slight heaviness in my stomach. My morning sickness seemed to be easing. Either that or we had cured it with crackers. There'd been one awkward moment when I'd thrown up at work. At least I didn't spoil the hallway floor I'd mopped a few moments before I took off running to the bathroom. Cleo saw me and followed. She made lots of noise flushing toilets and banging doors so no one would notice my retching—and they didn't. They probably thought Cleo was drunk or crazy, though.

Before we knew it, it was August. And hot. I remembered Jack's warning that there were times in Florida when the wind seemed to stop and the sun baked everything below. Those days were upon us. I didn't mind the days—I'd become a champ at finding shade. The nights were the worst. Our house with its high ceilings and big windows was open to any breeze. But without one, the rooms held the heat. I would lie awake at night waiting for the air to cool down, but by the time it did, right before dawn, I had to get up for work. Cleo had taken to sleeping on the living room couch since we probably could have baked cookies in her room upstairs—without an oven.

The war was heating up as well. Ruth had started a scrapbook of newspaper clippings about the war in the Pacific. The rest of the paper had to be collected for reuse. We were learning new names like Midway and Guadalcanal. There was no telling which battles Davey might be in so we eagerly read about every one. News from the war in Europe crowded the airwaves. Sometimes our regular radio programs would be delayed up to an hour so the news could be broadcast. A lot of it was bad news, and that left us worrying about Jack and Tully. The British and the Americans were dropping everything they had on the German war machine with seemingly little effect. Rommel, the infamous German commander in North Africa, had attacked the Brits at a place called El Alamein.

Jack wrote home quite a bit—we could tell he was homesick. But his letters lost their flirty humor. They'd made him a B-17 bomber pilot, and I think the responsibility must have taken the laughter out of him.

I'd gotten two letters from Tully. I, of course, was thrilled to get them, but he still sounded stumped by the whole situation. Mostly, he seemed to be worried about my health. So I sent boring letters about the weather and how many planes we'd turned out that week at work. Neither of us even mentioned feelings. I'd gotten friendlier letters from my brother.

"How're you doing this morning?" Ruth asked.

"Good, actually." It had been so long since I'd had any energy in the morning, it was nice to feel almost normal. Especially on a Saturday when I didn't have to work.

"Cleo and I want to talk to you about something." Ruth patted the couch next to her and I sat down. Cleo was in the armchair facing us. Ruth smiled and rested her hand on my slightly rounded belly. "Remember when we told your mother that I *thought* I was expecting?"

"How could I forget?"

"Well, I think it's time I tell her that in fact I *am* expecting." She stopped and stared at me for a minute. "I think I should announce it to the Silers, too."

"What?" I sat up straighter and her hand fell away. "Why?"

"This is part of our camouflage plan. If they think I'm in the family way, they won't be surprised by some of the things that go on around here. We need to have a doctor look at you. I'll make the appointment, the two of us can go together—when they call my name you can go in to see him. Things like that."

"But how can we fool the Silers? I'll be the one getting fatter."

"Yes, I realize that, but I can stuff a little extra material or a towel inside my clothes to look the part. It should work for a while, I think. Most people are too polite to point out figure flaws."

"What better way to hide than in plain sight?" Cleo added. "Just don't let them get a good look at you."

The whole idea made me nervous. Fooling my mother was one thing—she wasn't here to look us in the eye. Fooling the Silers seemed like a pipe dream. I'd already been spotted raiding the mashed potatoes. "Randy points out everything. What if they catch on and throw us out?" I asked, feeling like a cornered criminal.

"If they do, it'll only speed up what must happen anyway."

Outnumbered, I agreed to their plan to announce Ruth's counterfeit condition after Sunday dinner. That left me with a whole Saturday and Saturday night to worry. It already seemed like I'd worried enough for one lifetime. I couldn't even remember how it had felt to have nothing greater on my mind than what movie I wanted to see or whether my mother would make me go to confession for buying yet another pair of shoes.

"Do you think we could take the bus and see an early movie before Cleo has to go to the pier?" I asked. It was a dodge but at least when I sat in the dark I could lose myself in the movie and not dread the next day. Beyond that, the movie theater was air-cooled.

"You know? That's a great idea," Cleo said. "That'll take our minds off our troubles."

By the time we'd borrowed the Silers' paper and were set on seeing *Springtime in the Rockies* with Betty Grable and John Payne, Randy had become part of our enterprise. Since he couldn't take the bus, with Mr. Siler's help we loaded him into Cleo's Ford. We had to tie his wheelchair on the back like a fifth wheel.

"Cleo, you drive like a fighter pilot," Randy commented as we pulled in front of the movie theater. "I swear if any dogs or little old ladies had walked out in front of you, you'd have made wallpaper paste out of 'em."

I'd learned the hard way that teasing was Randy's method of flirting. I was glad to let Cleo duck his observations instead of me for a while. He obviously had a crush on her, even though she was married.

Cleo gave him a devil-may-care grin. "I got us here, didn't I? And ten minutes early."

It took us longer to get the chair untied than it had taken Mr. Siler to attach the darned thing. I left Cleo tangled in rope and rolled the chair around to the door and positioned myself to help Randy from the car.

"Uh-uh."

When I turned both Cleo and Ruth stood there with their hands on their hips. Finally Cleo, looking like a drill sergeant said, "You," meaning me, "out of the way."

"But—"

Ruth shook her head. "We don't need your help."

I understood then, why they didn't want my help. They were babying me and my baby. I nodded and moved out of the way.

Under the watchful eye of the man selling movie tickets in the booth and a few people passing on the sidewalk, Cleo and Ruth each took one of Randy's arms to help him slide into his chair. Things went wrong from the start. Ruth had her back to the chair and Cleo faced it, so when they lifted, they each pulled a different way.

I stood frozen as Cleo stumbled and Randy landed on the arm of the chair instead of the seat. The chair went over and the three of them tumbled to the sidewalk in a pile.

"Help! These women are trying to kill me!" Randy called out and struggled to get untangled.

A few people ran over to help. But our joker, Randy, couldn't keep a straight face. He started laughing, then Ruth and Cleo joined him. They were all laughing so hard they didn't seem able to get up on their own. I sat down on the curb next to the heap.

"Why didn't you help us?" Randy accused me between gasps of air.

"It happened so fast. One minute you were there, the next you were rolling around on the ground with two married women. You ought to be ashamed of yourself."

He winked at me. "I am, can't you tell?"

Somehow I didn't believe he was sincere. With the help of a few concerned strangers (one man acted like he thought we really were trying to kill poor Randy), we rescued Randy from the ground and got him into his chair. The movie didn't turn out to be nearly as funny as our gymnastics seemed to be. We chuckled about our "fall from grace" all the way home then made a pact not to tell Randy's parents.

The next day at Sunday dinner Ruth, Cleo, and I were as skittish as three canaries in a coal mine. Me more than anyone else. Before we sat down to eat, my two roommates spent so much time standing in front of me that I'd gotten used to talking to the backs of their heads. After an uneventful dinner, Ruth's grand announcement—made over coffee—came off without a hitch. Well, almost.

"Why, congratulations, dear," Mrs. Siler said, obviously in favor of the enterprise.

"Thank you," Ruth replied. "Davey will be over the moon when I tell him."

"He doesn't know?"

Ruth lowered her voice. "I didn't want to tell anyone, especially him, until I knew for sure." She patted her padded stomach. "I'm already three months along."

Mrs. Siler tsked. "You should tell him right away. It'll give him more reason to hurry home."

I watched Ruth's expression change briefly, like wind rippling calm water. A second later she regained her smile. "Yes, I plan to. I was wondering if you could recommend a good doctor. I don't want to take any chances."

That's when Randy almost ruined our lovely plan. "Did you hurt yourself when you fell yesterday?"

The look of concern on his face made me want to hug him but I held my breath instead. He could ruin everything.

Ruth looked suitably puzzled. "What do you mean?"

"When we fell down."

Mrs. Siler waded into the conversation. "You fell down? When?"

Randy told an abbreviated version of the story but included the part where they'd all hit the ground. The whole time he kept his worried attention on Ruth.

When it looked like Mrs. Siler was going to demand to examine Randy and Ruth, Ruth cut in.

"I assure you, Mrs. Siler. I'm fine. I actually landed mostly on Randy. You might want to make sure he's okay."

Mrs. Siler unexpectedly turned her frown on me and unfortunately, I jumped. "Maddy, now that Ruth's expecting, you're going to have to watch out for her. She should never have been trying to lift Randy." She looked at her husband. "Charles? I want you to teach Maddy and Cleo how to lift and move Randy the next time they go out. Ruth is not allowed to participate."

It was a good thing she went on without waiting for me to comment because I had nothing to say. Ruth gave me a "don't worry" look. I could see that she was not going to stand for me being taught to lift anything heavier than a broom.

The talk turned to doctors and babies and I stayed out of it. Oh, I listened, but I knew I had to be like the invisible man.

There, but not there. Even though they were discussing my future.

It still didn't feel quite real to me. Yes, in theory I knew there was a baby inside me. Frankie's baby. I could feel the changes in my body but I couldn't envision being a mother. That seemed like something Ruth was more suited for. Oh, I'd played with dolls when I was a girl, but I'd imagined babies as sort of like cute kittens. You brought one home, played with it and fed it, and it grew into a cat that could take care of itself. I hadn't even had much experience at baby-sitting. Jeanne and I had been in charge of her three cousins a couple of times but only for a few hours. And, mostly they'd been so annoying we'd talked about locking them in the basement until their parents came back to get them.

"Well, it's a good thing Maddy has her job at the aircraft factory," Mrs. Siler was saying. "At least you won't have to worry about money."

Ruth smiled at me like she knew what I was thinking. "Yes, Maddy is my mainstay. I'm a lucky woman to have a sister like her."

A good thing Maddy has her job. Ha! I had no idea how long I'd be able to keep it.

It wasn't like no one had noticed me. From the start, most of the women who worked at the plant had counted up and figured out I was the youngest one on the manufacturing line. So they'd taken me under their wing. If they'd known my real age, they'd probably have taken up a collection and sent me home to my mother. Not because the work was too hard. Sure, it was hot and dirty—no place for a lady. But the real danger to a girl like me, young and single, was the men.

The 4-F wolves, Cleo called 'em. These men were classified as unsuitable for military service for a variety of reasons: Too old, too many children to feed, flat-footed, or with a weakness in their heart. The men weren't all wolves, mind you. Many of them said they'd wanted to serve, but since they couldn't, they'd volunteered to help supply the war machine. A fine sentiment. Not unlike my own reasons for working. It didn't hurt that war work paid very well.

But then there were those who saw the war as an opportunity—a chance to be big fish in a little pond. With most of the men gone and so many women taking over the jobs that needed to be done . . .

"When the husbands are away, the cats will play," Cleo said as we walked out of the ladies' room. It was the end of lunch break and most of the women were busy reapplying their makeup and lipstick. Like the airplanes would care.

I was used to hearing a whistle or two when I walked down the line on my way back to my workstation. Or sometimes a "Hey, Winnie!" for Winnie the Welder. A couple of the guys had even learned my name and called hello to me. One morning I found a nosegay of flowers stuck in my welding shield.

"One of those yahoos in electrical," my male welding partner informed me.

I didn't have the heart to throw them away, but I didn't want to act too interested in them either. So I stuffed 'em in my empty coffee cup without water and went to work as they wilted.

Cleo had been wading through men to get to her workstation for months now. She didn't have to tell me it wouldn't do to get to know anyone, especially a man. I was already in a tangle because of the wrong man and I felt like a criminal, like everyone would find out my secret sooner or later. If not for Ruth and Cleo I think I might have thrown in the towel. But with the two of them working so hard to help me, I knew I had to keep my head down and stay unremarkable, for as long as I could.

— RUTH —

Dear Ruth,
I've given it a good deal of thought and for the life of me I can't figure out how you two girls are going to manage down there

alone. I know Davey's military pay will only go so far. Maddy has mentioned having a job but she hasn't told me where or what. I can't tell you how worried I've been about you both. You need proper care and Maddy needs supervision.

I wish you'd reconsider about coming home. Please keep me up to date on how you're feeling and as soon as possible, please let me buy you train tickets. Surely Davey would want you in a safe place.

Love,
Mother Marshall
PS—I'm sending some money to help out by Western Union.

"We write little notes and put them in with each box of bullets," Leah Dowland, Nickie's mother, said. "Or use a marker and write things on the bigger shells, like *Give 'Em Hell Boys* or *Greetings to Hitler*." She laughed. "Some of the girls even put lipstick kisses on the boxes. I don't know if it makes the soldiers feel better, but it does a lot for our morale."

I knew I needed to broach the subject I'd been considering for days now. I'd been waiting for the right time. Mother Marshall's letter was not so off the mark. I had no idea how long we could hide Maddy's pregnancy, but when the jig was up we'd need to make some fast decisions. I intended to keep the old switcheroo going that Cleo and I had devised—Maddy taking my place when it was necessary and me taking hers.

"I was wondering if you'd consider allowing Maddy to take my place looking after Nickie?" There, the words were out of my mouth.

Leah looked at me in surprise. "Are you unhappy with us?"

"No. No. It's not that. It's just that—" I couldn't think of any plausible excuse.

She fumbled through her purse and pulled out her pay slip. "I could give you a little more money—"

"It's not the money." I didn't know how to tell her the reason without *telling* her the reason. And in the long run, Leah belonged to the Silers' church. Better to wait until the cat was out of the bag. "I promise to explain why, but I can't right now." By the time Maddy needed this job there would be no hiding the reason.

Leah looked puzzled but she let it be. "We don't want to lose you. Do we, Nickie?"

"Don't go away, Ruth, we haven't finished the Three Bears yet."

"And I can't give up my job. It's not just the money. I feel like I'm doing something important to help the men who had to go. Our men."

I pulled Nickie closer and gave his stalwart little shoulders a squeeze. "Don't worry, I'm not going anywhere for a good while yet. We'll get to each one of the three bears and the funny farm friends, too." I hoped I was telling the truth. "Besides, you'll love Maddy. When she reads, she acts out all the parts."

That evening, we were a somber group as we readied our table for cards night. The war news was dire, especially from the Pacific. The reports of a tremendous naval battle at a place called Midway gave me nightmares. Even though I could be reasonably sure Davey wasn't involved, there were enough other hot spots to make me nervous about my daily examination of the photograph.

In the newspapers the roll call had begun: Two Miami Men Missing over France. Miami Navy Officer Reported Jap Prisoner. Corporal Prisoner in Nazi Camp. Miami Airman Killed in Raid. Beach Youth Dies in Action.

To top it off, every song on the most popular radio station seemed to be a "sentimental favorite," like "Green Eyes" and "I'll Never Smile Again." Luckily, we had Randy to cheer us up.

"Come on, deal them shingles. I swear you girls are slower than granny's molasses."

Cleo, the dealer, pinned him with a stern look. "You know it's a short roll out to the river. How would you like to go for a swim with Old Joe?"

Randy laughed. "Hey, you girls are the ones who should be doing the swimming. The three of you look a little heftier since you moved in. My mother's cooking isn't THAT good."

Without losing her card count or even glancing in Maddy's direction, Cleo explained, "Well, Ruth's eating extra for the baby." Then she smiled at Maddy. "Maddy and I are eating extra for Ruth. You got a problem with that?"

He raised his hands in self-defense. "Okay, okay."

As everyone picked up their cards, Cleo gave one last jab. "And if we catch you cheating again, I'll tell your mother what you said about her cooking."

Case closed. Randy rolled his eyes and we laughed.

Dear Mother Marshall,

Thank you so much for sending the extra money. I assure you we've put it to good use. I have an appointment with the doctor to-morrow and will let you know everything he tells me.

I've been feeling very well except for a bit of morning sickness. I don't want you to worry.

Maddy says hello and that she's doing her best to make you proud of her.

I'll write again soon.

With love,

Ruth

Maddy and I took the bus to see a Doctor Perkins the next Monday. Maddy had to beg a day off from work, but I brought Nickie along with us since I wouldn't be the one in the examining room. I could have taken her to the naval hospital since she was using my name and my husband was in the Marines. But somehow I felt that would be disrespectful to every man in uniform, especially Davey. It would make him an unknowing partner in our deception. So we went to the doctor Mrs. Siler had recommended. His office was in a portion of his home.

Maddy was red-faced and quiet when the doctor escorted her back to the small waiting room in the hallway.

"She's doing fine, Mrs.—"

Since Maddy had used my name, Marshall, I went back to my maiden name. "Mrs. Thornton," I answered as I shook his hand. "I'm Maddy's sister."

He smiled at Maddy and patted her shoulder. "Your sister is young but she's fine. She needs to drink her milk, eat her spinach, and take it easy. That baby is already strong."

"Where's the baby?" Nickie said.

Dr. Perkins smiled and stooped down. He rested his hand on Maddy's stomach. "Right in here," he said to Nickie. "That's where you came from, your Mommy's stomach."

Nickie frowned and for a moment I thought he would argue. But then he put his hand next to the doctor's. "Helloooo, baby," he yoo-hooed like someone calling down a mountain. Then he petted Maddy's stomach like he was stroking a cat or a dog.

Even Maddy smiled.

Dr. Perkins stood up. "Come back to see me in a couple of months, Mrs. Marshall. Sooner if you have any problems."

"Thank you so much, Doctor." I shook his hand.

Maddy looked worried again. The doctor turned to her. "Don't be concerned. I know it's fearful to face this without a husband to help, but women were made to have babies. And first babies usually have a mind of their own. You'll do fine."

Dear Davey,

I'm missing you more than ever tonight. I don't know, something is in the air. Not just the war, although that is certainly on my mind. I guess it's wanting to feel like a wife again, in my own home, with the man I love. This bachelorette existence doesn't suit me in the least.

It had been bittersweet to hear the doctor talk to Maddy about her baby but use my name. Hearing that her baby was strong and she'd do fine was wonderful, but it also brought back the words of the doctors who'd tried unsuccessfully to save my babies.

Beyond that, I was feeling so strong—fully recovered from my long illness—that my heart ached to try again. If Davey had been within a thousand miles of me, I would have found a way to get to him.

Right now I'm thinking that it took the Marines to get you far enough away to keep you safe from me. If you were here I'm afraid you'd be my captive. And there would be no thought of being "careful."

I hope I haven't shocked you. As I sit here and read this letter I can feel my face warming. Know that these words are only for you, my love. I haven't the least interest in any other. My heart is yours.

Come back to me, Davey—by hook or by crook—and I promise you won't regret it.

All my love,
Ruth

Chapter Eleven

— RUTH —

My Dearest Ruth,

Well I suppose you've been wondering where I ended up. All I can say is, I don't think I'm "there" yet. Wherever "there" happens to be. Either our destination keeps changing or we're trying to confuse the Japs. That confusion tactic has certainly worked on us "Jireens." So far we're like a bunch of sardines in a can—salty and glassy eyed—waiting for somebody to let us out of here. Aboard ship a lot of us sleep on deck cause it's cooler and cause we're only allowed a short shower every other day. I know things will most likely go from bad to worse but I have to tell you the breeze from belowdecks smells pretty rank.

I've been dreaming of a soft bed, clean sheets, a floor that doesn't rock and, of course, my darling wife. It seems like years since we had our own little place to call home. You're such a great wife— I'm such a lucky man. I've shown your picture and recommended marriage to these dopes who don't think they want to be tied down. I'd be the luckiest and happiest man to be back home, tied to you with an anchor chain. Your captive so to speak. I can't think of a better jailer.

Tell Mads hello and that I got her last letter. (We get mail pretty regular—twice a week.) I'll write to her soon. Right now, thanks to your letter the only thing I can think of is you.

Your grateful but smelly husband,

Davey

Maddy, Cleo, and I had just gotten home and were busy reading our treasure trove of mail when I heard Maddy say, "Oh, no." I had been smiling because of Davey's letter, but the look on Maddy's face made my heart skip a beat. *Bad news.* Rather than tell me what was wrong, she handed me the letter.

"It's from Jack."

Dear Maddy,

I've hooked up with Tully over here and a more hang-dog Englishman I've yet to see. You'd think he'd left his sweetheart behind in the USA or somethin. Ha. Ha. Both of us have been put in bombers although we'll rarely see each other. The Brits fly at night and the rest of us "Yanks" go off at sunrise.

I guess there's no point beating around the bush. Tully told me that you shared your secret with him. He nearly knocked me to the ground for not letting him in on it when he could have done some good. As a matter of fact, I think that's why he came to see me first thing when he got back home. To sock me in the jaw. He's been torturing himself over your welfare and wanted my advice on how to help. I have to say I'm worried about you myself.

So I hope you can forgive me for breaking a promise. I've written my mother and explained your situation—with one change. I told her that you're expecting MY baby. That way, no matter what happens to Tully and me, you'll be taken care of.

Be my girl, just till the war is over. I promise (there's that word again) that we'll straighten everything out then.

Ever your friend,

Jack

I stared at the paper not believing what I'd read. What was the military term I'd seen in the paper? FUBAR. Fouled Up Beyond Repair? *Oh, no* was right.

"What are we going to do now?" Maddy looked like she was beginning to panic.

I felt like wringing Jack's neck. Wasn't it so like a man to decide on something and then drop it on our heads without any discussion?

A loud banging on the back door made both Maddy and I jump. "Ruth? Maddy?" It was Mrs. Siler.

"Go up to Cleo's room and tell her what's happened. Stay up there until I call you."

"Just a minute!" I called as I shuffled Maddy toward the stairs. I waited for her to disappear upward then counted to three. I had no idea how to deal with this surprise but I was determined to appear calm. I lost my determination when I saw that Mrs. Siler had a letter in her hand.

Oh, Jack. What have you done?

"Come in," I managed and swung the screen door outward.

Mrs. Siler marched inside looking more upset than I think I'd ever seen her. The letter she was holding had to be from Jack. She stared past me, searching for Maddy I assumed, then she waved the paper at me demanding my attention.

She needn't have worried. She'd had my complete attention since she'd banged on the door. And, at the moment, she was staring at my midsection—enough to make any spinner of pregnancy lies nervous. "So both of you are pregnant?" she asked.

I drew in a slow breath, then reached for Mrs. Siler's arm. "Come, sit down," I said in my most soothing tone. Both of us needed to be calmer before I brought Maddy into the discussion.

Mrs. Siler let me guide her to the sofa but remained standing. She shook the letter again. "Well? I demand an answer. I knew it was a mistake to have women in this house," she snapped.

I felt the flutter of our carefully guarded reputation as it flew out the window. When I merely watched her and waited instead of rising to the bait, she sat.

I took the chair at the end of the sofa. "May I see that letter?" I asked. I was purposely avoiding her question until I felt settled enough to address it. She shoved the paper in my direction.

Dear Mother,

Of course I recognized Jack's handwriting.

I'm writing this letter addressed only to you since I have some-thing I need your help with. Being a woman, I'm sure you'll know how to handle a delicate situation and handle Dad and Randy as well.

I'm afraid I've done something I sincerely regret but cannot change. It concerns our little boarder, Maddy. She's written me with some distressing news and I'm too far away to help her. She's going to have a baby—and the baby is mine.

Please try to forgive me. You've told me many times that my charm and love for the girls would get me in trouble. Well, I've gone and done it this time. It wasn't in any way Maddy's fault. She's a sweet kid. Heck, if it hadn't been for this war, I'm sure the whole thing wouldn't have happened.

I know you don't approve of this kind of behavior. But, as a favor to me, your loving son, I ask that you take care of Maddy in any way necessary. She doesn't want to go back North in her con-dition as her mother might reject her. If something should happen to me, please consider her your daughter and protect her.

I'm sorry to have to deliver such upsetting news. I know you've always expected the best of me. I hope I can make you proud.

Love,

Jackie

"Well? Exactly what has been going on over here?"

At least Jack had done his best to protect Maddy from blame. But Mrs. Siler didn't seem inclined to be charitable.

"I'm afraid I don't know what you mean," I said. "My hus-band and I—"

"I'm talking about your sister."

I heard a sound behind me. Maddy, walking arm and arm with Cleo, approached the couch. "Mrs. Siler, I—"

"Before you say anything," I warned Maddy, "you need to read Jack's letter." I handed her the paper. As she read, her eyes filled up with tears.

"Oh, Jack," she whispered.

I wasn't sure if the tears were for our ruse being discovered or because Jack had done everything he could to protect her. Cleo clamped an arm around Maddy's shoulders as she handed the letter back.

"Jack is such a great guy," Maddy said.

"I've been aware of that for quite a while," Mrs. Siler said. "He's also a soft touch when it comes to women." Her eyes narrowed. "How can we be sure this baby belongs to him? What about that lieutenant?"

Maddy sucked in a breath like she'd been slapped. Of course it wasn't Jack's baby, or Tully's, but now Maddy would be forced to defend another lie. Our web of deception was tightening like a noose around our already stretched necks. Maddy gazed at me as a new rush of tears rolled down her cheeks.

I was suddenly on my feet facing Mrs. Siler. "You will not speak to Maddy in any accusatory fashion. You can believe your son, or not. That's your business. But Maddy is a good girl. I'm sure you're upset, angry even, but I've lost two children to miscarriages and I will not allow you to endanger Maddy or her baby with some kind of cruel cross-examination."

Mrs. Siler raised one hand to her throat in what looked like shock. "Why, I would never mean to do her any harm . . ." Her own eyes filled with tears. "It's just that Jackie— I so hoped that Jackie would settle down and marry a local girl . . ." As she dug in her pocket for a hanky, Maddy left Cleo's protection and went to her. Then something happened I thought I'd never see—Maddy and Mrs. Siler hugging and crying.

I let them cry. I'd made my stand and had to stick to it. Mrs. Siler could throw us in the street if she wanted. I didn't care.

Cleo came over and gave me a quick hug of support. "See, and everyone thinks you're milquetoast." She lowered her voice. "I'd be willing to bet your husband has seen that tiger who lives in your heart, though." She winked. "At least I hope he has."

It wasn't fair for Cleo to make me smile at such a moment, but she did and it lightened my heart. We'd be okay—as the soldiers say—come hell or high water.

After everyone got their emotions under control, I continued on where I'd left off. "The truth is, Mrs. Siler, I'm not expecting. I was . . . pretending . . . to take some of the spotlight off Maddy."

Mrs. Siler nodded as though she understood that roundabout logic. I wondered then if she'd had any sisters.

I kept rolling. "And if you don't mind, we'd like to keep Maddy's condition a secret for as long as we can. I'm sure you agree. She needs to keep her job and we don't want to cause your family any problems with gossip." As our landlady, she'd warned us when we moved in that her community standing was more important than our presence in her family home.

"I certainly agree," Mrs. Siler said. "The way people talk will only be upsetting. I'll help any way I can." She looked at Maddy. "I realize Jack should be here to bear the responsibility of what the two of you have done. But since he isn't, his family will have to stand in."

Maddy gave me one miserable glance then nodded to Mrs. Siler. "Thank you."

Mrs. Siler fixed her gaze on Maddy's stomach. "When will it—"

"The doctor said sometime in February," Maddy answered.

"February . . . well, then, we have something to look forward to."

— MADDY —

Everything changed from that day forward. Mrs. Siler treated me, if not like a long-lost daughter, then at least as someone else's long-lost daughter who happened to meet her beloved son once. I know it was hard for her because it was even harder for me. Jack had been wonderful about wanting to take care of me, but living an even bigger lie—one that others pinned their hopes on—hurt me like a constant toothache.

Each special thing Mrs. Siler cooked for me and every concerned look she gave when I wasn't hungry or if I got too tired weighed on my conscience. What would happen when the truth came out? Life had gotten so complicated, between the war and my condition, that I couldn't keep up. My body seemed to be taking over my brain anyway. I did what Ruth and Mrs. Siler asked me to do and gratefully stopped thinking. My main job was to write letters. Or to read them and cry . . .

Dearest Maddy,

I know I've been a bit distant since I left. In my defense I must say that I was overwhelmed by the enormity of your situation and my inability to help. I wanted to help. Your refusal to marry me hurt more than expected. But I understand and believe I've passed that painful point now.

I miss you dreadfully and have done so each day and each hour of the day since I left you. Even as I lie down to sleep I hope for dreams of your sweet face. I know this sounds like so much bunk but I have to say what I feel—now while I can at least put it down on paper. I'd much rather say it to your face. And there would be the matter of kissing you—at the bare minimum of once between each word.

I don't want to sound too maudlin but things are becoming rather rough here. Enough so that I cannot make any plans for the future even on paper. I do, however, want you to know that if the worst happens, you are the only one I will hold in my mind and heart as I face my destiny. My last thought will be of you.

I hope I haven't made you cry once again. I didn't mean to. Forgive me.

With all my heart,

Tully

I swear, it was almost too much to stand. Watching movies of lovers tragically parted had always seemed so romantic. Now that I knew what separation truly meant and how it turned your heart inside out, I'd lost any interest in seeing the cinema version.

I walked across the room and picked up the photograph. Tully looked so handsome, and happy. I brought the photo closer and stared at his face. There was something about his eyes, they looked a little sad. Maybe that's what had tripped me up and made me fall in love with him. I don't think I could ever get tired of looking into those eyes. I studied his face, his uniform, then I noticed something I hadn't seen before. I'd barely known him the night the photo had been taken. He'd been standing behind me but his hand rested on the back of my chair, and it looked like one side of it barely touched my shoulder. I hadn't noticed at the time. Now the sight made my heart go mushy. That ugly Frankie may have thrown his arm around me, but Tully had been there, standing behind me.

I stared at the image for several minutes, wondering how to make it show me what Ruth said she could see. The present or the future—anything about Tully. But nothing changed, no one disappeared or stopped smiling. Tully's hand remained steady and I looked like I owned the world.

Standing there, three and a half months later, I felt like I'd been put through the ringer and hung out to dry. I missed Tully, and Jack and Davey. And, hard as it was to admit, I missed my mother. Not that she could save me. No, I'd dug my own pit and couldn't ask to be excused. I guess I wanted her to do what she'd done in the past—make me a glass of warm milk, pat me on the cheek or shoulder, and tell me that things would work out. Somehow she'd *order* them to work out.

I couldn't imagine what she'd make of my problem. *Oh, Momma what a mess I've made of things this time. If it hadn't been for Ruth and Cleo I'd probably be in the asylum or on the streets or in the ocean swimming for England.*

I kissed the cool glass covering Tully's face then replaced the photo on the cabinet. If I couldn't change my own situation, I could do my best to help his.

Dearest Tully,

I'm mad at you. All this talk about destiny has got to stop. As the doctor treating your funny bone I prescribe that you finish this inconvenient war and get back here to Florida—"on the double" as the Army officers say. You'll donate your uniform to the infirm, buy an Indian grass hat, and sit on the beach next to me to watch the tide roll in and out—for approximately forty years. During this convalescence, you will have the opportunity to kiss me at your whim, morning, noon, or night. And I will require same.

Seriously, my dear, I believe the Germans don't have a chance with both you and Jack at 'em. I think of you constantly and ask the angels to watch over my very favorite fly-boy. I know you have a job to do, but please take care. Don't rush into any destiny without a care. I care enough for us both.

Love,
Maddy

Dear Maddy,

It's been almost two weeks since I've heard from you. That is unacceptable. You promised to keep me informed of Ruth's progress in her pregnancy and I insist that you write more often. I'm sure you can't imagine how "left behind" I feel but I assure you it's not pleasant. I think I should have named my new kitten Worry since he and my imagination are my only companions.

Ruth should be nearly four months along by now. Is she resting well? Are there any rationed items she needs? I could send them from my stamps.

Maddy, I'm depending on you. Please don't disappoint me. Ruth's health is very important—a life-or-death issue. Davey would never forgive either of us if anything happened because we were careless with her needs.

Write soon. I insist.

Mother

A life or death issue. My mother's not-so-casual reminder made my heart flutter. I'd been wholeheartedly thinking about the men we knew and loved—whether they might be killed in some foreign battle and leave us forever. I'd put Ruth's "death" from losing her baby out of my mind.

I could die.

I waited a moment, for the fear to overtake me. But by two minutes, nothing had changed, really. Whereas my mother's imagination produced thousands of tragedies, mine seemed stuck in limbo. My mind couldn't look past tomorrow or next week much less proceed to sometime in February when I would hold a baby in my arms. My baby.

Dear Mother,

Please forgive me for not writing more often. I'm afraid I've been sidetracked by war volunteering and letters to our brave fighting men. I guess I was thinking that no news is good news. But now I see that you need to know the good news and the bad so, here goes.

Ruth is doing very well. The doctor instructed her to drink milk and eat her spinach. He says women were made to have babies and she should do fine. I'll ask him any question you like the next time we go. Just write and tell me.

The whole Siler family has taken us in like we're their daughters. You don't have to worry about Ruth being underfed. Mrs. Siler guards our ration stamps and makes very healthy meals. Ruth has even written down some of the recipes so we can share them later.

Your new kitty sounds like a real pal. I can't wait to meet him when we get back. Speaking of pals—Ha Ha—have you heard anything from Jeanne and Sharon? I know I'm mad at them, but I get a little homesick sometimes and wonder what they're up to.

Well, that's it for now. Other than it's HOT here. We can hardly stand to wear clothes. (I'm joking, Mother.) Back in the middle of winter I thought it could never get too hot for my liking. Well, I've been proven wrong again.

I promise to write oftener, and oftener.

I miss you.

Love,

Maddy

As I folded the pages and slipped them into the envelope I had to wonder how my mother would take my changed attitude, telling her I was homesick and that I missed her. I hoped it would please her and not give her a heart attack or something. I wanted her to know I was different, that I'd learned a couple of things anyway. Because I knew I was about to learn a lot more.

* * *

Dear Sweet Maddy,

What in heaven's name is a "funny bone"? And are you quite sure Englishmen have them? If so, I would be most happy to have you attend to my wounded sense of humor. I've left my walking stick behind and as soon as we take care of this disturbance, I promise to be at your disposal for any further treatment you deem appropriate.

What a pleasure your letters are. I cannot tell you how much they brighten my day. Please keep up the good work.

Remember when I told you the best place for me was away from home? Well, I have received new orders and will be leaving shortly. I cannot explain where or how but it's another continent— one whose weather resembles Florida without the greenery. Oh, I wish I were coming west. There will be no ice cream or movies there. Even so, it's sure to remind me of you as everything else does. I'm so thankful you are in a safe place—that knowledge allows me to carry on. Please let Jack know I've gone, as I doubt I'll have the chance to see him before we debark.

You are ever in my thoughts. I will always be glad I met you.

Yours with a smile,

Tully

If America hadn't been invaded by an enemy yet, the war had certainly invaded every facet of our lives. In a way it helped me take my mind off myself and my problems. I was too busy. Two weeks before, I'd had to bow out of official Red Cross doughnut duty. My old skirts were too tight and I couldn't wear my factory coveralls to any social function.

"How can you stand to wear those heavy coveralls all the time?" Randy asked, one afternoon as we were sitting on the Silers' front porch, tying bundles of scrap newspaper we'd collected around the neighborhood. He and I had become a team. I'd push his wheelchair from house to house, the neighbors would stack their daily papers in his lap, then I'd wheel him back home.

"They're comfortable," I said, automatically, and hunched forward a bit. I was used to dodging Randy's eagle eyes.

As I pulled the string tight around a bundle of old *Miami Herald*s the two-inch-high headline on a front page trapped my attention.

U.S. MARINES INVADE AT GUADALCANAL

A shiver of fear went through me. Davey. My brother had always been the happiest person I knew, even when things were bad like when Ruth was sick. Davey seemed determined to find a good side to everything, including his headstrong little sister. I couldn't imagine how he'd find any good side to war. The paper was a few days old. The photo under the headline was grainy and faces were hard to distinguish, but it had been taken on a beach—far away from the one where we'd dug sand castles. An unnamed beach on Guadalcanal, halfway across the world, cluttered with blasted palm trees, broken equipment, and bodies.

U.S. MARINES

I let the string go and piled another layer of paper on top to hide the proof that men were dying. Men like my darling brother. Men like Frankie, the father of my baby. But as fast as I recoiled from that thought another alarming one took its place. The baby inside me. I hadn't been seriously thinking about the future. About the young woman or man this baby would become. The *soldier* it might become. I hugged my hands across my belly, leaned forward, and began to silently pray.

Please God, let this baby be a girl. Please don't punish me by giving me a son who has to go to war someday. Please God, I promise to—

"Are you okay?" Randy asked.

When I opened my eyes, he was staring down at me in concern.

"Mom?" he called out.

In three heartbeats, Mrs. Siler was at the door.

"Maddy looks sick," Randy added.

Then Mrs. Siler was there bending over me.

"No, really. I'm all right." I did my best to act normal since with Randy my secret was still in the bag.

"You look a little pale." Mrs. Siler offered her hands to pull me up from the porch. "Come in and lie down for a few minutes. It's probably the heat."

Mrs. Siler led me into the house, but instead of settling me on the couch in the living room, she took me into her own bedroom.

"It's cooler in here," she said as she helped me take my shoes off and lie down. She left the room for a moment and I heard water running, then she pulled a chair up close to the bed. "This should help." She placed a damp cloth on my forehead and it felt so wonderful that I stopped arguing.

"You know, both my boys were wonderful babies. They were happy and rambunctious." She smiled a smile I'd never seen before, one that made her look years younger. "And as they got older, they were fast friends. None of that sibling fighting people talk about. They didn't even beg for separate rooms, happy enough having each other to talk to." The smile changed, the loving light going out of it. "And then, when we almost lost Randy, our whole family was fearful. No—terrified. Jack most of all.

"I've given it some thought and I believe that's why Jackie hasn't been able to settle down. He's afraid to love someone else because he might lose them." She sighed. "He worries me so because he's not afraid of risking himself. He'd rather be the one to die a hero than lose those he loves." She stopped speaking for a while. Then she seemed to shake off the dark conversation.

"May I?" She moved her hand toward my belly.

I nodded and she rested her palm over a baby she thought was her son's. "I've decided this baby is a blessing in disguise. Do you know why?"

I was fairly afraid to ask so I shook my head.

"Because, like it or not, now Jack has someone else in his life to love. Someone who needs him." The happiness returned to her smile. "Jack will be a wonderful father."

My conscience flattened me like a locomotive at full throttle. I felt sunk—up to my neck and squirming in the quicksand of my lies. And I couldn't take it one more moment. Mrs. Siler deserved better, Jack deserved better. How could I start a new life feeling like a complete and total fraud?

I put my hand over hers and did my best to fight the tears I could feel on the horizon. I had to just say it and get it over with. "Mrs. Siler, this baby isn't—"

"Oh, dear—now I can see I've upset you talking about Jack and the war. No more talking," she decreed in her familiar drill-sergeant manner. In a businesslike motion she refolded the damp cloth to a cool section and replaced it on my forehead.

I was getting desperate. She was going to leave the room before my courage overcame my fear. "But you have to listen to me."

She frowned. "No. This is my house. You have to listen to *me*, young lady. Close your eyes and rest. That's an order." She put the chair back against the wall. "And from now on, either Charles or I will go with you on the paper drive. One of us will do the wheelchair pushing."

A moment later, she was gone.

— RUTH —

"Ruth, please help me tell Mrs. Siler the truth. I know it's keeping her from throwing us out but I don't think I can stand it. I'd rather find another place to live. Maybe I should even go back to Radley."

Now I knew this had to be serious, for Maddy to volunteer to face her mother under the circumstances. I didn't know what would be best. Although, some fateful sense inside me didn't want to upset the applecart. An upheaval now—and I was sure there would be one—might harm the baby or Maddy, or both.

"You know Jack is the one who started this. Technically, he's the one who lied . . ." It was a dodge and I knew it, and Maddy sidestepped the easy excuse.

"But he doesn't understand what it's done to his mother. She'll be heartbroken, not to mention mad as a wet hen, when I tell her the truth."

As she should be.

"I don't know the answer," I said. I honestly didn't. The more we tried to plan, the more things seemed to take on a life of their own. At this point I was willing to wait for more information before making another rash decision. "I have the feeling we should let it be for a little longer. Another month won't matter any more or less when the truth comes out."

Out of habit, when I had questions, I walked over to the photograph. As I stared into the familiar faces, reflections of light from the window sparkled on the glass. The image flickered for a moment, like an old silent movie—images moving and changing. When it settled, one more man was missing—a sailor, this time. Everyone else seemed more rumpled. Uniforms were missing insignias, jackets were torn or gone altogether. Jack, our mischievous benefactor, looked like he'd been to a weeklong party without sleep. A party he hadn't enjoyed.

And Davey . . . I must have gasped because Maddy rushed over to stand beside me.

"It's okay," I said quickly. But my heart had taken a hard jolt. "It's dirt," I said aloud although she couldn't know what I meant. *Dirt, not blood.* "He's just so dirty. He looks like he hasn't shaved in a month. I don't know how they can tell who is who without making them take a bath first." I tried to keep my tone light for Maddy's sake. But I'd been poring over each newspaper photo I could find of Marines anywhere in the Pacific. I studied every one before I pasted it into my scrapbook—looking for Davey among those dirty faces. But . . . it was impossible to tell. It made me want to cry because I should've been able to tell. So far the only place I'd been able to find my husband was in the photograph I held in my hands.

"Everyone's fine," I said. A sad lie. Somewhere a sailor's family would be getting a telegram and hanging a gold star in their window.

"Tully?"

I concentrated on the lieutenant's face. His eyes seemed the same. They'd always had a serious look about them. But he appeared gaunt, as though he wasn't eating or sleeping properly.

"He's lost weight. You need to tell him to take better care of himself. He'll need his strength." I stopped in surprise. I had no idea why I'd said that—except that every one of them would need strength to survive this war. "Tell him to eat more—he's too thin," I finished lamely, then put the photograph back on the cabinet.

Sept. 5, 1942

Dearest Ruth,

Darling, time is short but I wanted to drop you a line in case it's awhile before I get another chance to write. Well, we're in it good. You know I can't say where or when but let's just say I've met the enemy and he's as tough as they come. But us Marines are tougher—you'll see.

Please try not to worry. Tell everyone back home not to forget us. We're already having to ration due to shortages. If there's anything we don't want to be rationed it's bullets. We can't talk 'em to death.

I love you, wife. I'm doing my best to stay alive. Keep writing— the mail gets to us sooner or later—sometimes in one wonderful pile. What a Christmas party that is.

Your lonely husband,

Davey

Another month went by. Thankfully the weather slowly began to cool—the nights anyway. As the Allies celebrated their first major victories in the Pacific, the roll call continued: Miami Marine Cited in Pacific Heroism, Florida Flyers Get Medals, Miami Beach Boy Missing in Pacific, Plane Crash Fatal to Miamian, Miami Sergeant Dies in Action, Miami Doctor Prisoner of Japs.

Maddy and I kept our secrets. We went to church on Sundays—Maddy wearing a borrowed suit with a jacket she could hold in front of her—worked during the week, and made plans to swap occupations. Moving forward seemed our one alternative. There was no sure bet that Intercontinental would go along with our switcheroo, but even if they didn't, Cleo had brought home a paper announcing free courses offered to war workers in aircraft sheet metal, aircraft mechanics, industrial electrical control, and hydraulics. Applicants had to promise to work a minimum of eight weeks.

I was determined to do my part—to support us and the war.

"I guess it's time," I said to Maddy. She'd been called into the office at the end of the day because one of her female coworkers had, in effect, "ratted her out" about looking pregnant. "Do you think you can teach me welding?"

"Sure." Maddy waved my doubt away with one hand. "It's easy once you get the hang of things. Nothing pretty about it though, just hot and dirty. The pretty part is when they double-check the welds and give you a thumbs-up before moving on down the line. That and the paycheck, of course."

I touched her shoulder. "Will you miss it much?"

"Nah," she said, resting a hand on her stomach. "I think the baby is getting jumpy. I can feel it moving even when I'm not. And I suppose I should learn how to stay home and take care of children. Since I'll have one of my own." She sounded so sensible and grown-up I was surprised into silence. I knew she loved her job. Being a mother would be the first step into the great unknown. The old Maddy might have argued until the cows came home in order to do what she wanted to do.

"Ruth? What in the world am I going to do with a baby?" she asked, sounding more like her old self.

"I guess that depends on what you want to do," I said, carefully. We seemed to be constantly overtaken by one thing or another, I'd been hesitant to mention alternatives. The baby could be sent to one of the churches or orphanages to be adopted. But another possibility had been growing in my mind. I'd have to discuss it with Davey of course, but . . .

"I can't figure how I'll be able to work and take care of the baby at the same time." She looked at me with dread in her eyes. "And I know I said it, but I can't imagine going home to Mother. She'd hate me *and* the baby like poison for all the lies I've told."

Maddy had become a child again, right in front of me. It didn't seem the time to go into the many social barriers and pitfalls her predicament presented. I decided to address the immediate—her mother—and leave the rest of the world for another time. She'd have to face them sooner or later. I sat next to her. "Maddy, mothers don't hate their children for making mistakes. As a matter of fact, I'm not sure any mother can hate their own child for whatever reason."

Or their own grandchild.

Or one they *thought* was their grandchild—like Mrs. Siler. When Monday morning rolled around, Mrs. Siler—our chin-up champion—had made her way to the bus stop. She'd volunteered to watch Nickie for two weeks while Maddy, Cleo, and I went off to Intercontinental Aircraft.

This part of the "man's" world seemed like an unfriendly place. The rumors of Maddy's "condition" had obviously spread through the workers. Not only did the women stare at her or ignore her, the men did the same.

"I used to be aces around here," Maddy said as we sat down at a table in the lunchroom. She glanced around at the other tables. "But now they act like I've got scarlet fever or the bubonic plague."

My superstitious nature flared up. "Don't even joke about such a thing." In that moment I realized what a good thing it was that Maddy was leaving a job where she came in contact with so many people from different areas of the city. Catching some kind of sickness could put her and the baby in grave danger. If it came down to it, better me than her.

As it turned out, the welding supervisor at Intercontinental was glad to have me take her place on the welding line, especially since Maddy could train me herself and save him some time and effort.

Dearest Davey,

You're not going to believe this, but I'm training to become a welder. I'm working at the aircraft factory welding the wings of B-17s. I come home grimy but I have no reason to worry about my appearance with you so far away. Right now I wear coveralls and a scarf to protect my hair. But I promise to be in a new dress with a perfect hairdo and polished nails when you see me again.

It's thrilling to think that I may be working on an airplane that might bring supplies to you and help end the war sooner. And, on a mercenary note, the money is very good—$60 a week for my job. That means you don't have to worry about us. I can take care of Maddy and me, pay off the last of the doctor bills, and save some money for when you get home.

I hope you'll be happy with this news since I'm over the moon. My health has never been better.

I'll write again tonight.

Love you always,

Ruth

Chapter Twelve

— MADDY —

"Officer shoots skunk caught in trap, after claiming it was none of his business," Mr. Siler read from the newspaper.

"Peee-uuwww," Randy said, dramatically holding his nose.

Mr. Siler smiled. "And two sailors have been jailed after *borrowing* a city fire truck and smashing it into a pole."

It was his habit to read us anything amusing he found in the local papers. He declared there was enough bad news collected for the evening radio broadcasts—we didn't need any extra helpings. I tended to agree. I'd begun to notice that when I got scared or upset, the baby seemed restless, as though it could read my mind. Both of us were more comfortable when calm. I still felt horrid about going along with Jack's clever stunt to fool Mrs. Siler about the baby, but I'd stuffed my conscience in a box of "worries for later." The bunch of us were skating along well with each other, and following the blue-ribbon insanity of the previous months I was glad for the opportunity to coast.

It was a little less than a week before Halloween, Friday night, following Ruth's first successful week as a solo welder and my first successful engagement of imitating a baby-sitter (not being much of a disciplinarian, Nickie and I got along more like brother and sister) when we toasted our triumphs after dinner at the Silers'. Mrs. Siler had finagled enough sugar and cocoa and had traded a bushel of coconuts for a few extra tins of milk to make chocolate pudding. Cleo had reason to celebrate as well. It looked like she was happy living at the Samuel place and wasn't going anywhere soon. She'd had two men take the tires off her car and put it up on blocks for the duration. Then she'd donated the tires to the Red Cross.

Laughing like it was New Year's Eve, we clinked pudding cups rather than champagne glasses. The only things missing were the silly hats and noisemakers.

After a pleasant dinner, and a particularly funny episode of *The Burns and Allen Show*, Cleo, Ruth, and I were laughing as we returned to the Samuel house. It had become a habit for the three of us to spend an hour or so at the dining room table writing letters before hitting the sack. That way we could share paper and pens and Cleo could drop the letters in the box on the way to work. Tonight I *needed* to write some letters, especially to Mother. But I also wanted to remember a few of the hilarious lines from the radio show to continue my doctoring of Tully's funny bone.

Cleo switched on the overhead light and collected our penmanship supplies before sitting down next to me at the table. Ruth crossed the room to claim her North Star—the photograph. She always placed it within sight as she wrote her letters.

While we waited for Ruth, Cleo and I went over a few of the jokes we'd heard to make sure I remembered them right. I'd just written a Burns line, "Whadya call a blue-blooded lady?" when I heard a sound that made the hair on the back of my neck stand up.

When I looked up, Ruth had a hand over her mouth, like she might be able to hold in that terrible sound or stop the tears pouring from her eyes. She tore her gaze away from the photograph, clutched it to her breast, and looked toward us like we could help somehow. Then she swayed on her feet.

I tried to get up to help her, but I'd been frozen by that

sound. Cleo was faster. Her longs legs carried her across the room and she clamped a strong arm around Ruth. As Cleo helped her to the couch, Ruth kept repeating, "No. No. No."

Something terrible had happened. Someone we loved must have disappeared.

Tears filled my own eyes. I forced my feet to move, but when I reached the couch I couldn't make myself sit next to her. I couldn't take the news eye to eye. I sank to the floor at her feet.

Ruth made an effort to collect herself but it failed. That awful mewling sound came again, and the pain of it shot straight through me. I had to know.

"Is it Davey?" I demanded as I clutched her knee. "Is my brother dead?" I felt the same hysteria that seemed to be gripping Ruth and the baby kicked in uneasy response.

Ruth tried to answer but couldn't make any words come out. Struggling, she shook her head no.

I was so relieved I didn't stop to consider the other possibilities. Tully, or—

"It's Jack," she whispered.

The news felt like a boxcar landing on our heads. "Dead? Jack's dead?" I couldn't recognize my own shrill voice. Nothing seemed real. Jack couldn't be dead. Not happy-go-lucky Jack.

Ruth rubbed the tears out of her eyes, took a deep breath, then slowly, like a witness to a disaster, turned the photograph upward so she could study it again. After a moment she wiped at the glass with her sleeve before sitting forward on the couch. She perked up a little.

"He's almost completely disappeared but I can still see a faint image." She brought the frame closer to her face. When she lowered it she shook her head. "I can't say for sure but I think he's hurt, hurt bad. Maybe dying right now." She blinked and tears coursed down her cheeks again. "But I don't think he's— I don't think he's left this world yet."

"Whaddya mean disappeared?" Cleo asked.

She shifted her gaze to Cleo. "I guess you didn't know you'd moved in with a lunatic—a fortune-telling witch who sees soldiers disappear," she sighed, "and gets the bad news before anyone else."

Cleo took the picture in question from Ruth and scrutinized it. "Ruth," she said with a sigh, "I don't scare worth a nickel. If you say you can see people disappear then I believe it. I sure wish you could keep an eye on my Johnny."

From the edge of my vision I saw a light switch off at the Silers'. Poor Mr. and Mrs. Siler—and Randy. Tonight might be the last night they would happily go to sleep knowing they had a brother or a son. What were they going to do without Jack?

"Ruth, what do we do?" I asked.

She slid off the couch and onto her knees next to me before looking toward heaven. "We say our prayers and hope."

— RUTH —

Again, all we could do was wait for news. I wished more than ever to be wrong—at least wrong about Jack being in grave danger, or already dead. I prayed to be right in my conviction that until he faded completely from the photograph, however, he was alive. The three of us made a decision to keep away from the Silers as much as possible in case someone, most likely eagle-eye Randy, noticed our long faces and asked what was the matter. We'd told enough fibs to last a lifetime and the truth was too horrible to say. Midmorning on Saturday I assigned Maddy to keep a lookout for any unfamiliar cars while Cleo and I did our weekly laundry.

"You know, when it comes down to it, none of this is my business," Cleo said as she stuffed our work coveralls in the washing machine, "but if Jack has been killed, this whole baby story gets very complicated."

"As if it isn't already," I said, scheme-weary. I knew she was right though. And I'd been so upset about Jack himself, I hadn't even considered that part of the equation and its effect on us. We would never be able to straighten out the tangle of lies. The Silers believed Maddy was carrying Jack's child; he'd told them so. If he'd been killed they'd never willingly let her or the baby—the last tiny evidence of his life—go. The truth wouldn't matter. I dabbed the sweat from my forehead unable to hold back a sigh. "What a mess."

"Yeah," Cleo agreed. "And not one we can clean up with a little Tide either."

The official telegram came in the early afternoon.

Maddy called me to the front window and together we watched the Western Union man approach the Siler home. Each step closer felt like a blow to my heart. *Oh, Jack.* Before the man even knocked on the door we heard an anguished cry from inside the house. We could see Mr. Siler step onto the front porch to accept the bad news.

"Come on," I said, and took Maddy's hand. I briefly glanced at the photograph as we hurried by. Jack's image remained but more ghostly than real, like his spirit hovered, wavering. I had hope—I didn't know how much or for how long, though. "Don't leave us, Jack," I whispered.

Cleo opened the door and we hurried over to the Silers'.

The smell of scorched fabric greeted us. An ironing board was set up near the kitchen door and what looked like an almost completed maternity top was draped over the business end. The iron was resting hot plate down on the center of the material, which had begun to smoke. Mrs. Siler had collapsed on the sofa with her face buried in the pillows. Not knowing what else to do, I set the iron upright, then sank down next to her and put an arm around her shoulders. Out of habit, I suppose, Maddy went to Randy and slipped her hand into his.

Mr. Siler stood as straight as any ill-at-ease soldier to read the telegram. "WE REGRET TO INFORM YOU THAT ON OCTOBER 21, 1942, LIEUTENANT JACK LEWIS SILER WAS SHOT DOWN OVER ENEMY TERRITORY.

HE HAS BEEN REPORTED MISSING AND PRESUMED D-DEAD." He faltered on the last word, then he pulled a handkerchief out of his pocket and blew his nose.

October twenty-first—almost a week ago.

Mrs. Siler cried louder and I tightened my grip as Cleo crossed the room, linked her arm with Mr. Siler's, and guided him to his easy chair. He collapsed more than sat, staring at the telegram as though he could wake up from this terrible nightmare.

"He can't be dead, Dad," Randy said. He gazed up at Maddy. "He can't be."

"I'm so sorry," Maddy said as she hugged him.

"He can't be . . ." he said, as though he hadn't heard her.

Cleo and Maddy worked on coffee and dinner while I went through the Silers' address book and made phone calls—first to Pastor Williams, then to friends and neighbors. Soon the house was filled with murmuring voices and shifting footsteps. The sounds of grief taking the place of war news and *The Lone Ranger.* Everyone obviously wanted to help but didn't know what to do. There was no body to bury, no funeral to attend. By ten o'clock it was quiet once again, the Silers and their boarders left to look to their own comfort. Mr. Siler took up a vigil on the front porch, smoking cigarettes in the dark. Randy had rolled his chair outside to watch the river in the moonlight. Mrs. Siler remained where she'd crumpled earlier, on the couch.

"Wouldn't you like to lie down awhile now?" I asked her.

She stared at me with hollow eyes. "I suppose so," she said after a while. "But I don't imagine I'll be able to sleep."

I didn't try to argue with her or tell her that a little rest would do her good. Sleeping wouldn't ease her pain. She would wake up and her son would still be dead. Nothing would take the salt from the wound except for Jack to walk through the front door.

"Where's Maddy?" she asked, as though she'd just noticed

her absence. "She must be terribly upset. She loves Jack, too. Someone should be looking after her and the baby."

"She's with Randy and Cleo," I said, quickly. I didn't want to go into who had loved whom and how much.

"Here, let me help you." I took her arm and helped her to stand. She wobbled for a moment, as though her strength had been used up. Then with my support we slowly walked to her bedroom. Once inside, she sat on the edge of the bed and slipped her shoes off.

"May I?" I asked before pulling the pins from her hairdo. I didn't really expect an answer. Running on instinct alone, I picked up a brush from her dresser and drew it through her hair.

She closed her eyes and sighed. "Your mother must be very proud of you," she said in a sad, far-off voice.

"She died when I was young, but I like to think she would be."

Mrs. Siler opened her eyes briefly and patted my hand. "Know that she'd be proud of you this very moment. I'm grateful you're here." She stretched out on the bed. "Thank you, dear."

I stood there, holding the brush in my hand, wishing I could say something, anything to help. But I knew in my heart, if I'd lost my Davey, no amount of words or tears would ever make a difference. My heart would be forever broken.

"If you need anything . . ."

She nodded. I put down the brush and closed the door as I left the room.

I passed Maddy and Randy on the way back to the Samuel place. Randy had parked his chair on the walkway, and Maddy had taken up a place next to him. They had escaped to their own private world of rustling trees, slow-moving water, and moonlight.

No one could see you cry in the dark.

I gave Randy's shoulder a squeeze as I passed them. "Are you two all right?" I asked.

Randy looked up but he didn't speak. His eyes sparkled, moonlight or tears, I couldn't tell.

"We're okay," Maddy said. "I'll be along in awhile."

Too tired to argue, I said, "Okay," and walked on.

It was shocking how much difference a day could make in a life—or in ten lives. All it took was one dose of good or bad news. One truth that couldn't be changed or denied. One death. I felt like I'd aged a decade during this single long day.

I opened the screen door and found Cleo sitting at the dining room table writing letters.

She shrugged sheepishly. "I thought I'd write Johnny a few extra pages tonight, to let him know I'm thinking about him. Doesn't matter about the shortages, or working a man's job. This whole thing with Jack sure brings the war home. You know?"

The war.

Yeah, I knew. And I needed to write Davey—simply because I *could* write him. But first, fighting my reluctance, I walked over to the photograph. I wanted to look, but I didn't want to at the same time. What if he'd disappeared completely?

I picked up the familiar frame and stared. My heart took several slow thud, thud, thuds as I studied the place where Jack used to be. It looked different.

My heartbeat accelerated.

"Cleo? How long has it been since I saw Jack disappear?" I hurried over to hold the photograph under the brighter dining room light.

Cleo looked at her watch. "A little over twenty-four hours, I guess."

"Well, I can see him. He's alive—barely, but alive. I'm sure of it."

The photograph had changed again. The image of Jack, which before had nearly gone transparent, now had "thickened" ever so slightly—his features returning even though they remained ghostly. I was sure it had to mean something good.

"Hot damn," Cleo swore, then changed her tune. "I mean, Hallelujah!"

"Come on, Jack, *fight*," I ordered as I did my best to picture him whole and alive—smiling. If I could envision him that way, then maybe he'd feel my presence. "Stay alive."

A shaft of joy rushed through me. My first impulse was to run over to the Silers' shouting the news. Then doubt waded into my enthusiasm. What if I was wrong? Or what if I raised hopes and Jack died anyway?

What if nobody believed me?

I turned my attention to my husband. Davey had believed me. In the photo he looked slightly cleaner, but tired. I had to bite my lip. I missed him with a physical ache. I'd learned to live separated from him, but I knew I'd never learn to live without him.

Oh Davey, what should I do?

A clear memory of the "without-hope" look in Mrs. Siler's eyes sliced through me. If I were her, and there was some chance, even a crazy chance that would give me hope, I would beg for it. Good, bad, or indifferent.

Don't give up.

I tucked the frame under my arm and headed for the door.

— MADDY —

"*I* think you ought to marry me," Randy said, calm as the surface of the slow-moving river.

We'd been sitting in the dark talking about Jack, Randy telling me how as boys, the two of them had built a fort in a tree with only a rope for stairs so the imaginary natives couldn't get inside. The shift from Tarzan to a marriage proposal stumped me.

"What?" I asked, thinking I hadn't heard him right.

"I know I'm not supposed to know about the baby, but I do. I overheard my mother telling Father." I must have looked mortified, like I felt, because he quickly added, "I don't care about gossip. I still think you're great." He ducked his head for a moment. "And Jack—Jack was probably crazy about you."

Crazy about you. I captured his hand and squeezed. "Oh, Randy. Jack wasn't—" I caught myself before I accidentally told the truth. Jack didn't love me, he'd felt sorry for me. I suppose Randy felt the same way. I drew in a deep breath. "Let's not talk about this tonight. Everyone's upset." And I was past the point of defending or even explaining the ins and outs of our maze of lies. I was too tired and too sad.

He pulled himself together, turning to look at me. "That baby is a Siler and should have the Siler name. Let me do that for you, Maddy. I know you probably couldn't love a cripple like me, but let me give Jack's baby our name. For my brother's sake and the baby's."

With the rest of me whipped, my conscience expanded until it was about the size of Oklahoma, then it seemed to settle squarely on my shoulders and shout, *Tell him.*

It would be the "right" thing to do. Bad timing or not, I should just get it over with.

Just as I'd screwed myself up to say, "This isn't Jack's baby," a screen door slammed and Ruth came rushing out of the Samuel place toward us on the walkway. She looked more excited than I'd seen her in days. And, she was carrying the photograph.

She touched the top of my head as she passed and said, "There's hope."

Speechless, I watched her open the Silers' back door without knocking and disappear inside. *Hope.* She must have seen something else in the photograph and it looked like she was going to tell Mrs. Siler. I wondered if one more shock might finish our landlady off. Or whether she'd kick us out for being crazy. But, whatever the case, I believed Ruth knew what she was doing.

"What was that all about?" Randy asked, gazing toward the house.

Now I had a clear choice. I could tell him about who had fathered my baby, or that I'd already given my heart to Tully, or I could explain why Ruth might think there was hope his brother was still alive.

"You know that photograph Ruth had in her hand? Well, that's why I can't marry you. We don't believe Jack is dead."

Okay, it was the easy way out, but Jack meant more to Randy than any of my problems. By the time I told Randy the bare facts about the photograph and answered his usual twenty questions—the ones I could answer, that is—nearly an hour had passed. We were narrowing down theories of why it worked when I heard the squeak of the Silers' screen door as it opened. Mrs. Siler, in her robe with her hair wrapped in a turban, stepped out onto the walkway with Ruth.

"Randy? I think you should come in now and get some rest," she said.

Our landlady's voice sounded almost normal. Having one son in danger or dead had obviously not made her forget her other son.

I stood and dusted off my backside before turning Randy's chair toward home and giving it a push.

Ruth waited at the bottom of the ramp, the photograph cradled in her arms. She seemed calmer, much more at ease. Randy stopped next to her.

"Could I see the picture?"

"Sure," Ruth said. "Let's go inside where there's some light."

We gathered in the dining room around Randy's chair as Ruth handed him the frame.

Randy stared hard at the image then rubbed his thumb over the glass near his brother's face. "It just looks like a picture to me," he said, but you could see he was affected. Tears glimmered in his eyes.

Mrs. Siler hugged her son's shoulders. "Ruth is the only one who can see the people change," she said, as though the whole idea made some kinda sense.

Mr. Siler came through the front door and stopped in front of us. He looked like an old man—heartsick and weary. "Don't put your faith in hocus-pocus," he warned. "This war has killed our Jack and that's that. It was God's will. Might as well get used to the idea."

I would've thought he was angry except that he brought out his handkerchief again and blew his nose. Angry or grieving, Ruth stiffened next to me like she'd been physically struck. Mrs. Siler removed the photograph from her son's hands and returned it to Ruth.

"Charles, I'm not ready to get used to the idea," she said with an air of finality. She took her husband's arm and led him toward their room. "Come on, Daddy. Let's go to bed. We're all tired." He didn't argue.

We attended church on Sunday and as the congregation prayed for the country's boys in harm's way, we prayed for Jack.

The following week the newspaper continued the war's roll call: Three Killed as War Plane Falls into Bay, Miami Naval Officer Believed Lost at Sea, *Miamian With RAF In England Reported Shot Down,* Miami Seaman Reported Lost, Beach Youth Missing in Pacific.

By November I felt big as a house—and I had at least three months to go in this baby business. And I had one more reason to feel guilty but grateful. Jack's loss or the neighbor's good manners kept anyone from asking about *my* situation. As for Jack himself, he seemed to be hanging on according to Ruth. And Mrs. Siler remained a true believer. It had become a ritual for her to come over to the Samuel place, and after getting any information Ruth could glean from the photograph, she'd sit with the frame in her lap for at least thirty minutes, sometimes an hour. None of us knew whether she was praying for his return or trying to send the love of a mother to her son. We weren't about to ask. Sometimes I sat with her, sometimes not.

There was no new word from the Army, other than the arrival of a gold star, which Mrs. Siler refused to hang in the window until all hope was lost.

Mr. Siler merely shook his head any time the subject of the photograph came up. He'd told us he believed the whole thing was foolishness, but you could tell he'd lost the heart to argue.

One day, after Mrs. Siler left her vigil, Ruth held the photograph and said, "He's better. I can see he's better." She looked worried. "Why don't we hear something?"

I could tell she was afraid that her "sight" had left her. That maybe this whole thing had been wishful thinking on her part and she'd misled everyone. The very idea scared me so much I had to sit down. Ruth couldn't be wrong—I was living proof of that. She'd seen me with the baby—and Frankie . . .

We hadn't written any of the men about Jack. I knew Tully was too far away from England to help us gather any news. And Ruth said she didn't want Davey to worry about us. Gosh, we were each so busy worrying about the other it's a wonder we got anything done.

Dear Tully,

I dreamed of you last night. You were swinging through the trees like Tarzan, yodeling like a lunatic. I assume you were chasing Germans but for the life of me I couldn't figure out how you'd catch them when you were making so much noise. I thought you looked very handsome in your loincloth, however.

Do you know how to yodel? If so, you'll have to demonstrate when you get home.

I would imagine you're very busy. Here we have busy days but the evenings seem to drag on forever. We haven't been to the movies in weeks, so I have no reviews to post. We miss our guys, and I miss you very much.

Don't worry about me, I am as healthy as a horse—and about the size of one. Please, please, please take care of yourself.

Love,

Maddy

I knew my mother would worry one way or another so I'd told her right away about Jack being shot down. I found it actually made me feel better to be able to mention some portion of our real trials and tribulations to her.

Dear Mother,

This news of our friend Jack has given us a hard jolt. I know you've been thinking of Davey as I have. I get so scared sometimes and I hate to bother Ruth. She's being strong for the both of us— or I guess for the three of us. She and the baby are fine.

I'd learned to mix the truth up a bit. If I didn't, I'd have nothing safe to say. I told myself I wasn't really lying, Ruth and the baby were fine—except I was carrying the baby.

I'm doing my best to keep things running smoothly around here. Cleo, Ruth, and I have been handling a little more of the cooking chores these past weeks since Mrs. Siler isn't quite herself yet. You would be proud. I've learned to make biscuits—on my own. I've also learned that doing the laundry can be dangerous. I got my hand hung up in some wet, twisted sheets and nearly had it dragged through the ringer. Luckily, Cleo was there to shut off the motor.

I didn't add Cleo's vow that it was the last time I would do laundry until there were diapers to wash. She said I wasn't fast enough on my feet to stay out of trouble.

Well, as I said before, we're fine. And, we're used to looking out for each other. Please don't worry. By the time we come home I should be quite the homemaker. I'm sure you never dreamed that would happen.

Love,
Maddy

Chapter Thirteen

*I*t was the day before Thanksgiving, the week before Maddy's birthday, a little over a month since Jack had been reported missing, when the photograph changed significantly. As usual after I'd come in from work, before I even read my mail, I studied the picture for my nightly report to Mrs. Siler. There had been little change after the initial thickening of Jack's image and I'd begun to think the whole thing was wishful thinking on my part. Now, however, I finally had some real news, yet something I would never have chosen or guessed.

I studied Jack's unsmiling, ghostly, black-and-blue face and remembered Maddy's words after he'd shipped out.

Don't let the Germans get you.

Jack's clothes had changed. Before he'd been wearing his uniform and a flight jacket, then it had disappeared. Now he looked to be wearing gray coveralls with a black swastika painted on the upper-left-hand side of his chest—like a target.

The Nazis had captured Jack.

With a heavy heart, I placed the frame back in its usual place atop the radio cabinet and walked toward the back door. Maddy and Cleo glanced up as I passed.

"He's been captured by the Germans," I said.

Maddy gasped and Cleo shook her head with a low sad sound—half sigh, half whistle. They didn't even question how I might know anymore, they simply waited for news.

"At least he's alive enough for the Germans to want him," I added. "And, there should be some official notice of his capture."

"Is everyone else all right?" Maddy asked. Whether she was aware of it or not, her hand was resting on her midsection—automatically protecting or comforting her unborn child.

"The same as yesterday," I answered and resumed my path.

"Do you want us to come with you?" Maddy asked. She knew where I was headed and sounded as though I was about to face a firing squad rather than our landlady. I didn't know if the news would bring tears or celebration in the Siler household. On the one hand, their Jack was alive. On the other, he might not stay that way for long. And the merciless Germans might make him wish he was dead.

"No. I'm only going to tell Mrs. Siler, like I promised, and let her decide what to do about the news."

That night at dinner, it was more celebration than lament. Mrs. Siler smiled several times during the meal and served her special ginger cookies in observance of the news. Even Mr. Siler's frown had faded. He hadn't met my gaze directly since I'd mentioned my special connection to the photograph. But at dinner, for one extended moment he'd stared at me. He didn't smile, but I could see hope in his expression—and gratitude. If nothing else, I had given his wife her son back for a little while. And, as she had informed me, now she had something to quiz the Army about—a place to look for her "missing" son, rather than a gold star in payment for his life.

Caught up in the fear and excitement, I realized as we listened to the war news, I'd neglected to read my mail.

"British forces under Montgomery have broken through Axis lines at El Alamein. Allied troops under Lt. General Eisenhower have landed in Algeria and Morocco. Allied troops, mainly Australians, have gained the upper hand on New Guinea."

When the announcer mentioned Guadalcanal, I pushed out of my seat and made my excuses. I had letters waiting at home—hopefully from my husband—and that was better than any news on the radio.

I found two envelopes—military style—addressed in Davey's handwriting on the dining room table. I wasn't sure which to open first so I started with the one on top.

Dearest Ruth,

It's very hot here—in many ways. Sometimes I dream of snow falling—the coolness, the quiet. Nothing's ever quiet around here—the big guns on the ships seem to fire constantly. I hope they have plenty of extra ammo, because when they stop we usually get hit—and hard.

Right now we stay in our holes and keep our heads down. I've got sand in places I didn't know sand could get. One of the guys in my unit bought it from a Jap sniper yesterday but we took the sneaky b— out. Frankie and some of the other men have been braving a bullet or a booby trap to search through the Jap hideouts for rice or saki. The C-rations we get aren't fit for a dog but I'd rather bark and eat 'em than scrounge for enemy leftovers.

I'm sorry to go on so. I guess you can tell I miss home, and you. Heck, I even miss the Spam we had on board ship. Now that we've been dropped off in somewhere resembling nowhere with thousands of To-gos between us and dinner our stomachs are rubbing against our backbones. I'd ask you to send food or even a fishing line but that wouldn't work in V-mail.

I love you, wife, and I should be happier tomorrow because we're supposed to have mail call. Haven't gotten any letters in over a week.

Your loving husband,

Davey

As I opened the second envelope I felt a pang of guilt. Here we'd been having a celebration meal, with cookies even, and my husband was practically starving. I'd read in the paper about C-rations and K-rations. Basically a meal in a can or a box. But it hadn't crossed my mind as to how the stuff might taste. If possible I would've used every penny of the money I made to send Davey and his fellow Marines food. I'm sure Davey knew that, but I still wished there was something more I could do.

I picked up the second letter.

Ruth,

What the hell is going on?

The opening of the letter gave me a shock. Davey rarely used bad language and never directed toward me. I was almost afraid to read further.

I wrote to Mother about your welding job—proud as punch of my wife. She wrote me back that you're PREGNANT and shouldn't be working under any circumstances. How could that be Ruth? I told her you would never keep that kind of information from me. That we'd never had secrets.

So, tell me now. Have you been keeping secrets? Were you afraid to tell me the whole truth?

I swear I feel like I'm about to go crazy. I'm angry and worried. If you are pregnant then you MUST quit that job and go home. You know the doctor told us it was dangerous for you and any baby so soon after your illness. I can't believe you would take chances with your life this way.

If the Japs don't kill me then this might. I'm already out of my head. Please write immediately and help me understand why you would risk everything when I'm too far away to help.

Davey

Tears came to my eyes. Davey sounded so hurt and betrayed. It seemed no matter how clever our plan had looked in the beginning, it was unraveling faster than a spinning ball of yarn at the mercy of a tornado.

Oh, Davey. Thinking of him angry, miserable, too far away for explanations, filled me with guilt and dread. What if something happened to him before he knew the truth? Before he knew that I would never willingly do anything to make him so unhappy?

My dearest Davey,

You're right. We've never had secrets between us. I see now that I should have told you the whole story from the beginning, but I didn't want to worry you.

I have never lied to you—would never lie to you. But I have lied to your mother. You see, it's not me who is expecting, it's Maddy. Please don't rush to any judgments about her until you've heard the entire story. It seems absurd to say it wasn't her fault but that's the God's truth.

Do you remember the last night we went to the Servicemen's Pier together? When Maddy came home so late with Jack?

I went on to tell him the whole story. Everything, from Frankie's attack to Jack's attempt to cover for Maddy. I didn't have the heart to tell him Jack might never come home and straighten out his own lie, and truthfully there wasn't room for any extra information. As it was I had to write small and tight to fit the story on one page for V-mail. I couldn't stand the thought of putting half the explanation in one letter then half in another. It was hard enough knowing it might be weeks before he received the news.

If you could see her, you would be as proud of Maddy as I am. She's doing her best to cope with her situation. I know this might not be the ideal time to bring this up, but I had hoped that if Maddy decided to give up the baby we might be able to adopt it. I haven't mentioned anything to her yet because she doesn't need to worry about the future right now. She's due in February. Until then her main purpose is to stay healthy.

We had hoped to keep your mother in the dark for as long as possible—mainly for Maddy's sake. She's fearful of your mother's disapproval and I have to say I'm not looking forward to her reaction either. After your letter to her, I imagine we'll be hearing from her posthaste. Please don't tell her anything about Maddy yet. I've promised to let your sister decide when she's strong enough to explain it for herself.

Davey, I love you more than my own life and would give anything to have your son or daughter, but even so I would not risk our chance to grow old together by being foolish. I intend to have your baby, when the time is right. So, take care of yourself and come home to me. And please forgive me for the worry I've caused you.

 All my love,
 Ruth

— MADDY —

Thanksgiving looked to be a solemn affair. Ruth seemed a bit under the weather and the Silers were still getting used to the idea of Jack at the mercy of the German bullyboys. The bright spots of the day turned out to be our company. Mrs. Siler had instructed me to invite Nickie and his mother since they were alone for the holiday, and Cleo had picked a couple of young sailors from a line of men sponsored by the Red Cross hoping for a home-cooked meal.

I think the Silers were glad to be hosting the Navy rather than Army fliers who'd remind them of Jack. And I knew Ruth sighed every time she saw a Marine uniform that wasn't Davey. Personally, seeing such young guys in sailor hats made me feel like an old woman. It also brought back my memories of Lyle and our plans for the future. Plans that seemed like they'd been made a lifetime ago now. Watching these boys, I wondered how Lyle was doing so far from home—at war. And I wondered if he'd make it back home to Jeanne.

Good manners forced us to put on pleasant holiday faces. That, and our peculiar main dish.

There wasn't a turkey to be had in the city—not one that we could afford anyway. Earlier in the week we'd heard on the radio that several grocers had already been fined for price gouging or hoarding, and turkeys were at the top of the most-wanted list. No turkey, no pumpkin pie, or candied yams. So Mrs. Siler, determined to save Thanksgiving dinner, sent her husband to beg, borrow, or trade for a couple of roasting chickens.

I was in the kitchen helping peel potatoes when he'd come back and proudly presented her with three rabbits that he said he'd acquired in a deal for a similar number of truck spark plugs. "One plug each and old Joseph said they're better than chicken," he declared.

With some trepidation, I watched Mrs. Siler open the parcel. Thank goodness they were already dressed out. If I'd had to witness the killing and cleaning of furry little Easter bunnies I might've burst into tears. Who knows how a mother's water-works could affect the baby?

Mrs. Siler stared down at the unexpected substitution and frowned for a moment as though her plans for Thanksgiving had received a blow. But then she smiled. "Why, these'll do fine, Charles." She turned to me. "My daddy used to bring home all sorts of creatures when he took the boys hunting—he insisted on eating what they killed. I suppose we can give thanks over these rabbits as well as we could over a turkey."

"This feels just like home, ma'am," one of the sailors, a country boy from Tennessee named Clifford, said when Mrs. Siler placed the platter of fried rabbit in the center of the table. "The Navy brass could do worse than letting some of us go out huntin' once in a while—with the shortages and all."

"They're probably afraid we'd get lost in the woods and shoot each other," the other sailor, Seaman Wesley said. "They'd rather save us for the Japs."

"You Navy boys would be better off *fishin'* around here," Randy said. "Why my brother and I used to catch plenty of bream in the river right behind the house."

At the mention of Jack, Mrs. Siler reclaimed control of the conversation and the meal. I imagine she didn't want to think about how her son would spend Thanksgiving. "Randy? Would you say grace, please?"

"Yes, ma'am," Randy responded and dutifully bowed his head. "Lord, please bless this food and this day. Bless those of us gathered here and every one of those we miss who are so far from home. And please, bring Jack back to us safe and sound. Amen."

"Amen," Nickie echoed, breaking the silence. "Let's eat."

His mother shushed him but everyone chuckled. As the main dish made the rounds, I watched, dreading the moment it would be passed to me. Nickie spoke the thought in my mind.

"What's that?" he asked as his mother chose a piece of rabbit from the platter and put it on her son's plate. Leah, who'd begun cutting the meat from the bone, hesitated long enough for Nickie to get suspicious.

"Why, can't you tell a chicken when you see one?" Clifford said with a wink.

"Dudn't look like chicken," Nickie said, unsure. He gave it a halfhearted poke with his fork.

"That's because it's a Tennessee chicken. They look different than a scrawny old Florida bird. Why I grew up on 'em and look at me, off to fight for Uncle Sam. You just give it a try. I bet you'll like it better than any old *regular* chicken you had before."

Nickie, unwilling to disappoint a Navy man like his father, took a bite and chewed with serious concentration. The platter made its way around the table and as it was placed in my hands, he swallowed and said, "It's good."

"Atta boy," Clifford said. "You'll grow up to be a sailor yourself someday."

Nickie grinned like he'd been promised a ride to the moon.

"No, thank you," I said and gingerly passed the platter on to Cleo. Everyone turned to stare in my direction. I reached for the mashed potatoes which I'd already planned as my main dish, but Mrs. Siler was having none of it.

"Maddy? You should have some of the . . . uh . . ." She glanced at Clifford. "Some of the Tennessee chicken. There's plenty and remember, you're eating for two."

Cleo, after forking a piece onto her plate, held the platter for me instead of passing it on.

Clifford smiled. "Why, Maddy? Have you something against Tennessee?"

"Um . . . my stomach is a little upset . . ." I began. It wasn't my stomach, it was my mind. And I hated that Clifford was using the same technique he'd used on Nickie—on me, a grown woman. An expectant mother. About then the baby gave a kick as if to say, "Hey, don't turn down food, I'm hungry."

I was hungry, too, and it seemed like no one would eat until I tried the rabb— I mean, the chicken. I scrunched my face into a frown for Clifford's sake and chose the smallest piece of Thanksgiving rabbit on the platter. Thankfully, Cleo passed it on and I gratefully received the mashed potatoes. When the many dishes had made the rounds, everyone dug in.

"Come on, try it," Cleo said, close to my ear.

I gave her an impatient, "Oh, all right" look before cutting off a sliver and tasting it.

Then and there I learned another important lesson. Rabbit doesn't taste like chicken. It's better than chicken. As a matter of fact, it was downright wonderful. "This is really good," I said in surprise.

"Told ya so," Nickie said. For his two cents, Clifford winked again.

Mrs. Siler looked as proud as any Cordon Bleu chef.

After dinner over coffee, the Navy boys showed us pictures of their families and the girls they'd left behind. Before we could get maudlin about how many of our loved ones were so far away, the boys insisted on Randy showing them the best place to catch fish in the river. Soon Mr. Siler and Nickie were digging for worms and the rest were rigging bamboo poles. In the time it took to clear the table and wash the dinner dishes, the men of the household were lined up along the bank, fishing.

They stayed until the sun went down. Each of the fishermen, including Nickie, had caught at least one fish. Mr. Siler, Randy, and Clifford had brought in several.

"It's a shame you boys can't come back to visit for a fish fry," Mrs. Siler said as our company prepared to leave. Mr. Siler had offered them a ride back to the naval base but they'd insisted on accompanying Leah and Nickie to the bus stop.

"Heck, since I joined the Navy I've been on more buses than ships," Seaman Wesley said.

"Ain't that the truth," Clifford added. "And yes, ma'am, today was a grand day and we wish we could come back soon, but I think the Navy has other plans for us." He thumped Nickie on the bill of his cap. "I'd surely like to taste some of those *Florida* fish we caught."

"They're better than *Tennessee* fish I bet," Nickie said, pushing his hat out of his eyes and grinning. They'd obviously had that discussion before.

We wouldn't let them leave without our names and addresses so they could write and tell us how they were. Leah Dowland gave them her husband's name and ship, and I had them write down Lyle's next to mine so they could say hello if they met by chance.

The house felt too quiet after they left. The silence seemed to echo the memories of other voices, better days. To overcome the stillness, Mr. Siler turned on the radio and we set up the cards on the dining room table.

"Come on ladies, deal them shingles," Randy said. A day of manly pursuits must've taken his mind off sadder subjects. When I suggested using matchsticks instead of change because I was fresh out of coins, Randy would have none of it.

"That's worth about as much as a Japanese yen at Burdines' credit desk," he said, quoting some newspaper columnist he read faithfully. "I have plenty of change and I'll be happy to break a bill for you."

In the middle of the third hand of poker, the telephone rang.

— RUTH —

*M*y heart sank when Mrs. Siler said, "Hello Mrs. Marshall. Happy Thanksgiving."

I hadn't had time, or to be truthful, the mettle to explain our newest disaster to Maddy: The fact that Davey's mother had informed him I was expecting and I'd already told him I was working. After what could be called a "happy" day—if any of us could be truly happy with our men gone and one of them in the hands of the Germans—I cringed at the very thought of new lies and explanations. Maybe the men had it right after all. In that moment I'd rather have gone to war myself and left the explaining to others. But it was too late to enlist.

"I thank you for your prayers. We still have hope for our Jack, though. Yes, she's right here." Mrs. Siler put her hand over the bottom of the receiver. "Ruth? Mrs. Marshall wants to speak to you."

Trapped.

I put my cards down and slowly rose from the table. Maddy offered a worried glance as I passed her. Well, I'd started this tightrope act, and now since it had gotten off the beam I'd have to think of a way to fix it.

"Hello, Mother Marshall," I said. Everyone in the room had their eyes on me as I listened to Davey's mother complain about the telephone lines being busy the whole day, and then tell me about the letter I already knew she'd received from her son—my Davey.

"Yes, I know. I'm sorry he's so upset." Sorrier than she'd ever know. "And I'm sorry you're upset. But I did ask you not to tell him."

Mrs. Marshall sputtered at that one and I felt a twinge for spoiling her holiday, but I couldn't help it. By interfering she'd made my husband unhappy—mother or not—and she'd caused him to doubt me, his wife, when he was too far away for explanations.

"I was only worried about your health," she said stiffly.

"My health is fine and since the cat is out of the bag so to speak, you may as well know the truth."

Other than the music—"I'll Walk Alone" was playing on the radio—the room and the people in it were completely silent. I took a deep breath. "Maddy is the one." The sound of her name brought Maddy out of her chair. Cleo moved next to her and took her arm.

"Maddy is the one what?" Mrs. Marshall asked.

"Maddy is the one who's working at the aircraft factory." *There,* I thought, *another lie to toss on top of the pile.*

Maddy brought a hand to her throat and Cleo's arm tightened around her.

"We didn't think you'd approve so we didn't tell you."

"Of course I don't approve. A factory is no place for an innocent young girl. That's man's work. She'll have to quit at once. Both of you need to come home. I have Mr. Jenkins looking into return tickets."

I'd done my best to stay on good terms with my mother-in-law but it looked like those days were over—gone with the wind. "I'm not coming back to Radley until the baby is born and I need Maddy's help. There are many young boys and girls working for the war effort down here. (Lie number 3,822.) Our fighting men need all the support they can get. Maddy'll be eighteen in less than two weeks. That makes her old enough to decide for herself."

For several heartbeats I was treated to the sound of a few clicks and the faint buzz of an open phone line. I wondered if any of the party lines were listening, holding their breath like me.

"Let me speak to my daughter."

I put my hand over the bottom of the receiver, sighed and closed my eyes. It would be up to Maddy now. There was no real advice I could offer but I'd stand behind whatever she decided. I shook off my dread and held out the receiver.

"She wants to talk to you. You can tell her the truth if you want to go home. If you want to stay here, you'll have to stick to the story."

"Perhaps if I spoke to her . . ." Mrs. Siler offered.

I quickly shook my head no. I appreciated how far we'd come with our landlady—enough that she wanted to defend us, but there were too many opinions in this mess already.

Maddy swallowed and took the phone out of my hand.

Being on the outside of the conversation I had to guess at what Mrs. Marshall said to Maddy. I was sure it had a lot to do with acting her age and being a dutiful daughter. Maddy herself spoke only to acknowledge with a "yes, ma'am" or "no, ma'am." Then, after I imagined Mrs. Marshall had finished her what-I-expect-from-you speech, Maddy made her decision.

"I'm sorry, Mother, but I'm staying here with Ruth and I plan to continue working." Maddy glanced toward the Silers with a guilty expression because they knew she wasn't telling the truth. "Yes, I am. I promised Davey I would look after her like a sister and I can't break my promise when he's so far from home."

There was another longer pause and my heart clenched as tears rolled down Maddy's cheeks.

"Yes, I know my father would be disappointed in m-me—for disobeying you but I can't help that now. I love you, Mother." Then, Maddy broke the connection by hanging up the phone.

I put an arm around her and led her from the room.

Chapter Fourteen

— RUTH —

*M*addy was more melancholy than usual the next few days. So much so that I began to worry about her health and the baby's. She hadn't received any letters from Lt. Tully for over three weeks, which hadn't helped. That, combined with her mother's vocal disapproval on Thanksgiving, seemed to have knocked her spirit down.

Unable to stand watching her suffer in silence, I cornered her one afternoon. I'd been reluctant to bring up the future since it meant facing our many deceptions. I'd thought that once the baby was born we could make whatever decisions had to be made. Presently, I wasn't so sure.

"If she's so upset about me working in a factory, what do you think she'll say about this?" Maddy indicated her extended belly. "I can never go home. What am I going to do?"

"You're going to have a healthy baby," I said. "We haven't even discussed the many possibilities after that."

"Possibilities like what?" she asked, gazing at me with wary interest.

"First, tell me what you wish could happen."

The interest faded. "What I wish'll never happen," she said.

"At least say it out loud."

It didn't take long. She'd obviously been thinking and wishing for some time.

"I wish Tully would come back, and we could get married and live here, in Florida. I wish this baby would have a father and a mother who love it."

Well, there it was, I had my foot in the door but I was reluctant to push through. Unfortunately, I believed she was right. The possibility of her wish coming true was slim. I'd seen too many men disappear from the photograph to depend on any of them coming home safe. Except for Davey of course. He had to come home safe—I couldn't envision *any* future without him. "Okay," I said, "we'll keep your wish at the top of the list."

"List?"

"Yes, the list of alternatives. Now, you know some of the others. First, you could go home with the baby and live with your mother."

The horrified look on her face would have been comical, if it hadn't been so sad. She didn't answer, she shook her head.

"Next, you could give the baby up for adoption. There are many churches and organizations who will find a new home for a child—"

Her eyes filled with tears.

"I know I should give it away." She sniffed and looked down. "But how would I know if it was safe and loved?" She gazed up at me, misery in her eyes. "This baby is Frankie's and I'm still mad at him, but it's not the baby's fault. This baby is mine, too, ya know. I don't think I can give it away to strangers."

I patted her hand. "Yes, I know. That's why I want to bring up one more possibility." I waited for her to sniff and dry her tears then eased into my best wish. "You know how much Davey and I want children," I began.

She nodded.

"Well, we started with the story that I was pregnant. What if Davey and I adopt the baby? You know we would love it and you would be free to start over—here or anywhere. Your mother would never have to know."

— MADDY —

Free to start over.

Boy, did that sound good at the moment.

"You and Davey— You would do that for me?"

Ruth smiled. "Not just for you, silly. You know I've wanted children since Davey and I married. I'd feel blessed to have yours."

"But what does Davey think about it? Did you tell him what happened?"

"Yes, I'm sorry. I had to when your mother told him I was expecting. You can imagine how upset he was about me keeping secrets from him."

For a second, the image of my brother's face that morning in the hospital when Ruth had died came back to me. "Yeah, Davey can be a real pain in the neck sometimes."

"I haven't heard back from him yet, but I know he'll agree with me once he thinks it over," she said.

"There's one more thing . . ." I said. I hadn't told her before but I was sure the subject would come up again at some point. "When we thought Jack had been— You know, that he wasn't coming back? Well, Randy asked me to marry him to give the baby the Siler name."

Ruth blinked but didn't say anything for several seconds.

"Randy is a doll. Jack better come home—if for no other reason than so I can give him a piece of my mind," Ruth said, then sighed. "He certainly saved us from being thrown out on the street, but how in the world can we make things right without him?"

I wrote Tully that evening.

Dear Tully,

How can I know if we've healed your ailing funny bone if you don't report in to Ha-Ha Headquarters? Perhaps it's your broken arm that's in need of attention.

As you can probably tell, I'm in the dumps tonight. Could be

my birthday coming up, or having to act happy during the holi-
days when everyone else is sad. More than likely it's a lack of letters
from my favorite Brit. Are you okay? Ruth wants me to tell you
not to forget to rest and eat well when you can. She worries that
you're too thin.

There was so much I wanted to say—to tell him about
Jack and ask what I should do about the future. But Tully had
warned me he couldn't plan a future the war might take away.
And I didn't feel right asking him to comfort me when he had
enough to do fighting Germans and staying alive.

No one is going to accuse me of being too thin. I've been eating
for two as you can imagine, but I feel fine. I have a doctor's ap-
pointment soon for a checkup. While I'm there, I'll ask about your
funny bone and pass along any tips for treatment.

I can't figure out how to tell you how much I miss you, so I'll
end this letter by saying that each night before I close my eyes I pic-
ture your face and send you my love. In my dreams, you're smiling.
Love,
Maddy

Not much had changed by the time my birthday rolled around.
So even though I did get a short and sweet birthday letter from
my brother, Jack was still dead as far as the Army was concerned and Tully's letters were missing in action. Not to mention that my mother wasn't speaking to me and I had no firm
plan for the baby.

I'd been doing my best to stay upbeat. I didn't want to
stunt the baby's growth by being melancholy. It was kinda
tough though, being on the outs with my mother, then facing
a birthday that only reminded Americans of the infamous
Japanese attack the year before.

There were memorial services being held all over town.
Ruth and I went to early mass then to church with Cleo and
the Silers. I prayed for the families of the sailors lost, for our
own lost and found, and for the end of the war. I didn't know
what to ask concerning myself and the baby.

After church I found out my roommates had made plans to celebrate my birthday, dark clouds or no. At the Silers' we had orange pound cake that weighed in a good bit less than a pound because of the butter shortage. War–2, birthday–1. To even the score, Mr. Siler had picked up some candles at the five and dime so I wouldn't be deprived of my birthday wish.

As everyone waited for me to blow out the candles, I nodded to Ruth—she already knew what my first wish would be. I needed seventeen more tries to take care of the many other things weighing on my mind. But, since it was my day, I asked for my heart's dream. Tully. Then I cut the cake.

"All right, let's hit the road," Cleo said after taking the last sip of her coffee. She glanced at her watch then looked at me. "We don't want to be late and miss the newsreel."

Ruth obediently rose from her seat and began collecting the cups and cake plates.

"Don't worry about that, Ruth. You girls go on. Randy and I'll clean up."

"Yeah, I'm an expert dish dryer," Randy said. "Happy birthday, Maddy."

"Thank you."

I was in the dark even as Cleo pulled me to my feet. "Come on, birthday girl. It's your night out and we're headed to the movies."

On the way across the causeway in the Silers' car, Cleo drove while she and Ruth explained the dilemma they'd faced on how to celebrate my special day.

"We wanted to get you out of the house and do something fun but we couldn't go to the beach—it's too chilly to go swimming, even for us Yankees. Also, I'm not so sure we could find a bathing suit to fit you at this point." Her cocky smile took the sting out of the remark.

"We need to take you shopping but couldn't work that into the schedule for today," Ruth added, then after a hesitation, she went serious. "And we figured you wouldn't want to go to the pier."

"So, it had to be the movies," Cleo added.

"I've missed seeing the new pictures," I said, passing by the mention of the pier. Ruth was right, going back now would make me sad, about Frankie but more so about Tully. "I hope it's something funny."

"Better than that—it's got singing and dancing. Bing Crosby and Fred Astaire."

The young lady in the ticket booth sold us tickets, and after counting Ruth's change, she looked at me and said, "When is your baby due?"

I slid my hands into the pockets of my maternity top to hide the lack of a wedding ring before answering. "In February."

Her eyes lit up. "Ooh, I can't wait to get married and have my own. My boyfriend enlisted so I'll have to twiddle my thumbs till he comes home. How old are you?"

"Eighteen today."

"Yeah," Cleo added, "Eighteen going on thirty."

"Well, happy birthday and good luck," the girl said. "You better hurry, the show's about to start."

The lights were dimming as we found seats in the fourth row center.

"Perfect," Cleo sighed.

We sat in the dark as the newsreel footage ran. I should have been prepared after poring over the war coverage in the newspaper. But seeing it on the huge movie screen almost felt like being there.

"After the stunning defeat and surrender at Stalingrad, which ended the Germans' eastern push—" The screen filled with German soldiers, looking half starved, their hands in the air marching down a road lined with war wreckage and bodies.

"Here, the Germans fall back at El Alamein in North Africa before the British forces under Montgomery." I sat frozen in my seat watching tanks rumbling across the desert, and streaking overhead, the bombers and fighters of the RAF. Somehow I knew with certainty that Tully was in one of those planes. The memory of the day he'd taken me flying floated through my mind. Zooming through the air I'd felt like Amelia Earhart, like an adventurer who could do anything.

That was before I'd known about the baby. I picked out one plane in the center and decided it was Tully's. Then I silently wished him Godspeed.

The British were winning, that's what the announcer claimed, but the news was weeks if not months old. No telling what might be happening now, or if Tully— Before I realized it, I'd clutched Ruth's hand.

"On the other side of the world, the battle for Guadalcanal rages on—" The huge guns of a Navy ship flashed on the screen, firing again and again as the announcer continued, "After months of vicious fighting the Allies have the Japs pinned down without supplies—" The picture showed a Japanese ship sinking, then a suicide bomber crashing his plane into one of the Allied ships as anti-aircraft fire filled the sky with smoke.

From the corner of my eye, I saw Ruth slip her other hand into Cleo's—her Johnny could be on one of those ships.

"The Marines are in it for the duration. They've shown the Japs a thing or two about American tenacity—"

Like the photo I'd seen on the front page of the newspaper, the screen showed sand, rock, and blasted trees—and Marines dug in amid the debris, firing at the unseen enemy. Next, five or six Marines smoking cigarettes stood over at least twenty burned and blackened bodies. "The Japs choose death over surrender and our boys are determined to oblige—"

"Go get 'em, boys! Remember Pearl Harbor!" Someone yelled. There were several added cheers from servicemen and civilians in the theater.

I had to look away. I didn't want to imagine what my brother had suffered or what he'd had to do to defend our country. And I certainly didn't want to feel sorry for Frankie being thousands of miles from home and facing death.

The newsreel continued on to sports and the drive for war bonds. By the time Bugs Bunny, dressed as Stalin, took over the screen in "Herr Meets Hare," the three of us had recovered somewhat. With a fortifying squeeze, Ruth let go of my hand and whispered, "It's still your birthday. Let's put our worries away and be happy."

I wondered if I would ever be able to put my worries away until the war was over. Each day it intruded on our lives in one way or another. But I did my best. I wasn't the only one with worries. Besides, Ruth and Cleo had gone to a lot of trouble to help me celebrate. I wasn't going to ruin it for them.

The movie, *Holiday Inn,* was a little bit of heaven. I found I could put my troubles away, for a little while anyway. Watching Bing Crosby and Fred Astaire trying to steal a girl, Marjorie Reynolds, from each other made my heart smile. The baby was so calm it had to either be sleeping through the whole picture or enjoying it as well.

When Bing sang "White Christmas," my eyes filled with tears. At home in Radley they most likely had snow on the ground already. But my life had changed by more than geography. As it stood now I might not see a white Christmas for a very long time.

My overdue letter from Tully came three days later.

Dear Maddy,

I'm so sorry I haven't written sooner. I must claim king and country as my excuse. You must be beside yourself with worry, and I feel terrible having been the cause. I hope you can forgive me. I know if your letters were to cease I would be lost. You are the beacon I look to in this dark night.

To be truthful there is not much I can tell you—like where I am and what I'm doing. And what I could tell you about men and war isn't fit for you to read.

We are winning this fight, but at a terrible cost. Just yesterday three men in my unit were reported shot down. There are many empty chairs at any given meal.

I'm sure you must have had the news by now. I ran into one of the Yanks from Jack's squadron who'd flown in from England. When I asked about Jack this fella told me he'd "bought the farm" as they say back in the States. I am beyond words. I know you girls and the Silers must be devastated. Please give them my heartfelt condolences. Jack was surely one of a kind and a heckuva pilot.

I pray you are well and as happy as anyone can be with this war on. I know Ruth is looking after you. Please tell her hello from me.

I'm sorry but must close now. I promise to write more often. Never think that because I don't write that I'm not thinking of you—every day and of course, every night. I find myself humming "White Cliffs of Dover" on occasion. It doesn't remind me of home anymore—it reminds me of you.

All my heart,
Your Tully

I sat down and immediately wrote him back—since I knew he probably hadn't even received my most recent letters lecturing him for not writing. This letter seemed so different from the others, I was afraid the bottom had fallen out of his morale. I was sure that whatever he was doing, it was more dangerous than he let on.

And he knew about poor Jack. Part of it anyway.

Dear Tully,

You'll never guess what greeted me this afternoon. Not only a prized letter from you, but, a "lady" mailman. That's right, wearing pants, too. She said the regular mailman had joined the Merchant Marines and they were allowing women to take the place of any man who enlisted. Next they'll be having women in the Army. What do you think about a female PFC, anyway? I imagine it would be difficult for them to be pilots because their skirts would fly up over their heads.

I hope you'll excuse my last few letters. I'm afraid I got a little down about not hearing from you. So skip over the sad parts and hang on. I'm feeling better nowadays.

Now, about Jack. Yes, we heard he'd been shot down and let me tell you the doom and gloom around these parts was an awful thing to witness. But we've had some "sort of" good news since. We've heard he's not dead—he's actually been captured by the Germans. I understand that for many being captured would seem a fate worse than death but I can guarantee you, as a woman left behind, hearing the word "captured" is worlds better than the word "killed." I hope Jack feels the same way. We're keeping him in our prayers.

My birthday was a few days ago. Ruth and Cleo took me to the Columbia—the same theater we went to when you were here. We saw a picture called Holiday Inn *starring Bing Crosby and Fred Astaire, about a quaint inn located in Connecticut. The snow was so beautiful and when Bing sang a song called "White Christmas" it brought me to tears. I closed my eyes and imagined that you were sitting in the empty seat next to me holding my hand, and that we would someday see a white Christmas together.*

Well, enough of that or I'll be blubbering and smearing the ink on this page.

Oh, knock knock?

Who's there?

"Fival."

"Fival, who?"

"Fival get cha ten you're the one for me."

Take care, my love, and write, write, write. Your words are the next best thing to seeing your face.

Love,
Maddy

Chapter
Fifteen

— RUTH —

*A*s we prepared for Christmas, our vigil in front of the photograph continued. Each afternoon, after Maddy returned from Leah and Nickie's home and I got in from work, we'd join Mrs. Siler on the couch with the photograph facing us from the coffee table. Jack remained dressed in his prisoner clothes yet his image had grown stronger. Davey seemed to stay dirty but he was alive. And Tully looked more haggard than ever. I kept that observation to myself though. Maddy and her baby were in the home stretch and I wasn't about to upset her if I could help it.

Mrs. Siler had begun crocheting a yellow hat and booties for the baby, and she was determined to teach Maddy the stitches. Each day they made a little progress. Maddy started out all fumbling thumbs but she was showing no signs of giving up.

"I wish we knew if the baby is a boy or a girl," Mrs. Siler said as she worked the thread and needle with competent hands. "Then we'd know what color would be best. Did the doctor give you any hints?"

"No," Maddy answered. "He said it was hard to tell with the first one."

We'd been to Dr. Perkins for a checkup earlier in the week. The checkup had gone fine, although the questions afterward brought another looming problem into our lives. It had begun as a discussion of which hospital Maddy would go to for her delivery. There were military facilities but the better choice seemed to be Jackson Memorial.

"I know your husband is overseas, but we'll need some paperwork for the hospital, for the birth certificate and military notification. We have to know who will guarantee payment of the delivery bill. What branch of the service did you say your husband was in?"

A perfectly reasonable question, but one Maddy and I hadn't rehearsed lately. When Maddy looked at me, I thought she wanted me to answer for her. She couldn't have meant that, however, because we both spoke at the exact same time— Maddy said, "Army," and I said, "Marines."

Dr. Perkins looked up from the papers in front of him and waited.

Maddy's face turned beet red. She must've wanted to give some kind of answer. Or, she was thinking of Tully—or Jack. Lord, what a mess. I cleared my throat. "Marines," I said again.

The doctor stared at Maddy for longer than normal, I guess to see if she would contradict me, then he filled in the blank in front of him.

"We'll be paying the delivery bill ourselves," I said, making an effort to slip past the questions.

He seemed unconvinced.

"We've been saving up for it," I added.

"Well, we don't know exactly how much it will be yet. Don't worry, as long as the hospital has the paperwork, they'll wait. And as far as the military goes, having a child will add to your husband's points. It might help to bring him home sooner." He patted Maddy's hand. "But I want you to think about eating right and being well."

We'd skinned by on that one, even though Dr. Perkins had seemed suspicious. Several bumps loomed ahead in our particular road, however. One of them was sitting on our couch.

"Well, I have Jack's christening gown with its blue bows. We'll use it if we have a boy. If it's a girl, we'll have to buy something new," Mrs. Siler pronounced.

She seemed excited by either prospect and I had to hand it to Jack. He'd saved us and given his mother something joyful to consider rather than the war and his survival. Maybe I wouldn't give him a piece of my mind after all. Of course, we'd have to see how everything turned out in the end.

Christmas week, Mrs. Siler sent her husband out into the woods to cut a pine tree sapling to serve as a scraggly version of a Christmas tree. We decorated it with ornaments and one string of lights while the roll call in the newspaper continued: Miami Cadet's Rites on Tuesday. Pvt. Fuller Killed. 6 Miami Navy Station Fliers Die in Crash. North Miamian Gets 2 Awards from Army. Cuba Ships Ten Million Pounds of Holiday Candy to be Distributed Here and in Other Cities for Children.

Good will toward men was at war with every man for himself—make that every country. The world had gone mad and people seemed unsure whether they should celebrate or worry.

We were determined to celebrate, so our Christmas was pleasant and uneventful. We exchanged small gifts between us girls. Cleo and I went in together on a new maternity dress for Maddy to wear to church. I received a colorful nylon scarf for my hair and a package of hard-to-come-by hairpins. I had no idea how Cleo had found them. The government had halted production months before in order to use the steel to make machine guns. I had my Christmas revenge, however. Cleo nearly swooned over the lipstick and counterfeit perfume Maddy and I had found at Burdines.

For the rest of the day we did our best to stay busy and act happy by going to church with the Silers, singing carols along with the radio, then visiting the living nativity scene in front of the Methodist church on Miami Avenue. By some unspoken agreement, none of us mentioned our men although Mrs.

Siler excused herself from our off-key caroling and spent her usual time with the photograph—and Jack.

We finished off the evening breaking in Randy's Christmas present—a Monopoly game from his parents—and were roundly defeated for our efforts. I had hoped for a call from Mother Marshall, for Maddy's sake, but as with other news we waited to hear, it didn't come.

— MADDY —

Three days after Christmas I received a tardy present. Our lady postman handed me a letter postmarked from Pennsylvania—addressed in my mother's handwriting. I don't know if it was guilt or relief but the sight of my name in her familiar style made me feel like I'd swallowed a cat. Sniffing back my tears I tore open the envelope hoping she'd forgiven me, at least for defying her.

But other than addressing the envelope, my mother hadn't wasted any ink on words. Inside, there was another unopened, well-traveled letter addressed to me.

A letter from Lyle, dated December 7, 1942.

Dear Maddy,

I hope I can call you dear. I'm writing because it's your birthday and I still feel like an A-1 rat for how everything turned out between us. Not that any of it was your fault. I know you must hate me like the devil and I don't blame you one bit. That's why it's taken this long for me to work up the nerve to write. But here I am—a day late and a dollar short.

War does something to your conscience, I guess because you never know if you'll make it back. Anyhow, I wanted to say I'm sorry. And say I hope you're fine. You're a sweet, beautiful girl and I'm sure there are lots of others who want to take my place as your guy—maybe one already has. Here's some advice from an old "friend," don't believe everything they tell you. I know what it's like to be single and going to war.

Happy Birthday, Mads. I won't forget you.

Lyle

Single or married it didn't seem to matter. The war changed everything.

I sat down at the table and tried to imagine how different my life would've been if I'd stayed home in Radley and married Lyle before he went to fight. How my mother might still love me if this baby had been his. But I couldn't picture it—I was too tangled in the web we'd been weaving since then. The worst part was, I couldn't even be mad at Lyle and Jeanne anymore. Since the bombing of Pearl Harbor each of our lives had exploded in different directions. Every one of us was too busy clinging to the closest comfort and hoping to ride out the war.

Don't believe everything they tell you.

Too late for that flimsy advice. I didn't have to believe. I had to foolishly walk over to the wrong man at the wrong time.

You're a sweet, beautiful girl.

I looked down at my growing belly and shook my head before folding the letter and sliding it back into the envelope. *Ah, Lyle, if you could see me now.*

New Year's Day brought a lunch of hog jowl and black-eyed peas for money and luck. At the table, Mrs. Siler pronounced that I was "too far along" to be taking the bus to Leah and Nickie's house anymore.

"We've discussed it and as of the new year, Mrs. Dowland has offered to change her route to work in order to drop Nickie off here each morning. That's all right with you, isn't it, Maddy?"

"Yes, ma'am," I replied. Lately, I'd been having a harder time climbing the stairs to get on the bus.

"If he gets too rambunctious, Randy and I can help keep an eye on him. It'll be good to have a child in the house again."

A child in the house.

I felt my shoulders sag with the weight of my conscience and gave Ruth a miserable look. Would I ever be able to say the many truths I was holding back?

"Are you feeling okay, dear?" As usual, Mrs. Siler had been paying attention.

"I'm fine." I forced a smile and handed out my best excuse. "A little tired I guess."

"Not too tired for the parade?" Randy said. "You can't miss it!" He turned to his father. "What time should we leave, Dad?"

"I always like to get there early so we can sit in the front row," Mr. Siler answered. "Don't know how it'll be this year, with the war . . ." His voice drifted off, thinking of his other, absent son, no doubt.

With the ease of a long-married spouse, Mrs. Siler confiscated the conversation. "Why don't you go and lie down for a while, Maddy? You don't want to come all the way to Florida then miss our King Orange Jamboree. We'll leave around three-thirty, right, Daddy?"

Mr. Siler nodded. "I've already loaded up the blankets and folding chairs."

"You girls need to bring sweaters," Mrs. Siler continued. "It can get cold outside this time of year."

The parade was spectacular. As Mr. Siler promised, we found front-row seats on Flagler Street and huddled under blankets while at least fifty marching bands strutted their stuff—many of their drums painted with the slogan, BEAT JAPAN. I'd never seen anything so wonderful. There were singers and dancers, floats decorated with palm trees and filled with beautiful young girls dressed as pirates—those brought a great deal of applause from the servicemen lined along the route. There was even more applause for a float with the motto "Remember Pearl Harbor," and another, "Don't Forget Wake Island," manned by sailors and Marines.

By the time the last majorette had tossed the final baton, we were shivering and my feet were complaining—a sad reminder that in this pregnancy business even your feet gained weight. Anyhow, I was glad I went but even gladder to see the front door of our home away from home.

*   *   *

Nineteen forty-three, the new year had begun. The busywork of even our stunted holidays gave way to a January that seemed to drag more than usual. As much as I'd tried, I couldn't put off the preparations for the baby any longer. With money supplied by Ruth's job at the factory and advice from Mrs. Siler, I acquired several tiny gowns and a bassinet. Leah gave me four playsuits Nickie had long since outgrown. And one of the Silers' neighbors came up with a crib—thank goodness Jack's old crib had been given away years before. I'm not sure I could have borne one more false connection to our missing pilot.

Anyway, I stayed close to home, watched Nickie, and wrote letters.

Dear Lyle,

Thank you for your letter. Believe it or not, I've changed a lot since you knew me. I can't say I forgive and forget but I certainly don't hate you.

I'm living in Florida. We like it so much here that Ruth and I decided to stay for as long as we can. We have jobs and are doing our patriotic best to help the war effort.

Speaking of war, I hope you're safe as you can be in this mess. I know Jeanne must be worried about you. I won't forget you either. I pray every night for the war to end and for our "friends" to come home.

Best wishes,

Your friend Maddy

I guess I could've told him I'd given my heart to Tully so he needn't think I was pining for *him*, but I'd run out of spite months ago. In the scheme of things, Lyle had done less damage than certain other persons who'd remained nameless.

Like Frankie.

I wondered what my brother would say to his so-called buddy after he received Ruth's letter with the truth? Nothing I hoped. I decided Davey needed to hear it from the horse's mouth. I didn't know how to explain the mess we'd made and the lies we'd told so I kept to the high road.

Dear Davey,

Well, I guess you're pretty steamed at me and this whole situa-

tion. *All I can say is I'm sorry. Sorrier than you'll ever know. You were right, I shouldn't have stayed at the pier that night.*

That was a tough one. If I hadn't stayed I wouldn't have danced with Tully. If I hadn't gotten pregnant, Tully wouldn't have asked me to marry him. Thinking of small decisions that changed lives made my head hurt.

I'm sure you remember asking me to look after Ruth when you left and I've tried—truly I have—but everything is topsy-turvy. If you think of my condition like a war, then Ruth is my home-front Marine—ready to fight all comers to defend me. She's my number-one ally and friend and I can't imagine where I'd be without her. Thank you for marrying such a terrific woman. We're so lucky to have her in our family.

I don't know what to say about Mother except please leave her out of this. She would never understand and I doubt if she'll ever forgive me.

Keep your head down, brother dear. We miss you dreadfully and Ruth deserves the life the two of you have planned. She's earned it.

Love you,
Your kid sister

— RUTH —

Working for the war had its advantages. Not the least of which was a fat paycheck. In January, Intercontinental went on round-the-clock shifts and offered the night workers a raise. Since women weren't allowed on graveyard, the day shift lost many of its male employees in the migration. We women were allowed as much overtime as we wanted though, until they hired daytime replacements. Cleo and I started going in two hours earlier in the morning and staying at least an hour later in the afternoon. It raised our salaries by fifty percent and enabled me to buy a used sewing machine for Maddy to sew some baby clothes.

At the plant, our workplace seemed to change overnight. For

once the women outnumbered the men in several departments—welding, riveting, and wiring—and boy howdy, did we work. It became a personal source of pride to get more planes through our departments faster and with better workmanship than any other shift. During our shortened lunch breaks we were more likely trading tips on how to save food, or recipes, than reading newspapers, gossiping, or smoking cigarettes. We were on a mission—with dirty hands. At the end of the line, as a salute to victory, we signed our names on each plane and put good-luck notes in the bail-out kits. We might not be able to fight but we could make sure our men had what they needed to do the job and then come home.

There was no telling when Davey would get back home.

Dearest Ruth,

I'm so sorry to have doubted you. I received your letter concerning Maddy and honestly, I'm mad enough to spit nails. I'll do as you asked though and keep everything to myself—more for Maddy's sake than anyone. I'd much rather corner my "buddy" about it but I guess we already have enough fighting to go around without going at each other.

We're on the move again which is why I got a bunch of your letters at once—eight to be exact. I can't say where we're going but I don't think it could be much worse than where we've been. At least on the ship we get two squares a day and a beer once a week. I don't want you to worry about me starving. I intend to eat my way back to my old pants size.

Poor little Maddy. Please give her a hug from her big brother. She was always so gay and headstrong but even so I never pictured her in this kind of trouble. I figured she was smarter than that. I guess life takes over sometimes and dishes out the dirt. I'm so glad you're there with her. If anyone can help it's my sweet Ruth-E. I can't imagine what Mother would do or say, and I doubt Maddy would appreciate her getting involved. As for your suggestion of our becoming parents in absentia, I'm happy to go along with whatever you girls decide. I sure wish I could be there, though. All the times we talked about having a baby—I'd like to be there to see it.

I love you, darling wife, even when I'm worried about you. Never doubt that. I'll try to write more often while we're on board because mail call is twice a week and the letters will get home faster.

Your lonely husband,
Davey

Chapter Sixteen

— MADDY —

The best we could do about the baby, or about the war, was to worry and wait. Wait, wait, wait. Our main comfort came from each other and the letters we received. Rarely did a day go by without news from someone. When one of those days arrived in late January, however, it seemed to darken the mood in both households. Mrs. Siler spent the entire afternoon crocheting like a one-woman bootie factory with the photograph resting in her lap, while Nickie played war games on the living room rug at her feet. Under Mrs. Siler's orders I was *resting*—stretched out on my bed to give my back a rest. The pow-pow-pow sound of Nickie firing the guns on his wooden naval ship had nearly lulled me to sleep when the tone of his voice changed.

"Hey! Somebody's here!" he shouted in excitement. Little feet pounded across the floor, then I heard Mrs. Siler's low voice, probably shushing him.

A feeling of doom settled on me. No mail, and now what? *Please, not bad news.* What if it was the Western Union man or someone from the Marines? By the time I pushed my round self up and had my feet on the floor, Mrs. Siler was standing in the doorway of my room. She didn't say anything. I followed her down the hallway and we joined Nickie at the front windows.

"Do you know her?" Mrs. Siler asked as a woman in-structed the cab driver to unload her suitcase and put it on the Silers' front porch.

I sucked in a surprised breath. Surely, if there was any mercy in the world I would be struck dead on the spot. "Good grief! It's my mother! What's *she* doing here?"

The silence around me was complete. Then Nickie, who must've recognized the petrified look on my face said, "Uh-oh."

I crossed my hands over my belly like I could hide it and stepped back from the window at the same moment my mother turned to look at the Samuel place. I tried not to panic. "Oh, no! What am I going to do?"

"Sit down, Maddy," Mrs. Siler ordered, taking my arm and steering me to the nearest chair. She was right, I needed to sit before I keeled over from sheer terror. The baby twisted and started kicking, and I had to draw in a sharp breath. I did my best to calm down but my best just wasn't good enough.

"I can't face her without R-Ruth," I stuttered. "I can't face her, *period.*"

"It'll be fine," Mrs. Siler said, trying to soothe me. "Stay here and watch Nickie. I'll go over and keep her with me until Ruth gets home. I'll tell her you're at work."

It occurred to me then how insidious this whole lying business could be—now we even had Mrs. Siler making up things to save us. I grabbed her arm before she could walk away. "What will you tell her about Ruth? She's supposed to be—" I looked down at my stomach but couldn't say the word.

Mrs. Siler frowned. "I'll think of something."

Nickie stayed close to me for the next hour as we waited and watched the Siler house. I didn't know what to expect. I guess in the worst possible case, Mother would come march-ing over the walkway and disown me on the spot.

It was past time for me to have gone over to help start dinner when Leah showed up to take Nickie home.

"Maddy's mommy is here," Nickie told his mother as she picked up his toys. Leah paused and gazed up at me—I guess to see how I felt about the news. I shrugged like it didn't matter one way or another. From the beginning Leah had been too polite to ask any questions about my baby or the father, so we'd settled into a need-to-know silence. She'd obviously decided she didn't need to know.

"Is there anything I can do?" she asked.

"No." I tried to form a reassuring smile. "She's next door. I'm hiding out here till Ruth and Cleo get home."

Leah helped Nickie into his jacket then gathered their things to leave. "Well, if you need me, call me. Otherwise I'll see you in the morning as usual."

As usual. It was a comforting thought that things might go on as they had in the days before. But left alone with my runaway fears, the comfort didn't last long. At 6:30 when Ruth and Cleo hit the door I was already well on my way to a nervous breakdown.

"Mother's here!" I blurted as soon as I saw Ruth's face.

Cleo dropped her purse and Ruth stared at me as though she hadn't heard me right. I'd been holding myself together pretty well until reinforcements arrived. Now I felt my phony calm slip away.

"She's next door at the Silers'—Mrs. Siler is keeping her busy—" Tears burned my eyes. "What are we going to do?"

"Oh, dear, oh dear," Ruth said. She paced over to the window and peered out as though she might gauge the coming storm. "I can't believe she's come all the way down to Florida without even a warning."

"She must be really mad," I said. "You know how much Mother hates to travel."

Ruth shrugged. "Maybe her mother's instinct told her something fishy was going on." She walked over and put her hand on my shoulder. "Well, kiddo, it looks like the jig is up. There are no lies big enough to get us out of this one."

That shut me up. I'd dreaded seeing the look in my mother's eyes when she found out the truth. But the truth had been put off so many times it was hard to believe the moment had finally come. Then I realized that Ruth had said, "get *us* out of this one." Ruth was in big trouble as well—she'd lied and defied my mother the same as I had.

"I'm so s-sorry, Ruth. I've messed up everything." I wanted to wail but each time I wobbled on the edge of crying my heart out, the baby, with a well-placed foot, reminded me to keep my chin up.

"She had to find out sooner or later, I guess," Ruth said, but I could tell she was disappointed. "Maybe it's for the best."

Interrupted by a knock at the back door, we jumped like three nervous cats on an electric wire.

"Hey, open up in there!" It was Randy—out of breath from wheeling his chair like a demon from house to house.

"Mother said to tell you to come over—she said she'll straighten everything out."

I looked at Ruth. She seemed resigned. Next to her Cleo wearily shook her head. We followed Randy across the walkway like the condemned to our own execution. When we got there the best plan we could mastermind was for Cleo and Ruth to stand in front while I hid behind them—eight months pregnant and big as a house. Hiding was the least I could do. My dad had already died of heart problems. I didn't want to give my mother heart failure, too.

We stared at each other in silence for a moment. My mother'd had plenty of time to freshen up after her trip. She'd removed her hat and jacket, and probably washed her face— she still looked exhausted. Her happy expression, sparked by our arrival, faded on her tired face.

"Now, Mrs. Marshall. I understand this might be upsetting to you—" Mrs. Siler began, but my mother was already rising to her feet.

"Ruth? I thought you—"

Unable to hide for one more second, I pushed between Ruth and Cleo until my mother could see me clearly—head to toe.

The color drained from her face and she teetered. "Oh dear, I think I—"

Mr. Siler caught her as she collapsed. He and Mrs. Siler half carried her back to the couch. "You girls go get some wet towels," Mrs. Siler ordered.

Ruth and Cleo disappeared into the kitchen. I couldn't take my eyes off my mother's face. I was sure I'd killed her.

"Maddy, sit down before you fall down as well."

Mr. Siler guided me to his easy chair before I realized my head was spinning. Time seemed stuck in slow motion. Ruth brought two wet towels from the kitchen, and Cleo followed with a glass of cold water. Out of the seven people in the room, no one spoke. The clock on the end table ticked loudly in the tense air as Mrs. Siler placed one towel on my mother's forehead and used the other to wipe down her arms and hands.

Ruth moved closer to me and took my hand.

Slowly, my mother opened her eyes.

"There, that's better, now isn't it?" Mrs. Siler said.

"What happened?" My mother whispered. She stared at the room and the people in it as though she'd woken up in a foreign land. Then her gaze found Ruth and me—and she remembered. "Maddy?" She cleared her throat. "What have you done? How could you—" With a pained look she closed her eyes again, like the sight of me was too much to bear.

"I'm sorry, Mother." My voice didn't sound like it usually did. For one thing, the baby was kicking like a football player. For another, I was wishing I could sink into the floor and disappear. Too big and too late for that magic trick though.

My mother's eyes opened once more and she stared at me. Recovering, she shoved the cloth off her head and pushed to a sitting position.

"Now, Mrs. Marshall. You should let us explain . . ."

Mother shifted her gaze to Mrs. Siler. "It's up to my daughter to explain—"

"Well, yes," Mrs. Siler conceded. "But it also concerns my son."

"What?"

"My son Jack. He's the father."

*   *   *

Mother allowed Mrs. Siler to tell her about Jack and his re-morse over what had supposedly happened between us. She vowed to treat me like her very own daughter and that she'd accepted the baby as her grandchild. But she might as well have been talking about the weather. I could see that my mother had put on her mask of "civility," which I recognized from other traumatic days—my father's funeral, my brother's departure for the war.

Dinner was icily polite. Mother asked a few questions about Miami and mentioned the unusual warmth for this time of year, without ever looking my way or uttering my name. I spent most of the meal staring at the food on my plate. I could barely choke down a thing but found that making the effort kept my hands busy. The Silers might think Hurricane Edna (my mother) had passed, but I knew better.

Ruth remained my home guard—she stood next to me when I stood, sat next to me with Cleo guarding the other side when I sat, and she made sure I had food on my plate. If it came to it, I expected she'd be willing to throw herself in front of me to derail the speeding train of my mother's anger. Not that it would do any good.

After dinner, the occupants of the Samuel house, old and new, made their way across the walkway. Cleo carried Mother's suitcase and Ruth kept up a running travelogue of informa-tion about the house. I waddled behind them like an oversized duck wishing I could fly or even run—somewhere, anywhere. Even heaving myself in the river to be an appetizer for Old Joe the alligator seemed better than what I knew was coming.

Cleo volunteered to move my things to Ruth's room, leav-ing my room for my mother. While we waited, Ruth paced the living room, ending up in front of the radio cabinet and the photograph. I knew what she was doing, she was looking at Davey, probably for help. When she picked up the frame I thought for a moment she'd decided to tell Mother about her special connection to the photograph—to distract her from my condition. Instead, she sighed, placed the frame back on the cabinet and switched on the radio. Harry James was playing,

"I Don't Want To Walk Without You." I was happy for the music; it kept me from screaming to put a dent in the silence my mother was wearing like armor.

When Cleo announced she'd finished clearing out my room, my mother nodded and addressed the dining room table as though it had ears. "I believe I'll go to bed."

No one spoke for a moment. Then Cleo said, "I'll show you where to find the bathroom."

There wasn't much to say after that. Cleo and Ruth followed their usual routine and wrote letters for the next hour. I sat with them, listening to the music and watching the light under my mother's door. She may have gone to "bed" but she wasn't sleeping. Worn out by the weight of the baby in my belly and the rest of the world on my shoulders, I headed for the extra bed in Ruth's room.

I was dozing from sheer exhaustion, when I heard a loud thump in what used to be my room, next door. I opened my eyes and saw Ruth throw back her covers, heading for the sound. By the time I followed, the door to my mother's room had been flung open and Ruth was standing over Mother. She was half sitting, half crumpled on the bed, crying as though her heart was broken. Her suitcase rested on its side against the dresser with the contents spilled, like it had been thrown across the room. That would account for the thump.

Ruth carefully sat down on the bed and put an arm around Mother. I wanted to go to her as well but before I could screw up my nerve, her gaze caught me, sweeping upward from my extended belly to my face.

"How could you have done this?" she asked, her voice hoarse from crying. "You've ruined everything."

If she'd thrown the suitcase at me I couldn't have been more shocked. The furious, unforgiving expression on her face pinned me like a sword thrust. I stumbled backward under the weight of her disappointment. The baby felt like it was doing pirouettes. I had to either lie down or fall down. Like a hundred-year-old woman I shuffled back to Ruth's room and cried myself to sleep.

— RUTH —

The next five days were bearable, but just. We were like novice skaters on thin ice making careful, necessary moves. After her midnight outburst, Mother Marshall regained control, and other than almost completely ignoring Maddy, she remained polite. For their part, the Silers took up the slack and made over their "adopted" daughter at every opportunity. Mrs. Siler cooked special meals to tempt Maddy to eat and Randy kept her busy playing games. Mr. Siler presented her with a beautiful oak rocking chair—perfect for rocking babies to sleep. The trade had cost him five precious gallons of gasoline but he seemed happy to do it.

It took Mrs. Marshall a solid week to get around to her pregnant daughter. And when she did, I insisted on being included. She didn't argue. As it turned out, she had a few things to say to me as well.

"I've been thinking about what to do," she began.

Maddy and I were seated on the couch while Mrs. Marshall, ramrod straight, faced us from the armchair.

"It's obvious you can't come home in this condition," she said to Maddy, then as though unable to look at her for long, she switched her attention to me. "I would never have made the trip if I'd known the truth."

"I'm sorry I lied to you, Mrs. Marshall," I said, "I was trying to protect Maddy—"

"You should have been protecting her before—so this kind of thing couldn't have happened. It's too late now." Her eyes sparkled with moisture but she continued. "I'm very disappointed in you, Ruth. I'm sure Davey will be as well.

"As for the baby . . . it must be put up for adoption. The hospital can make the arrangements. There's no guarantee this Jack will marry Maddy after the war. By then it'll be too difficult to give the child up."

"The Germans have Jack," Maddy said, looking down at her hands.

In the few seconds of silence that followed I nearly blurted out the whole story: Frankie, lies, and all. Doing that now, though, would probably guarantee Mrs. Marshall wouldn't believe a word of it—or us, ever again.

"I'm sorry to hear that," Mrs. Marshall said. "But it's neither here nor there. He's not your husband and you're barely eighteen. I'm the one who's responsible for making the decision and I say you'll give the baby to an orphanage then come back to Radley where you belong." She gave me a stay-out-of-it look. "And I intend to remain here and see that it's done."

Next to me, Maddy sniffed back tears. I tightened my grip on her hand but remained silent.

"Ruth and Davey said they'd adopt the baby," Maddy challenged.

Mrs. Marshall had yet to regain her normal skin tone since the first shock of seeing Maddy. Now, if it was possible, she grew paler. "And have the reminder of our shame right under our noses?"

I couldn't stay silent. "No one would have to know—"

"*I* would know."

That seemed to be the end of the conversation as far as Mother Marshall was concerned. She kept her decision from the Silers though, staying silent when they spoke of the future, possible baby names, or when Jack might be home.

Maddy had fallen into silence as well. I concluded she'd withdrawn to some inner place to wait the future out. I didn't blame her. We'd run from pillar to post, planning and plotting, only to see those plans swept away. Even I felt worn out—too tired to cry.

— MADDY —

I was so tired of crying. My thin hope that somehow my mother would understand and help me had been pie in the sky. Every tear in the world wasn't going to make her love me again. Even so, the tears still came. I had the hysterical thought that the baby would be born crying—filled with my sadness.

How could this baby be anyone's joy, especially mine, when everyone was so unhappy?

At least my one source of happiness returned—letters.

My Dearest Maddy,

I would love to see your adorable face, even if the rest of you, as you say, is as big as a house. I can't tell you how much I wish I could be there. If not to help, then at least to witness that life does go on. That's what we're fighting for. I know you're in good hands, however, I worry.

It's hard to imagine that it's been mere months since we parted. I've been so caught up in my work that sometimes it feels as though I've always been here—somewhere—at war. Different faces and places but the same routine. Looking in the mirror to shave this morning gave me a shock. I'm not sure you'll recognize me when I return. I look like an old man. People will say, "What's that ancient codger doing with that young, beautiful girl?" I hope you won't turn up your pretty nose at this old war horse.

We'll be moving again very soon so you may have an interruption in letters. I'll do my best to write as often as I can.

It seems I've forgotten how to pray, but I promise to dust off my neglected soul and ask the angels to watch over you.

You are my heart,

Tully

Dear Mads,

I'm so sorry about your situation. If I were there I'd knock a few heads together and straighten things out. As it is, tell me what you want me to do and I'll give it my best. I know Mother will hit the roof and if you want, I'll write to her in your defense—but I won't say a word unless you tell me to.

As to the matter of "F," now that I've seen the other side of him, I have a hard time looking him in the face. It should be the other way around. Since you want me to stay silent I will. It's the least I can do. You didn't ask for any of this, and if anything, I should have taken better care of my baby sister. Well, the damage is done and I hope you can forgive me. If you change your mind and want a little retribution, let me know. I'd be more than happy to take the weasel responsible down a couple of notches.

Please write often and tell me how you are. I worry about being so far from home at a time like this. Follow Ruth's advice, she's the expert.

Love you, kiddo,

Davey

Chapter Seventeen

— MADDY —

Dear Tully,

Well, I'm in it good now. My mother has shown up in Florida!

I balled up the paper and threw it in the scrap heap. I couldn't write Tully about my mother—it made me sound even more like a child whaa-whaaing. Here I'd been doing my best to convince everyone I'd grown up, then my mother appears and my adulthood deserts under her disapproval. What happened to the backbone I thought I'd grown? What happened to my determination to never go back to Radley?

I rested my hand on my child-to-be and made a silent vow. *I promise to let you grow up when the time comes.*

That's when I realized that I was keeping this child—no matter what or who tried to stop me. I would not duck out on my responsibility and let my mother take over. This baby and I would go it alone. If people called us names or refused to speak to us, we'd just move somewhere with nicer manners. I'd worry about eternal damnation at a later date.

Of course it helped bolster my courage that Mother had gone shopping with Mrs. Siler, leaving the Samuel place empty except for Nickie and me. Without her glowering in my general direction, I could almost imagine my life, exactly as it was—a mother on her own.

You're mine, for better or worse.

The baby seemed to sense my decision because it twisted and kicked, giving me a pain low in my back.

Okay, calm down. It's only January 31st, we have most of a month to wait before we meet.

I went back to my letter.

Dearest Tully,

I promise not to "turn my nose up" at the old war horse. When this awful war is over and you show up at my door, I'll be too happy to care about what anyone thinks. We'll make a perfect pair, you and I.

A perfect pair—and baby makes three. I wasn't sure how to bring up that subject so I decided not to borrow trouble.

I finished off the letter with as much silly, everyday nonsense as I could report: like how my first attempt at crocheted booties turned out looking more like drunken doilies, all round and lumpy, or how Randy the Monopoly master had put me in the poorhouse before I'd managed to buy one single hotel—ruining any future financial investing on my part.

It was strange, but the effort to cheer him up made me feel better. Either that, or my decision to act like a grown-up tipped the scales. No more tears.

Smiling for the first time in what felt like an eternity, I pushed back from the dining room table and stood.

"Ow." The pain in my back returned. Nickie stopped fort building and glanced up at me. "I must have been sitting too long," I said. "Gave me a crick in my back."

"What's a crick?" he asked.

"A crick," I informed him as I pushed my chair under the table, "is a pain you get when you get old."

He looked me over with his four-going-on-forty stare. "You're not so old."

"No, but my back is." I changed the subject before he thought of another unanswerable question. "Hey, what do you say we have some lemonade?" Making lemonade would give us both something else to think about.

"Sure," Nickie said.

"Let's go out and pick some lemons."

— RUTH —

The moment our share-the-ride driver pulled up in front of the Samuel place to drop me and Cleo off from work, I knew something was wrong. First of all, both Mrs. Marshall and Mrs. Siler were out in the side yard and it looked like they were arguing. Then there was Maddy, wielding a long-handled stick with a hook on the end, busy yanking lemons out of a tree—ignoring both women.

"See ya Monday," Harry, our driver, called.

"Yeah, see ya," I said, but my attention was on the drama in our yard. Cleo and I, lunch pails in hand, crossed the lawn toward them. It didn't take long to hear that Mrs. Siler and Mrs. Marshall were arguing about Maddy.

"I don't care what you did when you were expecting, Maddy shouldn't be outside working like a field hand in her condition," Mrs. Marshall said.

"But she wants to. She needs something to keep her busy. A little fresh air and exercise is just what the doctor ordered—"

"Walking, yes, not manual labor. Maddy, I forbid it, do you hear me?"

As Maddy bent over to gather the fallen lemons into a bucket, I noticed she pressed a hand to her back as she straightened. I bypassed the arguing women and went to her.

"Whatcha doin'?" I asked, using the slang I'd learned around the plant. I hoped it would ease some of the tension in the air.

Maddy barely glanced at me before she spied another lemon she had to have. "I'm making"—she rose on her tiptoes and gave the lemon a hard tug—"lemonade."

I looked down at the bucket at her feet. It was well over half full of lemons. "Have you invited the neighborhood? There're enough lemons here to make lemonade for an army."

"This is my second batch," she said with pride, as though that made sense. "Nickie and I made some earlier."

I took the hook from her hands before she could spy another perfect piece of fruit. She looked at me then, and I could see the beginnings of panic in her eyes. I guess having her mother and Mrs. Siler chattering over her the whole day long had pushed her too far. "Come on inside. Cleo and I'll help. Won't we Clee?"

"Sure we will," Cleo said and picked up the bucket. "Come on, kiddo."

I took Maddy's arm and the three of us walked past the now quiet mothers. But when we delivered the bucket and Maddy to the kitchen of the Samuel place, we were in for another strange surprise. There were squeezed lemons everywhere: in the sink, on the counter, in the trash. It looked like Maddy had been at it the entire afternoon.

Something about the situation made me uneasy. I wondered if we'd done more harm than good by trying to save Maddy.

"Gosh, honey, it looks like you've already squeezed enough for at least a week of hard drinking." I was making an effort to keep things light, but Cleo and I exchanged a guarded look.

Maddy took the bucket from Cleo. "I have to finish this bunch." She poured the lemons into the sink and picked up the knife.

"All right then." I put my lunch pail on the counter. "Let us get washed up first, then you cut and Cleo and I'll squeeze."

We formed our own assembly line and made short work of the lemonade. When Maddy ran out of lemons she turned to me as though she didn't know what to do next. Her eyes shimmered with moisture but she seemed determined not to cry. I took the knife out of her hand and put it on the sink. Then I slid an arm around her shoulders.

"Why don't you go lie down for a while before dinner. Cleo

and I will clean up the rest." I didn't take no for an answer and deliberately walked her from the kitchen to our shared bedroom. Obediently, she sat on the bed, yet she looked reluctant to relax. "Just stretch out for a little while," I coaxed and waited. Slowly, she swung her feet up and leaned back to rest her head on the pillow. I slipped the shoes from her feet then kissed her cheek, breathing in the tangy smell of lemons and lemonade. On my way out, I heard my name.

"Ruth?" Maddy's voice sounded young and unsure. She was frowning.

I stepped back toward the bed. "What is it, sweetie?"

Several emotions flickered across her face, like she had something to say but couldn't find the words. I had to hide my rising anger toward Mother Marshall for the way she'd made an unpleasant situation nearly unbearable for her daughter. "Can I bring you something?" I asked.

She shook her head. "No, never mind," she answered in a defeated voice.

Maddy insisted on going to the Silers' for dinner with everyone else even though Cleo offered to bring her own plate and one for Maddy back to the Samuel house.

I thought she would've been grateful to escape Mother Marshall and even the watchful eyes of the Silers. Without a glance toward her mother, she'd explained she felt better when she moved.

Lemonade was served and dinner was relatively quiet, probably due to the arguments of the afternoon. Well, Mrs. Siler and Mrs. Marshall were grown women and would have to work out their grievances on their own. I kept an eye on Maddy and tried to get her to eat, but she remained pale. After dinner, Randy talked Cleo, Maddy, and me into a few games of gin rummy while the "parents" listened to *The Lone Ranger* and the war news on the radio. We returned to the Samuel place around 8:30.

"I think you should go to bed," Mrs. Marshall told Maddy.

"You look terrible. You'll make yourself sick—" She stopped before mentioning the baby.

For some unknown reason, Maddy seemed to have settled on the path of complete defiance. "I'd rather rest here on the couch for a while," she said. "I'll go to bed when Ruth and Cleo finish their letters."

Mrs. Marshall's color came back, in a rush. She pinned me with an accusing look. I guess I *had* been a bad influence on her daughter. But today I couldn't figure what caused Maddy to rebel.

"Well, *I'm* going to bed," Mother Marshall announced with a regal sniff.

She looked more shaken than angry, like keeping a queenly, stiff upper lip was more of an act than reality. It suddenly dawned on me that Mrs. Marshall, who'd always been in control of Maddy and their world, had unexpectedly walked into a madhouse where no one seemed to be in control. Certainly not herself. If she ever learned about the tangle of lies we'd concocted she'd probably throw herself on the next train hoping her visit had simply been a bad dream.

It was a wonder Maddy had managed to remain calm this long. She deserved a little rebellion.

"I'll watch over her," I said in a kinder voice than I'd been using.

Mrs. Marshall relaxed slightly, then with a nod she went to her room. We settled down to write our letters accompanied by the music of Bob Everly singing with Glenn Miller.

I was humming along with, "Don't Sit Under the Apple Tree with Anyone Else but Me" as I wrote my husband's name.

Dearest Davey,

Well, your mother is here in Miami with us. As you might guess she's not very happy with Maddy and me. I'm sure we'll work it out—she's only just arrived.

I had to tell the truth but I wasn't about to upset Davey— I had enough to worry me with Maddy acting so strange. Since letters are long-distance conversations, I fell back on the old adage, "When all else fails, talk about the weather."

At least she'll have the chance to enjoy the relatively warmer weather here in Florida. She said it was 28 degrees with snow on the ground when she boarded the train in Philly. To be honest, it made me a little homesick to hear her description. I'm not sure I could live in a place that stayed warm and green year-round.

Maddy is doing well.

I glanced at her image in the photograph as I wrote her name. She didn't look well to me. As a matter of fact—

I turned to her. She was half sitting, half reclining on the couch but she seemed uncomfortable. "Maddy, are you sure you're feeling all right?"

She didn't answer right away but she rubbed a hand over her belly. "I don't know," she finally admitted.

I left my letter unfinished and moved over next to her on the couch. "What is it? You're not bleeding or anything, are you?"

Cleo had caught the urgency in my voice. She stopped what she was doing and stood next to me ready to help.

"No. I'm— Everybody seems to be mad at me, even the baby. It's been kicking so hard—" Maddy hesitated then seemed to wilt. "I guess I'm just tired. I think I pulled my back making lemonade." She grasped my hand. "Don't tell Mother."

"I won't. You know that. But I think you need to rest. Let Cleo and me help you to bed, okay?"

After getting Maddy settled, I had a hard time settling myself. Cleo and I went back to finishing our letters but my mind was stuck on Maddy. What if something happened to her or the baby now? So late in the pregnancy? She could end up in the same situation I'd been in—I'd had a glimpse of heaven. What if we'd been so worried about Davey, Jack, and Tully, when it was Maddy who might be in mortal danger? I nervously checked her image in the photograph but she looked the same—not smiling, but the same. No, I couldn't think about that. I couldn't sit and watch for her to thin out, then disappear.

"Well, I'm gonna hit the sack," Cleo said as she folded her

last letter and sealed it in an envelope. "I have doughnut duty early but if you or Maddy need me, yell."

"I will, thanks." I let her go to bed without voicing any of my fears. I couldn't wake Mrs. Marshall and tell her either. It was my job to watch over Maddy. Toward that end, I went to the kitchen to brew a late cup of coffee.

Something woke me a few hours later. I'd fallen asleep, slumped over my unfinished letters. The overhead light was on and my empty coffee cup was turned on its side. I rubbed my tired eyes enough to focus on the photograph.

It had changed.

"It's the baby," I said to the empty room. Before I could act, I heard Maddy call my name.

"Ruth!"

In a rush I knocked over my chair as I raced for the bedroom. Maddy was sitting up in bed. She grabbed my arm as I switched on the lamp.

"Ruth, I'm bleeding, I think I'm dying!" She fell backward onto the pillow. "Oh!"

Terrified, I yanked back the wet covers. The bed was soaked, not with blood, with water. Maddy's water had broken.

"You're not bleeding, Maddy. The baby's coming. We've got to get you to the hospital."

Maddy stopped gritting her teeth long enough to rebel again. "No! If I go to the hospital, they'll take the baby away. Mother said so. Davey said to trust you, that you're the expert. You can help me."

I did my best to keep the panic out of my voice. "Maddy, listen to me, I went through two pregnancies and lost both the babies. I've never gone full term. You have to have a doctor."

Suddenly, Mrs. Marshall was standing next to me. "What's wrong?" she demanded.

Maddy lost the will to argue for a moment. "Oh, it hurts!"

"It's the baby," I said feeling stupid and helpless. *Some expert.* "We've got to get her to the hospital."

"Help me get these wet things off her," Mother Marshall

said. Then she took Maddy's chin in her hand and pushed the damp hair out of her eyes. "Maddy? How long have you been having pains?"

Maddy opened her eyes. "Most of the afternoon, I think. I didn't know what it was. I th-thought the baby was kicking harder." Tears rolled down her cheeks and I had to look away. I'd failed her, I hadn't even considered she might be in labor—not until I looked at the photograph. I steadied my guilty concentration on stripping soiled sheets and finding clean ones.

"Ruth, get me a dry gown for her, then tell Cleo to go call the doctor."

"I'll go," I said and turned.

"No!" Mrs. Marshall's urgent tone stopped me in my tracks. "I need you here with me."

I called up the stairs for Cleo. Like a fireman answering the alarm, she clattered down a moment later wearing a robe with her hair in pin curls.

I shoved a piece of paper into her hand. "Here's Dr. Perkins's number. Go to the Silers' and call. She's having the baby."

Cleo hit the door running.

— MADDY —

I was dying. Mother, Ruth, and Mrs. Siler were too scared to tell me but I knew I was at the center of a whirlwind that was tearing me apart. Surely, I couldn't survive. It hurt—bad. Each pain felt like it would split me open—any moment I expected to explode like one of those bombs in the newsreels.

My earlier decision not to cry had been replaced by the determination not to scream. It was scary enough that each time I moaned with the pain the women watching seemed to hover over me like it might be the last sound I'd make.

I was almost too weak to care.

They'd sent Mr. Siler on the errand of bringing the doctor, pronto. Then they'd pulled the bed—with me in it—into the middle of the room so they could stand on all sides. Mrs. Siler on my left, Mother on my right, and Ruth at the foot. Only my mother seemed halfway calm. And why shouldn't she be? So what if her disappointment of a daughter died? Not to mention her shameful baby.

"You're doing fine, sweetie," my mother crooned as she bathed my forehead with a wet rag.

Before I could register that she hadn't called me sweetie in a long, long time, another pain tore through me and my back arched in reaction.

"Try not to push yet," she continued as she let me squeeze her hand. "Let's wait for the doctor."

I gasped in enough air to speak. "Mama? I'm dying. I know I'm dying. I'm so sorry for—for everything."

"Don't think about any of that now," she ordered. "You're going to be fine. We're here with you."

Mrs. Siler grasped my left hand in hers. "Jack will be so proud when we tell him how brave you are. He may not be here, but soon you'll have a little one to hold in your arms."

I'm not sure what came over me then, whether it was hysteria or the surety that I was about to meet my maker, but I couldn't have the lies on my conscience for one more moment. I glanced at Ruth before facing Mrs. Siler.

"It's a lie," I managed before another pain halted my speech.

"Don't try to talk," Mrs. Siler said as though she didn't hear what I said.

When the pain subsided I went back to my confession. "This baby isn't Jack's!" I practically yelled.

I was conscious enough to see startled looks on both Mrs. Siler's and my mother's faces. As soon as the pain faded, I went on. I didn't want to die before telling the whole truth. "Jack lied to protect me—"

"No, he couldn't have—" Mrs. Siler began.

"Yes, he did. I'm so sorry, Mrs. Siler. I can't leave this world with that lie on my head. I wanted to tell you so many times. Jack is such a great guy and he's been a great fr-friend to Ruth and me. But I didn't get this baby from him."

Ruth cut in then. "She was raped."

Mrs. Siler seemed to have been shocked silent. My mother couldn't quite hold in an alarmed "My Lord!"

Soon, everyone in the room was crying along with me. In the calm before the next pain I stared at the amazing sight of my mother's tears—shed for me. "I couldn't tell," I whispered. "And I couldn't come home. I didn't know what to do."

"Was it that young English lieutenant? Tully—wasn't it?" Mrs. Siler seemed to be hiding her disappointment behind indignation that someone had hurt me on her turf.

I managed a "No" before I sailed off into pain-land again. Panting after it passed, I concluded, "No, Tully has been wonderful. He wanted to marry me, after he found out." The next pain scattered any thoughts I might have added about loving him. I had to arch and push.

"The baby's coming," my mother pronounced.

I already knew that. I could feel solid pressure between my legs. Suddenly I wanted to live long enough to at least have the baby.

My mother stood, pulled the covers back, and raised my right knee. She indicated for Mrs. Siler to raise the left.

"Where's the doctor," Ruth muttered as she helped pull my gown up.

A commotion at the door made us look up as Dr. Perkins stepped into the room. He took one look at me and the frightened faces surrounding me before tossing his black bag on the bed. Yanking it open, he handed a bottle to Ruth. "Pour this over my hands but save some for the forceps."

The last thing I saw was Dr. Perkins at the foot of the bed delivering my baby. He was still wearing his hat.

Chapter Eighteen

— MADDY —

"It's a healthy little girl," Ruth said as she placed the newborn in my arms. "The doctor said she's a couple of weeks early, but not enough to worry."

I drew in a slow, deep breath. The sun was coming up like on any other morning, the world continued to turn, and against my will, or not, I'd become a mother. I gazed down into the tiny face fringed with dark hair searching for the part of me living inside her—worried I might see reminders of Frankie. But she didn't take after either of us—she was simply herself. That's when I realized several of my prayers had been answered. I'd survived. And I'd given birth to a healthy baby *girl*. A girl who'd never have to go to war.

I smiled for the first time in what seemed like ages, then rubbed a finger along her downy cheek. "She's so red. She looks mad. I guess I can't blame her. After such a wild night she probably thinks she's been born into a family of lunatics." Now that the ordeal was over I could almost laugh, except every part of me hurt.

"How're you feeling?" Ruth asked.

As a test, I shifted slightly and grimaced. "Better, but very, very tired." I gazed down at my daughter. "I feel like I've been run over by the express bus," I said to her scrunched-up little face. "I can't believe you're actually here."

"Have you thought of a name for this particular bus yet?" Ruth asked, smiling.

I tore my gaze away from the baby and met Ruth's question with a question of my own. I had to know if another fight loomed on the horizon with the dawn. "How's Mother taking this? Is she over at the Silers' calling the people from the orphanage?"

Ruth shook her head. Her smile remained as she teased the baby's fist with her finger. The baby opened her tiny hand and took hold. "To tell you the truth, I think she's already fallen in love with this little munchkin—like the rest of us. She hasn't said a word about giving her away. She and Mrs. Siler are busy discussing different methods of feeding her until your milk comes down." Ruth grew serious for a moment. "I told her the whole story of what happened; I hope you don't mind. It felt good to get the truth out in the open."

"You can say that again."

"So you haven't answered my question. What's her name?"

To be honest, I hadn't gotten around to choosing names. I guess because the whole thing had seemed unreal to me until this moment. Looking at *my* daughter, my flesh and blood, filled me with an overwhelming love—bone deep. I realized what Ruth was asking.

"If I name her, it means I'm keeping her, right?"

Ruth nodded.

"Then I guess it'll have to be Dorothy because she's certainly landed in Oz," I answered.

"Well, then we can call her Dottie," Ruth declared.

I watched the loving expression on Ruth's face as she gazed down at my daughter. "You're not mad at me for keeping her, are you? I know you and Davey wanted her."

Ruth gazed at me then. "I just wanted to give you a way out of something you didn't ask for," she said. "Don't get me wrong, I would love to have her." She blinked and I could see tears gathering in her eyes. "But she's yours. I guess Davey and

I will have to make our own when he gets back." She gave me a watery smile. "Besides, I still get to help raise her—for a while anyway."

"Would you mind very much if I gave her the middle name of Ruth? I mean because of her being— I mean, because of our situation?"

She seemed surprised. "Hmmm, let me see, Dorothy Ruth Marshall, that's a lot of name to grow into. Are you sure you want to saddle her with such serious expectations?"

"I'm absolutely sure." I shifted the baby and held out my free arm for a hug.

Ruth hugged me back hard before whispering, "I'm honored."

Little Dottie seemed to have had enough conversation. She let out a thready wail that startled us both. Laughing, Ruth took her out of my arms.

"Yes, we know. You're hungry," she said, then smiled at me on her way to the door. "Let's go see what the grandmas have cooked up."

I woke to my mother's voice.

"Maddy?"

For a flicker of a moment I thought I'd been having a delirious dream about a daughter named Dorothy. A dream I didn't want to leave behind.

"I brought you some soup. You haven't eaten yet today."

When I reluctantly opened my eyes, my mother, tray in hand, was seated on the edge of my bed. My little, sleeping dream Dorothy was tucked into the bassinet next to me.

"Here, drink some water first," she coaxed, handing me a glass. "Or would you rather have lemonade?" My mother had a funny half smile on her face. It took me a moment to realize she was teasing me.

"No—" I had to clear the croak out of my throat. "No. I've had enough lemonade, thank you."

I pushed up a little straighter on the pillows and accepted

the glass. Next, she arranged the tray on my much deflated lap. The tempting smell of chicken soup made my stomach rumble. My mother busied herself tidying up the room as I ate. When the bowl was empty, she removed the tray and sat next to me on the bed again.

"Now that I have you alone, and you're wide awake, I want to talk to you."

The contented feeling I'd gained from filling my stomach disappeared. I rested a hand on Dorothy's bassinet in case she was about to be snatched away.

"About what?" I asked, more than a little afraid to hear the answer.

Mother drew in a long breath then stared at me for several seconds before answering. "I want to apologize."

"For what?"

"For the many terrible things I said to you. The way I treated you when—" Tears spilled down her cheeks.

"I'm the one who—"

"No," she said, then swiped at her tears with a hanky. "Be quiet and listen." When I stopped interrupting, she went on. "You should never have gone through something like this with strangers. Thank God Ruth was here with you. I can barely imagine what a terrible mother I've been that you both felt you couldn't tell me the truth."

I didn't have a ready answer to that one. We'd lied for many reasons but the biggest had been our fear of my mother's reaction.

"Any mother would have been upset . . ." I ventured.

"But any mother wouldn't have blamed and shamed her only daughter without ever knowing the whole story." She straightened her shoulders. "So, I'm apologizing for that—for being judgmental and downright hasty. I've asked God to forgive me until I can get to confession. I hope you can as well."

"Can you forgive *me*?" I asked, wanting more than anything to hear the words that would put me out of my misery.

She patted my hand. "Of course I can forgive you. You're my baby and I'll always love you, even when we don't agree.

And there's one other thing I have to say. It's not your fault. None of this—not what happened to you, not the baby, not my indignation, none of it—is your fault."

Now my eyes sprouted tears. In my many moments of making wishes, I'd never been brave enough to hope my mother would understand that I'd gotten hurt, too, and would know I hadn't meant to disappoint her. I'd just been a stupid, headstrong girl.

There was one more point I had to make before I could relax. "I've named her Dorothy Ruth and I'm keeping her." I nearly blurted out my hope to marry Tully when he finished his part of the war but knew the odds were against me. So I shut up and waited for the next explosion.

"Of course you're keeping her," Mother replied. "It won't be easy, but we'll manage."

So used to arguments or lectures, I blinked in surprise at her agreement. *We'll manage.*

She smiled wistfully at her much-awaited granddaughter. "She looks a bit like your father, around the eyes."

"Oh—" was the only reply I could muster before I boo-hooed in my mother's arms for several minutes—a pleasant eternity. Even being a mother myself didn't take away the need for my own mother's love. Dorothy must have sensed she was being left out of our happy reunion because she began to whimper.

Mother gave me a last parting squeeze before straightening and reaching for the baby.

"Unbutton your gown. Let's see if you have enough milk yet to feed this little angel. We've kept her busy with a sugar rag but she wants the real thing."

Before I could get too embarrassed by the whole process, my mother had arranged Dorothy within range of her goal. I jumped as she latched on to my nipple then laughed in surprise as the milk began to flow.

Chapter Nineteen

— RUTH —

Dearest Darling Davey,

Well, you're an uncle!! Maddy gave birth to a beautiful baby girl and has named her Dorothy Ruth after Dorothy in The Wizard of Oz *and Ruth after me.*

I went on to tell him about almost having to deliver the baby ourselves, and the news that Mother Marshall knew the whole truth and had made peace with Maddy.

She's even forgiven me for my part in the deception. I can't tell you how relieved I am to have the truth out in the open. I feel like we're a family again. Speaking of families, looking at little Dorothy simply takes my breath away. She's so perfect. I can't WAIT for us to try again. I'm sure the third time will be the charm.

Frankie came to mind, as I suppose he always would where the baby was concerned. If things had been different, if he and Maddy had been in love or even friends, the news of the birth would be joyous to him. I couldn't stop my wishful thinking. If only Lt. Tully had been the father, at least Maddy would have a loving moment to remember each time her daughter smiled.

Maddy is in good spirits and she's determined to keep the baby.

I believe it was love at first sight. None of us know how yet, but we're confident the future will take care of itself.

I promise to send a photo when we get some taken. Your mother is going to stay with us for a while, until Maddy is up and around and we've adjusted to having a newborn in the house.

It's impossible to tell you how much I miss you. I hate it that you've missed such a grand event in our lives. Please take extra special care. Each day, each moment is like an eternity without you.

With all my heart,
Your Ruth-E

Unable to fault our plan to remain in Miami, Mother Marshall stayed with us until the middle of March. Long enough to help me and Maddy with the aid of Mrs. Siler, through a crash course on baby care. And to arrange a private christening by the local Catholic priest for little Dorothy Ruth. By the time she boarded the train for home, the only secret left standing between my mother-in-law and myself had to do with the photograph. I'd decided to let sleeping dogs lie where that was concerned. We'd come so far and made peace, I'd been hesitant to bring up any further craziness.

"I'll look after the two of them," I assured her as Maddy, holding Dorothy, and I waited on the busy platform.

"I know you will, dear," Mother Marshall said, as she sniffed and brought out a hanky. Then she leaned closer and squeezed my hand. "And watch over Davey as well," she said.

Shocked speechless, I felt my mouth open but no words came out. Did she know? Recovering, I let down my guard. "With all my heart."

She smiled before hugging me. "You're a blessing."

I guess that meant I wasn't cursed.

Regaining her queenly manner, Mrs. Marshall put away her hanky and followed the porter on board. Maddy and I waved until the train pulled out, then Mr. Siler drove us back home. *Home.* That's the way I felt about the old Samuel place now. Another month and we'd celebrate our one-year anniversary of arriving in Miami. So much had happened since then. The house on Ninth Avenue had become the touchstone for all those we loved and missed. They'd left us here, but they would return, and we would work and wait for that day. In my quiet moments, when I dreamily stared out the front window, I imagined I could see Davey, walking up the sidewalk, smiling. Coming home to me.

As soon as we arrived at the house, I raced up that same sidewalk to check the photograph. I wanted to share my happy thoughts with my husband and after lifting the frame, I gazed at him first. He was shirtless, somewhat cleaner, but not smiling. My lonely heart pounded in response. *Oh, Davey.* I kissed his image and whispered, "I love you," in case he could somehow feel my devotion.

Then, following habit, I moved on to Jack. Something had changed. A shiver of anticipation passed through me as his image seemed to melt and shift before my eyes. When it settled, his clothes were different. This was the first time in months I'd seen an undeniable transformation in his appearance. But what did it mean?

The swastika was gone.

It had to be good news. At least I hoped so. Mrs. Siler had accepted the truth of what had really happened to Maddy. Yet even as disappointment over not having a flesh-and-blood grandchild set in, she'd rallied around Jack's heroic chivalry— his effort to save a young girl in trouble through no fault of her own. And she'd clung to the tenuous connection I'd maintained with her son through the photograph.

But weeks went by with no news from the Army—good or bad. Even after Mrs. Siler had written letters with questions, the military seemed to have settled the issue. Jack was dead. *We are very sorry for your loss.* This new change had confused the issue and I felt out of my element once more. Mrs. Siler, however, clung to her hope. And as always, life went on. By May we'd adjusted to our altered routines as best we could—one of the major adjustments being diaper duty. It never ceased to amaze me how many diapers a tiny baby could soil in a day, much less a week. Enough that Mr. Siler had to make a lop-sided trade for some hard-to-come-by steel wire to construct a tight, new clothesline in the side yard near the lemon trees. He announced it to be the last stop on the diaper-washing assembly line. Cleo, Maddy, and I made him stand still long enough for us to give him a buss on the cheek.

On May 15th, I received a letter from Davey.

My Dearest Ruth,

You're not going to be happy with me after you read this letter. I'm afraid I've broken a promise I made to you and Maddy. I punched Frankie in the nose, and in a few other places. I'm sorry Ruth, but he deserved it. A bunch of us were loitering around talking after our ration of one beer. Frankie had traded to get a couple extra. After getting a little drunk he started bragging about what a ladies' man he was. Some big operator. He had pictures of three different women he said were his lady friends. (He used a different word.) Somebody asked wasn't he married and he smarted off. "What does that have to do with anything? My wife's in New Jersey."

I guess I lost my mind and my temper about then. I just grabbed him and started punching. I honestly think I wanted to kill him, or at least make him sorry he'd ever touched my sister. The guys pulled us apart but if I can help it, I'll never have to look at his face again. We're preparing for another landing and I plan to stay as far away from him as possible.

Anyway, at least I didn't tell him about the baby. I could see by the look in his eyes though, that he knows what the beating was for. He knows I know what he did.

Ruth-E, sometimes I wonder why you love me. I hope after this you still do. It's up to you what you tell Maddy. I'm done with my confession. Yours is the opinion that matters most to me.

Love you, wife—only you.

Davey

— MADDY —

I missed my mother. After dreading her visit for so long, it took more time than I expected to get over her leaving us. It helped that Dottie kept me so busy. My welding job at Intercontinental had nothing on my present occupation. This motherhood business was turning out to be a twenty-four-hour shift. If I wasn't changing diapers, I was nursing. In one end and out the other. One day slid into another with little change in the routine. It didn't take long for me to forget details I was supposed to remember—like which breast to use to feed the baby. I was supposed to alternate, according to Mrs. Siler. Many times I was just too tired to figure it out. I let Dottie choose. But I didn't let on to anyone. Dottie and I had a right to our secrets.

Dear Tully,

The baby took her first steps today. Ha. Ha. Ha. No—I'm joking. She's only three months old. She did smile though. She makes the funniest faces. I'm sure if you were here she'd have your funny bone tickled pink before you knew it.

I wish you could see her.

Reminds me of that song, "If you could see me now . . ." The good news is, I'm nearly back down to normal size. The bad news is, I'm so tired I sometimes fall asleep over my dinner plate.

I'd written Tully about every detail of the birth. Well, not every detail, but the ones I could share with him, since he couldn't be there. I'd also told him about my mother's forgiveness so he wouldn't worry so much. I was determined to include him in my life—to give him my dream of the future to hold on to as he did what he had to do. I wanted him to know he had a reason to live—me—and a reason to come home.

The weather is getting warmer here. I know. I spend a lot of time outside hanging laundry. Diapers if you must know. Have you ever changed diapers on a squirming, squalling baby? I believe I'd pay good money to see that side show. I'd give much more just to see your face.

I hope this letter finds you well. I sure wish there were tele-phone lines from here to there—we could at least meet on the wire somewhere in the middle of the ocean.

Stay safe. Dottie and I have so much to show you.

Love,

Maddy

The first of June brought rainy days. Randy spent the better part of the morning watching clouds from our front porch, trying to outsmart the raindrops, while his mother helped me wash the next batch of diapers. It was his job to keep an eye on Dottie and give us enough warning to get the dry diapers off the line before they got rewashed by the rain. The sun had just slipped behind some high clouds building in the west when Randy sounded the alarm.

"It's starting to sprinkle!" he yelled.

As Mrs. Siler and I rushed through the house and out the front door armed with an empty basket, Randy opened an umbrella. "You might need this," he said.

"Not if we hurry," Mrs. Siler answered, without pausing. She was a woman on a mission. I followed her into the yard. We'd cleared one of the three lines when Randy spoke again.

"Mama?"

The sprinkle was turning into raindrops. Mrs. Siler didn't slow down. "I know, Randy. We're hurrying." We were work-ing our way up the second line when Randy called again.

"Mama!" Some emotion in his voice made us both stop and look at each other. We left the basket where it was, but Mrs. Siler still held a handful of clothespins and I had a dry diaper as we ducked under the remaining dry clothes on the way to the front porch.

Mrs. Siler stopped halfway there, the forgotten pins falling into the grass at her feet. A taxicab had pulled up in front of the Siler house and a man stood facing us.

"Oh my lord! It's Jack! Jackie!" Mrs. Siler and I both raced across the yard with Randy wahooing behind us.

"Jack's home," he hollered to no one and everyone within shouting distance. I saw the neighbor across the street open her front door.

By the time we reached Jack, rain had made spots on his new-looking uniform. His mother didn't notice, she fell into his arms nearly knocking him over. With tears and rain running down my cheeks I wanted to throw my arms around them both, but I pulled up short. This was a mother's moment, and Mrs. Siler had earned it, keeping her faith alive for months. She deserved to have him to herself. I sniffed and wiped my eyes on the diaper I'd brought across the yard with me.

"I knew you weren't dead," she blubbered into his uniform jacket. "The Army said you were, but we knew the truth."

Jack hugged his mother hard, then shot a paler imitation of his old smile in my direction. Wherever he'd been, he'd paid a price for it. I remembered Tully's words about looking older. Now I could see what he'd been talking about.

"Hey, little Maddy," he said and held out an arm to me.

I didn't waste any time joining the huddle.

The taxi driver stood in the rain, Jack's duffel in one hand and a grin on his face watching our family reunion. Finally, Jack made an announcement. "Hey, it's raining. Whaddaya say we go inside." He nodded to the driver. "How much do I owe ya, buddy?"

"Not a slap-dab thing," the man announced. "A ride is the least I can do for one of our homegrown heroes." He winked as he walked past us to put Jack's bag on the porch. "Welcome home, son."

"I guess you know I got shot down," Jack began, then cleared his throat. He'd promised to tell what happened to him after dinner when all of us would be together. "I've already spent a week repeating the story over and over for half of the Army Air Corps," he complained. I got the feeling he thought we might not be up to hearing the whole truth and nothing but the truth.

"Anyway, we were on the return run when we were hit. We'd already flown through a wall of flak and dumped our load on the Germans. That's probably the first reason some of us survived—a plane full of bombs doesn't take being shot at very well, or very long. We were somewhere over northern France on our way to the channel when we were hit from behind and below." Jack shook his head. "We never saw him. I pulled to starboard and went into a dive but it was too late. His shells took us apart. When one sheared off the port wing and the leaking fuel tank exploded, we knew we were goners."

Jack visibly swallowed. "Three of us bailed out of the plane. Our radioman's parachute got caught up in a burning piece of debris . . . Well, only two made it to the ground alive. The navigator, Raymond Cherry, and me. I didn't even realize I'd been hurt, bad, until I hit the dirt and couldn't get up." He slid a hand over his stomach. "I was bleedin' like a stuck pig and—"

His mother's soft gasp stopped him. He gazed at her for a long moment, giving her a chance to recover.

"I'm sorry. Go on," she coaxed.

"Some Frenchies found us before the German patrols got there. The whole countryside had watched our plane go down. I don't even know where they took us because I passed out when they picked me up. I remember a man as old as Methuselah that they called a doctor but not much else. I guess that was the second time my life was saved that night."

Jack picked up his coffee cup, his hand shaking slightly as he took a sip. After a determined swallow, he continued. "They kept me hidden for a couple of weeks but sent Cherry off with the underground. I think they expected me to die. When I didn't, they hid me in the back of an old farm wagon and tried to sneak me out past the Germans." He shook his head. "That didn't work though—we got stopped and the Gerrys' guard dog sniffed me out. They shot the French wagon driver but took me to a prison camp. They like to find live flyers . . ." His voice drifted off then and he seemed to be looking at nothing and everything at the same time. He shook his head like he was shaking off a bad dream.

"I'm sorry the Army told you I was dead, Mother. But to be honest, I was nearly dead, and staying alive in the care of German prison guards is iffy at best. Wasn't it better to get the bad news first, then find out it was wrong?" He didn't wait for an answer. "That's why I didn't call you from the hospital when I got back to England. I was determined to come home and show you in person that I was alive."

"Oh, Jackie . . . but we knew you weren't dead." She turned to gaze at Ruth. "Ruth could—"

"We were praying with all our might," Ruth interrupted. Then she shook her head no to Mrs. Siler's questioning look.

"That's right . . ." Mrs. Siler continued slowly. "We had our faith to sustain us."

Sharp as a tack, Randy shifted the subject. "How did you get away from the Germans?" he asked.

"Providence," Jack chuckled. "And some help from friendly fire. The Germans were moving us to a larger camp built next door to one of their war factories—to make us pay the price if any of our buddies bombed the area. One night about three hundred of us were loaded on a train for the transfer. But we never made it across the Rhineland. Some of those wild British boys in their Hampdens hadn't gotten the message that this particular train was full of POWs. They bombed and strafed us, took out the engine, killed several of the guards who were riding in the second car, and I don't know how many of the prisoners. But in the dark and confusion two other fellas and I dug ourselves into an old trash pile and were overlooked when they rounded up the survivors. I hope a lot more got away but I only knew of us three.

"We stayed in that filthy pile the rest of the night and the day after. Finally, we had to move or starve. It turned out we weren't too far from the border of France, and after walking and hiding for a week, we were back where we started from except we stumbled onto one of the old British airfields.

"The second smuggling act went without a hitch and we made it back to England."

Jack looked worn-out even though I was sure he hadn't told us everything. Mrs. Siler asked the question on all our minds. "Are you home for good?"

"No. I'm still in the Air Corps. Getting shot down isn't a free pass out of the Army. I got promoted to second lieutenant though, and I have a month's convalescence leave before I have to report for duty."

"They're not sending you back to England! Back to—"

"No, Mother. They won't assign me duty in Europe, but not for the reason you think. Since I've been shot down over enemy territory and managed to escape, I can't go back. If I got shot down again, the Germans could execute me as a spy."

"Thank goodness!" Mrs. Siler said. "I don't care what the reason is, you've done your duty—"

"That doesn't mean they won't ship me off to the Pacific," Jack said in a reluctant-to-share-bad-news tone.

Everyone fell silent over that pronouncement. Jack sat up straighter and stretched his arms above his head. He grimaced like the movement hurt. "Now, with the story told, I need to get some shut-eye. You girls don't mind if I say good night, do you?"

Of course we didn't, and his announcement gave Mrs. Siler a reason to cluck over her son like a mother hen.

"It's so good to have you back home," Ruth said for the tenth time.

"Yeah," I agreed.

"It's good to be here," Jack replied. "I'll see ya in the morning."

— RUTH —

Mr. and Mrs. Siler wasted little time alerting their many friends and neighbors that their son wasn't dead after all. I took myself straight to church—to give thanks that the "visions" I'd seen in the photograph had been true. I finally believed what Davey had said, that the connection was a blessing. I could look at the changing faces without fear that my mind was merely playing cruel tricks. Now that Jack was home.

For his part, Jack slept on and off for the next three days. He seemed to be beyond worn-out. We tiptoed around the Siler house when he was resting and did our best to spoil him when he was awake. He seemed fascinated by little Dottie, and the four of them—Maddy, Dottie, Jack, and Randy—spent many afternoons sitting on the front porch together talking, laughing, and waving at the neighbors.

It made my heart smile to find them there when I came home from work. And it made me hopeful once more that the war would soon be over and Davey could come back to me. My own happy ending.

On the 5th of June, Cleo and I returned from work to find the whole shebang at our house. Whew! You would have thought, by the noise level, that the war *was* over. The radio had been turned up for some jump and jive music. Jack was sitting at the table playing go fish with Nickie and Randy. Mrs. Siler and Maddy were folding diapers with Dottie next to them on the couch.

"Well, I recognize the baby and the diapers," Cleo laughed, "but otherwise, are you sure we're in the right house?"

I shook my head and smiled. I knew what she meant. We'd been sad for so long. "Hey, what's going on in here?" I yelled over the music.

We were greeted with a chorus of "go fish!" Then Jack said, "Come on, you girls, we could use some fresh blood. Nickie is taking us to the cleaners."

On the way to the kitchen I stopped near the table and looked down at the game in progress. "Don't tell me you're playing for money with a four-year-old card shark."

"I'm almost five," Nickie said.

I ruffled Nickie's hair. "Okay then, an almost-five-year-old card shark."

"No, we're playing for my Army men," Randy said. He

held up a small metal man that looked more like an Indian than a soldier. "Mom dug out the old cigar box I kept under my bed when I was a kid."

I saw that each of them had a pile of men on the table next to them—Nickie's pile was the largest of the three. "Well, Nickie, you play fair. Don't take all their soldiers and make them cry."

He gazed up at me with a serious expression. "I won't, I promise, Ruth."

"Nickie's staying for dinner with us, and your mail is on the radio cabinet," Maddy said in between songs.

"Thanks." I made my way across the room, hoping for a letter from Davey. I found not one, but two. As I shuffled through them, I glanced at the photograph.

Davey was dirty again—wearing his helmet, his uniform streaked with something dark like mud or soot. His expression was grim, but at least he was safe. I gave silent thanks for that and moved on. Jack's old cocky grin had returned—

Without warning, a shudder ran through me and I nearly dropped the letters in my hand. Faces changed and there was no mistaking the meaning of what I saw.

Frankie was gone. Disappeared—sometime between last night and this afternoon.

The music on the radio resumed, playing "Praise the Lord and Pass the Ammunition" by Kay Kyser. Behind me, the fish game went on, yet I stood transfixed. Rather than picking up the frame for a closer look, I turned and gazed at Maddy wondering how or when I should tell her that Frankie wouldn't be coming back home. Dottie's father was dead.

Then a terrible thought blindsided me. Davey had said he'd wanted to kill Frankie . . . I quickly tore open the first letter.

Dearest Ruth,

We put into the harbor of an unnamed island of newly recovered Allied real estate today. Can't say where, but it's a loooong way from Radley, Pennsylvania. I volunteered for the shore party to unload supplies before the ship moves on. Guess what? There are women here. Natives. The first females besides a few nurses that any of us have seen in months. The men went pretty wild over the sight since the island girls don't wear too many clothes. It is hot you know.

But don't worry, honey, you needn't wonder about me stray-ing. The U.S. government issued every woman on the island a regulation T-shirt to cover their assets, so to say.

I skipped the rest and tore open the second envelope. Davey wouldn't be teasing and talking about island girls if he had a confession to make.

The second letter was chatty and concerned mundane life on ship. Although it did mention the division was gearing up for another fight. I checked the date at the top of the page—two weeks ago. These letters were too early for Davey to give me the sad news. I'd have to wait for the answer.

Just when I thought I could stop worrying . . . Davey wasn't a murderer who would take Frankie's life. In my heart, I knew that. But he'd been so angry, and so far from home. Who knows how the war had changed him.

My gaze drifted up, away from Davey's letter, and met Jack's. For a fraction of a second, in his eyes, I witnessed what must've been his own personal nightmare—the parts of his capture and triumphant escape he'd left out for our benefit. Changes the war had burned into his soul. Then Randy said, "Go fish!" and Jack went back to his card game. I closed my eyes and prayed. *Please God, forgive my husband for his sins and forgive me for doubting him.*

The expected letter from Davey came three weeks later.

Dear Ruth,

I'm not sure what's the best way to say this, so I'll just have to tell you outright. Frankie's dead—him and several others from our unit. It's Frankie I want to talk about though.

But I guess I should start from the beginning. You know I'd been doing my best to stay away from him. He tried to chatter me up a couple of times but I pretty much ignored him. I feel bad about that now cause he was a Marine just like the rest of us over here. I guess my feelings were too strong about him and Maddy.

It happened like this. We'd landed on another godforsaken island to dig out the Japs but got pinned down by this one machine gun position. It must've been in a cave cause the Navy had spent all night pounding every square inch with their big guns before we landed.

We were ordered to hold up and wait for the artillery to soften 'em up a little more. But Frankie didn't listen. He snatched up his forty-five and one of the satchel charges we use to clear out the caves. Before anyone could figure out what he was doing, he'd climbed out of his foxhole and charged the position. I saw him just as he slid over the edge of his last protection and I swear he smiled. Then with a war whoop he headed uphill.

As you might imagine, he was cut down halfway up. He managed to throw the satchel charge but never made it anywhere close to the gun position. I can't figure out why he did it. The captain called it suicide. He said if any of the rest of us tried something that stupid he'd have to shoot them himself.

I don't know, maybe Frankie wanted to be a hero, or to prove he had what it takes. But now he's dead and I feel sorta bad about it.

Don't know how to break the news to Maddy. Since I'm so far away, I'll have to leave that to you.

I tell you, sweetie, life has gotten awful strange with this war stuff. Sometimes it seems like we've all been shipped straight to hell.

Forgive my bein' in the dumps. I'd be 100 percent better if I could only hold you in my arms again.

You're my reason for living.

Love,

Davey

Maddy took the news better than I'd expected.

"I guess I should feel better, like he's paid his debt, but I don't," she said, staring at me. "I feel sorry for him, and his family." She picked up little Dottie to give her a kiss and a hug as though to comfort her. "Now that I have Dottie, I'm not mad anymore."

Suddenly, she looked at me again. "You must have known this for a while, Ruth. Did you see him fade in the photograph?"

I'd given up lying for Lent and hopefully for the rest of my days. "Yes, I saw it weeks ago. I didn't want to say anything until I was sure."

Maddy took a moment to think about my admission. "Promise you'll tell me right away if something happens to Tully."

"But Maddy—"

"I need your promise." She pulled little Dottie closer. "Promise you won't let me wait thinking he's fine, when you know he's not."

I couldn't see any way out of it. "All right, I promise."

Chapter Twenty

— MADDY —

August 14, 1943

My Dearest Maddy,

I'm just able to dash off a quick note to tell you I am well and that I've been given a new assignment. I'm very excited because this new mission may help to win the war earlier than I dared hope.

The only unfortunate part is that I'll be out of communication for quite some time. How long, I don't know. I wanted you and Dottie to know, however, that just because I haven't written doesn't mean I'm not all right. It doesn't mean I'm not thinking of you every day. If you don't mind, please continue to write. The postmaster will store your letters and get them to me when this mission is over.

As always you are ever in my heart and mind. If I am successful, then perhaps I'll be in a position to be transferred stateside. To your side.

Be a good girl and miss me.

With love.

Your only,

Tully

* * *

By my birthday—December 7, 1943—one hundred and thirty-two men from Dade County had died. The number of injured and missing kept mounting, and the war seemed no closer to an end. If anything, the fighting had spread. The radio and newspapers kept us informed of faraway places with names like Ploesti or Bougainville, and the roll call continued: Honor Roll Tribute to Corporal Kohn, Captain Lost on Mission, Miami Soldier Dies in Action in North Africa, Miami Sergeant Dies in Jap Camp, Draft Boards Told to Take Younger Men, Biscuit Bomber Pilot Receives Air Medal, Shoe Rationing Goes into Effect Immediately, Service Wives and Babies Find Homes Closed Here.

I hadn't heard from Tully in four months.

Jack, as he'd predicted, had been transferred to the Pacific. And this time, instead of bombers, he'd be flying his first love—fighter planes. We'd sent him off with our prayers, and Mrs. Siler took up her vigil in front of the photograph.

Thousands of soldiers who'd been so eager to get to war were streaming back through the port of Miami and into the hospitals as casualties. Cleo's husband, Johnny, was one of them. His ship had been hit by a kamikaze pilot, and he'd been injured in the resulting munitions explosion. The ship had survived and so had Johnny, but he'd lost three fingers on one hand and had terrible burns on his arm and back. He told Cleo, who spent most of her free time at his bedside, that he'd never feel the same way about barbecue again, and he'd probably have to quit smoking for good.

Miami was bursting at the seams once more with a new wave of wives and children. The ones whose husbands and fathers were confined to beds in the city hospitals. We at the Samuel house decided to squeeze in one more boarder, or I guess I should say, one and a half. Peggy Fairchild and her three-year-old daughter, Penny, moved in with us the last week of November. We'd worked out a deal to take turns watching the children (we still kept Nickie for Leah) so the other mother could do volunteer work at the Biltmore Army hospital.

The bunch of us were determined to do our part. Even Mr. Siler took advantage of the extra gasoline provided to those with private cars who could take convalescent soldiers on Sunday tours of the city. Mrs. Siler would pack up cookies and lemonade, then with Randy as the tour guide, he and Mr. Siler would pick up a carload of hospital patients. In one afternoon they'd average a seventy-five-mile route from the seaplane base at Dinner Key, to the beaches, to Surfside, Hialeah, the Naval Air Station at Opa-Locka, and Coral Gables. I could just imagine Randy pointing out every bird, every tree, and each significant rock. Not to mention the airplanes.

Volunteering at the hospital made me feel useful and kept me from worrying too much about Tully. It wouldn't do any good to get down in the dumps. Besides, I had Ruth watching the photograph and firmly believed that no news was good news. Helping soldiers write home to loved ones, feeding the ones who couldn't feed themselves, or just joking around with boys who weren't much older than myself was the least I could do. Instead of collecting jokes to cure Tully's broken funny bone, I used them on the men in C ward. They took a vote and decided I was a sure cure for a case of the blues—an honor I was very proud to accept.

Two weeks into the new year of 1944 and one hour from the end of my shift, I was sitting next to a bed occupied by a boy named Jimmy Dombrowski. Jimmy, a former football player who'd turned twenty years old in North Africa during the Tunisian campaign, had joined the Army to go up against the Germans. Two years of fighting had cost him his right arm along with the ability to ever play football, or to write letters home again.

Dear Mom and Pop,

As you can imagine, the food is much better here in the hospital than what we got in the field. I can even see the ocean from the window at the end of the hall. And right now I have a pretty girl sitting next to me, writing down what I say. Ha. Ha. You can't beat that with a stick.

Jimmy grinned at me then winked. "Did you write that?" he asked.

I gave him a saucy salute with my pencil hand. "Why yes, sir. That's why I'm here, to write down your every word."

He smiled again and went back to his dictation. It still amazed me how most of these boys who'd suffered terrible injuries and barely survived, could still laugh. They seemed to be happy to be alive—and to be home at last.

Tell Sissy and Albert that I'll be home as soon as the doctors fit me with a new arm. I might be funny looking for a while, but they say I should do fine once I get the hang of it. They call it rehabilitation. I call it torture. I guess the Army knows best though.

Well that's all I can think of for this letter. I'll write again soon.

Then he watched me, with an arched eyebrow. "Now we get to the good part," he said.

It was my habit to help the boys to at least try to sign their letters home if at all possible. I knew if I got a letter written in a stranger's handwriting that any mark on the page showing my loved one had touched it would lift my spirits. So, what Jimmy called the good part was me leaning close to him and helping him steady the paper so he could sign his initials with his left hand.

"Uh-huh," I answered and slipped the pencil into his left hand. I leaned in close to him and held my writing pad under the pencil. "Okay," I said, "ready when you are."

He didn't move a muscle.

When I glanced up at him to see what was wrong, he wasn't even looking at the paper. He was staring at me.

"I swear, this is almost worth the fight," he said, grinning. When I didn't react he straightened up his act and looked back down at the paper.

I did my best not to smile. We'd been taught by the Red Cross not to encourage any personal contact with the men. But some of them—

"Excuse me, Maddy?" One of the other volunteers called from a few beds down. "Someone's asking for you."

"Okay, gimme a sec," I answered without looking up. With slow concentration, Jimmy had nearly finished the effort of writing his first name—an improvement over his initials. I didn't want to upset the applecart.

"That's great," I said as he finished. I removed the pencil and pad from him. "I've got to go see what's up. I'll see you—"

I glanced up toward the door and froze.

Tully was standing there.

"Tomorrow . . ." I finished. I couldn't believe my eyes. For a moment I thought I was dreaming.

"Tully?" I whispered, almost afraid he'd disappear.

He came a couple of steps farther into the room and smiled as though he wasn't sure of his welcome. Somewhere in my addled brain I remembered him worrying—*You wouldn't turn your nose up at an old war horse . . .*

"Tully!"

He looked more than wonderful to me. I dropped the pad and pencil and ran to him. Seconds later, I was in his arms. "I can't believe you're really here," I blathered.

He pushed me back to stare at me. "I told you I'd come back if I could." Then he kissed me. I don't know for how long. I just knew I never wanted it to end.

"Hey, buddy! That's my girl you're muggin'."

Tully slowly drew away and glanced over my shoulder toward Jimmy Dombrowski. "Sorry, old pal. I claimed this one a long time ago. You'll have to find your own." With a slow smile he gazed down into my eyes. "Isn't that right, Maddy?"

"You bet," I agreed on a shaky breath.

— RUTH —

*M*addy and Tully were married on a Saturday two weeks after his return, in the office of Tully's new commanding officer. The ceremony was officiated by an Army Air Corps chaplain. I stood up as matron of honor holding Dottie, and Randy served as best man. After the short ceremony and official congratulations from the Army officers present, Mr. Siler drove us back to the Samuel place where Mrs. Siler, Cleo, Leah, Peggy, and a few of the neighbors had pooled their stamps to put on a reception dinner complete with a respectable-sized wedding cake.

You could almost forget there was a war on.

Enterprising Cleo had even dug up a record to play a special song for Maddy's bridal dance—"White Cliffs of Dover."

I don't think I'd ever seen Maddy so happy. Unless it was when she'd introduced Tully to Dottie the first afternoon he'd arrived. Afterward I decided we'd witnessed another case of love at first sight. Settled into the tall stranger's arms, Dottie studied this new face in her life for a long moment before breaking into a grin. Then with a squeal of pure delight she reached for the brass wings pinned to Tully's uniform jacket and held on.

"That's how I feel when I look at him, too, Dots," Maddy said, her eyes growing misty.

Tully smiled like a man who'd been released from his own dark prison cell. I knew without a doubt that as long as the three of them were together, the light of their love would keep the darkness at bay.

"I think we better hurry up and get married," Tully said that day. "Little Dottie here will expect a brother or sister without delay."

Maddy's face grew pink. "That would be fine with me," she said shyly.

Auntie Ruth coaxed Dottie from her comfortable position in Tully's arms, and we left them to work out the details.

And there we were, on Maddy's wedding day. The only people missing were Maddy's mother, Jack, and my Davey. I so wished he could be there, but I worked to keep my sadness at bay. I was determined not to do anything to put a blemish on this happy occasion, and I knew he was there in our hearts.

Everyone ate and drank and danced until the sun went

down. Sometime after that I casually removed the photograph from its resting place and slipped outside into the moonlight. I wanted to be alone with my husband.

I made it halfway to the river before I wearily sank down on my knees in the cool sand to let the tears flow. Alone, in the dark, I pressed the glass covering the photograph to my fore-head and prayed.

Dear God,

I thank you again for Dottie's safe birth and for Tully's return. With your help, I've done my best to see to Maddy's happiness and security. Now I need to keep my fears at bay. I miss Davey so much. If there is any blessing in this photograph, let him feel my love. Send your angels to watch over him, to protect him from harm. Please help us to hurry and end this war so the world might live in peace again. Please . . . bring Davey home to me.

Epilogue

— MADDY —

My brother Davey came home on April 18, 1945, after three years at war. Tully and I, with Dottie and her brother Stevie in tow, went with Ruth to meet the ship at the Port of Miami. We had to struggle to find a place on the crowded dock as the Navy ship, decks lined with waving, shouting Marines, tied up to unload. I was afraid we'd never find him in the crush, but Ruth kept winnowing her way closer and we followed in her wake. Finally we could see the gangplank being lowered and the first Marines stepping onto U.S. soil.

Ruth grabbed my hand, and I could feel her shaking with excitement. We'd stayed busy all morning, styling her hair and ironing her new dress. But now we were back to waiting. I knew she was fighting back tears because we'd both promised not to boo-hoo until we saw Davey in person. Talk about a flimsy promise. I could feel my eyes brimming already.

As each smiling Marine made his own landing, a Red Cross volunteer handed the new arrival a travel kit and a banana. I suppose the travel kit was to help them get on the road to their homes; the banana it turns out was like a vitamin pill. The doctors had determined that many men returning from war had health deficiencies. The banana was the beginning of better meals and better days ahead.

Forty-five minutes and what seemed like a thousand Marines later, Ruth spotted Davey and pushed through the crowd, calling his name. It took Tully, the kids, and me a couple of moments to catch up. By the time we did, Davey had dropped his seabag and enveloped Ruth in a bear hug. I gave in and let my tears fall.

"Look at you," Davey kept repeating. Then he pushed back to gaze into Ruth's face. I could see tears in his eyes as well.

"No, look at *you*," Ruth said, smiling and crying at the same time. Then, Davey kissed her and it took awhile for them to realize there were other people in the world.

"Mads!" Davey laughed when he came up for air. "Gosh," he said. "You're all grown-up."

"I should hope so," I said, ready and willing to give him the old gargoyle face. At the last second, I recovered my grown-up self-control. "I'm a married woman with two kids," I announced as though it doubled my age somehow. "Do you remember Tully?"

"Of course I do," he said as he extended his hand. "Welcome to the family."

"Welcome back," Tully replied.

"And who's this?" Davey asked, grinning at Stevie.

"This is Stevie," Tully said. Finding himself at the center of attention, Stevie hid his face against his father's shoulder.

"He's a little shy," I said as I coaxed Dottie forward. "And this is Dottie. Dottie, say hello to your uncle Davey."

"Hello, Uncle Davey," Dottie said just as we'd rehearsed.

My brother studied Dottie with a strange expression on his face. Then he stooped down to look into her eyes. "Hello, Dottie." He held out his hand. "It's nice to finally meet you." Davey seemed like he wanted to say something else but thought better of it.

Dottie leaned against my leg for moral support, but she put out her hand and let Davey shake it. "Why are you so wrinkly?" she asked.

Davey chuckled as he stood. He halfheartedly brushed at the jacket of his uniform coat. "I'm afraid my dress uniform has been stuffed in my seabag for three years. I didn't think I'd need it anymore." He gave Ruth a sheepish shrug. "There aren't any irons on board a warship."

Ruth smiled, and sliding her arm around Davey's waist said, "I'll iron it for you tomorrow. You won't need it tonight."

We all laughed as Davey made a quick grab for his seabag.

Ruth and Davey stayed in Miami for another month before heading back to Radley and my mother's joyous reunion. They stayed long enough to greet Jack when he returned from the Pacific as a hero. He and Randy were busy making plans for a flying clipper shipping business. The war was finally winding down, but none of us knew how or when it would actually end.

The Silers had become honorary grandparents although the Samuel house was nearly empty, except for the newest boarder, Peggy, and her daughter. Cleo and her Johnny had taken the train back to California when he'd been released from the hospital. Cleo vowed they'd come back for a visit. Leah Dowland's husband—Nickie's father—was due to return any day now. He'd survived D-Day and the daily war of the Atlantic shipping lanes.

Many of the boys, however, wouldn't be coming back. In my brother's platoon, of the three men he'd called friends— one of them being Frankie—none returned. My mother had written that eight of the many hometown boys who'd eagerly run off to enlist wouldn't be coming home. One of those boys was Lyle Nesbitt. He'd been lost at sea after his ship was torpedoed in the Pacific. I'd had to put away my pride and write to Jeanne with my heartfelt condolences. Poor Lyle.

I refused to feel guilty for being happy, however. Tully and I were planning to buy a house as soon as he received his official discharge papers from England. And he was applying to become an American citizen to fulfill our dream of living in Miami for the rest of our lives. He never told me what his last special mission had been, and one of my first wifely decisions had been to let it be. I knew about keeping secrets. We had the rest of our lives—he would tell me when he was ready.

Late one afternoon, as we sat in portable chairs on the beach watching the children play at the edge of the water, I breathed a huge sigh. "Do you remember the night we met?" I said, feeling dreamy and content.

"Yes," he answered. "You were determined to dance with every man in the room but me."

"That's not true!" I argued, my dreamy feeling falling back a notch. "I was too nervous to dance with you."

"And you had a boyfriend back home."

My memory of Lyle and our ill-fated plans to be married had mellowed and faded like an old photograph. As though he'd read my mind, Tully asked, "What happened to that photograph we had taken?"

I slipped my hand into his and smiled at the ocean, and at my babies, feeling oh-so-grateful to have gotten my heart's wish, my Hollywood ending.

"Before she left, Ruth and I answered an ad in the paper put in by a lady at the Edison Hotel. She was asking for scrapbooks, memorabilia, and photos of the war years for a museum exhibit. She said she wanted the world to know how we'd all worked together and survived."

"But why would they want a photograph of our mugs in a museum?" Tully chuckled.

I shrugged without explaining. I couldn't tell him that Ruth had insisted on donating the photograph and I hadn't argued even though it was the only evidence left of Dottie's actual father. To me it was a rerun of the unhappy past. The fear and uncertainty, the infernal waiting we'd suffered after that night. I intended to keep my eye on the future.

It was just like Ruth to have a different bead on the situation. She'd gazed at the photograph and seen all she needed to know about our future—and a secret about her own. She was already expecting again.

Now that our men were home, Ruth believed that the

moment—a bunch of kids in a dance hall with hope and fear in their eyes, forever frozen in time by a camera flash—was an uncommon blessing to be shared. She'd lived the blessing.

Over lunch at the hotel, Ruth had patiently told the collector the entire story of her special connection to the image and the people in it. (Except for the part about the new baby.) The woman seemed unconvinced and had stared long and hard at the image before smiling faintly.

"Yes, I think you're right. It does belong in our museum."

I don't know what changed her mind, but later, on the ride home, Ruth said, "Just think, Maddy. People will be able to look at the photograph and see where the past and the future met. Who knows what they'll find?"

I smiled at her uncharacteristic make-believe. I'd never seen anything change in the photograph. But that didn't put the kibosh on the occasion. At the end of the conversation, after the collector had written down notes and carefully cataloged the cardboard-mounted picture, she'd made a confession. She'd explained that she worked for the National Archives and The Smithsonian in Washington, D.C.

We were gonna be famous—part of history. Whaddaya know about that?

About the Author

Award-winning author Virginia Ellis has written a dozen romance novels under the name Lyn Ellis, and her literary short stories have been included in collections of modern southern writers. Her books have been translated into ten languages. She is also a founding partner of Belle-Books, a small press devoted to publishing the unique voices of southern women.